Dead Weight

Matt Casamassina

Dead Weight

http://mattcasa.com

Cover by Hampton Lamoureux
Formatting by Polgarus Studio

To my wife, Edie, who will never read this, and my kids, Zoe, Fiona, and Rocco, who aren't allowed.

1
Table for One

She was dead.

Had to be, Zephyr thought, as he rummaged through her sleeping bag for the third time that morning and found only clothes. The heavy sweatshirt and pink panties. The silver ankle bracelet he gave her when she turned seventeen. A pair of old jeans. All there, still sleeping without the body that wore them. No long, black hair with a red streak. No big, brown eyes to stare right through him. No slender arms to wrap around him. No Keiko.

Not even the heat of her. The bag inside was as cold as the air outside. Whatever she did, wherever she went, hours had passed, and the thought of her out there in the morning light with the chirping birds and dewing trees and the biting wind, no clothes to warm her, attacked his heart. What did she do? Where did she go? No answer he conjured sufficed, and only the darkest visions surfaced before he swept them away.

A crumpled ball of tinfoil lay beside an extinguished bonfire. Nearby sat the unused condom package he'd flung from the tent in the night, buzzed and stupid and still too scared to pursue the possibility. Even now, he still didn't know if she was a virgin — he just couldn't devise an elegant way to broach the subject — and meanwhile, he thought he might die one.

He replayed the night's events. There'd been a fair amount of drinking, some kissing and touching, and a full stop after that. Had she told him that she needed to leave early? No — intoxicated or not, he was sure he'd remember that. No hint of an early departure. He thought they might have dozed off talking about where they wanted to go after the school year ended, although he admitted to himself that his memory lacked consistency and swore off alcohol forever.

Zephyr searched the campsite and then the dirt path down to the lake where she sometimes bit her nails and smoked. He called after her until his throat felt raw. He tried the stone route back to his car. She wasn't waiting there, and he knew that he couldn't either. Whatever was going on, he needed help. From an adult. If she wasn't home, he'd have to tell her parents everything. That she hadn't slept at Luca's house last night.

His dirty old Volvo was the only parked car — unsurprising given the fact that it was now probably midday on a Tuesday, a ripe hour for work and school, the latter of which was minus at least one and possibly two this afternoon. He tried to power on his mobile, but it hadn't taken enough electrical juice yet, so he backed up and started down the road again.

Firefly Valley, population 26,000, his home of seventeen years, waited just beyond the intersection at Brussels Street. A small gathering of local stores and shops — the Durango Market, Jan's Pastries, Big 5 Sporting Goods, McDonald's and Smile Rite Dentist — flowed into each other on one side of Ridge Street just past the intersection, and as he slowed for a red light, he saw that something was wrong. Several vehicles were stalled on the road and sidewalk in front of the market. A red F-150 had crashed into a power pole adjacent to McDonald's and the impact had not only crumpled the truck's front end, but unhinged the pole, which now leaned to one side.

A fraction of a second held three connected thoughts. What? Then, where is everyone? And finally, no ambulance? The accident might be fresh, but he wasn't so sure, and he was just as troubled by the recklessness surrounding the crash. Empty vehicles dead on the sidewalk. Not a single person outside and none that he could see in any shops. No other cars passing by. The whole block looked static, produced – fake.

He sat there and gawked for what might have been forever. Finally, the light changed color and he drove beyond the intersection, where he rolled the car to a stop in the street – if everybody else can do it, so could he – stepped out and surveyed the wrecked truck.

The front end was mangled around the telephone pole, the windshield shattered onto the hood and street, and the driver seat's airbag inflated. It was a mess.

He peered through the passenger-side window, which had either been rolled down or altogether blown out, and saw no bodies inside. He did, however, find something else — something that caused the tiny hairs on his nape to stand rigid. In the driver's seat, a weathered cowboy hat, belt and buckle, green flannel and a pair of faded jeans. Not folded, but stretched and worn. Two dirty black boots overturned on the floor mat. The keys were still in the ignition, but the vehicle was off.

Zephyr Rockwell thought again of his girlfriend, reduced to a pile of clothes in the woods, as anxiety engulfed him.

2

His phone finally powered on. He paced between the truck, a blue minivan and some wannabe muscle car, its paint stripped to primer, and made phone calls, but found nobody off or on the line. The cars were empty except for clothes and jewelry — meaningless, he told himself, and yet his heart thumped harder every time he ducked his head into a window and saw no one. Keiko's house returned an old answering machine recording. He called his mom's office and it just rang. His dad's mobile went straight to voicemail. Finally, he mass-texted all nineteen numbers in his address book. The message—*Hello?*— sought only a response.

Arriving at the obvious and wondering why it hadn't occurred to him earlier, Zephyr dialed 9-1-1. It rang thirteen times before he relented, cursed and hung up. His frustration was compounded by the fact that no texts had come back.

"Zeph, this is not good. Not, not, not good, man," he said. "Go home. Go. Now."

And with that, he raced back to his car and sped away, leaving the wrecks and the mystery lingering in his rear view mirror.

3

He exhaled as he saw his parent's cars in the driveway, pulled in right behind them and ran for the front door. Their place on Fairfield Court was the farthest back in the middle of a gated cul-de-sac. It was a coveted neighborhood — not extravagantly rich, but certainly upper-class — and their house, a two-story Victorian built in the 1920s, was immaculate. He intended to fling the entryway open and burst in, where he imagined he'd discover his dad watching the afternoon news and maybe his mom tending to something that smelled wonderful in the kitchen. Instead, he realized too late that the handle was locked and couldn't reverse his momentum before his right shoulder crashed into the door.

"Come on!" he cried as he fumbled for the key and then unlocked it.

His dad was not in their expansive living room, home to a wall-eclipsing flat screen television — presently off, he observed. A crystal chandelier dangled from their vaulted ceilings, its lights equally powerless.

"Hello! I'm here!" he shouted. "Is anybody home?"

No replies came, but he ignored that little fact for the moment and canvassed the first floor of the house. The dining room, kitchen, den and family room were all parentless, much to his growing dismay. He sprinted upstairs, calling for them, and then stopped at their bedroom door. Please, God, he thought. Please. Please. Let them be here. Please. Please. Please. I won't ask anything of You again, I swear. I swear.

He opened it.

Their television was on, the volume low. The ceiling fan spun around as its pull-string clanked against the side of the light, itself off. The shutters were drawn and the room held the dark, but he could nevertheless see that the bed was disheveled, yet uninhabited.

His heart pounded in his chest and his vision skipped off track and then back again with each powerful beat. He felt dizzy, but the sensation was fleeting and after a pause he hurried into their bathroom, again hoping to find them at the matching sinks, perhaps prepping for a dinner party. This time, however, he wasn't surprised when they weren't there.

On the television, Judge Judy appeared to be giving an obese black woman a stern lecture about integrity and the importance of returning borrowed items. Zephyr sat on his mom's side of the bed with a squeak, grabbed the remote off her night-stand, and flipped through the channels for a local station. Some movie starring Harrison Ford – it might've been *Clear and Present Danger*. Then *SpongeBob SquarePants*. The next channel was black. More cartoons that he didn't recognize. Then a screen with the words, *Please Stand By*. That was odd. He searched without any purpose through additional cartoons and movies, the occasional sitcom, and more blank channels, until he finally came upon a broadcast that cut through him like the blade of a sharpened axe.

"What the—" he whispered.

It was a live studio newsroom accompanied by a scrolling ticker. *Florida Shooter Apprehended After Standoff. Neighbors Say Alleged Shooter Emptied Home. Three Soldiers Missing in Afghanistan. House Healthcare Vote May Be Delayed.* The same depressing reports. That wasn't the issue. Nothing out of the ordinary there. No, the issue was what couldn't be seen or heard. No news anchors. No voices. And no acknowledgement of these omissions. Just an empty, static, mute room. A camera locked on a neglected desk and two bodiless chairs. Words danced across the screen – nothing else moved or breathed.

4

Zephyr was terrified of flying. Every summer he travelled with his parents to his uncle's house in California, and he dreaded the trip because of the plane ride. It was a reoccurring nightmare. He'd board the airliner, find his seat, buckle firmly in, and in the minutes leading up to take off, drowsiness would fall upon him. He'd close his eyes, begin to drift off, and think, maybe I'll really sleep this time. I'm so tired. I think it might happen. But the moment the jet engines throttled and the craft gained momentum, he'd perk up, claw into the seat rails like a scared cat and whip his head from window to window. From then on, there was no hope of rest – only sweaty palms and torment— every airborne second a potential disaster. In those stretching minutes, a mild bump, let alone any real turbulence, was all it took to set his mind off again and then he couldn't focus on anything else.

Now, with his girlfriend and parents missing, absentee cars littering at least one intersection in his hometown, and an empty, unchanging newsroom on TV, Zephyr felt the familiar calm before the storm sweep over him and embraced it. In some weird way, it was reassuring to know that whatever happened, he was in it, and there was no turning back.

The sun threatened to take shelter behind a rocky mountain on one side of the valley. Zephyr checked his mobile and saw that it was 4:22

p.m. He also realized, painfully, no missed calls, voicemails or text messages.

His laptop rested on the kitchen countertop — his mom had obviously kidnapped it sometime recently, which always annoyed him. He powered it and loaded his favorite news site. *U.N. Calls for Sanctions Against Iran* headlined the page. Underneath an image of an older Middle Eastern man in a white turban were other popular stories. *Adam Sandler Takes Weekend Box Office. Will it Snow in Los Angeles? Ticker: House Chief of Staff Dies.* And so on. But nothing about any goings-on in his town. Nothing about abandoned newsrooms. Nothing about the fact that 9-1-1 was on vacation.

He searched for *"everybody missing"* and got nothing. He tried a general query on *Firefly Valley* to see if any results explained the predicament and none did. He loaded the website for the local paper and it was grossly outdated. He tried the social networks and surveyed his friends' news feeds but nothing announced itself as unusual.

"This is fantastic," he said.

A disturbing hypothesis kicked at his mind and he set out to test it, scared of the result. He reloaded the news site, clicked on a headline and scoured the story, finally narrowing in on his target: the timestamp that accompanied every article. And just as he feared, it was old. It was tagged from the day prior. All of the articles were. The other websites, too. Even the social feeds. All stuck in time. Such a possibility seemed so foreign to him that he closed his browser, cleared its cache and reopened it to the same results. Inexplicably, it was all yesterday's news.

His stomach growled and groaned, he couldn't remember when he ate last, and he needed a shower and some new clothes, but all of these truths buzzed like tiny gnats through the back of his mind. Persistent, troublesome, yet ultimately just background noise. Zephyr didn't know what to do. He pulled a barstool and slumped over the kitchen countertop, his face in his hands. He felt like crying.

His friends spent most nights prepping for tests, but when he read something once, it stuck forever. And he loved to read. By the time he started middle school, he'd already devoured hundreds of classic and modern novels, understood the fundamentals of advanced mathematics, and was well on his way to speaking fluent Italian — a linguistic preference that annoyed his mom, who would have preferred he learned French. This ability afforded him the time to screw around with friends and Keiko, the latter of whom was a recent obsession.

So he'd told his parents that he and his best friend Eric were going camping the previous night – a blatant lie. And now he was overwhelmed with guilt about everything. About the lie, but also the foggy drunkenness and most of all for losing his new girlfriend. She could be out there, he thought. You could've left her out there.

The suggestion triggered a wave of nausea that didn't last. Under ordinary circumstances, yes, he'd be back in his car and retracing his path up Ridge Street to the park by now. But only if he had talked to Kay's parents. Her younger brother. Anybody. No – whatever was going on here, it involved his girlfriend, yet didn't revolve around her. The crashed cars. His parents. And the damned newsroom. It was all encapsulating and it couldn't be explained away.

5

He drove around town as the night grew darker, the air colder and his outlook grimmer. The phenomenon was absolutely not limited to the crash at the Brussels Street intersection or the houses on Fairfield Court. A three-mile stretch of Flora Avenue was seemingly abandoned, too. No moving vehicles – just those parked in driveways and the occasional rolled stop or crash. The backend of a green truck poked out from the comfort of a living room it had smashed through. Zephyr decelerated as he passed it, but didn't even step out to check for survivors – he knew there'd be nobody.

Nobody was home, anywhere. Not Keiko. Not his uncle. The only signs of life he encountered were the fluttering moths drawn to their porch lights.

On Main Street, more stalled cars, crashes, and desolation. Most of the lights were out at the mini mall, but the Taco Bell remained illuminated. He slowed to study it as he drove by and saw nobody inside. It occurred to him that the eatery didn't close until 2:00 a.m., which probably meant that whatever had transpired — this event, as he had started to think about it — had likely done so before then.

He felt alone. In the cradle of darkness, the situation seemed bleaker, his fear heavier. Something was going on. He didn't know what. He didn't know why.

6

Zephyr's stomach performed backflips as he parked in his parent's driveway. He was terrified, confused and defeated, and he knew the emotional tidal wave that crashed against his nerves played its part, too.

Outside, the street lamps continued to spotlight the sidewalks and pavement. The moon, however, had taken refuge behind a thick veil of ominous clouds. He stepped inside, shut the door and instinctively locked it – both the door knob and the deadbolt. He could still hear his parent's bedroom ceiling fan clanking upstairs and the sound was calming, even if he knew it was a lie.

In the kitchen, he devoured an apple and some string cheese before gulping down a can of orange soda. When he was finished, he cracked open another and halved it, wincing at the carbonation, before he finally sat back in the chair and considered his options.

He knew the smart thing to do was to stay put and to wait. Turn the TV on. Sit with your phone. And don't do anything else, he told himself. Be smart. Even if it's just this once. It was the logical move and he knew it, but all the same his mind argued that he should do anything but sit still; that he should sprint to his car, find the nearest freeway and floor it all the way to the city a hundred miles out.

A year ago he'd come down with an inexplicable illness. A pink blotch had appeared on his lower back and he spent the better half of a week fighting off overwhelming nausea and diarrhea. Always an aspiring hypochondriac, he'd convinced himself that he'd caught every disease and virus in existence, including, of course, some new form of super cancer or AIDS or maybe even Ebola. He clearly remembered waking in those bright mornings when such notions seemed absolutely ludicrous. But then, inevitably, the sun would fade into night and as he lay alone in bed, his mental defenses receded, his shields thinned, until those impossible outcomes suddenly seemed possible. In the blackness, they took on crushing weight and became inescapable.

Now, as Zephyr looked beyond the radiance of his living room into those shadowy upstairs crevices, nothing seemed preposterous. Up there, the impossible could transform into the probable — those shadows might choke away reality and create it anew. So he walked the stairs and canvassed the rooms, turned on lights, looked under beds and into closets, and peeled back drapes. He wasn't even sure why he did these things.

When the check was done and just about every light in the house burned brightly, Zephyr moved back into his bedroom. He plopped onto his bed and flipped the TV on with the remote. A quick scan of the channels revealed few deviations from earlier, except for more dead broadcasts. There seemed to be more blank channels than before, but he wasn't entirely sure if that was true. And the newsroom was still live with yesterday's hottest stories and a few invisible anchors. He finally noticed the watermark in the lower-right screen and smiled.

"Fox News," he said. "Well, it's an improvement, anyway."

He closed his eyes.

His window rattled against the restless wind, a chorus of moaning ghosts, and he jerked. His alarm clock read 9:47 p.m. Had he drifted? His leaden eyelids threatened to close again. He felt drained to the point of vacuity. His phone still showed no missed calls or texts. He stood up, cracked his wooden shutters and peered outside, not expecting to see anything below, and it was precisely what he didn't see that got him thinking. The streetlights. The porch lights. And no more. He realized that in stark contrast, his house must look like Disneyland, and it scared him.

Zephyr didn't subscribe to the horror-movie cliché that illumination was the last great obstacle of the serial killer. Rather, he always wondered why the giant-bosomed babysitters in countless forgettable slasher flicks clung to telephones and pranced around within the confines of an overly bright house while the deranged stalker sneaked around under cover of darkness somewhere outside. He told himself that he would never follow those same broken conventions. Yet, as he idled in his room, he understood that his house was visible both outside and in and he wondered if that was a good thing. The more he thought about it, the more he figured the answer was no. He wasn't sure what the hell had happened to his friends, his family and the city at large, and until he was he wanted to blend, not diverge.

He canvassed his house, turning off lights. One by one the brightness gave way to blackness and the effect was simultaneously reassuring and maddening. When at last the final spark of sight was extinguished, his eyes struggled for traction as he shuffled through the inky embrace of night.

Upstairs, he reached under his bed and grasped the cold aluminum of his baseball bat, which he drew and swung slow and careful, as a batter might before the first pitch is ever thrown. It wasn't much, but he took comfort in the makeshift weapon.

He lay in his clothes and shoes with the bat at his side. Periodically, he rose from the depths of weary exhaustion and peered down at the unchanged street. Creaking wood stirred him from dreams of Keiko, her black hair and prominent red stripe, her one crooked tooth, her willowy body, her flowery perfume. He fought against sleep and searched the blackness with his ears. A tree branch scraping against the trim of the house. Or was it footsteps creeping up the stairs? The wind screamed and cackled at him.

As he twisted in and out of rest, the night seemed to stretch on eternally. And when the thin veil of dreams at last threatened to dissipate into nothingness, the white noise outside his window was violated.

Boom.

The sound thundered through his neighborhood and shook him.

Zephyr shot up and let go of something guttural.

Deep. Powerful. An explosion. Or a car backfiring. Or maybe a crash. He couldn't move. His mind stuttered.

Two more blasts. Pounding echoes ricocheted everywhere.

Gunshots, he thought, his eyes wide. Big ones. Probably not a pistol. Maybe a shotgun.

Sleep was exorcised from his body at the speed of light. He rolled across the bed and thumbed open the shutters. Nothing new. But even so, something had happened out there. Somebody had a gun – and not too far off.

"I'm not alone."

7
Shopping

The city's caliginous veil evaporated into pink daylight that drew faint pastel lines on his bedroom wall. Zephyr rubbed his beaten eyes and stood, a dull thud as the baseball bat rolled onto the carpet. He reached into his pocket, produced his mobile and once more found the battery dead, so he walked downstairs and charged it. It was early. The sliver of dawn, let alone crack. It had been about two hours since he heard the trio of gunshots. He hadn't slept, but no more interruptions came in the night.

He turned on the television in the living room and looked for changes in the patterns. More channels had blinked out. It was indisputable. At least half of them were airing dead space now. It was getting worse, not better.

Zephyr's body and mind waged relentless war – the former battling for tenacious slumber as the latter charged against it with all of its might. He had, in the hours since those blasts exploded in the distance, considered too many possibilities to count and nearly acted on every one of them. He felt compelled to drive about the desolate city again and investigate. He needed to speed toward the freeway and beyond the confines of his circumstance. Twice, he nearly did it. His car keys jangling in hand, he opened the entry door and looked outward to darkness, but then reconsidered. He walked the house, still afraid to turn on the lights, and stared out misty windows for signs of anything extraordinary. He telephoned everybody and got nobody.

Despite all of his long considerations and contemplations in the night, he knew the moment he heard those gunshots that his next action would lead him neither to the freeway nor to the executor of those mysterious shots.

He was a teenager, but hardly a naive one, and the signs were everywhere, not just in Firefly Valley. The failing TV networks. The one-way phone calls. Even all the dated websites. It stretched beyond his town. He didn't need to drive for two hours on a freeway to confirm that.

And although he longed to dismantle if not altogether obliterate his growing sense of isolation, he had no plans to seek companionship at his own peril. The fact was, he didn't know if the proprietor of the blasts was friend or foe. Could be either and you know this, Zeph, he thought. He might've been triple-tapping an old lady for her groceries. Hell, it could've been a freakin' gunfight, he thought. Or, you pessimist, maybe it was a cry for attention or maybe somebody needed help.

He stopped, an epiphany upon him.

Three successive shots. Three in a row. It was an S. O. S. It was a standard hunter distress signal. The valley was surrounded by forest, for crying out loud. He'd grown up with this stuff. That should've occurred to him right away!

"You idiot," he hissed. "Stupid. Stupid!"

Were the shots really back-to-back, though? He'd been adrift in dreams and couldn't rightly remember. Did the first linger, and then two more? He thought that was right, but he'd been jolted awake and his senses delayed. Either possibility was just as likely.

In the end, it didn't matter. It was the lingering threat of an enemy or perhaps even enemies lurking in the city that compelled him beyond Main Street, onto Market Avenue and finally into Foothill Plaza as the sun took shape over the mountains. It was another mini-mall, five or six businesses wedged into a thin line of dilapidated storefronts and barely enough parking spaces to accommodate them. The plaza stared across the street at an immense structure that was a K-Mart in another economic era. House of Smoke Cigars, Cindy's Laundry, 4 You Newsstand, The Cyclist, and at last, Firefly Guns, about to earn its first customer of the day. Scratch that – first and likely only visitor of the day.

Zephyr came prepared – not with a wad of cash or credit cards, but towing a massive sledgehammer he'd scavenged from his toolshed. He parked his car in front of the shop and stepped out with the makeshift weapon slung over his shoulder. He leaned it against the dusty storefront window and surveyed the area.

Firefly Guns was one of three such sellers in town. He chose it simply because it was nearest his house. As far as he knew, the place had been open for business longer than he'd been alive. It sat imprisoned by faded bricks that stretched into white stone. Hefty blue posts supported an overhang that provided shade on scorching summer days, which were not scheduled to return to the area any time soon. A sign on the glass double-doors read, *Closed.* He tried them anyway and found them locked. To their right was a large storefront window with more signs hanging. *Hunters #1 Resource* and *No Permits Necessary*, they claimed. Zephyr was relieved to see that neither the doors nor window were reinforced with security bars – one of the benefits, he supposed, of living in a small city.

"My good luck continues," he said and picked up the sledgehammer.

Maybe no bars, but what Firefly Guns did have was a security system equipped with an obnoxiously loud alarm. He chose the window over the doors, swung the hammer forward and the glass imploded. He imagined himself punching hole after hole through the translucent barrier until he had created a precise space large enough to duck through. That's not what happened. As soon as the hammer connected, the impact zone cracked and then shattered. Then, the entirety of the glass window followed suit, falling unto itself as it converted from a smooth, solid mass to tiny chunks and shards. He might've laughed at the outcome if not for the alarm, which bellowed a siren that violated his ears and got him moving.

"Crap!" he shouted and jumped into the new entryway, his heart thumping in his chest.

He ran and stumbled along the displays and surveyed the weapons. All he could think about was the piercing alarm and how it must be drawing all of the city's collective attention to the area, if indeed anyone's attention could be had.

He leapt over one display case and stole four handguns of unique shapes and colors, absolutely no idea what models, and clasped them to his chest with one hand as he ran back toward his car. Outside again, he fumbled for his keys and dropped all four guns on the sidewalk, where they clanked to a rest. He popped the trunk, picked up the weapons and tossed them into the space. Then he sprinted back inside and repeated the process, this time choosing rifles. He had intended to carry four additional pieces out, but they proved too ungainly, so he only took two, oblivious to their make. He tossed them into his trunk, slammed it shut and opened the car's front door when he realized he hadn't picked up any bullets.

"This isn't happening," he said and jumped through the window again.

He pawed all manners of bullet boxes. Red ones. Blue ones. Yellow ones. Green ones. Some were bulkier than others. Some leaner. Some heavier. The numbers that adorned them were perfectly meaningless –

they might've been long lost mathematical codes from an ancient alien civilization.

He braved two trips with the siren blaring and as he climbed out of the window with a myriad of boxes held against his chest, he looked up, and then he dropped them. Beside his car waited an old green station wagon with bald tires and worn paint. And leaning against its front bumper was a man, his arms outstretched and his hands held high, palms open and flat. It was a universal gesture that said with no words at all, stop, calm down – don't be afraid.

"Whoa, whoa, whoa — it's fine, chief. Fiiiine. Just wanna talk. Didn't mean to startle ya!" the man shouted over the siren.

He was older. Mid-fifties or early sixties, probably. Tall. Almost bald, save for a strip of black hair that faded into gray and circled the back of his head, itself tanned and spotted. Heavy stubble peppered his face and double-chin. He had a body like a pear and a belly that hung defiantly over his denim shorts, but Zephyr thought his girth belied muscles of the kind that take a lifetime of hard labor to define. He wore flip-flops.

"I don't mean ya no harm. Name's Ross. I live across the way." The man pointed to a grouping of houses adjacent to the abandoned K-Mart. "I heard the alarm is all." He stepped forward with an infectious smile and extended his weathered hand.

A box of bullets crashed to the ground as the boy forgot them and shook the man's hand instead.

"I'm Zephyr. I live a few miles from here. I just cam—"

"Boy, I'm so happy to see you I could kiss you!" Ross said and clamped both of his bulky arms together around Zephyr in a great bear hug. "I thought it were just me. But when I saw you – oh, dear Jesus! Dear sweet Jesus!" he almost sang as he swung the boy effortlessly around.

Zephyr felt tears rush to his eyes and fought them off, blinking.

Relief cascaded over him. He'd been struggling against everything: lack of knowledge, isolation, the endless possibilities and his growing fears. The dark of night was pure brightness compared to the blackness of the ordeal. Humanity had gone missing but a day yet it felt like decades to him, and here at last was a ray of authentic light wrapped in a tight shirt and sandals.

When the man finally set Zephyr down again, the boy could see him wiping away his own tears.

"Sir, I… well, thank you. I don't know what's going on and it's just been—" He paused, an idea forming. "Listen, are you hungry?"

8

Zephyr insisted on driving and the older man relented, but not before mandating that the boy trail him to his house first so that he could return his own car. Firefly Guns continued shrieking as the two drove off, its high-pitched drones fading slightly but never dissipating. Ross hadn't lied. His house — small, single-story, dilapidated, cacti and an assortment of colored rocks in lieu of grass – was several blocks away. The man pulled into a cracked driveway stained in oil and then hurried over to Zephyr's car, plunked down in the passenger seat — the entire car seemed to sway with him — and smiled.

"All right, let's eat," he said.

As Zephyr drove, he explained how he'd awakened at Ridge Park to find his girlfriend missing – censoring the fact that he'd been drinking the night before – and then detailed the events that comprised the remainder of his restless day and night. It was a summarized recounting that culminated in gunshots.

"So you thought you'd get you some of your own guns this morning, and that's when you run into me," Ross said.

"Right. It seems kind of stupid now that I'm talking about it with you, but it didn't feel stupid when I heard those gunshots last night," Zephyr said. "Did you hear them?"

"Well," Ross said, rubbing his hands over his scalp, "I heard something, sure enough. I got woke up out of bed in the middle of the night just like you, but I wasn't sure it was a gun or not."

"I think it was."

"Yep. Well, if that's true, we got company 'round here somewhere," Ross said.

A few minutes later, the Volvo pulled into a tiny parking lot off Flora Avenue, just four parking spaces and a thin stone walkway that continued to the front door of a restaurant aptly named *Early Bird Cafe*. The glass door was closed and locked.

"OK, boy. I guess you better do your thing," Ross said.

Zephyr had come prepared and he didn't hesitate. He swung the sledgehammer forward and it slammed into the rusty steel guard of the door. It was a direct hit. The metal barrier broke and the lock gave, at which point the door came loose and slid two inches inward. Ross pushed it open, cackling and shaking his head.

"You getting pretty good at this funny business, ain't ya?" Ross mused as he held the door and gestured for Zephyr to go on in.

Blessedly, there was no alarm. The two spent the next twenty minutes flipping on lights and then scouring the restaurant's storage room, freezer and pantry, and finally laid out several heavy frying pans on a series of oversized burners, turned them on – thankfully the gas worked just fine – and started cooking. Bacon and sausage sizzled, butter simmered and eggs fried. Ross toasted some English muffins and Zephyr poured two glasses of cold orange juice. The hypnotic smell permeated the place and the boy realized he was starving.

Shortly thereafter, as the two of them ate, Zephyr finally asked it.

"Sir, if you—"

"Boy, my name's Ross," the man said through a mouthful of eggs. "I know it's just you being nice and all, but there ain't no need for sirs with me."

"All right, sorry. Ross, do you have any idea what's going on?"

The man stabbed his fork into an overcooked piece of sausage, slid it around a plate soaked in maple syrup. They hadn't made pancakes or waffles, but apparently he had a sweet tooth. Then, he shoved the entire link into his mouth.

"I wish I could say yep. I woke up yesterday and everybody was gone." The words came muffled as he chewed. The man held up his hand, index finger outstretched, finally swallowed and then continued. "I looked all over, like you. TV and phone weren't any help. So I got on the interstate going north and that didn't last long. So then I come back—"

"Wait, why didn't it last long?" Zephyr asked.

"Damned trucks all over the place. Cars, too, but mostly just big old diesels. Some of 'em were just stopped in the middle of the lanes. A few more were stuck in the rails. I even saw some turned upside-down," he said, paused while he forked some food around and then went on. "I drove up and over the hill and let me tell you, it was hard going – probably twenty-five of those giants, at least. I spent more time trying to get around 'em than I did getting anywhere."

Zephyr had already seen this phenomenon in the city streets for himself. Not diesels, but an assortment of cars – a handful of them overturned, more crashed, but most rolled to a stop and vacant. He was going to ask if Ross had seen any evidence of survivors when the man started to speak again.

"So I just gave up and come back. But I'd already committed myself going northbound and there weren't no exits any time soon." He took a generous bite of muffin, wiped some jelly from his cheek and then licked the side of his hand. "So, I turned around and drove back down the wrong way. I always wanted to do that, but there weren't nothing fun about it. I thought I might get stuck between those trucks and there I'd be."

Zephyr found the image horrifying and incredible. All the law of the land, the rules of the road, forgotten, he thought. He finally asked if Ross had spotted anything resembling life and the man said no – just clothing, shoes, jewelry, all the same remnants the boy had encountered. As he'd suspected, the highways and likely the nearest cities too were not immune to whatever had happened — whatever was still happening.

The man said that after he'd finally traversed the freeway, he drove around town and looked for people but couldn't find anyone, a situation Zephyr knew too well. He tried the police station and it was open. When he stepped inside, though, he discovered it empty. Most of the shops were closed, he said. As the day passed on, he investigated the hospital, which was also vacant.

"It was eerie in there. I'm not gonna lie, I walked down a hallway and then I turned around and left. I'm a grown man, but I ain't embarrassed to admit it," he said.

So he'd gone home, sank into his sofa, turned on the television and waited. And then he fell asleep. He woke several hours later to the howling wind and it had grown dark outside. He made dinner and waited some more. Nothing happened. He dialed around and nobody answered. He even tried calling his ex-wife.

"And, boy, that should tell you just how scared I was by then," he said, threw back his head and laughed.

Ross Williams was fifty-eight, a bachelor, father to a single son who died in the Gulf War, and retired. He'd tried on a variety of professions throughout his life, he cheerfully explained, including cameos as a mechanic, salesman, and his personal favorite, a concierge for some "fancy hotel" from a different era and place. But, he said, the bulk of his career life could be divided in two: his younger days in construction and the last twenty years, which were spent in the postal industry. He'd been a mailman.

Zephyr returned his small talk with details of his own much shorter life. That he was an only child. His aspiration to be journalist. His first and only girlfriend, now missing. His parents, both doctors, also vanished. But he found his own story dull, especially because the older man recounted his stretching history with such gusto and a depth of enthusiasm that Zephyr found he could not parallel. Maybe his life was a bore. Perhaps, but it's certainly not boring now, he thought.

When their words finally ceased, Ross stared through the window a long time and Zephyr walked to the checkout register, found a pack of chewing gum and pocketed it. He had already shed any guilt about such things. For now at least, those old restrictions didn't apply. When he returned to the table again, Ross said, "Well, at least we know dogs ain't been taken away. Probably just people."

When Zephyr didn't follow, the man pointed to the window. There, out beyond the little parking lot and trotting along a sidewalk across Flora Avenue, was a bulky German Shepherd, its tongue dangling from its open jaws. As they watched, it hurried along an intersection and out of view.

"It could still be like us," Zephyr said. "Maybe some of the dogs are gone. But not all of them."

"Maybe," Ross agreed, but he didn't look convinced.

The two were halfway back to the car when the man stopped, turned and walked back into the restaurant, calling behind for Zephyr to wait just a minute. Shortly thereafter, he reappeared with an oversized bowl full of their leftovers – some scrambled eggs, charred bacon, sausage and even three pieces of toasted sourdough bread softened in butter.

"Just in case the little pooch comes back. Maybe he'll find this snack," Ross said. "He's gotta eat, too."

Fifteen minutes later, the boy's car turned onto Main Street as they searched the city for other survivors. The older man chewed two sticks of gum into a wet mass, his lips smacking, as the car coasted and they talked.

"Ross, what do you think happened?" Zephyr asked. It was the question that had been on his mind for hours, but also the one he'd been afraid to voice because he was sure no answer could suffice.

Ross continued chewing and seemed to consider the question.

"I don't really know, but if I were to guess at it, I'd reckon it's God's work," he said at last.

"Do you mean, like, the Rapture?" the boy asked.

Zephyr was agnostic, but he'd caught himself hypocritically praying to God nearly every time he soared into a rough patch of turbulence on his flights to visit family in California. He sometimes wondered if he didn't secretly believe – hidden, locked away – yet, he also found some of the stories populating the bible absurd.

Take, for example, the Rapture, a biblical prophecy predicting that at some point in the future, those who believe in Jesus Christ will simply float into the air and be saved, vanishing instantly from the planet. According to the same scripture, non-believers will, in stark contrast, be forced to endure years of turmoil, war, plague and more before Christ revisits the world and casts the sinful away into a lake of fire. In other words, good times.

"Well, I don't know nothing about that," Ross said. He turned his head to look at Zephyr. "But I'll tell you one thing, boy. Look around you. Who else but God could have done this?"

9

The town protected its secrets. If people persisted, they stayed hidden as the man and the boy patrolled desolate streets crowded only by cars and the intermittent motorcycle frozen in awkward death rolls. The occasional crash interrupted the surreal presentation of the leftover world. There lay no bodies to be discovered, but Zephyr nevertheless could not shake the feeling that people were out there – maybe drowning in their own plight, maybe hiding, maybe watching.

The car radio hissed and popped as they drove and only a single station played music – an endlessly looped tune from Bruce Springsteen. Zephyr wondered if the song might play forever, until the electricity crackled and blinked out or the broadcast satellites plummeted back to Earth in fiery streaks. Would it take a month? A year? A century of *Dancing in the Dark*?

As the sun inched past solar noon, the boy started to worry about the night to come. He wasn't convinced that he could hole up in isolation and wait out the morning again. Now that he'd found someone with whom he could share the burden of the nightmarish situation, he dreaded the prospect of reclaiming full ownership. Yet, he wasn't certain that Ross would second his newfound commitment to inseparability. The man might choose instead his own residence and to embrace some solitary semblance of the life that existed, for better or worse, just two days ago.

They backtracked the city, drove down Market Avenue and, with dust swirling beneath their tires, turned into Foothill Plaza, home to Firefly Guns, now and forever literally open for business. Zephyr rolled down the driver's side window and heard no deafening siren, only the grinding of grit and gravel under the weight of the car.

"Alarm finally shut itself off. That's a relief, anyhoo," Ross said.

Zephyr wasn't quite as relieved. The boy wondered if the system had shut down or if someone had turned it off. The latter possibility struck him as particularly frightening because it suggested that somebody out there was acting with a level of calm, methodical discipline that escaped his grasp.

"You think we should check it out?" Zephyr asked.

"I ain't got nowhere better to be," Ross mused.

Ten minutes later, they emerged from the store carrying even more guns and bullets. As far as the boy could tell, nobody had been there. Weapons and ammo still littered the walls and shelves. Shards of glass blanketed the floor just beyond the frame. Probably, the alarm had just run its course.

They popped the trunk and looked over the growing mass of handguns, rifles and ammo boxes of all colors. Zephyr still didn't know if any guns matched their bullets so he hoisted up a long, heavy rifle and examined it, searching for some kind of make and model number. A dark wooden grip bled into black steel. It was double-barreled. A single thin slot revealed a chamber for bullets. He turned the contraption over and then upside-down like an awestruck caveman intoxicated by a gadget from a science fiction future.

"It's a 30-30," Ross said, chuckling. "I can tell already you don't know shit about guns, chief. And here's another tip for you. You see all them yellow-trimmed boxes in your trunk?"

"What about them?"

"Those're blanks. They're useless."

In addition to all the blanks, what the man called "glorified noise-makers," they discovered that the majority of the bullets Zephyr had run away with were incompatible with most of his weapons. Ross found this truth tantamount to the funniest joke ever told. He laughed until his face turned red and his eyes watered and then he slapped the boy hard on the back.

"Boy, you got yourself more guns in that trunk than a man'd know what to do with but only a-one of 'em gonna fire," he said. "Maybe we oughta just get you a nice little BB gun so you don't go shooting your foot off, or something worse."

"I'm glad I amuse you," Zephyr said, smiling. "Oh, hey – here's an idea! If you can stop laughing for just a minute, maybe you could actually help me find the right bullets."

Ross eventually obliged him. The man combed through his weapons and identified them one by one. Two Glock 9mm pistols, a .357 Magnum, a Smith and Wesson long frame pistol, three 22-caliber rifles and a shotgun in addition to the 30-30 he'd already named. He'd also carried an assortment of his own weapons to the car, presumably much smarter choices.

"How the heck do you know what all these guns are?" Zephyr asked, astonished.

Ross stopped and looked at him, an eyebrow raised.

"Where do we live?" he asked. "Here's a hint, boy: it ain't New York. How don't you know what they are?"

Zephyr recollected that Firefly Valley's small population somehow still required so many guns and so much ammunition that three dedicated stores had surfaced and flourished over the years.

"Touché," he said.

Ross climbed through the store's open window and returned a few minutes later with a wide stack of boxes that he held between his hands, drawing on brute force to crush each container into the next in an explosive cardboard accordion. He dumped the packages into Zephyr's trunk and then he turned around and climbed into the storefront hole again. By his fourth trip, Zephyr could no longer bite his tongue.

"Are you planning to start a war, Ross?" he asked.

"Well, you already shown me you ain't too smart when guns is concerned, but I gotta give you credit for having a good idea. If somebody's here shooting their gun off at night, I don't know about you, but I'll sleep a little better with plenty of my own firepower," he said, paused and then added, "And since you already got all the blanks, I guess I'll just have to settle for whatever's left."

"Don't come crying to me when you've used up all your bullets and you want some of my blanks," Zephyr retaliated.

"Boy, let's hope I don't gotta use any of these bullets."

10

Tumorous clouds intercepted the sun's rays and cast the valley in shade as the wind took flight and the day grew older. They had spent the afternoon in a viscous blur, driving along deserted streets and emptied lots and rolling by lifeless storefronts like meticulous window browsers.

When another street light changed from green to yellow and Zephyr again slowed the car in observance, Ross said, "You ain't gonna get a ticket if you run a red light."

"What? Oh."

He'd been doing it all day, he realized. No — for the last two days. Obeying all the street signs and stop lights even as he robbed gun stores and ransacked restaurants.

"Sorry," he said and laughed. "It's ridiculous. I swear, I just… it never even occurred to me."

So he stomped on the gas pedal, his engine roared and he blew through the light. The overhang camera snapped a picture that nobody would ever see and issued a ticket that no law enforcement agency would ever enforce. A teenage boy at the wheel of a white sedan. Next to him, a stocky bald man. Both of them were grinning.

Thirty minutes later, with dark clouds upon them and drizzle coating the windshield, they rolled about town as Zephyr played a new driving game. If he saw a red light, he'd gas it and try to pass underneath before it could change to green again. The problem was that the lights didn't glow red very long. He didn't know if the city's traffic infrastructure operated via timers, whether it was based on the time of day or if hidden cameras or sensors triggered the lights. Regardless, the game wasn't easy and his new ambition did not go unnoticed by his passenger.

"Now you've gone from one extreme to the other," Ross said and rolled his eyes, but he never told Zephyr to slow down.

Eventually Ross said that they weren't accomplishing anything and suggested a trip to the grocery store, which was a good idea. They needed to stock up on food and water to carry them through the week, if not longer. And Ross also wanted to loot some beer. They took a corner back onto Main Street and Zephyr was so focused on the stoplight ahead of him that he didn't see the figure standing in the middle of the intersection.

"Look out!" Ross yelled and in a second flat the boy finally observed the pedestrian, jerked the steering wheel to the right and slammed on the breaks. If it'd been a driving test, he'd have failed for sure. The car drifted, skidding sideways over the crosswalk, spinning and spraying water as it went, and missed the man standing before it by no more than ten feet. The engine humming. Zephyr's heart nearly jumped out of his chest.

He turned to Ross. "Jesus! Are you all right?"

His passenger didn't answer. Neither did he move; only stared beyond the boy and through the driver's side window, his face frozen. When Zephyr started to turn again, Ross stopped him.

"No, no," he whispered. His eyes never moved. "Look at me, boy. Don't turn around. He's got a gun."

They had plenty of guns, too. Pistols, rifles, shotguns – just about anything a hunter, survivalist or nut job with an agenda could possibly want or need. But in a stroke of genius, they had loaded all of their weapons and bullets, blanks included, into the trunk, where they currently sat.

Zephyr turned to face the newcomer and the man met his gaze. Average height. Lean. Thinning brown hair, cut short, and an equally sparse beard. Mid-thirties, maybe. He wore a black business suit with tie and dress shoes, all soaked from the rain. Both arms hung at their sides. In his right hand, though, he gripped a black revolver. To Zephyr, his face looked… blank. Completely unreadable. And he didn't move.

"What did I tell you?" Ross said. "Jesus Almighty, get us outta here!"

The boy stomped on the gas pedal and back wheels spun, but the slippery street offered no traction. He stopped, then repeated with less pressure and the tires finally caught pavement. The vehicle's rear end drifted clockwise in a perfect circle before he realized that he'd forgotten to straighten out the steering wheel and locked them in a perpetual donut. Zephyr yanked the wheel to the left this time and the car at last chose a direction and sped off, zipping straight away into a center divide. The Volvo hit the curb hard and both occupants bounced around in their seats before it came down on the other side with brutal gravity and smashed into a parked mini-van.

"Pop the trunk!" Ross yelled, and Zephyr fumbled for the release.

His senses lagged. He felt like he'd been kicked in the stomach. When he finally stepped from the car and peered across the street through the rain at the man in the suit, the figure glared back, gun still dangling at his side, but made no move to advance on them. He might've been a statue. The boy heard heavy metallic pumping noises from the rear of the car and then Ross stepped out, butt of a shotgun held at his shoulder, aim locked and firm, and walked toward the well-dressed enigma.

"I got my gun on ya!" he called. "Don't try nothin' funny or you're gonna wish you didn't!"

The figure either didn't hear him or didn't care. He lowered his gaze, seeming to survey the street, but he looked neither scared nor mad.

"We don't want no trouble!" Ross repeated and edged closer. "Ya hear? Just drop that gun of yours, all right?"

It occurred to Zephyr that he had inadvertently become a passive observer to this scene, so he dashed forward and soon shadowed Ross, who stood less than eight feet from the drenched businessman. Now the rain poured down in curtains, splattering, pounding, and crushing visibility. Cold water hammered them, great gobs of it exploding on the barrel of Ross's shotgun. Zephyr pulled his hoodie over his head and it was soaked in seconds. But the figure in the suit kept on staring.

"Mister," Ross said. "Are you all right?"

There came no immediate reply.

"Miste—"

"Go ahead and do it," the suit said and there was something in his tone that stopped Zephyr cold. It was short. Defiant. Perhaps even provocative.

"Go ahead, what?" Ross asked.

The suit's gun hand twitched just a little as he locked eyes with them. They were tired, bloodshot eyes attached to a gaunt face. "Aim that fucking gun and pull the trigger," he spat.

"There ain't no rea—"

"Do it, or I'll do you," the suit said. Calm. But underneath, something else.

Ross hesitated. "Like I said, we don't want no trouble."

"You found it!"

And with a level of speed previously unobserved, he whipped his gun up and took aim at Ross. He might've been a gunslinger drawing his weapon in an old Western. It happened with such speed that Zephyr's only new-world companion stepped backward and nearly tripped over him.

The two men stood there, guns held, each locked on the other, neither blinking, a boy caught in the background. To Zephyr, this standoff seemed to last months, the rainfall not a storm, but a season. In actuality, it played out in seconds and it was Ross who finally broke form. The boy braced for an eardrum-rupturing blast, but one never came. Instead, the older man shook his head and slowly lowered his weapon with one hand, looked away, grimacing, and used the other, palm open, to block his face in a primitive shield against the suit's revolver.

"Please, don't shoot. We don't want no trouble," he pleaded. "We was just driving around. That's all. We didn't see you."

Zephyr braced for something horrible. A piercing crack followed by a nightmare, perhaps. He wanted to run, but his legs wouldn't respond; they seemed disconnected in another world and time. The gunman's aim was steady. He's going to do it, he thought. He's actually going to do it. You have to do something!

But no gunshot sounded. Instead, the assailant surveyed them both once more, his composure faltered, and just as quickly as he had raised it, he lowered his revolver.

"Gone," he said.

That was it — a breath of a declaration that proved nearly inaudible. For the first time, though, Zephyr saw authenticity cross the man's face, now a contortion of agony. As the rain pelted him, the gunman fell to his knees with a splash. The man looked up to meet their eyes and Zephyr finally understood.

"Please, don't make me. Don't make me do it myself."

"Mister," Ross said as he bent to one knee and redistributed half of his body weight to the shotgun, butt down — now a makeshift crutch. "I don't know what happened to you, but I can guess at it. Bad stuff's been happening all around. This boy here woke up and his parents was gone, too. Even a miserable sumbitch like me lost loved ones. It looks like the shit hit the fan pretty good and now we're all covered in it. But this thing you're planning, it ain't the answer. It just ain't."

Ross put a hand on the man's shoulder and water surged from his suit jacket like a wet sponge wrung out. "What's your name, fella?"

The man looked away, fixated once more on the concrete. "Jerry… Saunders."

"Take my hand and let's get out of this storm so we can do some talking, Jerry," Ross said and after only a moment's hesitation, Jerry Saunders did.

They broke into a McDonald's across the street from the crash site and it was dryer inside. The restaurant speakers played a low static and the florescent lights buzzed overhead. Zephyr peered over the counter, discovered a ruffled uniform on the floor, disrobed and tried it on. It was a perfect fit. Afterward, he surveyed the kitchen quarters and scooped up six cheeseburgers, fully wrapped and still warm under the glow of the red food lights. Then he crawled back over the counter.

"Oh, sweet Jesus," Ross said as the boy brought the food back to their table. "I think you found your calling, boy. You reckon they got one of those in my size?"

Zephyr grinned. "Afraid not."

Jerry just sat there, hands clasped on the table, his brown hair and suit still dripping. He didn't seem to notice or care that he was soaked. Zephyr sat beside the men and tossed the burgers on the table. Ross unwrapped one and halved it in a single bite.

"Eat, ya'll," he said, pointing to the pile as though introducing them to it.

Begrudgingly, Jerry unwrapped a burger and bit into it. This man still worried Zephyr. The boy wanted to ask what happened to him, but he was still afraid to broach the subject. It was only twenty minutes ago that he had drawn a gun on Ross. That he seemed on the verge of some botched suicide only added to the boy's reservations about him. He still looked dazed, sluggish, a little out of it. And the fact that he remained in possession of the revolver, now tucked away in his soggy suit pocket, had not escaped the boy's attention, either.

"I shouldn't have done any of that," Jerry said at last. The man's eyes were still red, his face haggard.

"Well, it's all right now," Ross said, wolfing down his second burger in as many minutes. "I'm not gonna lie, though – I just about pissed my pants out there." He slapped his hand on the table and then laughed with a mouthful of food until he coughed and choked.

"Excuse me, sir. I don't mean to be rude, but why would you – well, why would you want to do what you tried?" Zephyr asked, fidgeting in his chair. "My parents vanished. So did my girlfriend. Everyone I know is gone, actually. But we don't know what the heck is happening around here. Maybe there's a reason that makes some kind of sense and… I mean, what if everyone is coming back?"

Jerry considered the question for a moment and then spoke. His words came with concentrated effort. "This… is worldwide. It's everywhere. Your parents aren't coming back. My girls… aren't coming back. Nobody's coming back." He looked directly into Zephyr's eyes. "It's just us. It's our hell now."

The boy felt as if he'd been sucker-punched. The possibility that his parents could be forever missing always lingered, but nobody had given power to the notion until now. The implications of eternity clawed at the depths of him. He's saying they're dead, he thought. That they could be dead. He wasn't willing to accept that. Not yet.

"But how can you know?" Zephyr asked.

The man dismissed his question with a wave of the hand and then ran his fingers through his wet hair and sighed. "My girls are gone. My wife is gone. That, I know. And that's all that matters." There was a finality to his words that brought a full stop to Zephyr's line of questions.

"He went camping and when he woke up his little girlfriend was missing," he said, and nodded in Zephyr's direction. "Me, I didn't realize nothing was wrong until almost noon and only because the damn TV stations was out. What about you, Jerry?"

The man began to talk. Slowly at first, but then faster.

Jerry Saunders, dentist, husband, and father, woke at six-thirty in the morning, as he always did on weekdays. Dressed in his bathrobe and slippers, he tiptoed past two rooms housing his sleeping daughters and then to the downstairs kitchen, where he brewed his morning coffee. He cracked the front door for the newspaper, but couldn't find it, which never happened. He'd wait forty-five minutes and if it still hadn't shown up, he'd call and complain, he decided. Fifteen minutes later, he sat at his dining room table with a cup of coffee and his laptop, powered on and opened to *The Wall Street Journal*, which displayed yesterday's news.

It went from bad to worse. Like Zephyr, he checked all of the big news websites and found them outdated. But he also tried the international ones, including The Guardian and BBC News, and they were equally abandoned. So he turned on the television.

"Did you see the newsroom?" Zephyr asked.

The man nodded. "That's when I ran to get my wife," he said, stared at the table, shrugged, and added, "And… you know the rest."

He recounted the remainder of the last two days, detailing actions that Zephyr had also taken. Then he addressed a question never asked. The man owned one of those hulking satellite dishes – the kind that existed before *DirecTV* and *Dish Network* — and it allowed him access to all the international feeds. As the day wore on and nightfall bloomed, he tuned in to the global streams and confirmed only sporadic broadcasts and regular signs of a mass populace exodus, or "extinction," as he called it.

"You thought the newsroom was bad? BBC is stuck on some kind of crime scene. The title bar says it's live and something about hostages, but the camera is on the ground and everything is tilted kind of sideways. You can see police cars in the background." He leaned into the table, meeting Zephyr's eyes. "What got me is that right up front on the ground is a big microphone and a wad of clothes."

"The reporter."

Jerry nodded. "Just like every damn-body-else who vanished."

"Christ, Jesus," Ross said in disbelief. "It can't be."

"It is."

Tears flooded Zephyr's eyes, he leaned into his palmed hands and covered his face. He wanted to cry but he wouldn't let himself, so he stifled his emotions like some offensive sneeze. He took great, gasping breaths and held onto them. He'd clung to some tiny thread of hope, however minuscule, that the event was isolated. All of his logic required that. With that, he could concoct theories and explanations. Without that, the well ran dry, the antithesis to his watering eyes. Now, at last, he'd been forced to reconsider his optimism and the last strings of normality that came with it in favor of the unknown, where anything, even the utterly outlandish, was imaginable. His parents would not be resting in some hotel a hundred miles off while the city worked to clear a toxic spill or an outbreak of some virus if it wasn't just his hometown or even home state that was missing, but the entire world.

Ross put his hand on Zephyr's shoulder. He started to say something and then didn't.

11

Zephyr's tears receded as quickly as they had advanced and after a while he felt guilty for them. He had, since everything walloped him that early morning in the park, fought to keep his composure and his wits, to think and act older than he was, but the outburst had given him away. It was a reminder that he was, as Ross often said, just a boy, and he hated that.

Jerry had more news. In his time alone the first night, as he watched international television and drank himself stupid – Zephyr briefly imagined the man playing Russian roulette through a blur of drunken misery and rage – bright lights radiated his living room and rolled across his wall. He leapt from his recliner and ran to the window, where he saw two red dots speeding into the darkness. A car. Another person alive. And prior to his game of chicken with Ross a short while ago, a woman in a truck had rolled by the man as he wandered around the town.

"She tried to talk to me, I think."

"Did you happen to pull your gun on her maybe?" Zephyr asked.

"Possibly," Jerry said.

"Possibly?"

"That's what I said."

The man slumped back into his chair, then exhaled long and slow as he stared at the ceiling. "I swallowed a whole bunch of Vicodin this morning. Nine-hundred milligrams – definitely the good stuff. Everything's been a little hazy since. So I really can't remember," he finally said. "Red truck, and blonde. For all the good that'll do you."

"Well, least we know God hasn't taken away Eve," Ross said. To Zephyr, it sounded like a joke, but when he met the man's gaze he saw that he was serious.

"Eve was banished from Eden, along with Adam," Jerry said.

Several minutes later, the sodas finally caught up to Zephyr, who couldn't find the keys to the outside bathrooms. Finally, he resolved to relieve himself in the bushes near the drive-thru as he held several layers of newspaper over his head.

He could see that Jerry believed, as Ross did, that the disappearances were religious in nature. Both men obviously had shouldered some weighty sins in their day because they so readily accepted that they'd been forsaken. Zephyr endeavored to justify his own predicament as religious ramification, though, and found it difficult. Just two nights ago, he'd been drunk and frisky. It wasn't smart, and in hindsight, he wasn't particularly proud of himself. That all being true, though, neither of these acts was theft or murder.

He was pondering whether he was ignorant to the sins as defined by the bible and in the next blink he was kissing pavement, the newspaper tossed to the side in a forgotten pile, his train of thought obliterated. An explosion inside rattled the windows of the restaurant. He jumped to his feet, threw open the doors and ran inside. Ross stared back at him from his place at the table, his eyes wide, both hands up.

Jerry appeared fast asleep against the chair, his head slung all the way back over the headrest as he ogled the ceiling, mouth ajar. His two front teeth were missing and thick, dark blood hemorrhaged from his cavity, as well as a new one on the back of his head. It dribbled down his chin and onto his damp undershirt. A red spray of gore and fleshy chunks painted the wall directly behind him. His revolver lay on the tile beside the chair, finally surrendered.

He'd blown his brains out.

12

The two of them decided not to do anything with the man's body. What, really, could be done? Ross couldn't wait to leave. He turned from the scene and pretended to study the rain outside. Zephyr asked him if he wanted to say a prayer and he shook his head.

"I just wanna go."

He looked stunned — in shock, maybe — and for good reason. He was right there, Zeph, he told himself. Right there. Sitting right across from him when he did that. He has to live with that forever. Of course he's stunned. Of course he's in shock. You saw the aftermath and you're in shock.

The boy wanted to ask Ross how it transpired. He wanted to know how Jerry had done himself in. Had Ross said something to him? Was there some kind of conversational trigger or had he just smiled, winked, pulled out the gun and sent a bullet into his mouth and through the backside of his skull? He needed to tell the older man that he was sorry, and that it wasn't his fault, that Jerry had obviously made up his mind about this final action well before he had even met them, but he couldn't think of a way to begin.

He knew they should leave so he fumbled for his car keys, but when he pulled them out he understood that they didn't belong to him at all. At once, the day's events came flooding back to him. The stupid car crash. The fact that he now wore some vanished teenager's uniform. The keys dangling before him must belong to that person. Zephyr pressed the lock button and heard a car horn sound outside. He tapped it repeatedly as he ran to the window and saw headlights blink on and off. They belonged to a blue pickup truck.

"I found us a new ride, I think," he told Ross.

The man nodded.

"Ross, I hate to do this, especially in light of what just happened, but do you think we should go back to my car and get our… stuff?"

At first, he wasn't sure if Ross heard him. The older man continued wiping his shirt, as though cleansing the blood would also cleanse the memory. After a moment, though, he stopped rubbing, sighed and said, "Yep. I reckon we better."

"Is there anything I can do?"

"No. Ain't much can be done now. Let's just go."

Zephyr handed the older man the keys, suggested he try to start the truck and said he'd be right behind him. Ross pushed open the restaurant doors and scurried to the vehicle. He wasn't fast on his feet, even when he meant to be, and he was soaked all over again by the time he finally humped himself into the car seat.

The boy turned away and looked upon Jerry's lifeless body – slumped backward, arms dangling, jaw gaping, blood pooling on the tile below. If not for all the rich, dark red that painted his jaw and suit, he might've been a man so exhausted that he'd fallen asleep in his chair. Not light rest, but the hard kind interrupted only by desperate gasps of air and erratic snores so loud that they assaulted the ears.

Staring at the man, Zephyr had several unrelated thoughts. The first was that he should do or say something to honor a life lost — he just couldn't think of what. Then, his eyes came upon the black revolver, discarded on the tile, and he thought he should take the weapon and throw it away so that nobody else would ever use it. And yet, he didn't want his fingerprints on it supposing the suicide was ever investigated. Absurd, he knew. Seriously. Who the hell is going to investigate this, Zeph? I don't know if you've noticed, but both *Law & Order* and *CSI* have been cancelled, dude. He knew it was a ridiculous notion, but it didn't matter.

In the end, he said nothing, did nothing, and left Jerry Saunders in McDonald's at a table for one where he would sleep eternally. He hoped that if there was a God, he might take pity on the man.

13

Ross drove, which was just as well because the truck was a stick-shift and Zephyr had no idea how to operate it. It was a rough ride overrun with hard bursts and slows as the gears caught and ground. Eventually, the vehicle pulled parallel to the Volvo, forever locked in steely intercourse with the overweight minivan, and they transported all of the guns into the backseat.

"What now?" Zephyr asked as he slumped back into his seat.

"Well," Ross said, "I need a drink, so I guess we oughta go shopping." The tufts of hair around his scalp had dried some, but his clothes were still wet. He looked pale.

"OK. Sounds good." He wasn't going to say anything else, and then he did anyway. "Ross, don't be mad, but what happened? Why did he do that?"

His friend put the truck in gear. "I don't know, boy. One minute I was tellin' that damn fool about my ex-wife and the next he shot his head off. That's when you come in. You ain't miss much, but be thankful for what you did."

"Did he say anything?" Zephyr asked.

"Not a damned thing." Ross made the shape of a gun with his index and thumb and pointed at his mouth. "Just... pow."

Five minutes later, the truck rolled off Main Street into a large parking lot home to more scattered cars. Rain pounded the windshield, but Zephyr could nevertheless see clearly enough through the overworked wipers that the grocery store was open, its fluorescent lights still shining behind big, dirty windows. A hulking sign displayed a glowing red logo for *Ralphs*. The store bled into several other shops including a nail salon and a *Radio Shack*.

The doors opened automatically as they hurried toward them and they browsed independently, freely pillaging the aisles of the abandoned market, their steel carts loaded with food and drinks of all sorts.

Under the circumstances, Zephyr thought that a trip to the grocery store was an inevitability for anyone left standing and yet coming here just two days after everyone disappeared seemed altogether premature to him. Left to his own devices, he probably wouldn't have ventured over for another week or more. He wondered if other survivors had already visited the store. If anybody had, they hadn't really upset the place. Everything seemed in nearly perfect order.

The contents of their carts were telling. In Zephyr's, cereal boxes, milk, soda, chips, fruit, candy, bread, peanut butter and jelly, chunky and raspberry respectively. Ross had filled his cart with boxes of beer, some beef jerky, hot dogs, paper plates and various soup cans. The beer, however, greatly outnumbered all of the other contents combined and Zephyr suspected the man would be good and drunk before he drifted away to sleep that night.

The clouds no longer blocked the sun, but the moon, as they raced to stow their groceries inside the truck. When at last they finished and took refuge, Zephyr knew he could no longer avoid the possibility of a lonely, sleepless night.

"All right. Done with that," he said. "I was really kind of hoping I could hang with you tonight. If that's OK. If not, that's cool, but… I was really kind of hoping." His head down, the words came dumb, and had Ross seen his face in the shade of night, he might've looked altogether sunburned.

"Well, it's been a hell of a day and I ain't gonna be much company tonight, boy," Ross said. "What do you say we pick up tomorrow instead?"

"Sure, OK. That's not a problem. I'm just kind of freaked out to be alone." He hoped his voice didn't quiver. He didn't think it did.

Ross surveyed him a moment, scratched his head and then started the truck.

"I got an idea," he said. "Hang on now. This might get bumpy."

He rolled the truck along the cement walkway, coasted past the nail salon and slowed at the Radio Shack. There, he turned inward, stopped, then put the vehicle in reverse and backed all the way into the lot until the tires rubbed against a nearby parking divider. The store sat directly ahead, its lights off. He revved the engine and then put the truck in gear, ignoring Zephyr's questions. It sped forward, and when it did, the boy screamed and shielded himself. He thought Ross had lost his mind, that he intended to plow the truck right into the store and come racing out the other side. Instead, the man slowed the vehicle as it came to the walkway. It retained more than enough speed to smash through the entrance— a thin wire lock snapped as the doors came off their hinges, glass shattering – and yet the truck stopped firm and only its front end penetrated the doors.

Ross laughed hard, beat on the horn twice and shouted, "Yessir! That's how we do it, eh, boy!"

"What the heck are you doing!" Zephyr screamed back. "Are you insane?"

"No alarm, either. Hoo-wee! Little bit o' luck, and 'bout time!"

The man finally turned to the boy. "Now, I was thinking you wouldn't be scared if you could talk to me anytime and anywhere you want, and then it hit me. We just get us some of those fancy walkie-talkies. Then it'll be like we're together even when we ain't." He pointed toward the gaping hole that used to be an entrance.

Zephyr finally breathed. "Got it. All right, yes, good idea. But geez, can you clue me in a little earlier next time? I saw my life flash before my eyes there."

The boy returned to the truck a few minutes later with two boxes and some batteries. After they powered them on, Ross held in the talk button and squeaky, irritating feedback overpowered both speakers.

"What's your twenty, good buddy?" he joked, ignoring the noise.

"All right, all right – turn it off. They work."

A little while later, the truck rolled to a stop outside the wrought-iron gate that protected Fairfield Court. The boy reached into his pocket for his keys but found it empty. Then, he remembered that he wore a uniform and not his jeans and hoodie, presently soaked and tossed on the floor at the nearest McDonald's, a dead man watching over them.

Crap! Well, that's that, he thought. My mobile, too. They're gone for good now because there's no way in hell I'm stepping foot in there again. Ever. I guess it's not like my phone was ringing off the hook, anyway.

"So on your left there is the keypad to open the gate," Zephyr said and pointed. A silver box enclosed a small pad with numbers on it. "The code is 2020. Like the vision you wish you had." Ross chuckled, rolled down the window and keyed it in. A moment later the gate slid open with all the stuttering grace of any giant mechanism. A minute after that the truck stopped curbside in front of Zephyr's house.

"Nice place ya got there. What'd your parents do, own a bank or something?" Ross asked.

"They're doctors."

"Yep, 'course they are."

The rain broke against the windshield like heavy water balloons and the noise was so loud that it blotted conversation. Ross turned on the interior light, reached back into the cab and eventually pulled out one of the Glock 9mm handguns. Midnight black, cold steel, and heavy. With the unthinking ease of a man well-versed in the practice, he ejected the magazine, and thumbed bullets into the cartridge one-by-one. Afterward, he snapped the cartridge back into the handle of the gun with a satisfying click and then flipped on the safety.

"You ain't gonna need this, but just so you'll feel better. To shoot, you just undo the safety here and then back the slide here," he said, unlatched the lock and then demonstrated. "Now you've got a bullet in the chamber. All you gotta do is point and pull the trigger." He returned the safety and then handed the weapon to Zephyr.

The boy's heart hammered as he closed his hand around the grip. He knew that Ross was trying to offer him some small, misguided sliver of peace through the night, but the weapon induced just the opposite effect. It seemed to drive home the seriousness of the situation. If he really didn't need it, why did the man give it to him?

"All right. Thanks, Ross. I'm still kinda freaked out, but I'll live."

"You're gonna be fine. And don't forget your walkie. If you need me, I'm just a click away."

"What about all the other guns?" Zephyr asked.

"Your call, chief. If you want 'em now, they're yours, but running 'em up to your mansion over there ain't gonna be fun in this rain. Otherwise, I'll just bring 'em by tomorrow and then we'll go get us some more of that wonderful breakfast."

"Yeah, that's cool. Just bring them by tomorrow."

"Bright and early." Ross put his hand on the boy's shoulder. "Listen, no hard feelings or anything, ya hear? I just saw some things I wish I could forget and I'm gonna try and drink 'em away tonight. Ain't no reason for you to be around for that."

"I understand. I mean, I wouldn't care. I'd probably just sleep, but it's all right. I'll just see you tomorrow."

Ross waited as Zephyr sprinted from the truck with a Glock in one hand and two bags of groceries in the other. Thankfully, his door wasn't locked, although he almost wished it had been. The rain seemed to draw a murky curtain around the neighborhood, but as the older man finally drove away, the boy could still make out the dim red halo of his taillights.

When he finished putting his groceries away, he found an oversized mixing bowl and poured generous helpings of cereal and milk into it. Then he sat at his dining room table and ate in a daze as he dialed the phone numbers of friends and family no longer answering. When he was finally full, he took the gun and canvassed the house, once more searching out every room, every corner, every potential hiding spot. At last satisfied, he drew the lights, walked upstairs, powered the television and fell onto his bed.

"Boy, ya there?" the walkie-talkie hissed and squeaked. Zephyr about dropped onto the floor before he realized what and who it was.

He pressed the button on his own device. "Yeah. Where are you? Sounds pretty good on my end."

Several seconds passed. "At home already. Working like a charm. Sometimes I'm so smart I amaze even myself, know what I mean?"

"Yeah, a real genius. You ever hear of safety in numbers, smart guy?"

More hissing and pops.

"Now don't go getting all butt-hurt over nothin'. You're not the one who saw a fella shoot his head off today. Cut me some slack, boy."

"I'm just kidding," Zephyr said. "But these do work pretty well. I'll be hanging around so if you get bored, you can always say hi."

"You got it. Over and out," Ross said and then he was gone.

Sleep was myth; it teetered on the edge of reality, ever elusive. Midnight faded into one and two in the morning as he lay in bed with restless legs, the overwhelming compulsion to kick and to move as he struggled to find comfort. This frustrating sensation always tormented him whenever he dared sleep in his shoes, but he wanted to stay ready to race if the situation necessitated it. Eventually, though, he decided that preparedness simply wasn't worth sacrificing all chances at sleep, rose from bed, undressed – the McDonald's garb wasn't becoming anyway – and put on a new pair of jeans and a v-neck sweater. Then he lay down again and began to browse the television once more.

The walkie-talkie beeped and squeaked.

"Dipshit." The line hissed. "Little… damn it, pick up."

Zephyr jumped out of bed and yanked the talkie from the top of the dresser. "Here, here. What's up? Little late. Had a few drinks, did ya?"

Static. Then: "Damn right, I done. Fuckin' hell right!"

Oh yeah, he's ripped. Guy's out of his gourd, Zephyr thought. He already wished he hadn't responded – that'd he'd just left the man to sleep it off.

"What's up, Ross? You get any sleep?" He suspected that'd be a no.

Whatever the man meant to reply wasn't decipherable. Several pops came over the walkie-talkie and then a series of noises that sounded like scrapes. Zephyr thought he heard Ross saying something to himself in the background, but he couldn't be sure.

"You there? I think you broke up. Say again," the boy said.

No response.

"Ross, you there? I think we've got a bad connection."

Static hissed back. "Fuck yer congestion, boy." Ross laughed hard at this. "I heard just fine. Takin' a piss out over here."

"OK, sorry." Zephyr caught himself pacing around his room and then sat down on his bed. He pressed the talk button. "So what's up? Are you feeling any better about earlier?" He winced as soon as the words tripped over his clumsy lips. Oh, you dummy. You dummy! Right now? You just asked that now? Of all the things, Zeph. Seriously?

"Feel great," Ross replied. Nothing more.

"OK. Good." He paused. "Glad to hear it. So, it's pretty late. So I think I'm going to call it a night."

The talkie hissed. Then: "Why wouldn't I feel great, you—t? Why wouldn't I—" Broken, cut off. More words came, but they were so loud and distorted that Zephyr couldn't understand them. What did come through loud and clear was that Ross was screaming into his handset. The garbled, one-sided tirade continued for a little while longer before the correspondence returned to silence.

Zephyr stared at his talkie and said nothing. Instead, he sat on his bed, his heart beating hard, and considered an appropriate response. He waffled between replying in turn with a few stern words and apologizing – groveling, maybe. In the end, he did neither. He just sat there, now wide awake.

The talkie squeaked back again. "Ya fuckin' wi— m—oy?"

Zephyr didn't respond. He grabbed for the television remote and then muted it.

"Boy. Ya fuckin' with me?"

"No," he said. "No, man. I'm not. I'm just sleeping, Ross. It's really late."

Static filled in the gaps. "Yeh, that's what I thought." He muttered something else that Zephyr couldn't make out. "You ain't wanna be fuckin' with ol' Rossy. Yer boy earlier, he learned that lesson the hard way, but he sure as shit learned it all right."

My boy earlier? Huh? Does he mean Jerry? Zephyr's stomach felt as though it had been pushed off a cliff. "Listen, man. Go to sleep already. I don't even know what you're talking about."

"Ain't talkin' 'bout nothin'. Just tellin' ya how it is."

"All right. Sounds good." He considered his next words, and then said, "Hey man. I'm really sorry if I upset you. Try to get some sleep and sober up. We'll get some breakfast tomorrow, on me."

The line remained dormant for a moment and then it squeaked on.

"Well, I guess some sleep will do me s'good."

Zephyr sat in his room, the TV casting dim light all around him, and waited. He half expected Ross to burst back on the talkie with some drunken tirade, screaming and raging, but one never came. After fifteen minutes, his mind abuzz with horrible possibilities, he decided that the man had probably finally succumbed to the alcohol and passed out. If only he could be so lucky. He glanced at his alarm clock: it was 2:57 am. He wasn't tired anymore.

Ross was the culprit this time. Not loneliness or fear of a horrifying situation, but a fat, bald man in his late fifties. A man with a penchant for alcohol and a talent for guns. What was it he said? *Your boy earlier learned that lesson the hard way.* Was he actually talking about Jerry and if so, why would Jerry's suicide serve as a lesson in not messing with Ross? Zephyr thought the old man was talking nonsense fueled by too many beers.

And then the boy's eyes widened as a terrifying image came to him. It was Jerry's teeth. He'd blown them clean out when he'd killed himself. He hadn't thought much of it at the time — the raw violence of the act took center stage — but in hindsight, it was bizarre. Who the hell shoots through their own teeth when they off themselves? Nobody does, that's who, Zephyr thought.

The hair on his arms stood up as a chill slid down his spine. There's no way. No way Ross would do that. Just, no. I don't believe it, he thought. And even if he could, how? You'd have noticed something, for crying out loud.

He replayed the scene. He'd been outside pissing when the blast occurred. He made it back inside seconds later and Jerry was dead, blood everywhere, the gun on the floor, and Ross looked sick to his stomach. That was it. It was just suicide.

But Jerry's teeth.

OK then. The recoil from the gun knocked his teeth out, he argued.

That's a hell of a lot more logical and likely than a nice old man murdering a guy with his own gun, especially when the same nice old man had a chance to shoot the guy in a full-fledged standoff minutes earlier and didn't.

Dude, his mind persisted, you've known Ross for two days. Two measly days. Don't presume that you really know anything about him. That nice old man just screamed so loud into your walkie that he just about blew out the speaker on the thing. And there's no way a gun that small would kick hard enough to punch out two front teeth — even you know that.

He's the only person here and he helped me, he thought. He wouldn't have done that to Jerry. He stood down against him and he could probably out-shoot all of us. I just can't believe he'd murder a guy in cold blood after something like that. He's just not that evil. He went out of his way for me. Without him, all my guns would be useless.

And then, don't you mean all of his guns, Zeph? In case you forgot, they're all sitting in the back of his truck.

14

Zephyr's pillow was a rock, his blankets sandpaper as the prospect of sleep fled like he wished he could. More than ever, he missed his parents. His dad watching television downstairs, his mom slumbering across the hallway. His face contorted and he fought off tears. He felt so powerless and he knew that he wouldn't be able to lasso proper rest until daylight arrived.

Although his mind argued incessantly about the real Ross and what he might or might not be capable of, no fundamental decisions about that man had yet been reached. Zephyr knew only that he would likely be taking a raincheck on breakfast, a truth that filled him with a dilution of fear, sadness and guilt. He'd enjoyed making up a meal with the old guy. He was funny, he told great stories, and he didn't seem overwhelmed by everything going on around them. Zephyr liked him. The problem, of course, was that he just wasn't sure he could trust him anymore.

You're overreacting. He was drunk and out of his mind.

Do you really want to take a chance on something like that?

Stop it. He's you're only friend here and he's been nothing but helpful.

You don't know what his motives really are. You need to use your head and play it safe.

On and on the left and the right hemispheres of his brain dueled. Every time he closed his eyes and willed consciousness away, those arguments seemed to increase in speed and in volume and deep sleep proved evasive. As rays of light finally darted through the holes in his shutters, he put his feet to the floor and scurried downstairs to the fridge in search of soda and more precisely some caffeine to jumpstart his system. It was becoming an unnatural ritual.

It was three days now without any real news. He sat down at the kitchen table with a cold cola and tried to clear his head so that he could think about his next move. He'd happily surrendered control to Ross shortly after he met him, but the old man's drunken outburst in the night had triggered a reversal of that ownership. Zephyr no longer thought of the future as something they would face together, but rather something he might need to endure alone.

He also realized that he hadn't really considered the future – at least not one minus so many millions of people. Not really, anyway. Everything he'd done so far had been reactionary in nature and only to immediate problems. In a bubble. He couldn't find anybody so he looked for them. His clothes were soaked so he stole new ones. He heard gunshots in the night so he looted a weapon of his own. All fine. All logical. But nothing he could really call a plan, especially if the situation at hand didn't resolve itself tomorrow, or next week, or next year, or ever.

One of his dad's favorite mottos was: hope for the best, plan for the worst, and that, he thought, was exactly what he needed to do now. How to begin, though? He ran his hands through his thick hair and imagined a shower, but pushed the thought away. Come on, man. Get serious.

He rifled through one of the kitchen drawers, retrieved a pencil and notepad, sat down again and began to construct a list of pros and cons – the former on the left and the latter on the right side of the page.

Under pros, he wrote *electricity*. He stood, walked to the kitchen sink and ran the faucet. Fresh water poured out. He sat down again and wrote, *water*. Then *gas, food, Internet, phones,* and *television*.

He stared at the cons section for several seconds and then he simply drew long, squiggly arrows from all of the items he'd penciled on the left. Everything going for him now, it was all temporary. It was going to break down, to dry up, and to waste away. And it scared the shit out of him.

"You went to the store last night and what did you get, dude? Candy bars?" He shook his head. "Jesus."

He'd rendered some foggy index of what he might require in a world without easy access to the basic necessities. The obvious musts like shelter, clean water, canned foods, warm clothes, the means to make fire and so on, of course. He also thought it would be smart for various reasons to secure a generator. He'd seen it done in the movies, but the divide between what transpired on the silver screen and what played out in reality was not just a crack, but a canyon. He had no idea how to use one, for starters. He only knew it'd require gasoline, which might not be an easy commodity to come by in a world short on electricity and in turn credit card transactions, but he'd think about that later. He'd also need guns. He had one of those, that was something, but he knew he'd probably need more, as well as bullets.

He imagined some bearded future version of himself sniping deer and deboning fish and nearly laughed.

Something crackled upstairs and Zephyr's stomach took a dive as he realized what it was. He raced to his room just in time to hear the tail end of a fuzzy communication.

"—ere?"

He could've guessed what it was but there was no need.

"Boy. You there? Wake up. Let's get some eats."

The talkie squeaked into radio silence as the man waited for a response. Zephyr's heart jackhammered against his chest. He picked up the device and then held it in his hand, undecided about what to do next.

"Come on, boy!" the box hissed. "Come on now! My belly'll thank ya if—"

"Ross, hey. Sorry. Still in bed over here. Can you hear me?"

For a second, nothing. Then, "Well, hallelujah. He lives! All right. All right. You hungry?"

Zephyr pulled the talkie to his mouth and then yawned into the receiver for dramatic effect. "I'm actually not feeling so hot this morning. I didn't sleep much and I keep feeling like I want to throw up this morning so I think I'm gonna sit out breakfast— can't think about eating right now. Maybe try me again for lunch or dinner." He winced at his acting – the Academy wouldn't be calling any time soon – but he hoped Ross didn't notice.

He waited for the old man's reply but none came, and his mind raced with possibilities. Maybe he didn't hear me. Maybe he dropped his walkie. Maybe his batteries died. Maybe, maybe, maybe. Zephyr pressed the button on his talkie again. "Hey, you there?"

For a second, he didn't think Ross was going to engage, but the old man's voice finally squeaked back into his room. "Well, shoot. I'm real sorry to hear that," he said. "Could be you should try and eat something anyway. Sometimes your body wants it even when you think it don't, ya know?"

Zephyr's muscles relaxed ever so slightly – he hadn't realized they'd gone rigid. "I wish I could. I don't exactly love the idea of being alone, trust me, but I'm no good right now. I just need to rest, maybe drink some water. I'm sure I've got a long date with the bathroom. Hit me up a little later."

"All right, boy. Yeah, you drink some water and get some bread in you. You want me to bring you some breakfast, at least? I gotta drop by your guns, anyway."

"No, that's OK. Just give me a little recovery time and try me again this afternoon. If I feel any better, I'll holler so keep your walkie with you," he said.

"You got it. Take it easy over there. I'll be at the Early Bird if you change your mind."

"All right. Talk soon."

And that was that. Had Ross bought it? He didn't know. Good. Go ahead and add it to the scroll of other things you haven't been certain about recently. It was fair cynicism.

Zephyr let go of his breath and tossed the talkie back on his mattress. He'd gained some time. Now what? His heart raced onward as his feet led the way, his mind stumbling behind. First to his bedroom closet, where he found a weathered, stringy backpack and then to his dresser, where he gathered clumps of shirts and two pairs of jeans before stuffing them into his bag. He hurried downstairs again, eyed his notepad, and shook his head at the short list.

The gun, he thought, and then sprinted back upstairs again. He returned to the kitchen a minute later and then realized he'd left the talkie on his bed so he ascended the stairs once more. It was so frustrating – no, it was damned infuriating that he could not seem to gain legitimate control of the situation.

"Just ask 'your boy Jerry' what happens to people who aren't ready for the shit storm," he said and then pushed the thought away.

He sat at the table and considered what he was about to do as his pulse spiked. That inexplicable marriage of terror and raw bioelectric current had taken hold of him and it was in some twisted way a relief. It seemed to heighten his senses and surround the chaos with a protective web – a dose of nicotine before a sky dive. Yet that wasn't all of it. He also found solace in the closure of the situation. Whatever happened next, good or bad, he was fully resolute in his decision and momentum, and that felt good.

He made a mental catalog of all the items in the house, everything he might find useful in some capacity, except for food and water, of course, because he'd already resolved to throw some snacks and sodas into a plastic grocery store bag. He might've sat there for a few seconds or twenty minutes. In the end, he walked upstairs one final time and took his baseball bat from the floor. Five minutes later, a backpack bloated with clothes, a grocery bag full of food, his gun, walkie-talkie and bat, he locked and shut the front door to his parent's house and started toward the sidewalk.

He would never come home again.

15
Best Laid Plans

The rain had dissipated in the cold night but fierce clouds still held the sun and sky at bay. His neighborhood looked ordinary. The same old cars in driveways, the same old porch lights fighting against daylight to be recognized. A few birds were perched on the electrical wire overhanging the houses directly opposite him. The wind blew soft but cold against his face and he was thankful that he'd dressed himself for weather. The wrought-iron gate that shielded the cul-de-sac from the rest of the city remained closed, which he liked. Of course, Ross knew the code. That, he didn't like.

He crossed the street with his gear and stopped at the towering home in direct line of sight from his own. The place belonged to the Middletons: Gary, Jennifer and their two kids, Hannah and Stacey. The door was locked, so he walked around to the side gate.

"Climbing time."

An hour passed. He pilfered their fridge and cupboard and made himself a bologna and cheese sandwich and some chips topped off with a soda. Their TV showed more failing broadcasts. He dialed the police and it just rang. Deja vu. He accepted all of this with a sigh, but somewhere deep inside panic swelled and raged, waiting for its chance to seize control.

Zephyr wondered what day it was. He couldn't remember if it was Wednesday or Thursday. Or was it Friday? Did it matter? Probably not. Yet, the uncertainty nagged at him until he hit the menu button on the television and looked for the date. He finally found it in the upper corner of the screen: 9:39 a.m., Thursday, October 5.

His belly bulged and his eyelids might've held the weight of the world as he slumped on the couch and stared at the television, uncomprehending whatever program played out on its glossy screen – just happy to have background familiarity. He was so exhausted. He thought of Keiko and his parents. He thought of his friends. It was almost the weekend. One more day of classes. Just a quick nap will do the trick. I can deal with the rest after, his mind insisted, and he was asleep before he could mount a counter argument.

He woke to the familiar blips and hisses of the walkie-talkie as the old man muttered something indecipherable, and then fell promptly off the couch. He rubbed his eyes. What time was it? He fumbled for the television remote and found the menu button. 1:44 p.m. Not good.

"Helloooo! Sleeping beauty. Wakey-wakey!"

He pushed himself back onto the couch and pulled the talkie to his mouth.

"Ross, hey. I'm up, I'm up. I'm here."

"Well, hot damn. How ya feel?"

"Let's see," Zephyr began. "Barfed twice and been to the can as many times. That answer your question?"

"Aw, shoot. That ain't right."

"No, it sure isn't."

"Well, listen," Ross said. "I already ate lunch – figured I'd just let you sleep it off. Do you want me to bring something over? Aspirin? Or maybe, I dunno, soup? Shit. You tell me and I'll get it."

Zephyr allowed a considered pause. "No thanks, man. I appreciate it, but I just wanna sleep. I feel like dog crap."

"All right, all right. You got it. I'm gonna just dash by and drop off your guns and then leave you to it. If you wanna do dinner later, I'm your man."

Zephyr's entire body stiffened. That wasn't going to work.

"Hey, let's just do the gun drop off later if I'm feeling better. I'm not up to it right now," he said.

The talkie hissed a moment. "You ain't gonna have to do a thing, boy. I'll be two minutes, not a second longer. I really don't like keeping a full arsenal out in the open."

Shit! This was bad, Zephyr thought. If Ross finds out you're not home, this whole song and dance is over. He didn't know what to say though. None of the excuses he could muster sounded genuine at all. After what seemed like a lifetime, he eventually settled on: "OK, if you just want to throw the whole shebang on my front porch, fine, but I'm not getting out of bed for anything."

"Christ boy, you really are a Nancy, you know that? If that's how it's gonna be then I'll just hold onto the damned guns for you. Jesus. It's like pulling teeth," he said, his tone both amused but also frustrated. "Go on and get on back to bed, sleeping beauty, and I'll call again come dinner. If you change your mind, you know how to find me."

Zephyr let go of his breath and slumped again. "Thanks, Ross. For the record, I'm not a Nancy. Just a bit of a zombie at the moment."

Charade preserved. Probably. Well, let's just say maybe, he thought. Truth be told, he wasn't convinced that Ross was convinced but he'd already played his hand and there wasn't anything else to be done about it. Zephyr considered jogging back over to his parent's house and conjuring up some kind of explanatory note to post on the front door. *Ross — went to get some medicine and food; didn't want to bother you. Be back later.* Or maybe just, *Ross, couldn't sleep here alone another night so I decided to find a hotel and will hit you up tomorrow.* Or hell, maybe just *Gone fishing.* What was the difference? If the old man could not be deterred from dropping by that evening, he'd discover him missing and then he'd know something was wrong. It was not part of the strategy, but he would be ready with an audible if necessary. He hoped it wouldn't come to that.

The objective was twofold and altogether simple. Part one called for him to leave his parent's house as a safety precaution. It was his dad's life motto in effect. He wanted to believe that Ross was the good-natured old man he seemed to be, and yet he needed to prepare for the very real possibility that he wasn't; that he might just be a closet sociopath capable of gunning down a man in cold blood and then covering it up. Ross knew where Zephyr lived, plain and simple, so staying there was not the smart choice. Better to be paranoid than dead.

Part two called for him to get the fuck out of town as soon as he could. He'd given some thought to his escape and finally concluded that he couldn't do it under the eye of daylight and that he probably shouldn't do it with a car or motorcycle. It all came back to his sweet new friend, the grinning man who couldn't wait to bring him some piping hot soup to warm his belly and soul but also howled and screamed at him in drunken rages. Ross was old and slow, check and yes, but he also knew everything there was to know about guns and he could sure as shit shoot them. Zephyr imagined himself pulling out of Fairfield Court in his car and right into a big pickup truck with Ross at the wheel, a gun at his side and a conman's smile plastered across his face. No. Thank. You.

No, better to go in darkness and on foot. He'd wait until one or two in the morning and then he'd scale some backyard fences out of the neighborhood, take the side streets to the gully and follow it through the mountains where it intersected with the freeway again several miles out of town. With just a little luck, he could probably find some abandoned car or motorcycle, get it started, and put some serious distance between them. It would be slow. It might take all night to cover that kind of distance as he tripped over unseen stones, sticks, weeds and trash, the castaway junk of the city, but that was all right.

He felt like sleeping but couldn't, so after what was probably an hour he began rummaging through the bedrooms for a distraction. Nothing of interest. Just sad photographs of lost people. He knew his presence here was invasive and it made him uneasy, but he liked the upstairs vantage point — that he could flip the shutters and gaze onto his block if he so desired, which, as a matter of fact, he did. And when he cracked those wooden blockers and peered beyond, his heart nearly caught in his throat because there, creeping slowly up Fairfield Court, was the dirty blue truck he and Ross had commandeered the night before.

Zephyr was a statue as his mind struggled to accept this latest information. He couldn't seem to catch his breath. He finally moved, drawing the shutters just enough so that he could see without being seen. The blue pickup coasted to a stop outside his parent's house and the old man stepped out.

He saw two things. First, Ross had changed. His loose shorts and sandals had been replaced by a red and black flannel, faded jeans and cowboy boots. He wore a blue Chicago Cubs hat, the iconic red 'C' clearly legible from Zephyr's perspective, the bill bent and warped as only years of regular abuse can do. He looked like a genuine hunter. A true good old boy. All he needed was a case of cheap beer in the backseat, and Zephyr guessed it was probably there. His second observation, more disturbing, was that he tucked a silver handgun into the backside of his jeans as he stepped from the vehicle.

His instinct was to run. Tip-toe downstairs, scale the fence in the backyard, sprint as far as his legs would take him and never look back. And he might've just done it if Ross had given him time. But the man had already raised his own walkie to his mouth.

"Boy. Zephyr. You up?"

As the question squeaked loud and clear through the talkie, he fell away from the window and dug into his pocket for what might have been a bomb about to explode. Finally, he thumbed the volume down and cursed himself, then peeked through the cracks in the window again, ready to bolt if Ross gave any sign that he'd heard anything, but the man was walking up the path that led to the front door of his parent's house. Zephyr ran back into the den and grabbed his Glock and then returned to the window as quickly as he had gone. Ross was already at the entryway.

"Wake on up now!" his walkie blipped.

Zephyr felt checkmated. He dared not reply. His only real option was to remain unresponsive and hope that Ross believed him in deep sleep. So he just stood there, staring, leaving all possibilities to the old man.

"Boy! I'm here. Wake your sissy ass up a minute and come down here so you can get these guns and be done with it."

Again with the guns? Really? Zephyr wished he'd just unloaded them all last night, raining or not. He'd have a beefy arsenal at his fingertips and Ross would not be stalking him.

He is stalking you, – you know that, right? He couldn't wait to be done with you last night – didn't seem to care about the guns then, did he? Now he's determined to have breakfast, lunch and dinner with you and he acts like he's carrying a freakin' nuke in the back of the truck. Who cares if he's got a trunkful of weapons? Who's going to take them?

"Damn it, boy! I know you can hear me. Come open your door and I'll carry everything in myself," Ross insisted. Static hissed back over the airwaves as he waited for a response that never came. "Come on now. You'll thank me for it later." For the first time, Zephyr thought that good cheer sounded fabricated, a stupid disguise, and the grip on his gun tightened.

He was prepared to wait all day and night for the next move and was beginning to think that Ross might actually shoot down the door as a response to his lack of one when the man turned away and descended the steps to his truck again. Zephyr breathed for what felt like the first time since the man arrived. Thank you, God, he thought. Thank you, thank you, thank you.

The old man reached into the truck, hesitated, and then turned back for the house. This time, however, he ignored the path to the entryway and instead hurried up the driveway to the side gate. Zephyr knew there was no pad on the thing. Bless his dad; he always turned that porch light on, but never thought to buy a lock for the gate. Still, he felt violated as Ross slipped past it. It was just plain uncool. So completely thoughtless. Especially given that for all he knew, Zephyr was up there puking his guts out or half-dead with fever. Whatever, though. He knew that the sliding glass door was locked. He'd made sure of it himself before he left. So unless Ross had brought a hammer or rock or was just planning to shoot through the glass, he was still going to find himself on the outside looking in.

A minute or two passed as Zephyr stared out from his second-story window and waited for Ross to plead his case over the talkie again. No communications, though. Radio silence, good buddy. Whatever the old bastard was doing, he apparently didn't see fit to tell him about it. This, of course, troubled him on many levels. First, that Ross felt so compelled to deliver these guns he was willing to break in to do it. That was not the action of a completely sane human being, was it? Second, that he'd gone incommunicado as he committed this old-world felony. Now, that part -journeyed beyond rude, beyond wrong, and smack-dab into creepy country. Third and most obvious, he didn't seem to be carrying any of the aforementioned weapons into the backyard. Well, maybe a handgun. So what was he doing back there?

Zeph, it's time to stop the pretense, man, he thought. Your good pal here is seriously off. He never wanted to give you any guns and you know it. It's all been bait and since you aren't biting he's moved on to

Plan B. It's just that simple. And if he actually breaks in and doesn't find you up there, shit is going to get real.

He despised that interpretation but also accepted the possibility. Suppose it was true. How had he gotten here? Zephyr imagined Ross waking earlier with a ruthless hangover and his own icky feelings about his drunken ramblings the night before. Maybe he'd realized that he'd somehow revealed himself, reached out to Zephyr for verification, and found it multiple times when he'd refused the man's invitations. How different would this day have played out if he'd just accepted the breakfast offer and pretended nothing had ever happened? He almost wished he had. The boy was still pondering this when Ross emerged from the side of the house and trudged back toward the truck.

The walkie blipped back on. "Hey now. You get some more of that comfy old sleep, huh? Rest is the best thing for ya right now and nothing beats home sweet home for that," Ross said.

Zephyr was terrified that merely moving his talkie might generate some kind of reverb and signal his acknowledgement and proximity. He finally set it carefully on the bed near the window and resumed spying.

"Yeah. I ain't gonna bug you no more about those guns. I'll just hold onto 'em, let you snooze. I honestly don't think you're even gonna need 'em, anyhoo. You still got that pinky-dink Glock, ain't ya? That'll suit a boy like you just fine. Me, on the other hand – well, I'm the hunting type, as ya know. Long-range rifle with a scope; the kind of gun that could shoot the ticks off a deer's ass from a quarter a mile off. Now, that's a weapon for someone with purpose. Someone who'll do whatever he's gotta to survive. You wouldn't know what to do with a gun like that."

There was something in the man's voice now. Was it anger? Condescension? Sarcasm? Maybe. Probably. Even so, Zephyr didn't think that was all of it. It was also what he couldn't detect, which was the trademark jolliness. Not so much as a particle of it. It'd been blown away. This man was not the happy-go-lucky senior with whom he'd shared breakfast and stories.

"Yep. You just keep on sleeping in that big ol' bed of yours and you concentrate on feeling so much better," Ross spat. "I'll be here when you're up and about and feeling right again – just me and these rifles. We ain't going nowhere, that's for sure. Just around this here city. Matter fact, never really know when I might get the urge to take a drive, maybe swing by your neighborhood and look around. Check in on ya. Just the type of guy I am – always looking out for my friends. Like to keep 'em in my sights."

He might've kept on talking. Zephyr thought about it later but couldn't be sure. The truth was that Ross could've confessed to killing Kennedy just then and there and he wouldn't have heard a word of it because his ears had diverted all bandwidth to his eyes as they stared wide at his parent's house, now billowing deep, black smoke from somewhere on the rear side.

For all of his preparation, he was perfectly unprepared for this — demonstrated repeatedly by his obtuse line of thinking upon seeing the darkening smoke. He thought, there's been a car crash. Then, no, I think a house is on fire. Then, wait, is it my house? Shit! Oh my God! It's my house! Followed by, why isn't Ross doing anything? Does he not see the smoke? And finally, the overdue, sickening realization: you stupid, stupid dummy. He did this, man. That asshole is burning down your freakin' house!

Zephyr thought again of the old man reaching back into his truck for something and now pictured that unseen something as a plastic tank of gasoline.

"You…" he began, looked at the gun in his hand as though discovering it, and moved to the window.

Ross remained in his truck, undoubtedly ready to admire his handiwork.

Zephyr pulled back from the window again, unlatched the safety on the weapon and then shuffled forward once more. His heart fluttered and somewhere in the depths of his mind, reason and fear gave way to thundering red chaos—- a flashing mass that drowned out everything as a nuclear explosion does ground zero. The aftermath of all actions seemed inconsequential. All that mattered was that Ross was vile and dangerous and that he wasn't at all a friend but the grim reaper with a smile; that he had just set fire to the last remnants of Zephyr's missing family.

The bastard was going to pay. Now.

Zephyr cracked the shutters. Slow. Don't be hasty. That asshole's not going anywhere. He looked again to make sure the old man remained in place and as he did his talkie blipped on the bed.

"Boy. You there?" Ross asked.

He gave no reply. Instead, he pocketed the device and focused on the man in his truck. Ross seemed to be locked on his parent's house, so Zephyr quietly raised the window pane. When he was finished, there was a six-inch gap between the pane and the frame, a layer of screen the only barrier between him and the outside world. He could hear the breeze outside now. He poked the barrel of the gun between one of the high cracks in the shutters and pressed it to the screen, lined up his right eye to the sight and adjusted it until he had a bead on the old man's head. If his aim was true, he'd catch Ross on the left cheek. It would not be pretty.

He had no confidence with a weapon, very well expected to miss and decided to up his chances with numbers. Not one shot, but five. Take aim and keep shooting – hope something hits. Something would have to hit. Are you sure, though? Take a breath and be sure this is the right thing, he thought, but this line of reasoning was obliterated in a flash. He's burning down your parent's house and he thinks you're hiding somewhere inside. He's trying to kill you, dude. What's the difference? Do it!

He checked and rechecked his aim. Ross hadn't moved. Was he asleep or just transfixed on the house? He couldn't tell. What did it matter at this point? He was going to be wide awake one way or another in a matter of seconds. Zephyr held his breath. Then he squeezed the trigger.

Blam!

He closed his eyes and pulled again. Four more explosions.

The sudden silence was agonizing. He couldn't believe he did it. He opened his eyes and peered through the window, prepared for the horrific aftermath of his actions. But there was no change. No shattered truck window. No bloodied Ross.

He'd missed!

He let go of his breath as his legs wobbled and threatened to give way. What the hell had gone wrong? Confusion everywhere — the entire ordeal dreamlike, disorienting, and nightmarish. Why the hell wasn't Ross outside clutching his face and screaming right now?

The old man stepped from his truck and as he did Zephyr fell back from the window. He could see the hole his shots had torn through the screen, but he hadn't hit anything. Not Ross. Not even his damned truck. How was that possible?

It finally dawned on him.

"Oh my God," he whispered. "They're blanks."

And then he ran.

He was halfway down the stairs when the bedroom window exploded behind him amidst a cacophony of gunshots. His feet felt heavy and stupid and he nearly stumbled twice. Reality seemed to have slowed as he struggled for footing. At last, he made it to ground again and then bolted for the rear sliding door. Gunfire rang out and more glass shattered somewhere toward the front of the house, maybe the entryway or living room window. Ross might've been shouting something. He didn't care. It didn't matter. He pulled against the door, it didn't budge, and panic seized him. Time stopped and his mind agonized for the answer to the riddle, but no solution presented itself. He aimed his gun at the glass, ready to shoot, and then thought, it's locked, Zephyr. It's just locked! His shaking hands unhinged the latch and the door slid open. More gunfire in the background, but he never turned around. Instead, he sprinted into the backyard and beelined for the stone wall on the opposite end.

Zephyr never felt slower or more vulnerable as he raced for that wall. He was a deer in a hunter's sights. Somewhere behind him, gunshots and yelling. Ross was closer, maybe inside the house. He couldn't tell and he dared not look back. He just had to get over the wall and he'd be all right. If he could just get to it.

The barrier was tall, thick and presented no real challenge for him. Pieces of stone jutted out at irregular angles that he used for easy grip and footing. Within seconds, he had scaled the wall and landed in a muddy flower bed on the opposite side. He hunched over and caught his breath. His heart raged in his chest, but he didn't pause. Instead, he raced through the backyard and into the clearing that comprised Green Field Court, another gated cul-de-sac adjacent to the one that engulfed the now-smoldering remains of his parent's house. It entertained more lavish houses that looked like his own. He hurried toward a huge bush at the edge of the home's front yard and peered to the left and right for signs of the old man or his truck. He wasn't there.

He kept going, running from street to street, scaling fences and walls, and moving from backyard to front yard, as the houses become decreasingly lavish. On and on he did this until the sweat on his brow ran down his face and the sun in the sky dipped below some mountains in the distance. All the while, he was careful. He approached clearings with caution and didn't navigate a traceable pattern. Every few blocks, he'd choose a different path and angle off in a new direction. He knew the area well enough that he had some idea where it would lead him.

Eventually, his feet landed on cement and he found himself in a weeded, dilapidated backyard with an empty pool and several rusted, dismantled dirt bikes. He sat, drew his knees, leaned back on his hands and sucked in air. He'd been going forever and it had all finally caught up with him. He needed a break. Cover of night was closer than ever now, but he could still see well enough to know that he'd come a long way from the old neighborhood. That was good, at least. He didn't think there'd be any way for Ross to follow him. He was tired, though, not to mention hungry and thirsty.

The backdoor to the house wasn't locked. As he stepped inside, the stale air smelled of old cigarettes.

"Hello! Anybody here?" He said it loud enough to be heard by any occupants, but not so loud that the sound could be carried outside. There was no reply.

The kitchen was a cliché. Disrupted, messy, gross – empty beer cans, dirty plates and discarded fast food wrappers blanketed the countertops and filled the sink. A few glass ashtrays overflowed with cigarettes, some smeared in lipstick. It was a dump. He heard the hum of the refrigerator and opened it. Inside, a pizza box, a case of beer, two cans of soda, some mustard and a jar of pickles.

He wolfed down pizza, drank soda and thought about the day's events. Specifically, the real possibility that his gun had fired blanks and what that suggested about Ross. The old man had loaded the weapon in front of him. Zephyr had watched him do it. If they were just blanks, what did that even mean? He figured that Ross had finally turned on him after he repeatedly refused to meet him, but if he'd sabotaged his gun the night before...

He reached into his back pocket, found the walkie-talkie and turned it on.

"—amn shame there's nobody to put out the flames. On the bright side, ain't like you can't find another house to sleep at, right, boy?"

Chills.

The old bastard had probably been talking at him all afternoon. Zephyr wished he'd flipped the talkie back on hours ago. He was positive Ross had said more than a few things he'd never be able to take back, made threats, revealed himself to be a full-blown sociopath. A psychopath. A killer.

"I knew ya wasn't up in that old mansion of yours," Ross said.

Yeah, right, Zephyr thought. You knew shit.

"Not cuz I went up there and had a look around, either. I just took a whiff of the place and knew you wasn't there because I couldn't smell no coward up in there. It's got its own stench. Kind of like dog shit, but more putrid. Powerful as a skunk. Yeah, soon as I couldn't smell that, I knew you musta' high-tailed it out."

Zephyr pressed the talk button on the walkie and then let go.

A pause. "Well, now, that you, boy? You finally thinking 'bout growing a pair and saying hello to your old pal?"

"Hey Ross," Zephyr said, unable to resist. "Yeah, how you been, old man?"

"He lives! Well, would ya look at that. I wasn't so su—"

"Hey Ross. Do you have a twin, by chance?" Zephyr started. The fear was gone now. "I mean, because here I was camped out at my neighbor's house and along comes this fat, bald, ugly and stupid motherfucker, and do you know what, Ross? That dumb piece of shit looked exactly like you. A perfect doppelgänger. Can you guess what I watched this walking turd do?"

Ross might've started into a reply but Zephyr didn't wait.

"I'll tell you. This twin of yours, he goes into my parent's house, has a look around, lights the place on fire and then waddles back to his truck so he can sit on his fat ass and watch the place burn down. Does that sound like something a brother of yours might do?"

Nothing for several seconds. "Well," Ross finally said, "I sure ain't got no brothers like that."

"Well," Zephyr said in a mock tone, his heart racing, "why don't you just go fuck yourself, then? Take one of those guns you've been trying to give me all day – what a nice guy you are, looking out for me like that – and go blow your brains out."

"That's no way to talk to your friend, now is it? I swear. I try to—"

"Seriously, just cut the crap. We both know what you did."

"Whatever you say, boy. All I know is I come to your house to try and drop off your guns and the place is on fire. So I go in to try and wake you up and you're not in there. Next thing I know, you're shooting your gun off at me."

"My gun loaded with blanks, you mean? Thanks again for looking out for me like that, old friend."

Ross chuckled into the talkie. "I was afraid you'd shoot your feet off if I gave out real bullets. Can you blame me? Good thing I didn't, too, or you'd have shot me instead. And by the way, I don't appreciate all that." He sighed for effect. "Listen, boy, this is all a big misunderstanding. I'm not the boogie man. Let's just talk this all out, man to man."

"Uh-huh. Like the man-to-man you had with Jerry. I think I'll pass on that one, thanks."

"What're you talking about now, boy?"

"Are you seriously going to keep this up?" This charade wasn't just tiresome, it was infuriating. "Listen, I don't have the energy to argue against your lies. We both know you're a low life and one way or another you're going to pay the price for what you've done. You better hope that people never reappear because if they do I'm bringing the entire police force to your house."

The old man cackled into his microphone. "OK, boy. You do that. In the meantime, you just remember there ain't nobody but us. So maybe you oughta zip that big mouth of yours before I find you and shoot it right the fuck off."

There it was. A little taste of the real Ross. Even after all of it, all the lying and conniving, all that he'd seen the man do, those unexpected outbursts shocked him. He still wanted to believe that the day was one big mishap, the aftermath of a sitcom-level misunderstanding. But he knew better, and it was outbursts like those that reassured him.

It was stupid to engage Ross at all. He should've stayed silent, left the bastard to his diatribes. He just couldn't do it, though. Not after all that had transpired. Not when he saw the man set fire to his parent's home. Not after the blanks and not after the smug gloating. The way Ross painted it, Zephyr deserved everything he got because he didn't invite the man over for breakfast – a meeting that, in hindsight, might well have ended in his extermination. No, screw that. He couldn't take proper revenge, but he could at least let him know that the secret was out. He could call Ross on everything he'd done and maybe put him back in his place, even if just a little.

"Yeah, I thought so, boy. You bark a lot of bullshit until someone barks back. But we both know that even if you had the balls to do a damned thing 'bout it – and let's be honest, you don't – you ain't got no spirit, no plan, and no weapons. Nothing. Hell, I'll tell you where I am right now if I actually thought you'd show up to meet me like a man."

Zephyr ignored the insults. If they were designed to goad him, they failed. He couldn't have cared less what Ross thought of him. That being true, the old man did have a point: he was weaponless. Well, shy of useable bullets, anyway. Of course, Ross didn't really know that, did he? Not for certain. Not now. After all, a lot of time had passed since he'd sprinted from Fairfield Court.

"You can think what you want, old man," Zephyr said. "I'm sure you're feeling pretty high and mighty right now with all you've accomplished. I mean, it's pretty spectacular when you think about it. First, shooting a guy in the face who just lost his entire family. Nice one! Gave yourself a little pat on the back last night for that one, I'm sure. But you didn't stop there. No, sir. This morning, you woke up – with a massive hangover, I've no doubt – and thought, 'Shit, ya know what would make a nice encore to murdering that tormented guy I met? How's about terrorizing that teenage kid who thought I was his friend? Hell, yeah. Plot to kill him. Maybe burn down his house. Now we're getting somewhere!'"

Zephyr released the talk button and waited for Ross to say something. He didn't, so the boy continued.

"Wait, no long-winded explanation for me? Some total bullshit to chew on? Have I hit the lottery?" The question was rhetorical and he didn't wait for a reply. "Speaking of the lottery, I gotta say, it's been like Black Friday with all these empty houses in this great, hunt-happy town of ours. One huge fucking gun shop, old man. No blanks either. Just all kinds of rifles, every last one preloaded with bullets that put more than tiny holes in screen doors. Gun racks in the living rooms of some of these places, can you believe it?"

No hesitation this time. "Bring it, you little shit. You think you can threaten me?" Cold now. Defiant. Hard. "Please. You couldn't shoot a picture, let alone a gun. Shit."

"Yeah, that's a good one," Zephyr said, ignoring him. "I guess we'll just have to see how good my aim really is. I have to agree with what you said earlier, though, about those long-range rifles. I've been looking at your shitty house using one of the scopes and the thing is awesome. Now, I'm no expert, but it seems easy enough. You just line up the crosshairs and pull the trigger, right? I feel like even I can do that."

"That's funny," Ross said. "I guess we're both housesitting tonight. I'm here watching this big ol' ritzy mansion burn itself out. Now that it's good and dark outside, she's a beauty of a sight, if I do say so. You should come on by, get you some marshmallows, and we'll roast 'em up while we watch."

The cheerful old facade had returned, but Zephyr detected anger underneath. He knew his words had been received and at least some doubt about his intentions and his resources seeded.

"You get used to that burning, asshole, because there's plenty of it where you're going," he said, and replied no more.

It was all a sham, of course. Zephyr only thought to investigate for weapons of any kind after he'd made the bluff. He searched the house, now blanketed in darkness – he was too frightened to turn on any lights, dim or otherwise – and came away empty-handed. So he found a bed and lay there listening to the occasional comment or vague threat from Ross. "You ain't sleeping, boy," and "You know, if you come at me, it's not gonna end well for you," and "I just love driving around this here city at night," and so on. No more long diatribes – only enough to let Zephyr know he was still there, still awake, still looking for him.

The boy turned down the volume on the walkie so that the interruptions were nearly inaudible and stared into the blackness. He thought again of the disappearances, of his parents and his girlfriend, of all the crashed cars and vacant buildings. He missed his family with desperation. He wondered how much safer he'd be now if he'd only explored the highway that first day instead of holing up at home.

Eventually, he stood and then shuffled into the surrounding blackness, his arms outstretched, his feet ready for contact with whatever waited unseen. The bathroom was adjacent to the master bedroom, itself tucked away in the rear of the house. He flipped the light. It was dim, but it tickled his eyes anyway and he shielded them with his forearm before his vision adjusted and he squinted into the room. It was small. A single sink and a thin wall mirror that stretched from his torso up.

"Jesus, man," he whispered. "You've looked… better."

And he had. A brown v-neck sweater clung to his frame. Some worn jeans. He'd donned them both in the early morning — and was it really just this morning? It seemed like a lifetime ago. His dark, thick hair, now noticeably dirtier and greasier than normal, hung at shoulder length. He might've been a hipster who forewent a shower if not for his face. Pale skin, bloodshot eyes, bags underneath. Coupled with the neglected hair, he looked more like a stylish drug addict than he wanted to admit. It aged him up a couple years, at the very least.

He longed for a phone. Just to give it another try— maybe something had finally changed, maybe someone would answer now. There it was again: the old, steady hope, still refusing to die. He flipped off the light and lay back on the bed, determined to wait, to bide his time, and to move only after he felt confident that Ross had finally turned in for the night.

He didn't believe he'd actually scared the old man, who was arrogant, yes, but much as he hated to admit it, smart in his own way. The bastard had outplayed him several times over since they first met. He only needed him distracted, though. So long as Ross believed that he was planning revenge, fantastic. Whether he hunkered down at his house and waited him out, found another place altogether to hatch his own dirty plan, or drove around town looking for him, fine, good, perfect, even. Zephyr thought he could handle any of those scenarios. What he dreaded was the possibility that Ross had seen through his lies and somehow anticipated his exit. If the psycho maneuvered through the pile-ups on the highway and waited for him a few miles out, he'd be in trouble.

He thought about all of this and more for a long time while the mattress warmed beneath his weight. The wind rose and fell, leaves swirling and tickling the window. Jerry had seen another person— the girl in the truck. She was out there somewhere. Were there others? He believed so, yes. Maybe not many, but some. Hiding, like him. Scared, like him. Or maybe they'd taken to the highways in search of answers. If so, he was eager to join them. Time flowed, thoughts spun out of control, his heartbeat slowed and quickened, the pattern repeated.

Two-eighteen in the morning and still no word from Ross. It was time to move, so he turned the talkie off and stuffed it into the backpack with the gun, safety on— blanks or no blanks, better to be careful. A minute later, he was outside, lightning caught in his veins, ready to race if necessary. Darkness spread everywhere, extinguished only in small pockets by flickering street and porch lights. The weather, brisk and breezy, reminded Zephyr of Halloween, still a few weeks out, and under normal circumstances he would have found the climate altogether exhilarating.

He scaled a fence. His palms were still raw from the fast retreat he'd been forced into earlier. A dark backyard with lumpy grass. He kept going. A decrepit brick wall leaned inward. He climbed it and jumped down to the other side. Gravel now. Weeds. He winced at all the noise the rocks made under his feet. The moan of the wind blotted most of it out, but he stopped and looked around anyway. The old railroad tracks ran perpendicular into the night. Just beyond them waited Main Street, wider and more illuminated than he wanted.

He squatted behind a nearby bush and then peeked up and down the street for signs of anything out of the ordinary. Like the entire city vanishing, he thought. That would be pretty out of the ordinary, wouldn't you say, Zeph? His eyes darted back and forth in search of irregular motion or radiance, like approaching headlights. He stared wide in both directions and studied the geography. Thankfully, blessedly, even, there were none.

He was about to stand again when he heard the sound of grinding rocks behind him.

16

Zephyr spun and saw a figure silhouetted against the darkness. He froze. He wanted to duck for cover, to dive out of the way, to sprint for his life, but his arms and legs ignored all of these impulses. It was not possible. How had Ross found him, let alone secured the jump on him? He flashed through unlikely scenarios at lightning speeds. Had the old man tracked him using his walkie-talkie signal? He'd heard of people doing that before. His hopes disintegrated. He raised his arms into the air, and braced for the worst.

"Sorry," the silhouette said. "I'm sorry, don't be mad." He could barely make out the words over the wind. But it was not Ross.

It was a girl.

Zephyr felt like throwing up. "Get down!" he hissed.

"What?"

He waved her his way. "Over here! Hurry!"

She ran to him, hunched, and sat beside him. Up close, he could see her a little better, although her face was still a mystery. Zephyr thought she was too small to be anything but a kid. His panic gave way to flabbergast. Another living person. He almost touched her in disbelief.

"You were in my backyard and you were..." she said and stopped. "You we—w-were grown up..." She tried to maintain control of herself but it was a losing battle; she was segueing into hysterics. "S-since my mom was gone. So I chase—"

"It's OK. You scared the heck out of me, but it's OK," Zephyr said and without hesitation he embraced her. And when she wept back into his arms, he held on.

After some time, he couldn't have said how long, he let go of her and she pulled away. She stared at him from the weeds and rock in the cold of night, and when she spoke again her composure had come back.

"Do you know where my mom is? Can you help me find my mom?"

"No," he said. "I'm sorry, I don't. I wish I did. My parents are gone, too. Almost everyone is. But we don't have time to think about that right now. The two of us, we have to get out of here."

"Why?"

"There's a really bad man out here and he wants to hurt us." He waited for her response, but none came. She only nodded. "In a minute, we're going to run across the street, do you understand? You're going to hold my hand and run as fast as you've ever run. Then we're going to go into the wash where he can't get us, OK?"

"OK."

"Good."

He surveyed Main Street again. It looked clear. No signs of Ross either way. And although they might be seen as they sprinted across if anybody happened to be looking, the spot was nevertheless as navigable as he could ask for given the circumstances. It was a clear shot across a big road and into the trenches of safety on the other side.

"You ready?" he asked.

She nodded.

"OK." He reached out for her. "One. Two. Three. Run!"

She gripped his hand hard as their feet led them. She felt tiny—fragile, even. Zephyr moved so fast that by the time they reached the curb on the opposite side, he was practically dragging her. They finally slipped into more overgrown bushes and out of sight from the road. It was done.

"OK, good. Listen, what's your name?" Zephyr asked.

"Jordan."

"I'm Zephyr. You can call me Zeph, OK?"

"OK."

Her face was still a mask in the darkness but he guessed her eyes were still stained with tears. She must've been terrified, he thought, but she was a survivor and though he knew almost nothing else about her, he admired that.

"The hard part is over. That's the good news. The bad news is that we have a long walk ahead of us. Are you up for it?"

"Where are we going?"

"We're going to get out of this town and away from the bad man, and then we can try to figure out what's going on." He recalled the night after the event as he lay up in his room, alone, tortured. God, how old is she— nine or ten? How is that fair?

"My mom—" she started and he cut her off.

"I know. As soon as we can, we'll try to find her," he said, and hated himself for it. He couldn't leave her here, though. Not without anybody to take care of her and not with Ross on the loose.

"OK."

"All right. Le—wait, quiet." He cupped her mouth with one palm. "Don't move."

Zephyr cocked his head and listened. The wind hammered on, but there was something else now. The steady hum of an engine. Was that right? Yes. He thought it was. And it was growing louder.

"Stay here. Get down on the ground and don't make a sound," he whispered and then crawled back to the bushes.

It was baffling because the street showed no sign of any cars in either direction. Nothing out of place. It was still a midnight ghost town. As dark and motionless as ever. But wait— no, that wasn't true, he realized with sudden panic. There was a car. A truck, in fact. And it was rolling down Main Street at a leisurely pace. He hadn't noticed it because its headlights were off.

It had to be Ross, of course. The old bastard was cruising, but not for girls. He was still up and still searching, a truth that astounded and disturbed Zephyr. He realized with a pang of nausea that if he had hesitated by a minute, he'd have crossed Main Street exactly as Ross was rolling down it.

"Stay down!" he hissed at Jordan, despite the fact that she hadn't budged.

The truck moved down the road at a deliberate pace. He couldn't see Ross inside, couldn't distinguish much of anything beyond the vehicle, but he knew he was there, likely peering out the window, maybe even through a night scope. Why not? These streets belonged to him now. He could drive them as he saw fit.

Zephyr felt the old familiar paralysis grip hold. Yet again, Ross had every advantage save one, which was that he didn't know where Zephyr was, and the boy had no intention of revealing himself. For as much as he wanted revenge, for as much as the old man deserved his due justice, the reality was that if he went up against Ross, he was going to lose and he would lose with his life. So he stayed glued to the ground and veiled behind the bulkiness of branches and shrubs and he watched the tires roll by, the sound of rubber grating pavement. Too afraid to blink and to breathe, he never moved. And only when the truck was too far gone to see did his fear finally give way to relief, and then regret.

Not now, you son of a bitch. But maybe one day we'll see each other again, he thought. Maybe.

A half hour later, the boy and the girl marched in quiet lockstep across a snaking bike path that paralleled the gully system, leaving Firefly Valley and all of its mysteries to the bad man.

17
Going Nowhere

The walk was as long as the wind was frigid. The two of them traversed the path and then the rocky, weedy terrain of the gully into the night, at first whispering back and forth and then talking outright. Zephyr dominated the conversation. He asked question after question and made dumb jokes, but the girl seldom responded with more than a yes or a no and never laughed. It was understandable.

He'd been loath to make the trip through the ravine in the dead of darkness by himself, and yet he found that it really wasn't so daunting with company, even a companion as young as Jordan, who was, he confirmed, just ten. Once they had heard what sounded like either a dog or a coyote scrambling by in the surrounding hillsides and they had both halted, but that had been it, and by the time light radiated beyond the mountains again, Firefly Valley was well behind them.

The highway carved through and over the mountains while the gully lay in the valleys between them, a detail that Zephyr had prematurely dismissed. Their path disintegrated into a dirty ravine before the sun took shape and maneuvering through it was a chore— progression slow, yet steady. And while he was thankful that there was no more rain and no deep water to contend with, he worried about how long they might have to walk before their passage intersected once more with the roads.

Jordan's blonde hair blew around her freckled face and she tucked it behind her ears. Her eyes shone a bright blue and she stood to his chest. Zephyr figured she'd be a heartbreaker by the time she was sixteen, but for now, she was just a kid and a sad, dazed, exhausted one at that. He asked her if she wanted to rest and she shook her head, so they kept on as he lobbed questions at her.

She had dressed for school, made toast and milk and watched cartoons, as was the morning routine, she told him. Then, when she tried to wake her mom, she discovered her missing. Zephyr knew how the story progressed. She tried calling her grandmother and her best friend. She knocked on the doors of some neighborhood homes. She dialed the police. He got that much from her. He didn't ask about her first night alone because he didn't want to know. He thought about his own experience and couldn't fathom how a ten year-old girl could surmount such an ordeal by herself. The remaining details were irrelevant. The situation was devastating, but she had endured and that's all that mattered.

He glanced at her as she stepped over a jutting rock and was overcome with a potent mixture of sympathy and respect. He was not sure that he would've persisted at such a young age.

When they'd gone a little farther, she asked, "Where are we actually going?"

Zephyr considered it as they walked, and sighed. "That's a good question," he said. "For now, we're just going as far away from town as we can and then we're going to get on the freeway when we see it. After that, we'll have to see. I'm hoping we can get a car."

"Some food, too. I'm hungry," she said.

He smiled. "For sure. All the food we can find. What sounds good?"

"Um, macaroni and cheese and ice cream."

Zephyr bust out laughing. It felt good. "All right. We'll see if we can get that, but we might have to settle for something a little easier."

"OK, I can eat just about anything at this point," she said and then paused. "Zephyr, why was that man bad?"

"Don't worry about him. He's long gone," he said and glanced behind himself, prepared for the cruel possibility that Ross might be lingering off in the distance, a rifle at his shoulder. Only empty hillsides, though. "I just saw him hurt someone and he wanted to hurt me after that."

"Why did he hurt someone?"

"Because he's a bad man."

"Did he hurt someone you know?"

"No, just a man we met," Zephyr said.

"Oh." She seemed to consider it. "Do you think someone hurt my mom?"

"I don't think so. I just think she went somewhere, like my mom and dad did. Maybe they're all there together."

"Wherever they are, that's where I want to go," she said.

He flashed her his best smile. "Me too, kid."

They walked and talked some more as the day grew older. Zephyr possessed neither a watch nor a phone and had no view of the sun, itself shrouded behind ominous clouds. So as the hours passed on, he discovered that he really had no idea what time it was. It might've been breakfast, brunch or lunch. His growling stomach didn't care. His feet ached, his legs burned and the hillsides stretched on, the ravine they found themselves in the only sign of civilization. He wondered if he'd made a mistake. Maybe he should've taken the highway from the start. *Too risky. Not with your old friend roaming around,* he thought. *Just keep going. The gully intersects with the highways eventually— it can't be long now.*

But it was. And it was cold. As the day wore on, he began wondering if it might be closer to lunch or dinnertime. Jordan's hair danced in the wind as she wiped her nose with her jacket.

"Look!" she said, pointing. "See?"

They'd come around a curve in the hillsides and finally had a fuller view of the terrain ahead. He squinted. In the distance, the gully seemed to take on shape. He thought he saw the murky white of cement and almost smiled. Several hundred feet above the ravine, a road clung to the lip of the mountain, a metal railing running in parallel to its surface. It had to be the highway.

"I see it," he said, maybe a little louder than he'd intended. He couldn't help it. "That, my girl, is a freeway, which means we just found ourselves a light at the end of the tunnel."

She stared up at him.

"What I mean is, macaroni and ice cream, Jordan. Once we get up there, we can try to get some food and then take a break for a little while." He extended his hand, flat, and she slapped it hard, smiling.

"Who saw it first?" she asked.

"You totally did. Great work, kid."

Her smile widened. For the briefest of moments, he saw her as she was before the event had kidnapped her childhood. "Are we gonna climb up there?"

"Yeah. Hopefully won't be too bad, either. The angle looks pretty manageable," he said.

He was half right. An hour and a half later, the two of them stood at the base of the road, sweating and panting. The climb had been manageable, but it was by no means easy. He hadn't made a positive identification, but he thought he knew where he was. It was a two-lane system: one coming and one going. The road was grayer than it was black. Cracked. Used. Patches of weeds and shrubs loitered by the sidelines, afraid to venture any closer. The vegetation bystanders of the long-haul commuter, Zephyr thought. The street cornered to the left and behind the slope again a few hundred feet ahead. There were no cars to be found. Still, there was at least predictable, flat street, which beat trudging through old gullies every day of the week, and if his bearings were right there'd be an old gas station and the very real possibility of some vehicles soon.

"Now what do we do?" Jordan asked.

"We walk."

Thirty minutes later, and just as Zephyr started to question whether Ross had outright lied about mass pile-ups on the highway, they rounded another curve in the road and there, sprawled at a diagonal stop across both lanes, was a diesel truck. It was an 18-wheeler. Huge. Yellow with orange trim. A cartoony illustration stamped alongside the cargo unit depicted a Greek god reaching out for nothing. *Zeus Moving,* declared big, bold type. And just underneath that in smaller text, *Lightning Fast Transport For Mere Mortal Prices.*

Jordan tugged on his sweater again.

"I see it, I see it," he said.

It was an alarming scene, at least by normal circumstances. It wasn't every day, after all, that gargantuan haulers lay dormant in the middle of the street. It was therefore a testament to their rebooted state of minds and their collective submission to the world as it now behaved that neither one of them seemed concerned. They were excited. The boy pulled himself onto the driver's step and swung the door ajar with a heavy, dry squeak. He could smell stale cigar inside. Green leather seats, torn in several spots. A beaded golden crucifix dangled from the oversized rearview mirror. And, of course, he realized with dull acceptance, a thick red flannel and a pair of blue jeans lay crumpled on the driver's seat and floor respectively. Same old, same old.

He turned back to Jordan. "Nobody here. I'm gonna try and start it."

The keys remained in the ignition, but no matter what he did, he couldn't get it to start, which was just as well because he was positive he couldn't drive it, anyway.

"Yeah, not happening," he said, "but we can at least open up the back to see if there's anything useful inside."

He imagined a treasure trove of boxed kitchen goods. Cereal. Chips. Cookies. Anything that might keep in transport. No such luck. The truck held several beds, two couches, and a dining room table overrun with boxes, but no food. He scoured the compartments and came away wanting. Still, there were some valuable finds that made the examination well worth his time. He tugged a thick, navy-blue pea coat from one overstuffed box and it fit him perfectly. He offered a pair of hand mittens to Jordan, who happily donned them. With nightfall fast approaching, they'd do well to dress warm and he was thankful for the extra resources. They were what his dad called good-to-haves. Yet the clothes paled in comparison to the items wedged between the table and one of the couches.

"Hey kiddo. I think we're in business," he said, smiling.

He was still grinning ten minutes later as the two of them raced down the mountain on the bikes. It had been the perfect plunder. Warmth for the road and a faster means of travel. Zephyr coasted atop a lightweight mountain bike and Jordan zoomed alongside him on its twin, her hair flapping in the wind. If she noticed that it was a little too big for her, she didn't show it. The descent was gradual, but as the street curved and cornered the slope became more pronounced and it wasn't long before they moved so fast that Zephyr's bike wobbled off balance, and he squeezed the handbrakes. Jordan sped past him, completely oblivious.

"Hey daredevil! Be careful!" he shouted against the wind with no real hope that she heard him and no faith that she'd listen even if she did.

The freeway eventually bled into a lonely intersection overseen by a maltreated gas station. A few scattered houses that looked more like glorified shacks sat forgotten down one side of the perpendicular road before it disintegrated into shabby bush and then hillsides. It wasn't a town. It wasn't even a community. It was just a necessary pit stop on the way to somewhere better.

The station was old, dirty, and dilapidated, but it was also an oasis. The treasures encapsulated within those faded windows seemed boundless. Food and drinks. His mouth watered and his stomach grumbled in anticipation of tortilla chips, candy bars and soda. A big-rig and a Honda Civic had become permanent fixtures outside the pumps, and they ignored a crumpling of clothes near one of them as they dismounted and made for the entrance.

"OK," he said. "Let's grab some chow, kid."

The place was small, but well stocked. Florescent lights buzzed inside, illuminating a register surrounded by rows of gum and candy. Three sizable aisles held more junk food, and the refrigerator housed all manners of cold cola and beer. He tore open a big bag of nacho cheese Doritos and sat on the floor devouring them, breaking only to chug down mouthfuls of icy Mexican Orange Crush. In a glass bottle, too, he thought. This stuff is so much better in a bottle. Jordan alternated between bites of a Rocky Road bar and some pork rinds, of all things. A rather disgusting combination.

She stood and dusted her pants. "Is it OK if I get some Fun Dip?"

"What's that?"

"Yummy candy." She took it from the aisle and showed it to him. "Here."

"Oh, totally. Go for it. Eat whatever you want. You don't need to ask."

She sat on the floor beside him and ripped open the dip. Some of the powdery sugar spilled on her pants and floor, yet she hardly noticed. After some time, she asked, "Why do you think everybody is gone?"

He shrugged. "I really wish I had an answer for that one. I really, really do."

"That's OK," she said. "But where do you think everybody went then?"

How could he answer that? Heaven? Or maybe, what, flying saucers? Both seemed unbelievable possibilities. But then, the entire predicament defied normality. Whatever had happened to them all—his girlfriend, his parents, and for that matter the entire town, maybe the world— they'd all left in a hurry. And naked, he thought. Don't forget that little detail. They all left their clothes, too.

"I dunno, Jordan. Wish I did," he admitted. "But we're gonna try to find out, all right?"

"OK."

An idea struck him, and he rose to investigate the area behind the register. Ignoring another pile of clothes and shoes, not to mention a prosthetic leg, he rummaged through some unseen shelves and finally found it. A gun. A shotgun, to be more precise. And really, that was the extent of precision that his expertise on the subject allowed.

"Look what I found," he said and held up the weapon. It was heavy. Significant.

Jordan raised an eyebrow. "What do you need that for?"

"Just in case we run into any more bad men. It'll be good to have one of these." He turned the weapon over, treating the barrel with the same level of caution that one might pay the raised head of a cobra, found the safety, and flipped it on.

The sun was off for the night by the time they left the station. In the boy's left hand dangled some keys he'd discovered behind the counter and in the other hung an oversized plastic bag stretched to the tearing point with snacks and soda. Jordan carried bags of her own.

The door to the Honda Civic was unlocked. Zephyr acquainted himself with the driver's seat, set the bag on the passenger side, and tried the first key on the ring. Didn't fit. Neither did the second. The third, however, slid snugly into the ignition and when he turned it, the car sputtered to life, the radio blasting static. He recoiled, fumbled for the volume and turned it off.

"All right!" he shouted and honked the horn twice. Jordan set her bags on the ground and clapped.

The car's tank was half full. He pulled in beside a pump and killed the engine. Then the two of them returned to the station and packed three more bags full of junk food and soda. He lugged the gun to the car, unlocked the trunk and stored it. Then he made one last trip inside, where he pilfered the exorcised pants behind the register, snatched a credit card, and spent thirty minutes trying to trigger the pump. It was, he learned, ludicrous how something as trivial as accessing gas had transformed into a behemoth undertaking since the event. Eventually, though, he got it, pillaged two portable tanks and filled those with unleaded, too.

"Done and done," he said with satisfaction as he hurried back into the car seat. He was proud of them. They'd spent all day on foot, hungry and tired. Now, they were fed and full, stocked with food and drinks, armed, and with car. It was progress. He edged the vehicle back onto the highway and into the night.

18

"Now where?" Jordan asked.

They'd been on the road for ten minutes and she'd scrubbed the airwaves. The results were not encouraging, Zephyr thought, but he didn't say anything. Most of the stations sang static, which was probably to be expected. More than one, however, played a steady, toneless beep— the kind of noise he associated with the emergency broadcast system, the only difference being that no messages were being broadcast.

"South," he said. His high beams cut through the darkness and spotlighted the road ahead as he maintained a lethal grip on the steering wheel. "I have an aunt in New Mexico. I thought maybe..."

Except, he wasn't sure what to say. Thought maybe what, Zeph? An eight-hour drive to Las Cruces on the off-chance that your aunt— the same aunt who hasn't answered any of your calls — is just chilling? Maybe drinking some of her lemonade poolside? Yeah, this'll end well. OK, so it wasn't the best plan he'd ever hatched. Nevertheless, it was forward momentum, he assured himself. If nothing else, it took them farther away from Ross, and that was more than enough reason for him.

"She's probably not..." He hesitated. "But, you know, it's worth a shot. And if it doesn't work out, we'll keep on going."

"OK," Jordan said, dug through one of the plastic bags she'd taken along and surfaced a lollipop. If she had any concerns about his plan or lack thereof, she sure didn't show them. She was asleep fifteen minutes later, the lolly still lodged in her mouth.

The Civic didn't offer much pep. It chugged up the hills with great effort and every so often Zephyr gassed it and the car hiccuped as it struggled to change gears. It wasn't exactly a beater, but neither was it going to win any races. An hour into the drive, the boy made up his mind to find a newer, better vehicle at his earliest convenience. Eventually, though, he topped one final climb, his ears popping, and then there were no more ferocious slopes to contend with, only the steady application of brakes during what seemed an endless stretch of descending highway.

The traffic jams Ross said surrounded Firefly Valley had not yet been duplicated and he was glad for it. Still, there was enough congestion to worry him and, he thought, all it's gonna take is one big wreck, dude, and then what? He didn't have an answer. He supposed he could try to start any diesel that blocked their path. Of course, that hadn't gone so well before.

His heart beat faster every time a stalled vehicle forced their deceleration. He imagined terrible things in the darkness beyond the safe glow of their headlights. Zombies, their faces blood and bone, their eyes cataracts, waiting for them to slow enough so that they might shamble after and catch them.

The fuel gauge read a quarter of a tank when Jordan first rubbed her eyes and then opened them. Zephyr had chewed most of his nails into oblivion and was grinding down odds and ends.

"Where are we?" she asked.

"Welcome back," he said between bites and then forced himself to stop. "Don't really know. At least a couple hundred miles from the gas station. How ya feel?"

"Good." She shifted in her seat. "Are we driving all night?"

The answer was no, of course. It wouldn't be possible even if he thought he could, and he didn't. His eyelids were already heavier than he wanted them and it was still early, at least by the previous night's events. He thought they should find a place to hole up and then sleep.

"The short answer is th—"

The car convulsed, then lurched out of his hands and careened across the lane before Zephyr slammed on the brakes and they skidded to a halt.

"What the—" he shouted, suddenly wide awake, his heart pounding. "What the hell just happened?" He turned to her. "Are you all right?"

Jordan nodded, her eyes equally wide. The smell of burning rubber permeated the car and her candy blanketed the floor.

Zephyr's eyes darted everywhere for signs of anything on the outside that might explain the situation. Nothing presented itself. A street light illuminated a pocket of the highway, empty but for them. Beyond the light, darkness, and presumably miles of hills and mountains. Conspiracies raced through the boy's mind. Had they hit something? Did they blow a tire? Was someone actually shooting at them?

"Hey, I need you to get down and be quiet," Zephyr said as he unbuckled his safety belt and slumped out of view. He twisted so that his knees touched the mat, his stomach lay against the seat and his forearms held his weight. He fixed on the driver and passenger side windows and searched for motion. His weapon was in the trunk, unattainable again. How had he not learned yet?

"Zephyr," Jordan pleaded.

"Quiet," he whispered. "It's fine. Just— don't move."

They stayed there and listened to the wind cry all around them. When at last Zephyr felt confident that there was no threat outside, he edged ever higher and peeked through each window for explanations that remained unseen and unknown. If they'd run over a coyote, he couldn't spot it anywhere. And, he finally conceded, if somebody was actually out there in the brush beyond the road, he'd never find them.

Soon, they were moving again, but just that. The car limped forward and the steering wheel dragged hard to the left. He only centered it after a fight. It was definitely a flat, and he didn't care. It was a stolen car anyway, he figured, so if they totaled it on their way, well, so be it. He was going to drive the cursed thing as far as it would take them. If that meant they'd go until the wheel fell off, then that's what it meant. None of this frightened him. On the contrary, on some level he was actually glad it had happened because it made the decision to take the next exit bearing signs of civilization that much easier.

"Don't be scared. It's just a flat tire. We're gonna ride it out until we spot a new car we can take or we hit an off ramp. Whichever comes first." He glanced at her. "Don't worry. I promise it's not a big deal."

As they drove, the drag became more pronounced and the dull thud of hard rubber on pavement louder. The car shook whenever they slowed so Zephyr wrestled to stay the speed above thirty-five miles per hour. Fifteen minutes later, something loud popped up front, the car jerked off course before he corrected it, and then they drove in bumpy succession over large chunks and strips of rubber that used to be tire. It was a rough, but quick transition, followed by a light show. Zephyr rolled down the window and surveyed the damage. The rim was not just exposed, but naked, and sparks engulfed it before dancing away and blinking out into nothingness. The smell of incinerated rubber and cooked metal followed them.

They drove on like this, their windows down, the air frigid, until the dashboard gas light turned on. He finally swallowed a heavy drink of air and then slowed the vehicle.

"We're getting pretty low on gas so I'm gonna grab the tank from the trunk and fill up," he told Jordan, who nodded without reply.

It was even colder outside than Zephyr anticipated. He expected to see stars uninhibited by the glow of the city, but there were none. It was, except for their headlights and the short radiance of road ahead, black. He fumbled for the trunk, opened it and removed the fuel, suddenly very conscious of the mountains, the brush, and whatever might be skulking unseen.

"Just get it done, Zeph," he whispered and tilted the container into the gas tank. He had to pee something fierce and shifted his weight between legs as he waited for the fuel to pass. Here was another thing he didn't know: pouring gas from a carrier took forever.

His listened and looked with his ears. The wind was steady static so he searched beyond it for any subtle break in the monotony. Nothing. After what seemed a lifetime, he finished, screwed the cap back on the tank, tossed the container into the street and made for the door. Then he thought better of it. They might need to hold more gas in the future. Better to save it, just in case. He turned to retrieve it and then stopped dead.

"Shit!"

Zephyr sprinted for the trunk. The shotgun was stretched inside it alongside the box of bullets. He snapped both up, slammed the lid and then ran for the passenger side door.

"Jordan! Get out!" he yelled and yanked her door open.

She jumped from the car as though it were ablaze. "What? What's the matter?"

"Someone's coming," he said and pointed to the long stretch of road behind them. Somewhere in the distance, a pair of dim headlights cut through the night, and they were heading right for them.

"We need to get off the road." He directed her to the darkness adjacent the car. "There. Over there. Go, and I'll catch up. I'm going to get our stuff."

"No, come with me," she pleaded.

He had intended to pillage the car of anything else they might need, but reconsidered. No time.

"OK, let's go."

The road disintegrated into shoulder, gravel crunching under their shoes, as they descended into a slope blanketed in long grass or weeds. Zephyr squinted hard but couldn't see a damned thing. It was just too dark. Jordan gripped his hand and started to say something.

"Quiet, kid. Just a few more feet, then we'll stop."

He couldn't shake the absurd notion that Ross had somehow tracked them all this way, and his hand tightened on the shotgun. If it was the old man, if he'd followed them this far... *It's not him, you freakin' idiot. He's at home, drunk, probably still goading you on his stupid walkie-talkie.* But if it was him, Ross wouldn't know that he had Jordan, and he wanted to keep it that way. They descended deeper into the grassy blackness before Zephyr halted them.

"OK," he breathed. "I want you to move about ten feet to your left and lie down." He gripped her shoulders and held her front and center, her face close to his. "Jordan. Whatever happens, you do not say a word. Not. A. Word. Do you understand?"

Nothing.

Louder now. "Do you understand?" There was no time for this. If she didn't answer, he'd shake it out of her.

"Y-yes."

"Good. Get moving." And he nudged her in the general direction. Then he crawled two yards up the hillside, hidden in the brush, where he watched the headlights draw nearer.

He didn't blink. His hand molested the shotgun as he felt for the safety and unlocked it. He hoped it was unlocked, anyway. *If it's Ross, stay hidden — take a cheap shot if you have to, man,* he told himself. *And if it doesn't fire, grab Jordan and run. You run down the mountain.*

The car was close now. It slowed to a crawl and its headlights shone on Zephyr's own mistreated vehicle, casting shadows beyond it. The engine sputtered and then hummed. The newcomer finally drew alongside their car and stopped, the brakes squeaking in defiance of the action. The boy watched and waited, his muscles rigid, his vision skipping in lock with his heart. Then, without any warning, the night was alight with blue and red strobes and Zephyr ducked deeper into the weeds to conceal himself. The luminosity was nearly blinding and the colors unexpected but unmistakable: it was a cop car.

"Hey genius," a voice boomed over a megaphone and Zephyr recoiled, one ear cupped. "I know you're around here somewhere. You wanna come out and show yourself?" The speaker paused for a response and when one didn't come, he sighed and added, "Really makes no difference to me one way or the other, but it looks like you could use a hand."

Zephyr breathed. It's not him. It's not the old bastard, he thought. And it wasn't. A man waited on the other end of the megaphone, yes, but this one lacked any drawl and sounded younger than Ross. So what? That doesn't make him friendly, Zeph. You don't know that he's a real cop. You don't know that he doesn't have a gun aimed in your general direction right now. It was all true. He peered through the weeds but couldn't even identify the cop car behind the silhouette of his own. The reds and blues blazed and shadowy projections flickered and marched around the street.

Something moved nearby and he turned just in time to see Jordan upon him.

"What did I say?" he hissed.

"Sorry." She spoke so softly and still her voice wavered. It hurt his heart to hear it but there was no time to consider her feelings. "What are we—do you think we should—"

"Get down."

The megaphone erupted again. "All right, listen." The man hesitated. "I didn't make the best introduction there so let me just start over. Name's Merrick. I've got this nice police car with four working tires and you've got a three-wheeler. So I'm here offering you a ride, some warmth, maybe a little conversation. Truth is, it's a bit lonely out here, in case you haven't noticed. You can either take it or not. I hope you do, but if not, that's up to you. I'll give you two minutes and then I'm heading out."

Zephyr didn't move.

"Do you think we shou—"

"Quiet, Jordan," he whispered.

"But he said he's only gon—"

He cupped her mouth. The wind probably masked their exchange, but there was no sense in risking it. "Please. You have to be quiet."

Zephyr knew what Jordan wanted to do. He could hear it in her voice. He wasn't quite the optimist that she was, though. Chock it up to a bad week. The man or cop or whatever he was sounded friendly, but so did his old pal. Until, that is, he wasn't. Still, he wanted to believe him. Not just that— he needed to believe him. He'd been going for what seemed a lifetime and it was exhausting.

As Zephyr mulled over his options, the man with the megaphone walked the perimeter of his car until he stood in full view of the headlights. He threw his hands up in the air and turned in a circle as though modeling new clothes. The boy could see him much better in the light and was taken aback because he looked exactly like the lead singer of the heavy metal band System of a Down. It was remarkable. For a second, Zephyr wondered if it really was the rocker himself but dismissed it. Thick, dark, curly hair and a big, bushy beard that enveloped everything below his lower lip. He was skinny. Probably in his mid-thirties.

The boy made up his mind, drew Jordan close and whispered something into her ear, and then rose to a hunch. A second later, the girl waited on the grassy slope as he ran for the road, his shotgun pointed in the general direction of the newcomer.

"Don't move!" Zephyr cried.

It was terrifying and comical simultaneously.

The former because the boy understood the gravity of the situation, or so he presumed. The gusting wind and flashing lights threatened to overwhelm his senses as he ran, but he sidestepped the distractions and zeroed in on the man. Focused. Determined. If he reached for anything, there would be no hesitation— he'd pull the trigger and blow him apart. That he had come to this in such a short amount of time was horrifying, but that was a character dissection for another hour.

The latter because he really did look like the guy from System of a Down and Zephyr still hadn't outright abandoned the possibility that the two might in fact be one in the same. I really don't want to shoot you, dude, he thought. I might be a fan, for crying out loud. So please, please don't go for anything.

He didn't. The man finally turned to see Zephyr rushing him, threw up his hands, stepped backward and then tripped over his feet before falling hard on his ass.

"Don't shoot!" He held his hands in front of his face. "Take the car, I don't care. But don't shoot!"

The boy stood over him, the gun held firm. "Weapon!" he shouted. "Do you have a weapon?"

"Yes. In the back of the car. Jesus. I don't have anything on me, I swear." He lowered his hands and looked up. "You—you're a kid."

"A kid with a big gun so don't try anything you'll regret."

"Sure thing, buddy. Fuck. Just take it easy. We're all friends here." He nodded at something behind the boy. "That your sister?"

Zephyr stayed the weapon but glanced in the rear and there she was on her way toward them. "Damn it, Jordan, get back! I told you to stay down!"

"Sorry!" she whined. "I got scared."

"It's all right," said the man. "You guys, I'm on your side here and there's no need for any of this crap."

"How'd you know we were here?" Zephyr demanded.

"Your tail lights are on, kid. Kind of a dead giveaway. Lots of cars on the freeway, but none with juice still. And when I saw the busted wheel, it all came together. Can I stand up, please?"

"No."

"This is what a guy gets for trying to help someone," the man muttered. "No good deed goes unpunished, right?"

An idea occurred to the boy. "Actually, yeah, go ahead and stand up." He tightened his grip on the gun. "Let's go take a look inside your car."

"All right then, good." The man rose to his feet with effort, rubbed his backside and winced. "You wanna maybe point that thing somewhere else now?"

"Just move."

The front cabin was a picture of irony. A dashboard stamped by an oversized D.A.R.E. sticker and at least a dozen empty beer bottles strewn across the passenger seat and floor. System of a Down apparently liked his drink, Zephyr thought. The man hadn't lied about the weapons, though. There were two shotguns in the backseat. Inside the trunk, they found a spare tire, a first-aid kit and three large gas canisters.

"Are we good here?" the man asked.

"Getting there."

Zephyr lowered his aim. It was just for a second, but it was enough. The man lashed out and yanked the shotgun away from him before he had any time to react. Only a blink— a mere fraction of a moment— and everything had gone upside-down. He's fast, he thought. He's so freakin' fast! And then the boy had Jordan's hand in his own as the two of them sprinted away.

They hadn't managed more than a few steps when the shotgun crashed— it was a deafening ruckus that spread throughout the darkness and stopped them mid-stride. Zephyr didn't feel shot, though. No pain. No blood. He patted himself down with one hand as he surveyed Jordan, who seemed all right, too.

"OK, then. Turn around," the man said, and they did as he asked.

He stood there, the barrel of the gun raised to the sky, the beginnings of a smirk across his face. "Now, you see? I could've shot you if I'd wanted to, but like I've said all along, I'm on your side." And without another word, he reached over and returned the gun to Zephyr. "So, do you guys need a ride?"

19

Zephyr and Jordan refused to ride in the backseat, a mobile jail, and so driver and two passengers all sat up front. The rear cabin held the snacks and soda they transported from their ruined Civic, now a permanent metal obstruction on the highway. Zephyr had never ridden inside a police car before and found the experience both exciting and comforting. He knew it was a facade, yet cruising down the road in a black-and-white felt right in some fundamental way, as though the simple symbol of protection and service was all the proof they needed that lawfulness remained and the world was still doing just fine. It was ridiculous, of course, and he embraced it anyway.

The heater blasted hot air as Merrick drove and Jordan chomped gum. The man was not, to Zephyr's disappointment, a rock star, but the proprietor of a comic book store some five-hundred miles up the highway. He'd been on the road for two days and encountered several survivors, none of whom had assaulted him with weapons.

"I mean, is that really how you expect to handle people now?" he asked. "You seem like a good enough kid so let me give you a piece of advice. If you keep that kind of thing up, you're eventually gonna run into someone who's not nearly as nice and for that matter as forgiving as me, and you'll have some real trouble on your hands."

The boy's shotgun rested upright against the passenger door, forgotten for the time being. He still wasn't convinced that Merrick was trustworthy. He probably was. Yet as the road unfolded before them, the warm air enveloped them, and the fuel gauge dipped from nearly a full tank to a half, everything but his anvil-weighted eyelids dwindled into pure triviality. He heard Jordan say something about jumping a fence and then conversation was a distant whisper as the world blurred into blackness.

He woke sometime later with a start, the sensation of falling exorcised within, and he couldn't remember where he was. Then his mind skipped forward and it all flooded back.

"Heya, kid," Merrick whispered.

They were still on the road and it was still too dark to see beyond the radius of their headlights. Zephyr glanced at a watch he no longer owned as Jordan slept beside him.

"How long've we been driving?"

"Close to three hours," he said and yawned. "And I'd say it's getting pretty close to turn-in time."

"What time is it, anyway?" Zephyr asked.

"About two-thirty in the morning."

The boy straightened in his seat, careful not to wake Jordan. His exhaustion had remained a silent predator for the last two days, always stalking, never pouncing. That is, until he slumped into Merrick's warm police cruiser, at which point it had not just lunged, but devoured him. They'd scarcely begun the trip when he'd shut down, leaving proper introductions and stories for later. In hindsight, poor form, but he gave himself a pass. He pressed his hand against the passenger window, now painfully cold, and was glad for the comforts of the car.

"Probably take one of the next off-ramps and we can look for a place to sleep the night off."

Zephyr nodded. "What's your final destination?"

"Oh," Merrick said and then considered the question. "To be honest, I haven't really thought much about it. I'm just kind of following the road."

"That doesn't seem like much of a plan."

"No, I suppose not. It's served me all right so far, though."

"Well, you know we're on our way to New Mexico," Zephyr said.

"Oh? What's there, pray tell?"

"My aunt lives in Las Cruces. Or, she used to, anyway. I know it's a long shot, but thought we could check it out." The boy studied his lap a moment. "I'm not hopeful."

"No, can't see how you could be. There doesn't seem to be too many of us left around here."

"Do you have any idea what happened?" Zephyr asked.

"Not a fuckin' clue, kid. The world up and ditched us." Zephyr heard the clinking of glass as Merrick rummaged for something near his feet. The man returned upright with a bottle of beer and popped the cap while he steered with his knees. Then he took a big, thirsty swig and belched with loud oblivion. "You got any theories?"

"Hey, don't mind us over here. A teenager and a little girl. You enjoy yourself."

"Why thank you. Don't mind if I do." He tilted the bottle to his mouth and drank again while Zephyr rolled his eyes.

"Some people think it could be the Rapture," the boy proposed.

"Uh-huh. Heard that one, too. Just about every one of the survivors I've met so far has mentioned that as the most likely possibility."

"How many survivors have you met?"

"Oh, ten or fifteen. All of them nice enough, from what I could tell. Nobody tried to shoot me until you two came along."

"We didn't try to shoot you," Zephyr said but Merrick waved it away.

"I passed through a few smaller towns on the way when I had to fill up, eat, or pinch a loaf. I'm sure you know the drill. Haven't run into many survivors in the 'burbs. Just one older lady, actually. She pulled up to get some gas, saw me there, gave me this polite little wave like we were old neighbors or something and then she just drove off when I tried to talk to her. Like she decided, 'No thanks, not going near that asshole,' but didn't want to be rude about it."

Zephyr thought about how the disappearances and the extraordinary circumstances which followed affected people in very different ways.

"So what about the others then?" the boy asked.

"Denver," Merrick said and gulped down a mouthful of beer. "Bunch of people scattered around. Place was a total war zone."

"What do you mean?"

"I mean, it looked like Afghanistan or something. I could tell from fifteen miles out that it had gone to shit because you could see this epic black cloud hanging over the place and when I got closer, I figured out why."

He waited for Zephyr to respond, but the boy only considered his words.

"The city was destroyed. Buildings crumbled to the ground. Some on fire. And almost nobody there. The freeways were practically empty. It was beyond surreal. Like a movie."

"What the hell happened?"

Merrick looked at him. "Take a guess."

Zephyr could only conjure images of battlefields and bombs. "I have no idea. Just tell me."

"Think nine-eleven, kid."

He thought about it. "Planes?"

"Bingo," he said, and took another swig of beer.

"Fell right out of the sky when everyone disappeared, and Denver took a beating. Don't know if it was one plane or fifteen or fifty — I just know it was a cluster. And the difference is, no fire departments to the rescue. Not enough people left to put out a bonfire, let alone the firestorm that must've blazed after the planes came down. So everything just burned. And from the looks of it, the fire spread."

Zephyr remembered back to the morning of the event. Had he smelled smoke in the air? Maybe. Then he thought of all those empty planes plummeting toward mountains and valleys and oceans and cities and buildings. He hoped they had all been lifeless, anyway, and winced at the alternative. He tried to push away the vision of a lone passenger thrusting himself against the door to the cockpit, screaming, banging, but unable to penetrate the barrier even as the plane streaked across the sky toward doom.

"Yikes," he finally said in total disbelief.

"That about sums it up."

"What happened to the survivors?"

"What do you mean?"

"The survivors you met in Denver. Where'd they go?" Zephyr asked.

"What do you mean 'where'd they go?' I assume they're still there."

"None came with you?"

"Oh. Well, I wasn't exactly advertising my taxi services like I was for you and I don't think anybody would've come with me even if I had," Merrick said. "Everybody I met led me to believe they wanted to be there— that it was the smartest place they could be."

"How so?"

"I think they're all hoping help is coming and they don't have any intention of missing it."

"What about you?"

"Not really sure what to think," he said. "But I guess I wouldn't be on the road right now if I really believed that."

"So what's your plan then? Just keep driving?"

"Yeah, I guess. Why the hell not, right? Nobody seems to have a better plan and besides, I've always wanted to see the country. Now I'm finally doing it." He swallowed another mouthful of beer. "What about you? How'd you end up on the highway with three wheels and that stupid gun?"

"It's a long story."

"I'm a busy guy, but I'll clear my calendar," Merrick quipped.

"All right, fine— just remember you said that."

So Zephyr told him everything, and when, at last, he was finished with the story, he slumped back into his seat.

For some time, Merrick said nothing. He just sat there, one hand scratching his puffy beard as the road unraveled before them and Jordan slept. Just as Zephyr was going to ask if he'd been listening, the man spoke.

"Jesus Christ, kid. What a total shit show." It was so stupid and yet it was the way he said it, his voice imbued with genuine compassion, that nearly triggered tears in Zephyr's eyes. "Hey kid, I just want you to know that I'm sorry about giving you a hard time earlier. Jesus. You have every right to be careful. What the hell is this world coming to?"

Zephyr pointed out a sign that promised food, gas, and lodging several miles up and Merrick nodded.

"So, do you think it was the Rapture?" the boy asked.

"Seems like a pretty good explanation, no?"

"I guess so."

"Yeah. Sure does," Merrick paused. "Only problem is that I saw everything go down. I was awake when the shit hit the fan and I don't want to burst your bubble, but nobody flew up to Heaven. Not by a long shot."

Zephyr turned to face him, his eyes wide. "You saw it?"

"Yeah. Friend of mine threw a party and I was there. Bunch of us were still up drinking, playing Magic, listening to music, whatever. I was talking to this chick Hannah. Blonde hair, huge knockers." He glanced at Zephyr and smiled and when the boy didn't smile back he continued. "So anyway, she was showing me her stupid new phone and she was gonna take my picture and add it to her contacts. A few seconds later, she was a big mess of clothes on the ground."

Zephyr was about to ask for more details when Merrick continued. "It wasn't God, I can tell you that. There wasn't any floating, lights, angels, music— nothing of the sort. Just this loud sucking noise. Like all the air in the house was being siphoned out. It wasn't exactly going outside, though. It was more like it was being drawn inside her. One second she was smiling at me, the next her face was a total blank. But not her eyes. Man, I swear I saw understanding in those eyes. And, help us, fear. Fear, kid, and it's no lie. Then her pupils rolled back into whites and she blinked out of existence with this weird pop." He stuck his index finger inside the hollow of his cheek and pulled. "Everybody in the house went the same way. Everybody except me."

Now it was Zephyr who found himself speechless. All the evidence of the event lay dormant like some forgotten crime scene. The leftover clothes, abandoned homes and stalled cars. He had moved between these remnants, these reminders, for days and had come to accept, if not believe them. Yet, it was all the aftermath of some unseen thing. Except, the man riding next to him had seen it. And his retelling offered no closure and no solace.

They pulled off the interstate five minutes later and drove into another non-town of the kind that always seemed to loiter on the outskirts of such highways. Under the smile of the sun, there'd be nothing extraordinary about the place, just another rundown conglomerate of structures; just some dirty, shallow microcosm of the real world. By nightfall, however, it was all but invisible save for the beam of their headlights, and the display gave Zephyr chills. No glowing neon. No buzzing fluorescents. Tree branches swayed with the wind but no lights shone on the gas pumps, no windows stood illuminated, and no signs promised goods or sales with the glitz that only the spark of electricity can offer. The place was off the grid. Dark. Unnatural.

Merrick pulled the cruiser into a small parking lot home to a single-story motel whose name escaped the reach of their headlights. The place held maybe a dozen rooms that stretched to either side of the front door, itself a gateway to what was presumably a small office.

"Well, I guess we can forget about getting gas," he said as he killed the engine.

"Yeah, doesn't look too good," Zephyr said and then nudged Jordan, who woke with groggy disregard.

"Hi," she mumbled and stretched. "Are we there?"

"Yeah, we're somewhere, anyhow," Zephyr said. "We're gonna stop at a motel for the night so we can get some sleep in actual beds."

"Can I sleep with you?" she asked.

He grabbed his gun. "Yeah, of course. Come on. Let's get inside. It's cold out."

"There's three of us remember," Merrick joked, but they ignored him.

The office was dark, but they eventually discovered keys to adjoining rooms, and when Merrick suggested they share them, Zephyr reluctantly agreed. He swept away a grizzly image of a naked man slinking into bed beside Jordan in the middle of the night. Just stop it, dude. It's not gonna happen, he told himself. It was instinctual now, though, borne out of this new reality, and he realized with disappointment that his optimistic outlook on the world had likely been stripped of him forever.

The rooms held no power and more importantly no heater, but the water still ran cold as the midnight breeze. Zephyr removed his shoes and sank into the bed, too tired to disrobe, Jordan beside him, the extra blankets layered over them. I wouldn't mind taking a shower tomorrow, even if the water is freezing, he thought, closed his eyes and drifted.

When they woke in the late morning, the three of them raided a liquor store of chips, drinks, bread, mustard and Swiss cheese. The refrigerator was still cool, so the area must've dropped power recently, the boy thought. They carried the food back to the hotel room and made sandwiches.

"This is a long shot, I know," Zephyr said between big, hungry bites. "But you said you were drinking when it happened. Do you think you could've maybe imagined some of it or something?"

Merrick snorted. "What you're really saying is, you think I'm full of it."

"No, not at all. I just… I just don't want to believe you, I guess."

The man chugged the remainder of his beer, crushed the can with one hand and then tossed it on the carpet without a glance. "Look, was I drinking? Yes. Was I drunk? Probably. But not that kind of drunk. And believe me, I sobered up in about three seconds after that shit went down."

"No, I believe it. Just thought I'd ask."

"Trust me, kid, I wish I had blacked out and imagined the whole thing. I'd be happy to trade up this little road trip of ours, as much fun as it's been." He bit into a candy bar. "I wasn't exactly the King of Colorado or anything, but I had a nice group of friends. One or two of them more than friends. They're all gone now, just like everybody else."

"Zephyr said he's gonna help find my mom," Jordan interrupted.

"Did he now?" Merrick asked. "I'm sure he will then. You two just have to keep an eye out for her wherever you go."

"We will," Jordan said.

"Do you have family?" Zephyr asked.

"Just a brother in Nevada. Parent's passed away a while ago. No kids or anything like that."

"So have you thought about going to Nevada?"

"Yeah, I'll get around to it. I'm not too optimistic, but it's as good an excuse as any to drive around the country, I suppose. First stop is New Mexico, though, right?"

Zephyr smiled. "OK, yes. Good." He met the man's eyes, and he was glad he found them. "Merrick, thanks for helping us. And thanks for going with us."

His new friend gasped. "Jordan, did you hear that? I thought I heard a thank you, but it can't be!" He cradled his ear with one hand. "Did I really just hear actual gratitude from the little shotgunner over here?"

Both Zephyr and Jordan laughed.

"Can we go now? This town gives me the creeps," she said.

Sometime later Zephyr and Jordan waited in the cruiser as Merrick cursed and shouted from the rear. The boy was reminded again that real life was oftentimes opposite to the part-time realities portrayed by Hollywood, especially when the unessential details were concerned. Take, for example, the process of filling up on gas. Not a problem in any movie regardless of circumstance or environment. Arnold Schwarzenegger could surely siphon fuel from a rolling battle tank and transfer it to a jet airliner as it took flight and he could probably do it without space gear on the surface of Mars if need be. But cycle back to reality, take away the current of electricity and the convenience of plastic cards and you might as well blow up the gas pumps too because there was simply no accessing all that fuel.

They weren't in dire need of gas. The cruiser still held a quarter tank and they had a few full spare cans in the trunk, one of which now lay on the ground beside Merrick's feet as he fumbled with its nozzle, read and then reread the accompanying directions. Still, they'd all feel better with a couple spare tanks in the trunk.

"Mother—you piece of— who the hell designed this?" Merrick spat from somewhere behind them as Jordan giggled. "If there's any justice in this world, you've vanished forever so you can't do any more harm!"

Whether by dumb luck or genuine comprehension, Zephyr couldn't say, the older man finally figured it out and they left the station behind. A couple hours later, they crossed into New Mexico.

20
Little Green Men

They drove on as the highway grew and the trees around faded into rocks and desert. The landscape rolled by before them. Blackened, charcoaled vegetation as far as the eye could see. Fires, of course, but the flames had burned out well in advance of them. They saw more abandoned cars, trucks and enormous diesels by the hundreds in the miles that raced ahead of them, but no people. Always, Merrick maneuvered carefully around or between the obstructions without interruption. There was but one exception.

"What the hell is that?" the man asked and slowed the cruiser.

Directly in the road ahead rested a gargantuan white thing. From a distance, Zephyr thought it must be a boat. Perhaps someone had dragged it in tow before it became unhinged. Yet as they edged ever closer, he realized with sudden horror that it wasn't a boat at all, but the huge, splintered wing of an airplane, one oversized wheel still attached, now turned forever upside-down as though grasping for the sky it once kissed.

"Holy hell," Merrick said.

"What? What is it?" Jordan asked.

"I think it's an airplane wing," Zephyr replied.

The older man whistled. "Bingo, kid. Jesus, would you look at that?"

They coasted to a stop before it. The wing was colossal. It stretched across both lanes of the highway and then overhung the blackened desert weeds off one side. It was white with remnants of blue paint, but most of it had scraped or burned away to the primer beneath. The boy wondered if the landing gear had been triggered by the pilot or knocked outward with the impact of the crash.

"Where's the rest of it?" Jordan asked.

All three of them surveyed the radius of the wreckage and found no other remnants. No hulking chunks of steel. Not shattered glass. Not even a solitary seat. There was just the mammoth wing. And it was enough. Not only a reminder of the event itself, which had become a lingering shadow in the wake of survival, but their first unavoidable blockade. It could not be passed with any car. The highway's shoulder sloped into dirt and rocks that were too steep and rough for the cruiser. They would have to climb over the wing on foot and find another vehicle on the other side or turn back and search for another route.

"OK, so we'll back it up a bit, exit, then we can get back on going that way," Merrick said and pointed to the opposite side of the highway. "It'll feel a little weird, I know, but it'll work."

"If you say so," Zephyr agreed. In truth, it sounded like fun, he allowed himself.

It wasn't. They retraced their path, exited one of the onramps and then re-entered the freeway against traffic. There were no speeding cars to dodge, but even so their progress felt surreal and unnatural, if not altogether dangerous.

"It's kind of invigorating, don't you think?" Merrick said as he revved the car forward.

Jordan perked up. "What does inviger… invigergerating mean?"

"Like, exciting," the man replied.

"Totally!" she said, smiling.

The more Zephyr learned about Merrick, the more he liked him.

Even before the event, he was one of those men destined for eternal bachelorhood, happy in his small, decidedly geeky, certainly niche existence. Although he looked like he belonged in a metal band, he adored classical music, and delighted in the stories of superheroes, his favorite being the Green Arrow. He told the boy that he'd borrowed money from his parents, presently vanished, several times over so that he could keep his failing comic shop afloat — not just because he loved it, but because however few, others did, too. The business had proven secondary to the fandom.

"Dying art — people would rather watch the movie adaptations these days — and I love those, too, don't get me wrong," he said as they drove, "But kid, you haven't lived until you've trekked alongside Lobo on his quest to beat the shit out of Santa Claus. That's the kind of stuff you'll never see on the big screen. Especially not now."

After some prodding, the man confirmed that his recent travels weren't as spontaneous as he originally indicated. He hoped, he admitted, to build his collection, amassing rare comics and collectibles as he explored the country.

"You're thinking I'm ridiculous, or shallow, I know," he said and sighed. "You're probably right, but it's what makes me happy, and I don't think there's anything wrong with holding onto a little happiness now, ya know?"

The boy thought about it and nodded. They were all drifting through a new reality they didn't understand. He didn't think there was anything wrong with embracing old passions, especially ones so innocent. Anyway, if nobody ever came back, men like Merrick might be considered catalogers of history in the centuries to come.

"So what are you gonna do if we find this aunt of yours?" the man asked.

Zephyr shifted in his seat and tugged on his safety belt. He thought about it and wasn't sure how to respond because he held little hope of her survival. At last he said, “Eat a home-cooked meal, to start. After that, I don’t know.”

“I could use a home-cooked meal, that’s for sure.”

“Yeah, me too,” Zephyr agreed.

“Me three,” Jordan offered.

She was probably gone. Vanished. Evaporated. Or— what was it Merrick had said?— sucked back into herself until she blinked out.

“Here’s a question for you,” Zephyr said. “Why do you think some of us are still here if you don’t think the event is religious? Why wouldn’t all us have just disappeared together?”

Merrick shrugged. “Don’t look at me, kid. I don’t have the answers. I mean, I guess it could be religious, but if you saw what I saw, I think we’d be on the same page about that. I don’t know. The way they went. It lacked…” He struggled for words and finally said, “There was just no love in it.”

No love. That somehow resonated with him. He stared through the bug-soaked windshield and contemplated it. Would the believers and the saved be swept away to Heaven with terror animating their faces? Zephyr didn’t think so.

“What you should be trying to figure out,” Merrick said, “is what all of us have in common.”

“What do you mean?” Zephyr asked.

“Lots of people are gone. Maybe millions. Or even billions. We, on the other hand, are not. All of us. So what’s the same about us? What is special about the three of us that is keeping us here? You understand?”

Zephyr nodded.

“We’re all white!” Jordan nearly screamed, amazed by her own deductive powers.

“You’re right and that’s exactly the kind of thinking I’m talking about,” Merrick replied. “But there are definitely others out there. Mexicans for sure. I haven’t seen any black people yet, but I’ll bet we will." He rubbed the back of his neck with one hand as he drove. "Here's another thing. Why aren't animals affected?"

"Yeah, I've already wondered that. Maybe they are, though. We've seen some, but I haven't exactly been counting. Their numbers may have dwindled, too, for all we know," Zephyr offered.

"I've seen lots of dogs since this all happened. I don't think they've been reduced," Merrick said. "But let's suppose they have. Then the question we need to ask again is, why? And let's also suppose this thing— the event, as you called it— goes on indefinitely. Eventually, someone's gonna need to figure out which animals have and haven't been affected by all this, if any. Maybe Beagles are extinct but Huskies are totally unaffected. And if that's the case, again, why? There has to be some kind of commonality between all this stuff that we aren't seeing."

"You might be smarter than you look," Zephyr said.

"I get that a lot. I think it might be the beard."

The boy smiled. "You're right, though. I haven't been thinking about it that way, but I bet you're onto something. The thing is, though, even if we find the link between all of us, if there actually is one, that's all we'll have. Just a link. But we still won't know why. Let's say we find out that every last survivor loves the color red and that's what binds us all together. So what? The real question isn't why we're here but why everyone else isn't."

Merrick nodded. "Yeah, well, you're smarter than you look, too."

"Must be the hair."

It was a joke, but Zephyr realized that the mop atop his head really had been left unattended for the last week and it was greasier and longer than he preferred. On instinct, he tucked thick, brown strands of it behind his ears.

Merrick slowed and skirted a stalled red truck. "Like I said, I really don't know. I'm just throwing stuff out there. If it's God or a higher force that we don't understand or aliens or whatever, we can't control that. There may be a design here. Then again, there may be no design at all. But maybe we can find a few answers between us— and by us, I mean all the survivors— if we ask the right questions and look in the right places. That's all I'm saying."

"No, I totally agree," the boy remarked.

"Let's hope this is all moot in a few days, anyway. Maybe everything will go back to normal. I like to think I'm a realist, but you can't set any kind of realistic expectations when it's the end of the freakin' world, ya know?"

"It's not really the end of the world," Jordan said. "You're just kidding, right?"

"No, it's not the end of the world, sweetheart. But it might be the end of the world as we knew it," he said.

21

The freeway into Las Cruces was more congested than any Zephyr had seen since the disappearances, and the traffic slowed their progress. To his credit, Merrick proved a surefooted driver, and he zigzagged between stalled cars or wrecks without as much as a scrape. At first, the boy winced at every close call, but as time passed he came to trust in the man's ability.

"We're not gonna get a ticket, girlie. Wear it if you want, or don't. I honestly don't care," Merrick told her a couple hours earlier after she asked if she could unbuckle her safety belt for the third time. Zephyr was against this declaration from the start and suggested that Jordan re-clasp the harness without hesitation, but this advice ricocheted away from her and soon after she could be found bouncing back and forth inside the cabin, clearly drunk on her newfound freedom.

The car jerked to one direction before Merrick corrected it. "Whoa, whoa— there we go," he said, tapped Zephyr's arm and prompted him to turn around. Two miles behind them, a pair of headlights cut through the blackness.

"I see 'em."

"Hard to miss. We got another survivor."

Zephyr raised in his seat. "What do we do?"

Merrick ignored the question. Instead, he triggered the cruiser's emergency lights and slowed the car to a stop. This was not what Zephyr had envisioned.

"What the hell are you doing?"

The man beat on the horn and then opened the car door. "What's it look like? Let's go and say hello." And he was off before the boy could muster an argument.

Zephyr cursed him under his breath, then told Jordan to stay close. For a nanosecond, he couldn't find it and panic swept over him, but then his fingers curled around the butt of his shotgun and he withdrew from the vehicle with it. He and Jordan scurried away from the car, the center-divide and Merrick, a development not unnoticed by the man.

"OK, come on, where are you two going?" he called.

Zephyr shushed him. "Feel free to risk your life, but don't risk ours. When the coast is clear, give us a sign." He made for the darkness off the shoulder of the highway and then turned back again. "And don't tell anyone we're here!"

"Really? You're still doing this?" Merrick threw up his hands. "You know what? Fine. Try not to shoot anyone from the side of the road, if you can resist."

Zephyr held Jordan's hand and whispered commands to her — whatever happens, don't move and you have to be quieter than you've ever been in your life— as the two of them sat motionless under cover of darkness in the rocky shoulder off the highway.

The cold wind wedged itself between them as they watched the headlights approach. At first, minuscule candles flickering in the distance, but before too long the lights took on shape, size and halos. When at last the car was within throwing distance of the cruiser, the driver slowed and honked repeatedly before stopping. It wasn't just a car, though. Even from his position, Zephyr could see that it had real hulk and girth. The high beams stood level to the cruiser's top lights and the boy thought he could make out the shape of a huge truck, or maybe even a bus or tank between the pulses of reds and blues.

A door swung open and someone stepped out as Zephyr squinted for definition that eluded him. There was a figure engaged in conversation with Merrick, but he couldn't distinguish much more. Was it just one person or were there more? And why was Merrick such a fool? He remembered his own roadside encounter with the man. Had I been like Ross, you would probably be dead, my friend, and here you are again.

After too long, the older man walked to the newcomer's car and stood there for what seemed forever. Zephyr longed for a pair of binoculars and promised to track down some upon their arrival in Las Cruces. Just as he was contemplating where he might be able to loot some, another figure emerged from the vehicle and the three of them walked back to the cruiser, at which point Merrick leaned into the driver's side window and retrieved something.

A moment later, his voice boomed loud and clear over the megaphone. "All right, Road Warrior."

Oh, for crying out loud! The man just doesn't take anything seriously.

"The coast is clear. This is my official signal to come on back. Repeat. This is my official sign."

Then it was another voice that blasted against the wind. To Zephyr, he sounded distinctly teenage.

"So, do I just hold thi— OK, yeah, got it." He cleared his throat. "So dude. It's all good. It's just me and my brother and we're cool." He waited, perhaps expecting Zephyr to emerge from cover of darkness and when that didn't happen he continued. "OK, then, all right, so this is my brother, Brad. OK, so, yeah, here ya go."

A second later, one more voice blared into the darkness. "Yeah, we're stoked to see some more people on the road and trust me, we're totally cool, like my brother Dildo Face said."

Almost inaudible: "Shut up, jackass."

"Dildo Face has spoken so I better put this down. We'll be hanging here with Merrick so, cool. Peace out."

22

Brad and Ben Splinter looked like pro surfers. Lean, if not lanky, tanned, each with straight blonde hair that hung past their shoulders. Both donned loose shorts and t-shirts. They didn't just look like two brothers, but a mirrored image of one another, which made a lot of sense because they were identical twins. Zephyr guessed them in their late teens or very early twenties, but the subject of age hadn't yet come up. They all sat in the relative luxury of the parked Humvee the boys drove and snacked on some marshmallows.

They were staying with a friend in Henderson, Nevada, a suburb on the outskirts of Las Vegas, when "everyone popped," as Ben not-so-delicately put it. Like Merrick, they were wide awake and had their own recollections of the event.

"We were playing Battlefield online," began Brad.

"You were," his brother corrected. "I was browsing the Web."

"Dude, seriously? Does it matter? We were in the same freakin' room."

"If you want to be accurate, it does," Ben replied.

"Will you just let me tell the damned story?" He glared at his sibling. "As I was saying. I was online. My brain-dead brother was no doubt trolling for porn. And our friend, Jeff, was watching me play. I was on a truly gargantuan run, too. I mean, literally dominating dudes. And—"

"I bet you were," said Ben.

"Just shut up. So the next thing I know, there's this weird sound — like, everywhere. In the room and coming through my headset, too. Like a hissing. And then Jeff is gone."

"Nothing but clothes," his brother added.

"The sucking noise, right? Same thing I heard," Merrick said, nodding.

Ben nodded back. "Yep. And then like a bubble popping."

"Did you see your friend disappear? I mean, did you actually see him go?" Merrick asked.

The brothers shook their heads. "No," Ben said. "Just afterward. And, you know, nothing being left of him. We didn't actually see it, though. Brad was playing and I was online, so neither of us were really paying attention, and it happened so fast."

"I saw movement out of the corner of my eye, but that was it," his brother agreed.

Brad brushed his hands through his hair. "I was in the middle of a team match, though. One second earlier, we'd all been running through the desert and gunning down idiots. Like, totally owning these fools." He smiled, clearly impressed with himself. "Anyway, lots of chatter, lots of gunfire— just a big old mess of sound. Suddenly, it was all quiet. So I looked back at the screen and everyone is just standing there. My teammates, the guys we were battling. Nobody moving anymore."

"Even then," he continued, "we went downstairs looking for Jeff and his sister. They share a house together. Or, shared, maybe. Whatever the case, we obviously didn't find them. We just found Lisa's clothes in her bed. By that time, we were pretty freaked out. So, like everyone else still alive, we turned on the TV, tried calling peeps, etcetera. You know the story from there."

"Is your— I mean, your family— are they?" Zephyr started, fumbling for words.

"Yeah, no. Our dad died when we were kids and our mom died a few years ago. No brothers, or sisters. Or anybody, for that matter. Just the two of us," Brad explained.

"Gotcha," Zephyr said, unsure whether to offer condolences or congratulations. At least their grief was old and dulled and not fresh and sharp. He made apologies anyway.

"Nah, it's cool, dude," Brad said. "We figure this is one time it's good to be us. I would not be liking life right now if—"

"Yeah, we get it, Dr. Tact," his brother said and punched him in the arm.

"What?" he asked, rubbing his arm. Then it dawned on him. "Ohh, damn. Sorry, shit. I'm an idiot."

"Yeah you are," Ben agreed.

23

When they realized that the event was widespread, the twins drove from Henderson to Vegas to look for people and answers, but it proved mostly fruitless.

"Vegas looked like hell itself, dudes. It was, like, literally Sin City," Brad explained.

"I don't think you know how to use the word 'literally,'" his brother interrupted.

"Just shut. It was still dark outside, but this ginormous red cloud glowed over the city because all these fires were going. And there was this kind of fog covering a lot of stuff. Only after we got closer did it hit me that it wasn't fog— just smoke and dust, like when the Twin Towers fell."

"Planes," Merrick said, not really a question.

"Yeah. One of them hit Mandalay Bay, I think, because the entire hotel was just gone. Just completely missing except for piles of debris and shit." He drew his hands apart and sounded an explosion. "Meanwhile, a couple other hotels— MGM Grand, for example— were just roasting. Like, totally ablaze."

"Yeah, and that's when we started to see people running around," Ben said.

"In the hotel?" Zephyr asked.

"No, no. In the streets, mostly. We talked to some of them. This one girl was just wearing underwear and a bra and she said the terrorists got us and she was crying and not making much sense beyond that. We asked if we could help but she just ran off," Ben said.

"Yeah, she had mascara all down her face— she would've been hot, but it was just creepy," Brad added. Then, perhaps reading Zephyr's mind or just to change the subject, he said, "We saw probably fifty people or so, you think?"

"Nah, I'd say more than that. We saw thirty or forty walking together that one time and then tons of stragglers. I bet it's more than a hundred," Ben said.

"You're crazy. No way was it that much."

Ben looked at him. "Dude. There were like forty alone in the intersection in front of Wynn. Are you trying to tell me we only saw ten more people throughout the whole city?"

The brothers continued bantering and bickering this way for the next half hour, each allowing the other to advance portions of their story, but never without interruption. Zephyr eventually learned a little more about the situation in Vegas, although not very much. Vanishings and fires aside, the city lived on, according to the duo. Electricity flowed. Brad said that the strip was blanketed in clothes and shoes. Only a few hotels burned, but they were infernos. Wrecks lay unnoticed. Vacant cars littered the streets and sidewalks, their engines and headlights fighting to persist. They talked to passersby and nobody really knew what happened. Some people were leaving Vegas and others were staying.

Shortly after their arrival, the twins witnessed a small group of survivors loot a liquor store and this triggered a collective epiphany. It wasn't long before they found themselves drunk at one of the hotel casinos, where they spent the remainder of the night and early morning.

"It was surreal," Brad noted.

Ben sighed. "It sounds pretty bad, I know, and in hindsight it's probably not our best moment. But it seemed like the end of the world at the time and nobody was really thinking straight. So I guess we just sort of went with it."

"I mean, I won't bullshit you, either— it was kind of rad," Brad said and shrugged. "Just the total trip of doing whatever—not the peeps disappearing part."

Zephyr liked the twins. There was no air of pretense about them. Rather, they seemed to accept the reality of the event with a nod and a shrug. *Oh, the apocalypse has come? Bummer. That's that, I guess. Do you wanna grab a beer or something?* It wasn't noble or even particularly intelligent. They existed somewhere between pure fatalism and Darwinism. But for their faults, they were at least real. There was something else about them, though. Their attitude was infectious because despite it all, nothing had touched their optimism. They recounted everything not with incredulousness or horror. Oh, maybe a sprinkle of both in recognition of taste. Mostly, it was just astonishment, and underneath it all, excitement. For all of these reasons, he envied them, even if he didn't completely understand them.

"Didn't you guys wonder what happened, though?" he finally asked.

Brad smiled. "Oh, we know exactly what happened, dude. You've heard about Area 51, right?"

His brother rolled his eyes. "Come on, man. It's getting late and I'm hungry. Do we have to do this?"

"Can you just shut up for one minute? Jesus."

"Yeah, I saw *Independence Day*. Government facility in Nevada with a bunch of top-secret stuff," Zephyr said. "Guys, we already thought about aliens. There's also the possibility of the Rapture. And I'm sure a million more theories."

"This isn't a theory, my man," Brad said. "We've been there."

"You went to Area 51?" Merrick asked, unable to mask his skepticism.

"Hell, yes, we did. And we saw some pretty unexplainable shit, too."

"Uh, that's entirely debatable," Ben said.

After their drunken night in Vegas, the twins woke and resolved to utilize their newfound freedom to the fullest. They narrowed their options down to a nearby amusement park or the infamous government facility, and a coin flip decided it.

Brad recounted their travels to the hidden base, whose gates were mysteriously unlocked and swung outward, as though, "something had broken free." Merrick cackled at the suggestion but the twin ignored him. The two brothers explored the base, discovered security towers armed with turrets and piles of clothes strewn about the entryway and interior. They made their way deeper into its series of nondescript white buildings and found abandoned classrooms and barracks and hangars, all with more neatly-departed clothes.

It was one such hangar that served as the centerpiece to their narrative, though. Unlike the others, it housed no cutting-edge planes or jets. It was empty, and sloped down for a football field's length into what should have been earth.

"But it wasn't," Brad said, smiling. "We got to this open area filled with computer shit everywhere, tons of clothes all over the place, and then this big, black wall. But dudes, it wasn't a wall. It was like a screen. Imagine the biggest movie screen you ever saw, multiply that by at least fifteen, and you've got the size."

"So the government has a top-secret underground movie theater?" Merrick quipped.

"Dude," Brad said and stared at him. "It wasn't a movie screen. It was totally black. Even when we shined our phones on it. It was like made of some kind of weird glass, and we couldn't see behind it. Whatever it is, lots of people were working on it. Hundreds, based on the leftover laundry down there."

"My brother thinks it's a Stargate, basically," Ben said and shook his head.

"That's not what..." Brad punched his twin's arm. "You always have to... you're a damned idiot."

Merrick leaned back and sighed. "It's far-fetched. I mean, I believe you went down there, but I think you're stretching with the alien connection. I'm not hearing any proof."

"My dumb-shit brother acts like he wasn't weirded out now, but he was crapping his pants when we saw it, and for good reason. Whatever that thing was, it was the point of the base. And it couldn't have been manmade." He seemed to be pleading the case to himself. "It couldn't have been."

24

The twins were not only eager to join them, but also offered to drive. Merrick, of course, resisted this generosity from the start. He argued that the police cruiser had served them well so far and it would continue to do so. Additionally, he said, it would be a good idea to have two vehicles in case one broke down. All logical, but neither Zephyr nor Jordan, still groggy and keen to find a stopping point so that they might enjoy a full night's rest, were having it, and eventually the man relented.

"So we made it to Roswell but there really wasn't anything to see," Brad said as he drove, the highway ahead of them ablaze in the headlights of the Humvee. Ben and Merrick also sat up front, leaving Zephyr and Jordan to stretch out in the back. It was roomy and for that he was thankful. His gun lay flat on the floor as Jordan rummaged through their crinkly plastic snack bags for a candy bar.

"The place is really just a tourist trap."

"Not anymore," Merrick said, popped the cap on a beer bottle and chugged it. He belched and rolled down the window—Midwest etiquette, Zephyr thought. "Really, you two are off your rockers. If I had seen what you claimed to see — and I'm not saying I buy it — I wouldn't still be trying to find little green men."

"Well, to be fair, we weren't really trying to find anything. After we left Area 51 in our rearview, my bro made some crack about Roswell and that got us off again. But I think we were just happy to have a destination in mind."

"Yeah, totally. By the way, we probably stayed in Roswell for about twenty minutes before we tore out of there," Brad said. "Place was a bore."

Merrick laughed. "Damned Ping-Pong balls, bouncing all around."

"We just go with the flow, baby."

The chatter continued for a little while, although Zephyr stopped listening. He welcomed the veil of regularity, however thin. Some '90s grunge, he thought it was Soundgarden, played low but steady as the twins fought for airtime and the older man listened and occasionally interjected. Jordan chomped on some nutritionally-empty bag of chips while the car weaved through the last remains of traffic. Zephyr thought of Keiko and his parents and wondered if any of them had been awake when "everybody popped." He tried not to dwell on it, but couldn't escape a vision of Keiko's terrified eyes rolling back into their sockets and her body jerking in electrified rhythm before she vanished from the world.

Sometime later, they pulled off the highway and parked outside a La Quinta motel about fifty miles outside of Las Cruces. It offered little in the way of comforts, with its zapped electricity, moldy bread and turned milk. Someone had shattered several front-facing windows and one of the rooms the twins tried to claim had been altogether ransacked. Broken beer bottles lined the bedroom floor and they found the television floating amidst cold, gray water in the bathtub.

"If this is what the world has left, we may as well call it quits now," Merrick remarked upon seeing the aftermath. Zephyr thought the comment somewhat hypocritical coming from a man who regularly drove drunk, but he kept quiet.

The broken windows did nothing to stop the flow of bitter air into the rooms. "I can see my breath," Jordan said when she sat on her bed.

Eventually, the group searched the quaint lobby for more blankets. The reception area was small and unremarkable except for one unavoidable detail: someone had taken the time to write a message upon the wall in blood-red lipstick:

My World Now

Zephyr didn't want to meet the author, ever, and based on the sudden silence the words induced, he guessed he wasn't alone in his opinion. Shortly thereafter, they all resolved to sleep in the same room, which was fine by him. But sleep didn't come to any of them, and before too long Brad threw off his blankets, settled his flashlight on the floor so that it beamed at the ceiling, and finally stood.

"Sorry, peeps — I can't do it," he announced. "It's too flippin' cold in here."

Everyone agreed, even his brother, who normally dissected and debated everything he said, yet there was nothing to be done about it and they all knew it. Brad fetched more blankets for all of them and, still shivering, wrapped himself like a burrito before settling back onto the pile of pillows he'd strewn over the floor as a makeshift bed.

"This blows," he declared. "We should be on some tropical beach now, not freezing our asses off in the world's worst motel. The car would be better than this."

"You're welcome to it," his brother said.

"You're welcome to my middle finger."

"Yeah, I'll pass. No telling where that's been."

"Your mom knows," Brad replied.

"I shouldn't need to point out how wrong that is."

Merrick rolled over to glare at them. "I've got an idea — why don't both of you go to the car and leave the rest of us in peace?"

"What we need, is a bonfire up in here," Brad said, ignoring him.

"Yeah, if you want to smoke yourself out and burn down the motel," the older man retorted.

"Burning down the motel might not be a bad thing."

"At least we'd be warm," his twin agreed, and they both giggled.

"Hold up," Ben said, and then the room was overwhelmed by the sounds of crinkling paper and clanking glass as he rummaged through his grocery bag of goodies. He brought forth a tall, skinny bottle of vodka and smiled at the party. "This'll warm us up."

"Oh my God, I've waited my whole life for you to do something smart and now that it's finally happened, I don't know how to react," Brad quipped. "Am I dreaming? Jordan, come pinch me."

"OK," she said, and sprung from her heap of blankets to do as he asked. Zephyr was beginning to think she might have a little crush on Brad, or Ben, or maybe both of them.

The twins and Merrick took turns passing the bottle around and shivering while Zephyr and Jordan remained bundled side-by-side on one of the room's two queen beds.

Merrick winced. "This tastes like shit."

"Need to throw in the towel, old man?" Ben mused.

"Not too old to teach you both a lesson."

"That's because we're lovers, not fighters," Brad said.

Jordan, meanwhile, complained that whatever they were drinking smelled like window cleaner and pulled the blankets over her nose. This, of course, triggered more laughter from the group.

Zephyr dangled his legs over the bed and slumped forward, his blankets falling over his shoulders. He didn't feel like drinking, especially because it excluded Jordan, but neither was he tired. The ceiling shone a round gradient that resembled a tree's growth ring and the resulting radiance cast the room in dim, yellow light.

"Take a swig, dude," Ben told him but Zephyr shook his head.

"Your loss."

"If New Mexico doesn't pan out," Zephyr said. "What will you two do?"

Brad took another shot and then passed the bottle to Merrick. "I don't know," he said. "Our calendars are still pretty clear. We might have some cousins in North Dakota, I guess, so if all else fails, we could check that out."

"Except that it's North Dakota," Ben said.

"Yeah, except that."

"What we should do is hit Mexico proper. There are some sick beaches down there and we don't have to worry about getting our heads chopped off any more."

Zephyr chuckled. "Not from the cartels, anyway."

"Oh, here we go," Merrick said. "The pessimist speaks."

Ben ignored him. "Yeah, the old man told us about your… about your rough start in your hometown. I'm sorry that shit went down like that. On the bright side, you're here. You made it." He nodded in Jordan's direction. "And what you did for her, what you're doing for her, it's legit. One-hundred percent props."

"You're the real deal, man," his brother agreed.

"One day, we'll be upstanding citizens like you, but for now, we're cool with being more like Merrick here."

The older man was about to take another swig and stopped. "Hey, what the hell is that supposed to mean?"

25
Crossroads

Las Cruces did not greet them with open arms. The freeway into the city was littered with more jilted trucks and cars than they had grown accustomed to, yes, but that wasn't the problem. Rather, it was that someone had blocked the roads, both in and out of the city, with four adjoined yellow and black school buses. The rusty behemoths kissed nose-to-nose, two for each direction of the highway. Merrick thought they could veer off the road into the thick mixture of dirt, weeds and rock that substituted for a divide in order to maneuver around the blockades, but nobody else agreed. There was also another consideration, which was that someone had spray-painted the buses with big blue warnings that read *Stay the Fuck Out* and *Yer Not Welcome Here*.

Ben whistled at the last notice. "OK, then," he said.

"Uh, anybody up for some gambling? Vegas is looking a whole lot better suddenly," his brother added.

Merrick didn't comment but neither did he look disheartened by the predicament. He took the scene in with something resembling mild amusement and the boy wondered, not for the first time, if there was any alcohol remaining in the bottle that seemed to take permanent residence on his lap. Jordan asked what was going on and Zephyr shushed her. Something had caught his eye.

"I think the twins are right. We should turn around," he said, tapped Brad on the shoulder and then gestured the shape of a U-turn.

"Wait, wait, let's give it a second," Merrick argued, finally showing some signs of life. "It's just a damned bit of graffiti, for crying out loud. Let's jus—"

"No, let's go," Zephyr interrupted, meeting the man's eyes. "Please."

Merrick shook his head. "One minute. Let's just figure this out."

The boy pointed to the buses. "Something's wrong."

"Spill it then."

Zephyr wondered if Merrick was ignorant or just unshakably optimistic. Or maybe just dense. "You mean beyond the call for us to turn back?" He pointed toward the buses. "First, look there. See? The tires are all locked. Those big black bolts are called tire boots. Supposed to deter thieves. But I don't think that's the intention here. They just don't want anybody trying to move them."

"And?"

"You don't think that's strange?"

"Kid, this whole world is strange."

Zephyr ignored him. "And do you notice the lack of windows? No glass. It's all sheet metal with little rivets," he added, pointing. "Just big enough, I might add, for gun barrels."

"Really? Are we really doing this again? You always think everyone is out to kill you."

"That's because they are!" Zephyr shouted louder than he intended.

"OK, I get it. You've had a tough break, but let's remember that you thought I was the devil when we first met and then you pegged these two turds as bad news too when we caught sight of their headlights," he said, motioning to the twins, neither of whom seemed to care for the label. "Granted, it's not a party waiting for us here, but I don't think it's, I dunno, cannibals, either. I'm sure they're just paranoid and scared — not unlike you. If we could just chat with them, I'm sur—"

"It's just not right."

"This is all based on some locked tires and sheet metal. For all you know, these buses are junkyard specialties with broken windows. For all you know, the people behind this little stunt are scared shitless of other survivors."

When Zephyr gave no rebuttal, he continued. "Listen, I know, I'm Mr. Optimist, and yadda-yadda-yadda, but can we at least investigate this a little? We literally just got here. If anything looks fishy after we get a closer look, you have my word that we can roll out."

Zephyr considered it and shook his head. "I mean, are you reading the buses?"

"I get it, but what you're interpreting as hostile, I see as scared. Just… scared people trying to protect themselves. Besides, we came all this way for your aunt. Are we supposed to just turn around and forget her? Just give up? I honestly don't even know how to go around this city, so we'd have to go back."

The boy weighed his words and then reluctantly threw up his hands. "Fine. OK, yes," he conceded. "You're right. I just… forget it. What do you suggest?"

"Well, let's go knock on the front door and say hello," Merrick said with his trademark grin, and then he stepped out of the car.

He made it halfway to the buses, the twins and Zephyr united in their calls for him to return, when a shot rang out and the top of his head exploded.

26

Gunfire and agony waged war as reality swayed in slow-motion. Jordan was hysterical. Brad tried to throw the Hummer in reverse, but bullets deluged the windshield, first cracking, then shattering and finally penetrating the invisible glass barrier that protected them from the onslaught. He clutched his brother's arm and gasped as sprays of bullets punctured his face and chest with the heavy thud of meat and bone. Splattered in his twin's blood, Ben bellowed something indecipherable and swung open the passenger door, which was immediately blasted by more bullets.

"Fuck!" he screamed. "Fuck youuuuuuu!"

Zephyr thought Ben would run for it and was relieved instead to see him duck for cover beneath the glove compartment as glass shattered and spilled all around him.

Do something, damn you, the boy told himself, but he couldn't move. Then he caught sight of Merrick's limp body on the pavement before the bus, blood hemorrhaging in a thick red torrent from the gaping wound that used to be his hairline, and something inside him stirred.

Move! Do it now! And he did.

He fumbled for the rifle, unlatched the safety and thrust open the backseat door. He told Jordan to curl up behind the passenger seat. Then he turned to the twin.

"Ben!" he shouted. The bastards were still shooting at them, although the steady barrage had dwindled to intermittent discharges. "Ben! Listen to me. Can you hear me?"

"Fuck!" the older boy cried.

Good. Still alive and maybe just angry enough to do what needed to be done, Zephyr thought. "We have to get to these assholes on the other side of the bus. I'm going to do it, but I need a distraction. We're gonna need to crash into them. Do you understand?"

No reply, and he was sure Ben had either blacked out or gone fetal when the twin unfurled himself from the sanctity of the floorboard and slithered from passenger to driver's compartment. Sobbing and cursing, the older boy grunted and pushed his dead brother's limp body into the passenger seat before taking his place. When he finally managed to switch gears, the Humvee lurched before he reasserted his foot on the brake, and more wild gunfire peppered the hood as bullets whizzed through the windshield and tore into the upper seats.

"Motherfuckers! My turn!" Ben screamed, and in that moment, Zephyr loved him.

The vehicle sped backward for what struck Zephyr as an inordinate amount before the car stopped. He changed gears, the tires spun before they gained traction and the Humvee shot forward again like a bullet. The engine roared as the seconds passed and Zephyr's stomach turned as he fought without success to anticipate the point of impact. Jordan wailed next to him. He had just enough time to place her hand in his and squeeze before the world shook.

The Humvee struck the bus with bone-rattling ferocity and Zephyr's head slammed against the passenger seat before he came to rest atop Jordan and lost consciousness.

He opened his eyes seconds later, or probably it was minutes, he thought. Reality bled back in and blind imagery connected to context again. The good news was that the Hummer hadn't flipped. The better news was that the bus had. Somehow. Miraculously. The impact had actually knocked the damned thing on its side, boot-locked tires and all. He couldn't fucking believe it. As far as he could tell, the only damage to the Hummer was the missing door on his side—his own fault for opening it before the crash.

"Holy shit, Ben— you did it!" he shouted and when the twin gave no response, his heart skipped a beat. No, no, no—not you, too. Please, he thought, and then peeked around the seat into the front compartment. Ben's limp body remained slumped in the driver's recess, his face still kissing the recently-blown airbag. He was probably all right, just out cold.

Jordan's face was streaked with tears and her hair was frazzled, but otherwise Zephyr thought she looked no worse for wear and was relieved. OK, good, good, this is good—it's time to do it, he thought, and reached for the rifle.

It wasn't there.

27

"Jord. You need to stay here while I do a quick search. Absolutely do not move." He palmed her cheeks with his hands and stared into her eyes. "Do you understand me? Do. Not. Move. Say it. For real."

"Do not move," she said, but she was already weeping. "I don't want you to go. I don't wan—"

"I have to, but I'll be back, I promise. Jordan, listen to me. Do. Not. Move." He kissed her forehead and then slid out the side opening where the door used to be.

He caught sight of Merrick's body several feet away and wrestled with a fleeting ripple of dizziness before his eyes locked again on the bus and anger took him. Heavy black smoke billowed from the coach's underside before the air caught and dispersed it into nothingness. He thought he heard people crying and cocked his head to listen. Was it just the wind? No. For sure. He heard them in there. They were crying and shouting. Someone was calling for help. And now his anger gave way to rage. These damned subhumans possessed the temerity to first wage unprovoked war on the innocent and then beg for help when fate turned against them? His eyes darted around for the rifle and finally he spotted it almost buried within a stout tuft of yellow weeds in the center divide. It must've flown out at the impact. He sprinted to it and ran back to the bus just as fast, still aware of the danger before him.

The cries for help continued but he didn't respond to any of them. Instead, he sneaked around the bus and spied into the window of the rear exit. He could see the silhouetted outlines of multiple figures, all of them clinging to the interior sides of the overturned vehicle, no doubt crouching for cover and waiting for the opportune moment to attack. He ran back to the Humvee, crawled into the front seat and pressed the cigarette lighter. With that done, he took aim at the underbelly of the bus, sighted in on what he thought was the fuel tank, and pulled the trigger. He heard shouts and screams, but no gas trickled from the plastic wound. He took aim at another bulbous black canister, pulled the trigger and this time gas did flow from the opening and splattered on the gnarled street below.

"Help! Please!" cried one of the assaulters. "We're hurt in here. We're trapped! Let's talk about this!"

"Yeah, probably a little late for that!" Zephyr called back. "Maybe we should've had that conversation — oh, I don't know — before you murdered a couple of my friends? I would've been all for that. I really would've have. I gotta say, though, I'm not feeling very chatty anymore."

"We're—agghh—" The words that followed were unintelligible, just a medley of pain and aggravation. Then the speaker was back. "We're chained up in here! They said if we didn't shoot anybody who tried to pass, that if anybody got through, they were going to cut off our feet and watch us bleed out. Our feet! They'd do it, too. For Christ's sake, you have to believe me!"

"Who are they?" Zephyr asked.

A long pause with more agonized commotion. He heard chains rattling as someone pounded against the interior of the bus.

"Listen, I know you guys must be cold in there. It's freakin' freezing out here, that's for sure. Don't worry, though, because I got this," Zephyr shouted.

"No, wait! Some guys. We don't know who. They've got weapons and they're… "a new voice called back, and in a lower tone added, "They're deranged. They think the city is theirs and that the leftovers are their slaves. It's been like this for a week." Leftovers? Is that what they're calling the survivors?

Chains again as something slammed inside. "They took my damned sister. I had no choice."

So far, it was just the two voices, but Zephyr knew there were others in there. So what were they doing? He asked the latest speaker to identify everybody in the bus but the voice gave no response. And what about the other buses? Was there anybody in any of them? If so, why weren't they mounting any kind of counterattack? He was contemplating all of this when a hand closed on his shoulder and he squeezed the trigger of the rifle, sending a bullet into the air.

"It's me, dude," Ben said without inflection, plucked the lighter from Zephyr's hand and casually tossed it into the growing puddle of gas beneath the bus. The blaze was immediate.

A half dozen voices shouted to be released, screamed for mercy, and cursed them simultaneously. Seconds later, the tank exploded with a deafening crash and flames flared up before they engulfed the bus. It was fast. So damned fast.

Zephyr glowered at Ben, who either didn't notice or didn't care. The twin screamed at the bus instead. "Yeah, does it hurt? Good! Get used to it, you fucks!"

"Ben, they're chained up in there," Zephyr said. He wasn't sure if this statement was meant to discourage the twin or simply to inform him. Probably, something in the middle.

"I don't care. Those chains didn't stop them from trying to murder us. They killed Brad and Merrick. They killed my brother." He looked as though the realization had just struck him. "They killed my brother."

Zephyr nodded. He understood. He even agreed. And yet, he just couldn't go through with it. He couldn't let these people, however vile, die this way.

All he said was, "I'm sorry, Ben, but I can't." And then he ran for the back of the bus.

It was futile. Even if the doors hadn't been locked and chained shut, the temperature itself was impenetrable. Zephyr grabbed for the handle and burned his hand. He tugged off his shirt, wrapped it around his hand, and tried again. Even through the cloth, he could feel the heat, and this grip offered him no advantage against the lock and chains. He considered shooting the doors and as he did he remembered that they all had guns inside, too. Slowly, and with hot tears blurring his vision, he backed away.

The locks that barred him from a rescue were easily sidestepped by the inferno, which seemed to dance in rhythm to the tormented squeals of the shuttle's roasting occupants. Zephyr held Jordan hard and tried to shield her from the brutality. All of those voices in agonized harmony. They seemed to sing forever — a terrible, nightmarish song that he knew would never leave him.

Eventually, after a slow-motion infinity, the torture drained away into an uncomfortable quiet interrupted only by the crackle of flames and moan of the wind. The air itself smelled of barbecue for all the wrong reasons.

When enough time had passed, Zephyr ventured back to the overturned giant and shot out the rear window. Light bled in and he could see the charred remains of the assailants. There were four of them and yes, their left wrists and ankles were handcuffed to bars that had been welded to the interior of the bus. Poor bastards. Poor, pitiful bastards, he thought. He saw rifles strewn about the floor—what was actually the opposite side of the vehicle; and yes there were broken windows there, not just more metal— and realized why there hadn't been any more shooting. The crash must've scattered the weapons about and the cuffed assailants simply couldn't reach them.

"Jesus," he said.

"Not for them," Ben answered behind him.

Not, Zephyr thought, for any of us.

28

They spent minutes, not hours, arguing about what to do with the bodies and whether or not to turn back or go forward. They couldn't bury them. They lacked both time and tools. Zephyr was surprised when Ben didn't argue against the practicality of leaving his brother in the Humvee. He just nodded, walked back to the car and then climbed inside to say his good-byes. The boy couldn't watch it. He cursed Merrick, but wasn't angry with the older man. He felt like crying and held strong. Not in front of Jordan.

The other buses were empty. All of them. But Zephyr did discover that his presumption about the coaches on the opposite lane was correct. The windows had, in fact, been replaced by sheet metal on the reverse side. So the intention was to keep people in as well as out. But why weren't there any shooters in any of these other buses? Perhaps they weren't cuffed like the others and simply ran away at the first sign of danger. More likely, though, the group the attackers spoke of hadn't yet dedicated the manpower to the vehicles yet. If that really was the truth of it, he counted himself lucky. Had the shuttles been similarly armed, they would all be dead now.

Merrick had certainly paid the price. He stared at the departed man on the highway and puzzled over what to do with his body. Leaving him to the elements wasn't an option. He was cocksure if not downright patronizing at times, but Zephyr liked him all the same and wouldn't leave him to rot in the streets. While he meditated on it, Ben drew up beside him with three new rifles.

"I salvaged these from the bus. I thought they'd melted. Nope, though, just a little warm," he said. "They look like Uzis, but I don't know."

"What are you planning?"

Ben surveyed the clouds, his cheeks still streaked with dried tears. "A bit of a hunting trip." His words came in a monotone daze.

"So you're going in then?"

"Yep," the twin said.

"I don't think it's a good idea, Ben."

"Yeah, I could've guessed. You don't have to go."

"We don't even know if we'll ever find these guys. Las Cruces is a pretty big place. A hundred-thousand people. Maybe more."

"Not anymore, dude," he replied. "Maybe it used to be big, but I think the crowds are gone. I'm pretty sure all I have to do is lay low, keep quiet, and these guys will cross my path."

"And assuming they do, then what?"

"They all die. Or I do." He shrugged. "Either way."

"Won't bring your brother or Merrick back."

"I realize that."

Zephyr sighed. "OK. If we're gonna do this, let's be smart. And fast. For all we know, the crazy assholes are already en route to us."

Each gripping an armpit, they dragged Merrick back to the Hummer and lifted him to the driver's seat with a combination of clumsiness and care. The corpse threatened to slump over but they balanced him so that he stayed. When Zephyr saw that his eyes were still open, he tried to close them but they wouldn't remain shut. The man appeared to be feigning sleep and secretly spying through the lower slits of his vision. Of course, any such fiction disintegrated above his forehead.

Jordan followed Zephyr around like a lost puppy and cycled between confusion, fear and hysteria relative to their distance from the bodies, so he asked her to hold back as he stripped the Hummer of their gear and any sign that they had been passengers to the crash. After several minutes, the scene was finished to the best of his ability. To any investigators, it would look like Merrick and Brad had taken fatal gunshots but not before crashing into the bus, toppling it and igniting an accidental blaze. Or so he hoped, anyway.

The trek into Las Cruces proper paralleled Zephyr's escape from his hometown with the distinction that instead of eluding the nightmare one step at a time, they walked toward it. The journey was slow— the city stretched out several miles ahead of them and they were mindful of every sleeping car or conspicuous home, which sedated progress. But as the clouds grew ever darker and the chill in the air turned icy, they found themselves beyond the freeway and into the beginnings of an outlying neighborhood.

The streets were empty except for some residual cars and trash that blew around in the gusty air. No sign of the alleged slavers, as he had already taken to calling them. No sign of anybody. By the time they opened the squeaky door into a quaint yellow house amidst an old track development, the world was fading from gray to black and they welcomed the shelter from the dropping temperature.

The three of them utilized what remained of the natural light to feel out the unremarkable residence, small, with running water and gas, but no electricity. Zephyr needed to bathe, badly, as much for a psychological cleansing as a hygienic one. A quick search of the kitchen cabinetry yielded two functioning high-power flashlights. He set one of them atop the bathroom sink, its beam blasting the paint-peeled ceilings, and luxuriated in a steamy shower for as long as he could. Isolated from everybody else for the first time in too long, he felt no shame as the water washed away his tears.

After, he studied himself in the dim reflection of the bathroom mirror. His thick brown hair had grown some, he was inarguably thinner than ever and he looked older, which was unsurprising given everything he'd raced through in recent days... or was it weeks? He still hadn't decided. There was something else, though: he thought his eyes seemed a little wilder and his features a little harder. And why not? His soft life had been shot dead alongside some of his new friends.

Someone knocked on the bathroom door. "Hey, it's me," a muffled voice announced. "We got movement."

The community wasn't poised to make any future Best Of lists, but the house was serviceable and it did afford the trio one valuable convenience, which was a direct line-of-sight with the bridged freeway off-ramp before it sloped down to ground level again. While Zephyr and Jordan showered and bathed respectively, Ben rotated the flowery living room couch so that it faced the window, sat down and watched. Sooner than later, a pair of headlights disrupted the darkness as a vehicle traded freeway for city streets.

"Just the one?" Zephyr asked.

"Yep."

"Could you tell what kind of car it was?"

"Nope."

No way to know if it was the slavers or just another random survivor. The car had come from the direction of the buses, though, so if it was the former and they examined the wreckage at all, they might already know that someone had walked away from the crash alive and a few guns heavier. That alone could be enough to put them on guard. Then again, if their attackers had spoken true, and it was possible that they hadn't, their warped abductors believed themselves exceptional, everyone else disposable minions kept singularly for their pleasure. Buckets of arrogance typically accompanied this brand of fanaticism and Zephyr thought maybe such people might also ignore any threats that were not rubbing up against their collective noses because, after all, bad things couldn't happen to them, only others.

"Where's Jordan?"

"Getting dressed, I think. She has the flashlight," Ben said.

The boy was glad for it. He wanted to shield her as much as he could from anything he deemed dangerous, and more human encounters of any kind qualified. So far, roughly half of everybody they'd chanced upon had proven murderous. He wondered not for the first time if this was a mathematical statistic he should be focused on, if it meant something in the biblical sense or if was somehow by design, and promised himself to ponder it again when there were not other concerns.

His shotgun held only a single shell. One freakin' shot. Practically useless, he thought. The Uzis were better. One clip housed a full thirty-two bullets, another twenty-one and the last seventeen. He didn't know how far these rounds would go, though, and he was terrified that he might pull the trigger during a firefight and run bone dry of ammunition before he could even steady his aim.

"Our best chance is to figure out whatever the equivalent of Main Street is here, find a good place to hide and wait. I'm sure we'll get a hit in no time. Then, if it's our guys, we take them out," Ben said.

"What happens if they blow by us on the street? We'll never be able to follow them. And the other thing is, I don't know how far our guns are gonna go. I thin—"

"It'll work."

"Ben," he said, "I just think…" But he stopped, aware that his boyish friend was struggling to keep his composure, and as Zephyr noticed, he finally let go.

"Go—d… damn th—em," he barely choked out in spastic, breathless whimpers that circled the periphery of hyperventilation. "This whole fucking wor—ld is bull… bullshit!" He pounded his fists against the couch and cried in a great, silent trembling.

Sucker-punched by the display, Zephyr didn't know what to do or say. All he could think was, *I'm sorry. I'm sorry. I'm sorry this happened*, and the combination of guilt and shame was palpable. Finally, after several uncomfortable seconds that imitated minutes, he said, "I wish I could bring your brother back, Ben. It's not fair—none of this is fair. None of it." He felt his own eyes watering, his voice wavering. "I can't. I'm sorry. I'm sorry, man." He lay his hands on his friend's shoulders and added, "I can stand by you on this, though."

29

There is no romance at the end of the world. Nothing to love in leaving a bawling little girl to fend for herself in an abandoned house on the outskirts of nowhere, the prospect of battle and a premature death looming. It stank of ill-conceived priorities. It spat in the face of honor. Zephyr recognized the dirty brutality of the situation, and yet there was no way he could renege on his promise to Ben and no way Jordan could join them. She had to stay behind because he couldn't bear the thought of putting her directly in harm's way. Not again. Not when it wasn't imperative. So he scoured several homes in the neighborhood and stockpiled food and drinks, returned with a myriad of new clothes and blankets, and made more promises about their inevitable return. He told her to be brave, that she could do it, that she had already done it, that all she had to do was wait for them. And he said it all with the dark understanding that if they died in the streets of Las Cruces, she was doomed to a fate far lonelier than he wanted to imagine.

As he pillaged homes for gear, Zephyr stole a pair of keys that belonged to a plush Ford Flex with a half tank of gas in the neighbor's driveway and he and Ben drove it into the city. Along the way, the two of them worked through what they hoped was a much better plan. He bore no deep appreciation of the tactic— it was presumptuous, unpredictable and therefore riddled with danger, and yet he also saw its potential if everything fell into place. Of course, it was a big if.

The city's main street was, in fact, Main Street, and it was a black hole without the lifeblood of electricity. As he hugged himself in the darkness, he fought to keep his teeth from chattering out a novel in Morse code and thought of the last thing Jordan had said to him. *Don't leave me, too.* She had held her composure, but it was a facade. *Promise you'll come back and get me?* And, of course, he did. He could see that she was petrified — that she tried to conceal her terror only amplified his guilt. All of his practiced pledges seemed to crumble under the pressure of her heavy words. *Don't leave me, too. Too.* Just like everybody else. A little girl – the only person he knew for certain didn't deserve any of this, and he left her all alone. What is wrong with you? Seriously, just what the hell do you think you're doing? Get her now and go, he thought. Now. Before it's too late.

It was literally too late. Still no watch and therefore it was just a guess, but he thought it must be at least midnight. The public bench he chose as his waiting spot was hard and cold and there was no sign of anybody save for his trusty friend the wind, which had not abated its frigid attack. He drifted in and out of sleep and caught his head nodding forward several times before he jolted awake again and scanned the streets as though they held the answer to life and it would vanish in a flash if he didn't suddenly behold it.

"OK." He stood from the bench as needles prickled his lower legs. "This is a bust. Nobody's coming and I feel like I'm going to catch pneumonia if we don't get out of here."

Ben stepped out from behind a tree. "Yeah, totally, I'm freezing too," he admitted. "Fuck it. We'll try again tomorrow, but earlier."

A couple minutes later the Flex coasted back down Main Street. They didn't make it two blocks when a pair of headlights beamed back at them through the distant darkness.

"Shit, shit—stop the car," Ben hissed and Zephyr slowed. "No, no—park in the street at an angle, kind of diagonally." The boy did as he asked. When the car came to its full stop, the twin jettisoned himself out the front door, swung the back open and retrieved three of the guns. He left the fourth, the agreed-upon Uzi, for Zephyr, who snapped it up and concealed it by his side in the driver's seat. "OK, same plan, except you'll do it here."

Zephyr nodded. "Yeah, go."

"Turn on your emergency lights!" Ben called over his shoulder as he disappeared into the blackness across the street.

The headlights drew closer at a rapid pace. This was nothing like the excruciating lull that defined the crawl of Merrick's hijacked police car days ago. No, this driver was in a hurry and wasn't shy about showing it. The boy recognized the now-familiar rush, a marriage of fear and exhilaration, as the headlights grew larger. Then the high beams were on him in a blast of blinding light and halos, and the rhythm of his heart almost doubled. Killer, slaver—whatever, this guy was at the very least an asshole. The vehicle halted roughly fifteen feet ahead of the Flex, but the driver neither turned off his headlights nor removed himself from the car. Zephyr rolled down his own window and offered a friendly wave. Nothing happened, so he waited and it was torture. He counted down from ten. Nine. Eight. Motherfuckers. Seven. Six. Five. Four. Come on, you bitches. Three. Two.

The car launched forward and came screeching to a halt so that the driver sat window-to-window with Zephyr. And now the boy could finally see him. Them. There were two of them. The driver was an older man, pale white with a silvery beard, flannel and cowboy hat. There was another man in the passenger seat whose features remained silhouetted in darkness, yet Zephyr was sure he also donned a cowboy hat. The driver rolled down his window—it was a charcoal grey F150 raised slightly higher than Zephyr's own vantage point— and the thick smell of marijuana permeated the air.

The older man touched the tip of his hat and nodded. "Howdy."

"Hi there," Zephyr said and clutched the handle of the Uzi with his unseen hand. "It's good to see some people alive." He started for a handshake and realized he would have to release the grip on his gun unless he extended his left, which felt wrong, and decided against it. "My name's Zephyr." Stay calm stay calm stay calm. "Are you guys local or, uh, traveling through?"

Cowboy had no response to this. He just stared. Then another voice asked, "Whuch you doin' here, puto?" The driver apparently thought this question the height of hilarity and bellowed laughter.

"Looking for something to eat, actually. Then I'm hoping to be on my way."

"This here is our city, and you're trespassing," the older man said.

"We don' take kindly to trespassers," added the silhouette.

"Oh, no worries. I'll just pick up the rest of my group and we'll get out of your hair."

"Where's your group, son?" Cowboy asked.

"Holed up in one of the places over there, basically starving until I get back," Zephyr joked and pointed off into the distance.

"You think you can just ride in and squat in our houses, bitch?" the shadow asked and laughed, but Cowboy raised his hand and his lapdog quieted.

The driver smiled, revealing a mouthful of rotting teeth. "How about this: you take us over to your friends and we'll give ya'll a proper escort right out of town. How's that sound, curly?"

Curly? I don't have curly hair, you idiot, Zephyr thought, and dismissed it. "Listen, guys, I'm sorry if I upset you or something. I swear, I don't mean any harm. Just trying to survive here. I barely know what to do with myself these days." There was the bait. The question was, would they bite?

"Oh," Cowboy mused. "I think we can help you with that little problem."

"Yeh, puto, don' worry 'bout that," Lapdog echoed, giggling.

Was it enough? Zephyr thought yes—yes, it was, and killed his emergency lights. Just seconds now, he knew, so he decided to dive in hard. "Listen, guys, isn't the city big enough for a few more people?"

Cowboy stared at him without speaking for a long moment. Then he grinned. "Sure it is, son. Sure it is," he said. "Just, we got ourselves a pecking order here and I'm not so sorry to say but you and your little curly friends are at the bottom of the food chain."

"What's that supposed to mean?"

"It means you my bitch, bitch, and—" Lapdog started but was startled by someone knocking on his window.

"Who dis bitch now?" he asked and then actually rolled down his window.

Could he really be so stupid? This is spectacular, Zephyr thought, and drew his weapon in perfect harmony with his friend's on the other side of the truck.

30

It went down at light speed. The silhouetted man in the passenger seat grabbed for something between his legs, then shrieked as deafening gunshots tore through the air and muzzle fire strobed the front compartment in brilliant, blinding flashes.

Blat-blat-blat-blat-blat-blat.

Lapdog seemed to convulse in tune to the rhythm of the muzzle flashes. Zephyr barely had time to ponder the passenger's temporarily-illuminated features—dark hair, stubble, agony—when Cowboy jerked back and began squealing, too. Then he put it together. Ben had tried to aim in the general direction of Lapdog's unseen weapon, but in his haste he shredded the man's groin and upper thighs with bullets instead. He also forgot to consider the recoil and the barrel of the gun kicked up, sending a couple of rounds into Cowboy's right leg.

"You!" Cowboy roared in disbelief, cupped his leg with one hand and started to reach for something with the other when Zephyr pointed the Uzi at his face and he stopped.

"Yes, me," Ben said. "Whatever that means."

Lapdog squealed, beat his fists against the seat and arched his back, relaxed, gasped, then arched again as he rode out the throes of what could only be pure misery. Zephyr didn't envy the asshole, but neither did he really pity him—not if everything he suspected about these two was true.

The boy locked eyes with the driver. "Hey there, curly," he said, with emphasis on the latter word. "I'm going to open your door and you're going to step outside with your hands up. If you try anything dumb, you will die. Do you believe me?"

Cowboy nodded.

"Good. You should. Truth be known, I'm just looking for a reason to kill your worthless redneck ass, so you better not give me one." The door swung open and Cowboy stepped outside with his arms raised, wincing and moaning. Zephyr told him to take his shirt and pants off.

"W-what?"

"Take off your fucking clothes!"

He did as the boy demanded, although the process was slow and painful thanks to Ben's handiwork. The flannel came off easily enough, revealing a hairy, potbellied creature with man boobs decorated by a dangling golden crucifix. The jeans, tight to begin with and now blood-soaked, clung to Cowboy like plastic wrap. He kicked off his boots, sat on the cold ground and tugged the pants from his legs in a series of grunts and grimaces. All the while, Lapdog wailed and released a barrage of incoherent curses peppered with groans as he continued his spasmed assault on the truck's dashboard.

Gun aimed, Zephyr squatted several feet in front of Cowboy and smiled. "Guess that escort out of town will have to wait, huh?"

"What do you w-w-ant?" the man blubbered.

"I want to tell you a story. Don't worry, I know it's cold outside, so I'll make it brief. Then I'm going to ask you a question. Your answer to this question could save your life, so make sure you answer it honestly. You follow me?" When the man nodded, Zephyr continued. "It begins with a set of buses outside of Las Cruces and ends with a bunch of now-barbecued people chained up inside those buses. Have you heard it before?"

The bleeding man shifted as he considered how to respond to this and when no words came he finally nodded.

"Good! I thought you might. Now here's my question— and remember, curly, you don't want to get this one wrong or its lights out for you. Who chained those people up, and why?"

Cowboy frowned, then removed his hat and massaged his scalp and nape while he contemplated his answer. To Zephyr, he looked as though he was waging an inner battle of morality versus mortality: — to tell, or not to tell, that is the question. He raised a hand as one might to shield their eyes from the sun.

"Now, OK, first of all, just remember none of this was my idea," he began. "Just, a few of us got to thinking that with everybody gone and all, you know, we could live like kings, and then my nitwit brother said, 'Well, kings got subjects.' And everything just snowballed out of control from there. Next thing you know, we're making folks work for us. We ain't killed nobody, though. Just put 'em to work, is all."

I'm sure you pay competitively, Zephyr thought. "Chained them up and threatened to cut off their feet if they didn't shoot anyone who tried to enter the city, you mean?"

"What? No, sir." He feigned disgust. "We didn't make any threats like that. Shackled a couple fellas, yeah. And I admit, that was wrong. We shouldn't have done that."

"I'm sure the charred remains of those people would be happy to hear that you're sorry," Zephyr said. "And what happened to the wives and girlfriends of the men you enslaved?"

"Nothing. What wives?"

Just then, the familiar blat-blat-blat-blat and strobe effect of the Uzi.

Zephyr turned in surprise and witnessed Lapdog's mangled body jerking and twitching as the twin riddled it with an onslaught of steady bullets. It lasted seconds, yet the event seemed to transpire underwater and the boy's mind refused to accept what his eyes showed it. Had Cowboy been smarter or bolder, he could've tackled Zephyr then and wrestled the weapon away from him, but the man was also hypnotized by the turn of events.

The gun clicked, smoke wafting from its barrel, and the unnamed passenger stirred no more. When Ben finally looked his way, he must've seen something on Zephyr's face— disbelief, horror, or more likely a combination of the two— because he threw up his hands as if to say, what? "I warned the fucker, but he tried to go for that one's gun." Then he pointed at their remaining hostage, who looked as though he might piss himself.

"Please, God, don't hurt me," Cowboy begged. "Please, none of this was m—"

"Shut up," Zephyr said, thinking, Jesus, Ben, really? He wondered just how damaged the twin was and knew that the two of them would have a candid conversation later, but for now, he needed to use it.

"Do you think we're playing here? Do you!" He lunged within striking distance of the man and steadied the barrel inches from his face. "Now," he continued. "I'm going to ask you again. Where are the girls?"

"O-k-k sure—don't shoot! We got 'em. Just the two," the man sniveled. "We been takin' care of 'em while the men w-work, I swear. I can take you to 'em." Cowboy looked up and Zephyr saw something dawn in the man's eyes. "Y-you want them? They're yours."

It wasn't a good idea. Zephyr knew this, but he also understood that, live or die, Ben was determined to track down the remaining slavers and face them. The boy didn't think he would be satisfied until every one of them perished alongside their opportunistic minions. And even then, would that really be enough? The twin who remained in the wake of his brother's demise bore almost no relation to his former self.

Then there was Cowboy. Yes, it was still just Cowboy. Zephyr hadn't asked for the man's name and didn't want to know it. As far as he was concerned, he didn't deserve an identity beyond the stupid, shadowy cliché that embodied him thus far. The more Zephyr and Ben learned about their hostage's accomplices and their makeshift headquarters, the more the boy's stomach threatened to practice the summersault. The bastard was terrified that he would meet the same fate as his good friend Lapdog and therefore eager to please his new captors. So they discovered that there were two more of them. That the man's brother was allegedly three years his senior and carried a gun and that the other slaver was someone they picked up after the event and not very good with weapons. They were holed up in the local Target, an enormous department store.

"We got five or six generators in there so we can plug in lights, TV, microwave, what have you, and we cleared some of the crap into a corner and used the space all nice like a big old house," Cowboy explained as the three of them rolled down Main Street in the darkness. Ben had ripped off a few long, thin shreds of Lapdog's bloody flannel, fashioned them into a serviceable tie, and bound Cowboy's hands behind his back. Zephyr held his gun on the man as he sat in the Flex's back row without moving.

"Why Target?" he asked.

"It's got everything we need, is why. Number one: food. Full grocery store in there. Some of it's gone to shit already, sure. We got a lot stockpiled, though, and it'll keep us from starving for a long time. Number two is supplies. Clothes. Tools. Medicine. We got enough penicillin stockpiled to last us for the rest of our lives, if we're smart."

"Which you aren't," Ben interjected.

It was actually pretty smart. They didn't loot the place—they took outright ownership of it. Would he have tried something so brash had he stayed unharmed in Firefly Valley? He wasn't sure.

The gigantic, stretching parking lot was dark and empty except for a scattering of cars. They killed the Flex's engine on the periphery of the blacktop and surveyed the scene. Cowboy's home stood out like a lighthouse aglow in the midnight fog. Target was lit up inside. Not with the fluorescent beams that typically rained down sterile visibility upon shoppers, but with a series of standing lamps that had been placed behind the still-barred glass doors. Independently, they shed soft, gold light, but together they saturated the entranceway with bright luminescence and the signs of unmistakable life for anyone around to see it. Such travelers would, however, also notice the portable spotlights erected thirty feet outside of the store, supplied electricity via industrial extension cords, and there for the single purpose of irradiating a graffiti warning written in red and green spray-paint. The colors reminded Zephyr of Christmas. Someone had illustrated three crude skull and crossbones on as many large bedsheets, each pinned to tall pieces of thin plywood that stood at the store's curbside. Under each drawing, the message: *Occupied. Leave or Die.*

Real hospitable, these guys, Zephyr thought. "So, Cowboy. I hope you know that it's in your best interest to get us in there, and safely. Because if anything should happen—like, for example, some asshole taking a shot at us from afar—we'll leave your body behind as a parting gift."

Ben turned around and glowered at the man. "Believe him."

"Yeah, I do, I do, I swear."

"Where do they think you are and when do they expect you back?" Zephyr asked.

"They know me and Juan went out to feed the men…" he paused, perhaps thinking about how to phrase it. "The ones who got burned. But they don't know they're dead yet and they don't know nothin' about us running into you lot."

"And when would you normally be back?" Zephyr asked.

"Oh, right around now, give or take."

"What will they be doing now? Will they be waiting for you?"

The man shook his head. "Probably sleeping. Either that, or getting drunk and…" Another moment of consideration. "And tending to the ladies."

"You're a real piece of work, you know that?" Ben spat. "Demented little murdering rapists—that's all you are. You and your shitty brother."

Brother, Zephyr thought, his eyes widening. For whatever reason—sleep deprivation, fear, or any of the countless other post-event distractions—he had never focused on the significance of the fact that Ben and Brad were twins. None of them had. He figured it was just a lucky coincidence that both of them survived. But here was another example of that link and again two related survivors.

"Ben, I just thought of something," Zephyr said and explained himself. "Don't you think it's weird that just about everybody disappeared, yet you, Brad, Cowboy and his worthless brother all survived?"

The twin pondered it a moment. "I guess so," he said. "What are you getting at?"

"I don't know." It was true. He didn't. "I just think there's something to it. Something we're missing. You guys were twins. You're identical. So maybe something about you both— some kind of property—is what kept you here when everyone else popped."

"God works in mysterious ways," Cowboy said.

"Just shut the fuck up, you murdering douchebag. You better hope God isn't involved in any of this because if he is, you've got some serious atonement in your future," Ben countered, then recomposed himself and turned back to Zephyr. "So, what? Like, because we both have blond hair, we lived?"

"Maybe. Or blue eyes. Or hair on the back of your hands. Or—I don't know— moles. Or maybe seventeen moles." Zephyr continued. "Could be anything. I think it must be some kind of commonality, though. Some rare trait you guys shared that almost nobody has."

"But Cowboy and his brother have it, too?" Ben asked.

Zephyr nodded.

"Can't be a big dick then," the twin said, and for the first time all day, he smiled. It was infectious, and Zephyr caught himself beaming back. It was just so good to see any expression beyond blank indifference or blind rage on his friend's face.

"Hey Cowboy," Zephyr said. "The girls you guys are holding hostage. Do you know if they're related?" It was a long shot, he knew.

"I'm bleeding real bad here. Can I—"

"I understand that. Now, answer the question," Zephyr said.

The man shook his head. "No. One of 'em old enough to be your mother — she's been with us all week. The other is younger like you, we just met her today. They ain't related."

"This is intriguing, Zeph, but can we get this shit done and worry about this later?" Ben asked.

He was right. Although, he dreaded what lay in wait. The men in there were dangerous and for all they knew, they were stepping into an ambush. "Yes," he said and turned to Cowboy. "All right. Details. All of them."

Their prisoner reiterated that his brother and the other one—someone named Fran, which sounded like a girl's name to Zephyr—would probably be drunk by now, trying to "get in the pants of the MILF," as he explained it.

"What kind of security do you have?" Ben asked.

Cowboy stared at him, perplexed. "Security?"

"Cameras, alarms—freakin' turrets? Jesus. What do you think security means, you idiot?" His next words came slowly, as if he were trying to explain one of Einstein's equations to a caveman. "Do. You. Have. Any. Seh-cure-it-ee?"

"Let me phrase it another way," Zephyr said before Cowboy could answer. "How do we get in there unnoticed? And before you answer, remember that you'll be going in first, bound and with both of our guns trained on your back. So make sure you think this one through."

"Yeah, I know, I know," Cowboy said, winced as he tried to pivot in his seat, and continued. "We got a little system rigged up, is all. Nothing too fancy. When we lost the main power, we jimmied open one of the automatic doors. So now it's open all the time, forever. Then Fran went out and stole a few of those doohickeys that some stores got so when you walk through a door, it gives a little ding. You know what I mean?"

Zephyr nodded and explained it, mostly for Ben's consumption. "They've got door chimes. A little box on one side of the door frame beams an invisible signal to a receptor on the other side. If anybody walks through it, the interruption sounds a chime."

"Yeah, that's the kind," Cowboy said. "We got one of those and another that works the same way, but it triggers a strobe light."

"Wait, don't you just step over the beams to get past those?" Ben asked.

Zephyr nodded, and smiled. "Pretty much. I don't think we're gonna need Tom Cruise for this mission." Back to Cowboy. "Is that it?"

"We got the warning outside, too," the man said and shrugged. "Ain't nobody tried to come in yet."

"So to answer my own question then, no, there's no security," Ben said.

"The chime will be on the front door itself, but what's the range on the strobe? Where do you keep it?" Zephyr asked.

"We got our main setup about a couple hundred feet in there. Couches, some TVs, a few beds, oven, microwave, pretty much everything you could ever want. The strobe wouldn't work that far out, but it still worked when we dropped it back about thirty feet. We got it on a little coffee table, which faces our direction," the man explained, paused, and added, "We cleared out what used to be the women's clothes area and moved all of our stuff there. It feels more homely because it's got some carpet."

"Good for you, Martha Stewart," Ben said. When Cowboy started to say something, the twin waved him off. "Dude, just shut it. My wit is wasted on you, anyway."

They checked their weapons. Zephyr's Uzi still held all twenty-three bullets. Ben's clip, meanwhile, had dwindled from thirty-two to four, but he had another Uzi with seventeen more bullets. In addition, they kept the shotgun and its single round. Also, they'd been smart enough to pillage the weapons of their hostage and his dead friend before moving on, and had gained two handguns— one of them a Glock like the one Zephyr looted back in Firefly Valley. That one belonged to Lapdog. True to form, though, Cowboy's gun was a six-shooter like the ones Clint Eastwood used in the old Westerns Zephyr's dad loved. This did not go unnoticed by Ben, who made some crack about their hostage being a little too slow on the draw. They decided to leave the shotgun in the car and take everything else.

Cowboy limped, shuffled, and hopped his way across the parking lot. Every so often, he'd give a little yelp before threatening to fall over and one time Zephyr had to run to his aid before he did. It was a pitiful showing made worse by the fact that the man was dressed only in bloodstained underwear, hat and boots.

They originally positioned their hostage in the lead, but as they slid and strafed alongside Target's outer wall like professional burglars out to steal the Mona Lisa, they decided to reorder the man to the middle. Ben kept his weapon trained on him while they navigated the perimeter, white hot spotlights blasting them against the graffiti messages. Eventually, Zephyr dared to peek around the corner of the wall at the entryway.

He leaned back and whispered, "It's like Cowboy said, as far as I can tell. The opening is on our side. All we have to do is turn the wall and we'll be there."

"You see any of them?" Ben whispered back.

"No, not yet. When you walk in, there's a food court on the right and on the left, all the shopping carts. Just beyond those, there's a few lamps, but I didn't see any of them."

"That's too close," Cowboy breathed, shaking his head. "They're in the women's section. It's past the carts. You turn to the right, follow it for a little bit, and then you'll see them on the other side."

Zephyr undid the safety locks on both of his guns, which was difficult because his hands wouldn't stop trembling. When he caught Cowboy looking at him, he made an effort to steady himself and then tried for a casual comment about the freezing weather. The bleeding man barely acknowledged it. Instead, he begged them not to harm his brother.

"If you gotta get revenge here, Fran's your man," he said. "My brother is a dimwitted fool, I'll give ya that, but ever since we picked him up, it's the other one's who's been calling the shots. I told Dick to just get rid of him but for some reason he keeps him around."

"Shut the fuck up!" Ben hissed and Zephyr thought, Cowboy, you are trying to convince a wall, man. There was no way the twin would stop until he felt like his brother's death was repaid.

"I'll go first. Wait twenty seconds and then follow," Zephyr said to Ben. "Cowboy. You'll stay second. If you try anything funny, Ben shoots you." Their hostage was apparently accustomed to their death threats because he nodded as though he'd been asked if he liked chocolate.

"Not a whimper, dummy," Ben warned him. "You have to fart, you better hold it. Otherwise you'll find my gun barrel up your ass."

For all of their reservations about the mission, the ordeal itself was painless. At least for Zephyr, anyway. He simply dropped to his belly and pulled himself through. It took seconds. In contrast, Cowboy was all skin and blood, not to mention a hundred pounds heavier. He gritted his teeth and by the time he finally squirmed about halfway underneath the obstacle, sweat beaded on his forehead, he sucked air and stopped moving. So Zephyr grabbed his arm and tugged him through, leaving a streak of smeared blood on the cold tile of the store.

He looked at Cowboy as the man massaged his naked upper body and then at Ben, who just shook his head.

"How's the leg?" Zephyr finally whispered. "Good to walk?"

"I think so."

"Good," he said and pointed to the darkened aisles that waited off to one side of the radiance. "You say they're over there, so we're all going to walk that way instead." He fingered the opposite region of the store. "We'll go around and come at them from the inside."

The deeper they went, the darker it grew. Nobody said anything, the walkways they navigated so freely in light now transformed into potential obstacle courses, every step a new hazard. Zephyr imagined the loud clank of wrenches and screwdrivers jumping as his clumsy feet connected hard with an unseen toolbox, or the creaking wheels of a rusty clothing rack jarred from its hiding spot in the darkness, and moved ever slower.

Minutes passed as he held his breath and agonized over every step. He couldn't stop thinking about the other slavers and what untold and unseen advantages they might possess. For instance, night vision goggles. If either one of the men wore a pair, they could be watching three of them right now.

He turned toward the blanket of blackness beyond them and as he did there came a thud from behind followed by groans. He spun and pointed his gun but there was nothing to see; they might as well have been in the depths of a cave without a candle.

"Ben," he hissed and simultaneously grabbed at thin air. "Cowboy, where's—"

The thump, thump, thump of feet and then a cacophony of noise as something toppled in the darkness. Zephyr waved his gun toward the commotion. More movement, more things crashing over, and then Ben was shouting at him from the other direction, not even bothering to lower his voice.

"Fucker clocked me! The Cowboy! He's getting away!"

"Diiiick!" the escapee bellowed from somewhere in the darkness ahead, already winded but still moving. Zephyr's ears turned him to the sound and his feet started moving. When he felt someone brush by him, he knew it was Ben. "They got guns!" the man continued. "Help me! Get out here and help me!"

Brilliant light flashed in and out of existence and Zephyr recoiled as sprays or gunfire pierced the stillness. For a second, he thought he saw Cowboy taking refuge behind a clothing rack down the aisle, yet when the strobe of light returned the man was gone. If he had ever been there at all. He longed to drop his weapon and cup his ears. The discharges were so intense, so loud, and his eardrums were already ringing. The element of surprise was lost to them and Ben seemed oblivious to this fact as he screamed obscenities into the darkness and fired his weapon at what the boy thought must be imagined or purely arbitrary targets.

"Stop it!" he finally screamed and after a moment, Ben did.

"Listen," he whispered. "Just… listen."

At first, there was nothing, but then they heard it. Heavy breathing and the shuffling of heavier feet. Zephyr grabbed Ben by the shoulders and turned him so that the twin faced the direction of the new noise.

"He's that way," he whispered just as a lamp light flickered on some fifty feet ahead.

It wasn't bright, and yet Cowboy was caught between it and them like a pickled baseball player. Perhaps realizing this, the silhouetted figure shouted something indecipherable, started to run, tripped up, and then seemed to reconsider. In the end, he simply raised up his hands and turned around.

"Had to try, right. You can't blam—" he began before Ben pumped him full of bullets and he fell to the ground shuddering.

"Try that!" the twin barked as his gun clicked empty. "Try that, you stupid bitch!" He tossed it on the ground and pulled the spare Glock from his waistline.

People shouted nearby — cowboy's brother and the other man roused from their drunken slumber, no doubt. And they'd still be sleeping now if we hadn't blown it, he thought. The boy couldn't believe they had been so stupid as to trust the dead man before them to go along with their plan, especially when the plan involved killing his sibling.

"What should we do?" Ben asked.

He wanted to reply in turn, how the hell should I know? This is your thing, not mine. He wanted to scream it. To shake some sense into his friend. Then, there came the close clap of boots. Someone running. So instead, Zephyr pushed Ben to one side of the aisle and made for the shadows of the other. Then he fell back into the lane, crouched and waited.

Closer than expected, someone murmured something and another responded. He cocked his head and tried to focus on any noise. There was a whispered conversation, but he couldn't make out the words. He was about to slink forward when a great crash sent him skidding into the opposite direction as boxes exploded from the unseen end-cap ahead of him.

"You goin' die!" someone raged as another blast cleared away more boxes and with sudden horror Zephyr realized that his pursuers carried flashlights. The beams tore blinding holes into the blackness that had previously offered some cover. Any advantage they had was gone. The boy crawled backward so that he could take shelter behind the opposite end-cap. With any luck, they'd walk by him and he could either attack them from behind or run away, an option that grew more appealing with every breath.

Something clanked on the ground and another blast of gunfire sounded.

"Oh, you wanna play?" the voice called out from nowhere. "Well, then, let's play!" At this, another enormous blast seemed to shake Zephyr's world and consequently his resolve.

Clang, clang, clang, a new disruption echoed in the distance. More murmurs and then footsteps speeding after the noise. Was Ben just clumsy or throwing stuff? The latter, he figured, which was a lot more than he'd tried. The thought of the twin keeping his cool as he cowered behind a pyramid of diaper boxes brought Zephyr back to his senses and he strafed to the next aisle so that he could ascertain a better viewpoint of the man who remained behind. Without warning, a beam of light shone down the corridor as he whipped back to the safety of the end-cap, and a heartbeat later, the luminescence faded back to black.

More shouting, but the voices were different. Muffled somehow. Zephyr listened but couldn't make them out. Then a second set of footsteps returned.

"Shut those bitches up," one man muttered.

"Not now."

Zephyr was mustering the courage to creep ahead and take aim at the voices when another shot rang out and one of the men yelped.

"Right there!" someone screamed and then the scene was a symphony of piercing gunshots.

The boy had no idea how long this thundering war lasted, but it seemed to rage forever. Lifetimes. The explosions were peppered in shouts and calls and then terrible shrieks. All at once, he was running toward the source of the pandemonium, his gun ready to take part in the ensemble, and somehow he knew he was too late.

He rounded the corner and there stood a man who wasn't Ben. The figure swiveled on his heels and Zephyr shot him. A flashlight flew from the man's grasp as bullets sank into his chest, neck and face, and he was dead before he hit the ground. The other man already lay on the tile, badly wounded. Zephyr picked up the beam and shone it on him. Blood soaked his T-shirt but his eyes widened and he tried to move as Zephyr approached him. A shotgun lay only a few feet away. Zephyr picked it up and stared at him.

"I'm sorry you chose this for yourself," he said, aimed the weapon, and without any hesitation, blew his face off.

He didn't see any other bodies.

"Ben!" he called, tears already streaming down his cheeks. "Ben! Where are you!"

The teenager was sprawled on the floor beneath a rack of clothes, hidden but for his outstretched legs.

"Ben! We got 'em, man," he said, and pushed away the racked sweaters which covered the older boy. As soon as he did, he knew there was no hope. Ben's shirt was drenched in dark blood and he barely moved. Zephyr, too, seemed unable to move. Why did we do this? You made us do this, you damned idiot, he thought. And now look what's happened.

Ben's eyes darted and his mouth moved, although no words came.

"Ssshhh, no. It's OK. No, don't talk. No, don't try to talk," Zephyr said, his voice wobbly. He fell to the floor, slid over to his friend and held his head in his lap. When he did, Ben's foot kicked the flashlight and it rolled to a nearby stop, its beam a final spotlight on the disintegrated face of the slaver he just killed.

"You got 'em, Ben. You did it, man," he said while he stroked the boy's hair. The twin — his friend, however brief — seemed to nod in reaction, although Zephyr wasn't certain it was voluntary. He tried not to think about the inevitability before him. He searched instead for the right words but they eluded him. All he could do was stay, so that's what he did.

Some time passed— maybe seconds, maybe minutes. Ben struggled and choked for air and his body tensed and arched in regular order. Twice he tried to whisper something but couldn't get it out and instead pounded his fist against Zephyr's thigh, some final desperate act of defiance. And when at last he took his final exhausted gulp of air, his exit of the world wasn't noble or graceful, but smeared in dread, pain, and blood.

Zephyr sat with him for a long while and then he thought of Jordan, and slowly, he rose. He started toward the slavers' living space, doubled back, bent over and grasped the shoulder of his fallen companion. He didn't want to cry. He wouldn't.

Instead, he said, "You did it, Ben."

Then he turned and left him.

31

Cowboy's description of the space was accurate. What Zephyr didn't anticipate, though, was the smell, which was pungent. It reeked of food, sweat, sex, and above all else, rot. A few lamps shone, revealing messy accumulations of goods, as well as an array of cheap furniture and wiry electronics. Several big beds littered the premises. There were dressers, microwaves, and a row of behemoth refrigerators. Not one, but four big-screen flat-panel televisions waited at each side of the square perimeter and towering stacks of Blu-rays threatened to topple over a couple of the adjacent sets.

So this is what kings do with their spare time, he thought, and there was movement in his periphery. Gun drawn, his arm shot out and he was ready to fire before he realized what he was looking at. Not what, but who. It was one of the girls. She was cuffed to an enormous oven, and naked. He glanced away, blushing, and yet he'd seen enough to know that it was the older and consequently most unfortunate of the captives. In her thirties. Dirty blonde hair curled at her shoulders. There were bruises on her face and body. Something else, too— were they bite marks?

"Oh my God, are you OK?" he asked and moved to her.

When she flinched away, he stopped, tossed his weapon on the nearest bed, raised his hands and stared at the ground before her feet.

She seemed oblivious to her nakedness, but he wasn't, so he balled up a sheet and tossed it her way while he trained his eyes on some invisible object to her side.

"Ma'am, I'm not going to hurt you. I'm one of the good guys, I swear," he said. "The men who did this to you are dead." After a moment, he added, "It's over."

She didn't respond as she wrapped herself up.

"I'm gonna get you out of here. My name's Zephyr, by the way." She nodded but made no reply to this. After he surveyed the area, he noted, "I was told there's another person here."

"That'd be me," a girl's voice said and a hand waved out to him from behind the same oven.

"Show yourself, please."

"You think we're going to get the jump on you?" the voice asked.

"Please just do as I say."

A slender figure rose and turned to him, one hand still cuffed to the oven. Long, straight, brunette hair fell over her shoulders as she considered him. She was still dressed in a tank top and shorts, which was a good sign. On her face she wore a peppering of light freckles. She was, even in the dim light, unmistakably beautiful, but he had no time to dwell on it.

"We good?" she asked, waving her free hand as proof that she wasn't concealing anything.

"Yeah. All good. Let me get you guys out of here."

Naturally, Dick, presently a corpse, had the keys to their cuffs, so Zephyr spent the next five minutes digging through the blood-soaked pants of the man he'd just killed. With a shotgun, too. His face was a cavity of skull and blood. When he finally returned to the girls, his hands were painted red and still shaking. You figuratively and literally have blood on your hands, Zeph, he thought, and there was nothing humorous about it. He wanted to wash them, to scrub them.

"Got it," he said as he un-cuffed the woman, who thanked him, tried to stand, then nearly fell over.

So he led her to one of the beds and when she refused it he realized that he'd inadvertently guided her back to the scene of the crimes against her. Good job, Zeph. Really considerate there. He apologized and sat her in a nearby rocking chair instead. She asked for water.

"There are two of us," the younger girl said and pointed to her own cuffs, but he ignored her. Instead, he retrieved a couple bottles for them, realized he didn't know their names, and asked for them.

"Sarah," the older woman said.

"I'm Aurora," responded the other. "I'm sorry, but can I please get out of these?"

"Yeah, sorry." He unlocked the cuffs and tossed them to the ground as she stood and stretched. Fully erect, he was struck by how tall she was. She had a good half-inch on him.

Sarah shot to her feet, her eyes wide. "How many did you kill?"

"Four men."

The woman considered his response, exhaled and seemed on the verge of crying. "That's… good."

"I hope they suffered," Aurora added.

"Yeah, well, most of them did."

"The Mexican?"

"Was his name Juan?" Zephyr asked.

"Yeah, that's the scumbag."

"Then, yes. He suffered worst of all, I think."

"Good for him," she said, adding, "Not like any of them were good, but he was definitely the most rotten of the litter." She studied him a moment. "How old are you?"

"Why? Seventeen. I think? I guess I could be eighteen now. We need to get you two out of here."

"Thank you for… what you did," Aurora said. And she really was stunning. He didn't want to think about what these dead men might have done to her if he hadn't arrived when he did. What they likely had already done to her companion.

"We need to get out of here," he said. "I've got a little girl waiting on me and we need to go pick her up."

Sarah shook her head. "Can't. They've been holding my brother prisoner and I have to go get him."

"Where is he now?" Zephyr asked. Were there more prisoners here? His hand tightened on his weapon.

The older woman shook her head. "I think he's at the city limit. They were putting men in buses out there before they took me."

Zephyr flinched. He felt as though he'd been struck by lightning. Now his heart was beating faster than it had during any of the gun battles and he just wanted to disappear. Should he tell her? Could he tell her? It was his fault. After all, he didn't stop it. If only Ben hadn't lost his mind. You don't put this on him now— not when he died saving you, he thought. You didn't do a damned thing and you know it. It was true, and he accepted the responsibility of it, heavy as it was. Still, this poor lady had suffered enough already. Did she really need to know this now? Right now? As much as he wished the answer was different, he knew that it wasn't in him.

"Ma'am, I'm sorry," he began and something in his voice gave him away.

"What?"

"What's wrong?" Aurora asked.

"When we got here, we were ambushed by men in a bus," he said as he struggled to catch his breath. "They shot and killed two of my friends. So we rammed into them, and then the bus caught fire and…" He shook his head. It wasn't the whole truth, but it was close enough, and the result was the same. Sarah cupped her mouth as tears streamed down her cheeks and then she slid back to the floor.

"I'm so sorry. So, so, sorry," he said and he meant every word. "They were trying to kill us and we just — all we did was defend ourselves. We didn't know." And all at once he hated himself for allowing it to happen. The reality of his actions, or inactions as it were, lay directly before him: a brutalized woman whose only connection to the world had burned to ashes, all thanks to him. He wiped his eyes and nose on his shirt.

"Aw, God, this... wasn't what I wanted," he said.

He started away—he'd done enough damage already—when he felt a hand squeeze his shoulder.

"No, don't go, Zephyr," the younger girl whispered, her voice soft and genuine for the first time since they'd met. There was nothing judgmental in her tone. "Sarah, he's right," she continued. "There's no way he could've known. He came here and saved us. He saved us. He's not like them."

The other woman cried on, but after a while, her sobs subsided some, and then some more until finally she only sat, her face cradled in her hands.

Zephyr struggled for the right words. "Excuse me, ma'am — miss, what was his name?" he finally asked.

She looked up at him, eyes puffy. "Robert," she said and hesitated. "His name is Robert Weskler."

He nodded. "Robert Weskler," he repeated. "I swear, I won't ever forget it." It wasn't much, but his promise was genuine, and he saw that the truth of it registered on her face.

The woman rose to her feet again, a meticulous and painful undertaking by the look of it. Still wrapped in a bed sheet, she straightened, cupped his cheek in one hand and said, "It's OK. It's not your fault, honey." It was so unexpected—the antithesis to what he supposed she might say or do—that he found himself at a loss for words.

"You keep saying we. Who exactly is we, other than this little girl?" Aurora asked.

The question caught Zephyr off guard and resurfaced painful memories, but he ignored them.

"Yeah, her name is Jordan. Up until a couple days ago, there were five of us, including her," he began. "We lost two, Merrick and Brad, at the... buses." He glanced in Sarah's direction and was thankful that she seemed lost in her own thoughts. "Brad had a twin brother named Ben, who came with me tonight, but he's dead now, too." All dead, except for him and Jordan. All dead. All of them. "Ben was the one who you should be thanking. He's the one who took out most of the slavers."

"The slavers?" Aurora asked, her eyebrow raised.

"Yeah, these..." he searched for the right word. "Savages. That's what we've been calling them."

"I guess it's as good a name as any." She surveyed the scene and then focused on Sarah, who sat and stared in quiet oblivion. "Let's get her some clothes and then get the hell out of here, huh?"

When he was sure everybody was done shopping, the boy doubled back to the slavers' final living space, checked for any spare weapons and didn't find any. Instead, he wheeled one of the oversized generators to the parking lot, where the girls waited for him, they loaded it into the car, and drove away.

When he finally flung open the front door to the house, he found it static, so he called for the girl and when no answer came he sprinted up the stairs to the bedrooms. The search seemed to slow and stretch with every step until Zephyr thought time might freeze and then change direction. He barged through the first bedroom door and as it swung inward on its hinges he saw Jordan jolt awake from her resting spot. He scooped the little girl up, held her and felt hot tears on his cheek.

"I will never leave you again, Jordan," he promised and kissed the side of her head. "I swear."

"Never," she agreed. "Now put me down." After he finally did, she looked up at him, her eyes pink and tired, and asked, "Who are these people? And where's Ben?"

32
Alpha

They found his aunt's worn nightgown abandoned in her sheets and her slippers beside the bed. Zephyr was disappointed by all of this, but he hadn't expected anything else and was both too tired to brood and too dry to cry. He'd already wasted his supply of tears on Merrick, Brad and Ben, and what did all the tears bring? Not relief from the sorrow that cradled his heart. So he swallowed the lump in his throat and drew in air whenever he felt his eyes grow watery, and then he made a mental list of everything he needed to do so that he and the girls might survive. Water. Food. Guns. Warm clothes. Shelter. A purpose. A plan. To which the question always came: what exactly is your purpose and plan, Zeph?

Hours stretched into days and then weeks as his life transformed into a monotone blur. The four of them crashed through the formalities of fellowship to become something of a new world family. Perhaps this was out of necessity, the collective desire to find companionship in any form, but Zephyr thought there might be more to it. He was no longer confident that he could trust any man. Not after Ross, Cowboy and his gang, and even Ben to some degree; the twin had transformed in those final hours. Jordan, though? Yes. He trusted her. And Aurora and Sarah? Sure. They had no hidden agendas.

He suspected that they returned him their confidence as they wouldn't any other man. It wasn't difficult to understand why. He had, after all, saved them from the worst of men at the climax of despair. That made him the exception to the rule.

They spent long mornings in a lavish estate home they discovered and repurposed. Jordan called it a mansion and Zephyr thought the description was apt. Eight bedrooms, four living rooms, a huge indoor swimming pool and Jacuzzi, a tennis court and even a single-lane underground bowling alley. It was the epitome of American extravagance, and they all adored it. With the generator Zephyr stole and two more since, the house may as well have been back on the grid. The gas was out, so the water was always cold and their cooking options limited, but they could use the microwave, blow-dry their hair, watch what little remained of television, play video games, and even surf the Internet, which wasn't as finished as he thought.

It was a crapshoot of broken websites, but it still functioned. Google, Facebook, Twitter, CNN, The Guardian, and dozens of other popular online destinations were all down. Yahoo still seemed to work, but the search results it returned were incomplete and most of the links led to inoperative pages. When he searched for "missing people," though, he got a few hits. Someone had created a blog called *Me, Myself and I* and they were posting daily updates about their experiences in West Virginia. The site was offensively ugly, it subscribed to the AOL school of design, but the updates were informative.

The latest entry read:

There are more of us left than you think. People are shy, probably because nowadays you're just as likely to run into a killer as you are a friendly face. But here in Charleston, there are a few hundred of us, at least. If you're reading this, realize that you're not alone, and there are some good people left. Stay tough.

As if to illustrate this point, the visitor ticker at the bottom of the blog indicated that more than nine-thousand people had loaded the entry. Zephyr wondered if the counter considered unique IP addresses or if every refresh of the site added a number to the tally, and he was encouraged when the figure remained unchanged after he reloaded the page multiple times.

At lunchtime, they usually piled into the Flex and searched the city for signs of life, food, gear, weapons, and new toys for Jordan. As they emerged from a Wal-Mart with armfuls of items one afternoon, a motorcyclist slowed and chatted with them. His name was Scott, he wore his long black hair in a ponytail, and he seemed friendly. He said he was en route to Las Vegas because he'd read online that it was still going strong. Lots of people left and most of the hotels remained undamaged despite some initial fires. Best of all, he said, was that the electricity was still flowing because the city was powered by the Hoover Dam, which was self-sufficient.

"It'll keep going for years or maybe even decades, they say," the rider noted. Zephyr wondered who they were in this case, but he didn't ask. "You guys should come. It'll be easy living for sure."

They thanked him for the offer but declined. Perhaps they would move on, maybe even soon. He wanted to avoid Vegas, though, even if it did offer citywide juice. The prospect of finding more people, especially those lured to the City of Sin, was not as enticing to him as it might have been weeks ago.

The abundance of bedrooms in the house went unnoticed by Jordan, who asked if she could sleep with Zephyr every night, and he obliged her. The rooms were huge, and he encountered no hurdles when he transported a queen-sized bed from another space into his own. At night, as they lay in the darkness before drifting, they would play a game in which they quizzed each other about their favorite and least favorite things from the world before the event. Zephyr said he missed chili-cheese fries and milkshakes but didn't miss the

Kardashians. Jordan said she missed the Nickelodeon channel and Slurpees, but didn't miss homework or her mom's boyfriend, Dave.

One night as she curled up against him, she asked, "Do you think my mom is in heaven?"

"Maybe," he began. How to answer this one? The subject matter always triggered tsunamis of guilt. "I don't really know, to be honest. But I think yes. With my parents. And with all the other people."

He couldn't see her in the darkness but knew she was considering his response. When she finally spoke, her voice didn't waver or crack, as he feared. "Can you come back from Heaven? Is it allowed?"

"I'm not sure, Jord," he lied. "You and me, though— we're family now. Together forever, right?"

"Right," she agreed. "I just miss her—my mom."

"I know, kid." He wanted to say more. He wanted to tell her that he wished he could bring her back. He wanted to promise her that everything would be like it was. But he didn't say anything.

Sarah grew quieter and stayed in her room more. Sometimes when they ate, Zephyr noticed her across the table with a fork full of food dangling in one hand and her eyes staring off into nothingness. When he asked if she was all right, she'd snap back to life, say, "yes, of course," and then shovel whatever she could find into her mouth. He knew she suffered. When she forgot her bread in the toaster or put her dishes in the trash instead of the kitchen sink, he remembered her that first night, dazed, naked, and covered in torture.

What made it worse was that he blamed himself. Not just for failing to extract her before the slavers did their worst, but because he most likely had a hand in her brother's death, too. Every day, as she seemed to retreat internally more and more, so grew his guilt, and before long he had trouble meeting her eyes across the dinner table.

Aurora spent at least an hour every day in the bathroom and always smelled flowery and wonderful. It wasn't just that she loved conversation— she dominated the dining table with stories and jokes and questions—it was that she lived for engagement. Face-to-face time with eyes that penetrated their targets and picturesque smiles that rendered them speechless. At least, this was her impact on Zephyr, who tried to hold her attention but found his words stupid and awkward by comparison. That she barely noticed his efforts only amplified his growing sense of insignificance. And as a result, he would often excuse himself from dinner early or retreat to another room in the house as soon as she walked in. He knew this kind of behavior was borderline dysfunctional, but he couldn't help himself.

"Why're you so grumpy?" she asked over a late lunch one afternoon and punched him on the arm.

"What do you mean?"

"You're grumpy, dude."

"No, I'm not. Just a little tired," he said.

"I've seen you tired, and this expression…" She pushed his cheek with a pointed finger. "This expression. Here. Right here. The one I keep touching. It's grumpiness. And it's been going on for days. What gives?"

In a way, her optimism reminded him of the twins, neither of whom gave the event the gravity it deserved. Of course, that was partly true because they hadn't awakened to discover one or more of their loved ones missing. The difference was that Aurora had, and she was upbeat, anyway. Her mother died when she was seven and her father raised her. She doted on him, and she cried for hours after she realized that the vanishings were not some big hoax and that he wasn't coming back. Yet, when the sun rose the next day, she wasn't broken, but energized and committed to finding her place in the aftermath.

"Nothing gives," he said, and flashed her his best smile. "Seriously. Is this cranky?"

"The word dorky comes to mind," she joked. "OK, cute, too, I admit."

Then she bit her lip, as she always did when she wrestled with something. "It's just that I've seen the way you are with Jordan and you're... great. You're so great with her. And you don't even talk to me. I just... did I do something?"

"No," he nearly shouted. Absolutely not. I can't get you out of my mind is the real problem here, he thought. I should be figuring out our next move but instead I'm daydreaming about you, and I'm powerless. Instead, he said, "Jordan is like my little sister. I take care of her now. That's all."

"OK. You don't want to talk about it, that's cool."

"That's not what I said," he began and shifted in his chair. "I'm just— I mean, I get embarrassed around you sometimes." There. Finally! It was a microscopic revelation compared to the grand scope of his feelings, but it was something, and he was glad it was out there.

"I embarrass you?" she asked, feigning surprise as if to say, little old me? And she was smiling again.

He moved some of the food on his plate around with his fork and admitted, "Yes. Sometimes."

She was about to say something in response when Jordan walked in the room, and Zephyr found himself relieved and disappointed.

"What's for lunch?" the little girl asked.

"Delicious microwave pizza. Pepperoni, cheese and cardboard," Aurora said.

"You want one?" Zephyr asked.

She did.

The sun rose and fell, the moon shone and then faded into the morning blue, and the process repeated. Days. A week or more. The boy wasn't sure anymore. Some afternoons, they did nothing. Just lazed about the living spaces and watched the last remnants of television or played the video games they'd looted. With a little help from Jordan, Zephyr completed all four *Uncharted* titles for PlayStation 4 in just as many days, a feat he was proud of but seemed inconsequential to Aurora, who called the series a waste of time. One morning he singlehandedly transported an electric oven to the mansion and their damned generators wouldn't power it for reasons he didn't understand.

Other days were more fruitful. They scavenged a gun store— Zephyr already had some experience here— and came away armed with an assortment of rifles and handguns. After that, the three of them discovered a secluded ranch on the periphery of the city and wedged shooting practice into their daily routines.

Jordan's weapon was a Smith & Wesson .22 handgun and she was a capable shot. The little girl didn't look like much, but within a few days, she could knock a half dozen cans off their perch atop a wooden fence from fifty feet away. In contrast, Aurora's aim was of little importance to her. She much preferred the power of a shotgun despite the fact that she suffered for it. Her right shoulder was bruised and sore for days after their first practice, but this didn't seem to faze her and as more time passed, she adjusted her hold on the gun so that its recoil no longer battered her. Zephyr, meanwhile, trusted in his 30-30 rifle. Not nearly as destructive as Aurora's boomstick, it was nevertheless lethal and also more suited to long-range kills, as he proved time and again by nailing targets from nearly one-hundred and fifty yards away. He was, much to his surprise, a natural.

"OK, fine, you're the best shot among us," Aurora conceded one afternoon as she rolled her eyes.

"Don't sell yourself short. If we ever need to shoot an elephant, you're gonna be the one we turn to."

She stuck her tongue out at him. "You're hilarious. What's really gonna happen is that you're gonna be fumbling for your fancy scope when we're surrounded by three dudes and I'm gonna blast them to smithereens and save your little ass."

Zephyr waved this comment off. "Lucky for you, I'll have seen them coming and taken them out before they can draw their weapons," he said. "All you'll be doing is blasting the men I already shot. But whatever makes you happy."

"OK, smart ass." She called Jordan over and whispered something into her ear. A moment later, the little girl sped off into the distance with three beer bottles in her arms.

"Really? We're doing this?"

Aurora ignored him. After all the bottles were placed and Jordan returned, she asked, "You ready, sniper?"

"I think we both know the answer is a resounding yes."

Zephyr arranged a few heavy rocks on the ground, laid on his belly and positioned his weapon so that the long barrel rested on the stones. Then he assumed the familiar form— the butt of the rifle firm against his shoulder, his right eye focused on the scope, his breath held. He sighted on them almost immediately: three beer bottles placed about a foot apart, all atop a fallen tree in the distance. Even with the magnified lens, they were barely discernible. He exhaled, repositioned the scope against the socket of his eye and looked again. They gotta be a hundred and seventy yards out, he thought. And then, So what? I can do this. He sucked in air and held it. The crosshairs seemed to slide over the first bottle and then beyond it. The regular rhythm of his heart. Steady now. The world around him faded as he concentrated on the single point. He exhaled, his finger squeezed the trigger and—

"Boo!" the girls screamed in unison.

The crash of the gun. And the bottle exploded.

Zephyr grinned from ear to ear as the girls grumbled and groaned. Aurora shook her head and stared at him in what he thought must be exasperation and maybe even awe. He soaked it up, particularly because he wasn't sure he could ever replicate the shot.

"Are we done here?" he asked, hoping they were.

"No, we are not," the teenage girl said. "Do it again, and this time

I'm going to be right in your face."

"This gets fairer by the minute."

"Life isn't fair," she countered.

"I'll give you that. For instance, some of us are naturally gifted with guns and others aren't."

Her eyes narrowed in mock contempt. "Try shooting your gun, not your mouth."

So he resumed his position and attempted to reestablish the laser focus responsible for the previous shot. However, this was a much more difficult undertaking with Aurora's face hovering just a foot away from his own, her eyes once more penetrating him. It shouldn't have been much of a distraction, but it was, and he found that as hard as he tried and for all the methodology he employed, he couldn't align the crosshairs over the second bottle as it waited in the distance.

"Having some trouble?" Aurora asked and Jordan giggled off to one side of him. He could feel strands of her hair blowing against him.

"Just..." He sighted in, the crosshairs finally responding to his subtle direction. "Aiming."

He held his breath. The shot was good. The bullet would destroy the target, he knew. His finger touched the trigger and then he felt something wet and hot in his ear. He had just enough time to think, it's her tongue! Then the gun crashed again, but this time no bottle exploded. In fact, as far as he could tell, his barrel pulled high and the projectile soared skyward.

He looked up, his cheeks burning red, and could barely meet her gaze. Of course, she was laughing, scarcely able to keep herself from doubling over, even, but her eyes met his all the same and there was no shame in them.

"Well, that's too bad. I guess you're just not much under pressure."

Zephyr wiped out his ear and then stood, hoping he didn't look as silly as he felt. "Yeah, that was fair," he returned. "Let me stick my tongue down your ear while you try to shoot something from two-hundred yards out, and we'll see how you do."

"You can stick your tongue in my ear any time, baby," she joked, and blew him a kiss.

The weather took a turn for the worse three days later. Not just cold, but freezing, and with the fiercest of winds. Zephyr struggled to ignite a flame in the fireplace and eventually triggered it. By this time, Sarah had already picked at her dinner and gone upstairs to bed, as she often did. In her absence, the three of them made microwave popcorn, bathed themselves in heavy blankets and watched a movie as they stretched across enormous leather couches. In typical form, Aurora did not appear to care for Zephyr's selection for the evening, and her attention cycled between the ginormous television and the tablet in her lap.

"Dude. Candy Crush can wait. This is basically the greatest movie ever made here," Zephyr said. On the big screen, a teary-eyed Jodie Foster floated in space and declared that they should have sent a poet.

"No, wait—pause it. Something's up. You need to see this."

"What is it?" he asked and froze the movie.

She handed him the device, her eyes wide. "Check it out. I tried to load Yahoo and this is what I got instead."

The familiar search engine was gone, the iconic logo departed. The page was altogether void of any graphics or color. Just a sparse white background interrupted only by two short paragraphs made in a large black font. A blue hyperlink accompanied the words as a signature might a letter. The message read:

> *Why are we still here? How many of us are left? What do we do now? We don't have all the answers, but we have some. We also have a few strange theories that you might just believe. More important, we are planning for the future and if you are good and able, we need your help. Mankind is not extinct. We are,*

however, fractured and endangered. If we are going to survive, we need to unite, to share knowledge and trade skills, to rethink our way of life, and make children. This is a message of peace. Please join our democracy and our fight to persevere in the New World.

The collective citizens of Alpha, (formerly known as Santa Monica, California). December 11, Year 1, AD (After Disappearances).
Click here for directions.

Still wrapped in blankets, Jordan and Aurora situated themselves behind the sprawling kitchen bar while Zephyr doled out stale chocolate chip cookies and water— milk was no longer an option— and agonized over every detail of the posting. Those simple words had ripped any possibility of sleep away from him for the night, but that was all right, for within the electricity that hummed through his body and mind there also flowed the faint, steady pulse of something new. Something he hadn't allowed himself to feel since the vanishings, and even now remained afraid to fully acknowledge. It was hope. The girls were already infected. He could see that in the way their eyes sparkled and their smiles came easier and faster. And yet, this was a big deal and he didn't want to rush into anything. It was always better to consider every possibility, even the worst.

"Stop overanalyzing this," Aurora said as she bit into a cookie. "It's simple. A bunch of people are starting a new city. What's to discuss here?"

"I wanna go," Jordan said.

"You," Zephyr replied, "can go get Sarah. How's that sound?" The little girl sighed, but ran upstairs anyway.

When he was sure that she was safely out of sight, he turned back to

Aurora and whispered, "I hate to be the pessimist in the group, but shouldn't we consider whether or not this is some kind of trap before we go running blindly into it? This could all just be a big ruse— a smarter version of the men who kidnapped you— to lure in people."

"Yeah. I thought the same thing when I read the part about it being a message of peace." She rolled her eyes to emphasize the point.

Zephyr shrugged. "What? Nobody's ever lied before?"

"I believe it. And I also agree with Jordan."

"Of course you do," he said, plunked his elbows on the counter and rubbed his eyes. "Listen, I'm not saying it isn't legit. I hope it is. I even think it probably is. But let's just be smart here, OK?"

She smiled. "I'm always smart."

"You're always a smart ass, is more like it."

Sarah appeared at the foot of the stairs in worn sweats, her eyes tired and puffy. He read her the website post as Aurora interjected with comments like, "Isn't it amazing?" When he was finished, Sarah looked between them, nodded, and said, "So you want to go to California."

"Yes," Aurora beamed. "I mean, for one, it's California. I think it was just a matter of time before I wanted to go there, anyway. And two, they're rebuilding. This could be the closest thing we get to normal now."

"It's California, hon. Wouldn't count on normal," Sarah said.

"Do you think they have hot showers?" asked Jordan.

Aurora's smile widened. "For sure. And milk, too, I bet."

The little girl grinned and hopped up and down with her hands clasped together.

"I think that these guys have had similar run-ins with some bad people," Zephyr said. "Here. Look here." He pointed to the tablet's screen. "If you are good and able. You see that? Not just able, but good and able. Why specifically call out character unless you have reason to? I bet they're already guarding against messed up people."

"Maybe," Aurora said. "Then again, who cares? Why do you have to dissect everything?"

Now he was annoyed. "Maybe if you thought through things a little more, you wouldn't find yourself handcuffed to ovens in department stores," he said, and as soon as the words came out, he remembered that Sarah was right beside her. "I'm sorry—that was not cool," he told her. "I didn't mean you. Just..."

"It's OK," she said.

"No, it's not. I shouldn—"

"It's OK, Zephyr. Really. Don't worry about it."

"I don't forgive you," Aurora said.

"Didn't ask for your forgiveness." He didn't give her a chance to reply. "The message also indicates that they are looking for people to share knowledge and skills. They're basically saying they want to put us to work. And on top of that, make babies. Maybe you caught that part, Aurora."

"They're speaking generally. For the survival of the race," she said. "It's not like I'm going to be a baby farm for them. They're just saying that we— as in all of us, as in the human race—need to have children."

"That's presumptuous," Zephyr said, knowing full well that she was probably right but unwilling to back down.

"Are you actually trying to be an ass or does it come naturally?"

"Trying. Not all of us have your natural ability."

"OK, children," Sarah said.

"Yeah, Aurora," Zephyr agreed. "So we also know they're running a democracy, which is a good thing. No dictatorship, communism, or craziness like that. This might also suggest that their new city is far enough along that they already have some form of government. Which, you know, would be pretty amazing."

"Yeah, tell me something I don't know. You're forgetting the biggest and most important detail in the entire post," Aurora said.

"What's that?"

"It's December 11. That means it's almost Christmas. Have you gotten my presents yet?"

The conversation continued, derailed, unraveled, and all the while Jordan's eyes grew heavier and heavier. After a while, Zephyr picked her up, carried her to the couch, covered her in blankets and kissed her goodnight. When he returned to the kitchen, Aurora and Sarah were quietly locked in argument.

"What's happening?" he asked.

Aurora turned to him, tears in her eyes. "She says she's not coming."

Sarah stared at the floor, her arms crossed. "Yeah, hon, I'll be staying. But you should go."

"Why do you want to stay?"

"My life…" she began. "What's left of my life, anyway—is here. I don't belong in California. This city is where I belong."

"No offense, Sarah, but Las Cruces doesn't exactly hold the best of memories for you anymore," Aurora said. "You can start over in California, at least. And you'll have us. We want you to go." She turned to Zephyr. "Tell her I'm right."

The older woman raised a palmed hand to the boy and with the other, she brushed Aurora's hair out of her face. "I know, sweetie," she said. "I know you do, and I'm thankful that I've been fortunate enough to have all of you in my life. But I don't want to go. It's not what I want to do. Everything out there—I don't want any part of it. I just want…" She broke off, searching for the right words. "I just want to stay, that's all."

"OK, well, I think we should stick together," Zephyr said. "If that means we should stay, too, we can do that. We've been fine here so far."

"Absolutely not. You kids have always been passing through. Even if you didn't know it, I did." She smiled. It was a warm, pleasant smile and for the first time since they met, Zephyr caught a glimpse of the woman as she had existed before the disappearances, before pain and despair had marked and aged her. "Look at you. You're excited. You're happy. It's crazy, but it's impossible to miss. This is the right thing for you. For all of you. And I wouldn't have it—

wouldn't want it – any other way. No, you go. And don't worry about me. I'll be OK."

Aurora started to say something when Sarah cut her off. "No—this is the end of the conversation. The end. I'm going back to bed now and I'm sleeping in late. When I come downstairs to make something to eat, I don't want to see any of you. I want to know that you're on your way to a better place and that you're giving that sweet little girl a chance in this life. Now give me a hug. Both of you."

Zephyr choked the lump in his throat back down as he watched the two girls embrace and he held his composure even when Aurora shook in silence. It wasn't until Sarah bent down and kissed the sleeping child on the cheek, her eyes watery and tired, that he turned away.

33

When the sun rose, they ate dry cereal and drank canned juice. Then they tiptoed around as they stuffed bags full of food and spare clothes, assembled rifles and handguns, hauled a spare tank of gas to the car, and more. After they crammed the Flex's rear space with all manners of supplies and the car purred its readiness, the three of them did a final sweep of the house, and Jordan said she wanted to say goodbye to the older lady.

"No, she's sleeping. And she kissed you good-bye last night while you were knocked out," Zephyr told her.

"I know, but I want—"

"It's too hard for her, Jord. She told us last night that she didn't want to see us this morning." He nudged her toward the front door. "Come on, let's hit the road, kid. We have a long trip ahead of us."

Based on what he could ascertain from the map they carried, the drive to Santa Monica seemed easy enough. It was, after all, just a straight shot on Interstate 10 going west until they hit the coast. However, it was also an eight-hundred-mile trek on a highway still littered in forgotten vehicles, not to mention whatever else might lay in wait.

Usually, they could hug the left lane and bypass the big trucks, but leftover cars or even the odd 18-wheeler sometimes bled into their passage and they were forced to slow, switch lanes, or in some rare instances, veer into the shoulder to pass by. Their car never moved more than thirty miles per hour. And headway took another punch to the gut around lunchtime, when the dark clouds above made good on their threats and released a thick, steady downpour upon them.

"Are we there yet?" Jordan asked.

"Not even funny," Aurora said and turned to Zephyr, who continued to grip the steering wheel as a drowning man might a life preserver. And drowning they were: the windshield struggling to remove massive gobs of water. "This is ridiculous," she added.

"Yep," Zephyr agreed. "But look on the bright side. Only six-hundred or so miles to go. Speaking of, is it your turn to drive?"

They drove on for hours, the obstacles and rain never abating, as the clouds grew darker and the car's glass colder to the touch. Beautiful red rock formations surrounded the highway. Cacti, Joshua trees and wastelands stretched everywhere. Eventually, they passed out of New Mexico and into Arizona, which Zephyr considered a major accomplishment. A few hours later, the clouds could no longer be seen through the fog of night, and the boy nodded in and out of consciousness as the rain created monotonous music against their windshield and Aurora tended to the wheel.

After a while, she nudged him. "Hey, you awake?"

The words snapped him from some thin, hazy dream before he leaned forward and rubbed his eyes.

"Yeah. Am now." He turned around and Jordan was asleep in the backseat with a bag of chips on her lap.

"Sorry. I'm getting pretty tired and I can't see shit out here anyway. We should think about stopping for the night. Either find a place to sleep or just park somewhere."

"Yeah," he said and stared into the water-soaked darkness beyond the comfort of the car. "Any idea where we are?"

"Somewhere in Arizona, dude. That's all I've got."

"Awesome. Don't you read the signs we pass?"

"I've been pretty focused on not getting us killed for the last hour. Not sure if you've noticed, but we're in the middle of some kind of biblical storm."

"OK, touché," he said as he dug into a bag at his feet, pulled out a double-sized candy bar and bit into it. "So, I can drive for a bit and then we can look for a place to hole up. I think that sounds better than trying to sleep in the car. You cool with that?"

"Yup."

She rolled the Flex to a stop in the middle of lane and then flipped the hazards on. Zephyr was going to make a joke about how unnecessary that was, thought better of it and reached for the door handle, but by this time she had already unfastened her seatbelt, scooted over to his side of the car and straddled him. Her face was inches from his, her hair brushing against him.

"OK," she whispered. "Switch?"

"Yeah." He started to rise and his seatbelt pulled him back again.

"Here—let me help." She leaned into him, slid her arm across his leg and then pushed the buckle. The belt unfastened without interruption. He could smell her now, feel the warmth and weight of her, hear her breathing, and the world outside seemed inconsequential.

"Thanks." He didn't move—wasn't sure that he could.

"You know," she whispered. "You're pretty cute when you sleep. You have the tiniest, little snore."

"I don't snore," he said and knew his cheeks were already bright red.

"No, it's so little. I like it."

He didn't know how to respond and his mind considered a hundred options in a blink. He wanted to lock his arms around her and press her lips against his. Felt, in fact, like he might implode unless he did that very thing. But he was also terrified that she was toying with him, or that he was somehow misinterpreting everything she did and said, and these possibilities froze him in place.

"Well, thanks," he finally mustered. "I think." It was supposed to be funny, but it came out all wrong—arrogant almost, and he regretted the words as soon as he released them.

"All right, Zephyr," she sighed and started to rise again.

"What?"

"You know what. Take your seat then."

"Seriously, what did I do?" he asked.

"Nothing. That's the problem. That's always the problem."

"No, I want to talk about this. I wasn't trying to be rude. I'm sorry if it came out that way."

"Just…" she said. "Drive."

So he did.

Shortly thereafter, as Aurora slept in the passenger seat and Zephyr quietly cursed her for sending his mind and body into overdrive, he saw a sign for Tucson. He'd passed through the city before and knew it well enough. It was a metropolis with a massive population and it stretched for miles. Thankfully, the storm had finally dissipated and the moon cast soft light on the cityscape. A congress of tall and short buildings stood erect in the distance, but they were gray silhouettes on black, barely discernible in the night.

He found an off-ramp and exited, slowed to dodge a parked sedan and then stopped to observe a stoplight that no longer offered any instruction.

"Where are we?" Jordan asked from the backseat.

"Tucson. In Arizona," he said. "It's a big city. I'm going to stop at the nearest place and we'll figure out a way to get a couple rooms so we can rest through the night."

The next morning, the rain returned with a vengeance— somehow heavier, louder, fiercer, and more determined to disrupt them.

Amazingly, the water in the bathroom ran hot, and Aurora insisted upon a long, steamy shower before they left the motel behind. Zephyr explained that it was a pointless undertaking because they would undoubtedly be soaked and cold by the time they made it back to the car, anyway.

"I don't care—it's worth it," she countered. "It's been months since I've had a hot shower or bath. Months. Let me just say it one more time for emphasis. Months. You're getting this, right? There's no way I'm passing this opportunity up, so you two better get comfortable because I intend to enjoy this." And with that, she closed the bathroom door.

They both spoke true. By the time they pulled the doors closed on the Flex again, almost an hour had passed and yes, they were wet and chilled. Aurora didn't seem to mind. She fastened her seatbelt, her thick, moist hair pulled back in a ponytail, and beamed at him.

"So totally worth it, dude. Thanks for humoring me."

"Anything for you," he returned, and shook his head as he started the car and blasted the heater.

She cycled through stations on the satellite radio and when nothing played, she turned it off. "I love it when it storms like this. Reminds me of home."

"Me too," Zephyr said and turned to her. "When I don't have to drive in it, that is."

"Boo-hoo. We can take turns, like we did yesterday."

The three of them talked about whether or not to explore Tucson proper and decided against it. Their tank was nearly full again, they had ample food, supplies and weapons, and although they were curious to experience a metropolis in the aftermath of the disappearances, there were no genuine advantages to doing so. When Zephyr said it might be dangerous, he was relieved to see the girls nod in agreement. So they turned the car back onto the freeway and drove west as the city faded from view.

Jordan watched some movie on the tablet, oversized headphones dwarfing her head, and he and Aurora rode along in silence. After a while, she said, "Here's a question that I think I know the answer to, but I'll ask anyway. You consider yourself a half-empty or half-full guy?"

Zephyr frowned at her. "Do you even need to ask?"

"No, I guess not."

"You think that's a bad thing?"

"To be such a pessimist? Yeah."

"Better safe than sorry, my dad used to say. Those words are truer now than ever," Zephyr said. "I suppose you're half-full all the way, right?"

She shrugged. "Yeah. Sure, you could look at everything and ask, why me? Or, you could be thankful that you're still here. We basically own this entire world now. We can do anything we want."

That's what the slavers said, he thought. "That's sort of true, but everything around us is transforming. All the things we count on are depleting. Food, water, electricity, gas—you name it. We can't take any of it for granted any more. What's it gonna be like a year from now? What about five years? I don't know the answer, but very, very different is a certainty. Not for the better, either. New York, Chicago, San Francisco—in ten years, they might be ruins populated by wildlife, not people."

If his words had any impact on her, she didn't show it. "I think you're being a little dramatic," she finally said. "Think about how many people are left. Could it even be millions? I'm not so sure. I bet we're talking about thousands. But just for argument's sake, let's say a million people are still trolling around America. Compare that to a population of— a couple hundred million?"

"Three-hundred million."

"Yeah. Three-hundred million before everything went crazy. We're microscopic now. I think we'll have enough food and water to last us a lifetime, even if we're eating canned beans and corn into our sixties. And cities in ruins in ten years? No way, dude. We'll be dead by the time that kind of scenario plays out. Maybe our kids' kids will see that kind of world."

"Wait—this could be a deal-breaker. I never said I wanted kids."

"Shut up, jackass," she said and punched his arm. "You know what I meant."

"The twins—they died before we met—they spent some time in Vegas after the event. Merrick, also before you, he passed through Denver. They all spoke of plane crashes, big fires, people looting— just, anarchy." He glanced in his rear-view and verified that Jordan was still engaged. "It all breaks down, Aurora. Faster than you think. You don't take care of your lawn, it browns, weeds, becomes overgrowth, and it happens in weeks, not months, or years. Now imagine that on a global scale, and you watch how fast nature reclaims the world. I'm not saying we're gonna see tree branches growing out of skyscraper windows and bears and wolves roaming the streets for prey tomorrow, but yes, I do believe we're in the middle of a passing-of-the-torch and that if nothing changes, we'll see exactly these kinds of conditions in years, not decades. Maybe even months under the right circumstances."

She picked at her cuticles. "Agree to disagree on this one, I guess. Also, it's not like we're done as a species. We're on our way to a community of people who want to rebuild. To use your lawn metaphor, we're just putting gas back in the mower now and we'll be out there again cutting soon."

"Will we, though? The people of Alpha—their statement says that we need to rethink the way we live. For all you know, we could be churning milk and growing beards by the end of the week." He sighed. "Listen, I don't mean to be a Debbie Downer here. I'm just being the pessimist you know me to be."

"Let's say you're right. That Alpha is full of hippies who want to live off the land. Would that be so terrible?"

Zephyr considered it. "No," he said. "Actually, in the long term, this might be our best hope of surviving. To regrow crops, ranch, etcetera."

"OK, so how bad would it be if we churned milk or plowed land or what-the-hell-ever a few days a week and then we hung out on the beach, surfed, went drinking and dancing, or—I don't know— rode every ride at Disneyland all day long in our off hours?" She thumped his forehead with the tip of her index. "Stop over-thinking everything. Take a breath and enjoy what we've got, dude. I'll grant you that it's not always gonna be easy if you'll admit that, for whatever reason we're still alive, we have plenty of opportunities left."

She had a point. Survival was always his focus and priority. It never fully left him. But had they ever really been in danger of starving or freezing? No. In Las Cruces, they enjoyed a level of extravagance normally reserved for the rich. In many ways, she was right. They could do about anything they wanted.

"Yeah, I'll admit that," he said. "A hypothetical for you, then. If this Alpha thing doesn't work out, what do you wanna do? Lay on the beach and go dancing?"

She laughed. "I don't know, maybe. What about you?"

"I'm not sure. I mean, as long as we're all together, I really don't care what we do."

"And will we be together? I mean, even after the city?" she asked.

The possibility that they might separate hadn't ever occurred to him. He pictured Aurora splintered from the group in pursuit of another boy, or running around California with girlfriends, and a wave of nausea crashed over him.

"Yes," he said. "Well, I wouldn't want to split up, but I mean, I can't stop you from doing whatever you want to do. You know, if you decided you wanted to go, I would have to support that." Seriously? Are you trying to make it easier for her?

She looked away and said nothing, which was so completely opposite of what he anticipated that he wasn't sure how to proceed.

"What?" he finally asked.

"I just don't understand you sometimes."

"Why? I mean, what's to understand?"

"How you really feel, for starters. About anything. Except for Jordan."

"What's that supposed to mean?" he asked.

She glanced back at the little girl, who stared transfixed as SpongeBob Squarepants performed. "Do you really want to have this conversation here?" she whispered. "Because I'll do it."

"What conversation?" Zephyr asked, curious and alarmed by her tone.

"Do you want me to stay with you?"

"Is this a trick question? Of course, I do." he said.

"Then why would you tell me it's OK if I want to go do my own thing? How's that supposed to make me feel? Do you even…" she began and then shook her head. "Just forget it."

"Aurora," he said. "I don't want you to leave. You were the one who raised the topic, not me. I was just trying to be… respectful. What do you want me to say here?"

"Just forget it. Let's talk about something else."

Why did she always make him feel like the bad guy for trying to be nice? You were the one who brought up the possibility of leaving, he thought. You. Not me. And suddenly he was angry— at himself, because she was right, and at her for forcing him to acknowledge it.

"Fine. You want to have an uncomfortable conversation? Let's do it," he spat as he slowed the car to a stop and faced her while the rain continued its bombardment.

"No, I don't want you to freakin' leave. Jesus. How could you imply that? I felt like you ripped my heart in half when you even mentioned that possibility." He felt it coming out and couldn't stop himself. "Yes, it's hard for me to tell you how I feel because I feel everything for you. Everything. Since I first saw you. I wake up every morning wondering where you are and go to bed every night dreaming about you. Every morning and every night."

His heart raced and he focused on keeping his composure. The way she was staring at him— what was she thinking? Why couldn't he read her at all? Finally, he threw up his hands in defeat, resigned to the fact that he had just erected a mountain of uneasiness between them. Painfully aware now that she probably would leave the group, and all because of this little outburst.

"So, it's out there now," he said at last. "Happy? It shouldn't be awkward at all for the next ten hours, righ—"

Then she was on him, her arms around him, and kissing him. Before he could process it, he felt his arms envelop her, his hands caress her thick, dark hair, and then he pulled her closer and kissed her back. A sensation like hunger swept over him, but it was deeper and more powerful. His mind gave way to instinct and he led with his mouth and hands, meeting her every advance, relishing her breath, the pounding of the rain outpaced by the pounding of his heart.

"You stupid asshole," she whispered before her lips found his again. "Why'd..." She kissed him. "You... make this..." Again. "So... hard?"

"Sorry. I didn't think—" But she didn't give him time to respond. He felt her lips, her hot tears against his cheek, cupped her face and wiped them away with his thumbs. Then they were kissing again.

"What're you guys doing?" a voiced asked from far away and he ignored it. "Hello? Child in the backseat here."

Aurora pulled away from his face, giggling, so he tugged her back and kissed her again. When they finished, she leaned into his ear and whispered, "Jordan's watching us."

That broke him from the trance and when she leaned back again, he let her.

"I'm just showing Zephyr how much I appreciate his driving," Aurora joked and wiped at her eyes.

"Whatever," the little girl said. "Are you guys like boyfriend and girlfriend now?"

Aurora met Zephyr's gaze. "Yes?"

"Yes," he said, and then she kissed him again, hard.

The downpour and congestion followed them. Even so, the drive was beautiful, the conversation titillating, and he didn't care about the circumstances. When darkness fell again and they finally did cross into California, a five-hour trip transformed into an all-day affair, the car erupted with applause and Jordan and Aurora exchanged goofy high-fives. Somewhere between the unexpected lip-locking and the state border, they all decided that plowing straight through to Santa Monica was no longer the priority, even if they thought it was possible. Aurora wanted to track down a decent hotel with a large suite, see Jordan to bed and then stay up talking, and Zephyr thought this sounded like the greatest idea ever conceived.

He didn't know California well and couldn't really see much of it through the rain and blackness of night, but the details that did shine bright before they blurred by his vision suggested more desert. Flatlands, weeds and shrubs, rocks, and then darkness. For some stupid reason, he thought they might cross the border into blue oceans and sandy beaches and was imagining what they might look like when their high-beams lit up a huge barrier in the road.

He pumped the brakes and the Flex's rear-end drifted several feet before the tires caught the road again and the vehicle straightened out. With the car finally slowed, he focused on the impediment — the object so out of place that at first his mind refused to accept it.

"What the hell?" Aurora asked and then cupped her mouth, strangling a gasp.

"I see it," Zephyr said.

And he did. Someone had placed a portable basketball goal— the kind normally found curbside or in the backyards of neighbor's houses—in the middle of the street. The full system. A thick base and brackets held the long steel pipe that raised upward to the backboard, rim and net. This was an odd thing to be discarded on a freeway, yes, but that wasn't why Jordan screamed from her place in the backseat.

"Don't look at it, Jord! Close your eyes," Aurora called back. "Zephyr, get us out of here."

Dangling by a thick rope from the rim of the court was a soaked corpse, blackened, bloated and badly decomposed. Two things were wrapped around the dead man's neck, itself ripped, stretched, and threatening to tear away. The first was the rope which someone had used to hang him. The second was a big red sign that simply read, *Welcome to California.*

34
The Golden State

Hours later, when they pulled off the highway into Palm Springs, the mood was as dead as the man who received them. None of them talked a lot about the body or after it. And even now, with so much death, some of it by his own hands, it was a shock to see a corpse like that. Not just the loss of life, but murder. And for what? Some sick joke? Some warped message?

The rain had finally relented, at least. And the more they drove into the depths of California, the more lights they saw twinkling in the distance off either side of the highway. Somehow, electricity still burned and surged to these rickety settlements on the outskirts of nowhere.

Aurora pointed into the night. "I didn't realize how much I missed the city lights. You know?"

"Me too," Jordan added from the backseat. "And another thing. Maybe Disneyland still works, too."

"If Disneyland is still working, I promise you that we will go."

Hotel Red Leaf was modern, chic and pretentious. The kind of place people went to get away from reality for a few days. The kind of place whose inflated bill at the conclusion of the getaway brought reality back home. The reception lobby was awash in golden light from an assortment of featureless, square lamps and some brand of electronica played through unseen ceiling speakers. A huge fish tank was cemented into a cavity of a nearby opaque wall and a dozen or more large fish of various colors floated upside-down inside it. Of course, the reception desk was lifeless and when Zephyr scaled the counter to search for keys, he was not surprised to find a heap of uniforms and shoes sans their owners.

The old luxuries of the hotel belied the dangers of the new world beyond its walls, and as they searched the lobby, they carried their guns. Aurora escorted Jordan to the bathroom while Zephyr scoured the reception office for instructions on how to use the place's electric key system, and was amazed when he found a one-page tutorial that actually worked.

The suite was on the far side of the hotel and on the way, they passed the outside pool, still alight and positively alluring, even in the cold weather. Thick steam rose from the water as it waited motionless for someone to enjoy a swim. Cabanas and lounge chairs surrounded the pool and a barbecue rested in one corner. The pool itself was of the infinity kind and a waterside bar welcomed swimmers at one end. It was fully stocked, which did not go unnoticed.

"Yes, please," Aurora said and Zephyr imagined her in a bikini. Come on, dude. Focus. Pay attention.

The suite was a score. The place was gargantuan, luxurious, and altogether gorgeous. Vaulted ceilings and dark hardwood floors throughout. A stylish selection of modern furniture and art gave way to two expansive living spaces, three bedrooms, and french doors that opened poolside.

"Wow," Aurora said, after they'd completed their sweep of the place.

"Yeah. This is even cooler than our house in Las Cruces," Jordan seconded.

"It might be bigger, too," Aurora remarked.

"No kidding," Zephyr said, plopped into one of the sectionals, instinctively palmed the remote and turned on the television. It flickered into life with an electric hum and a brighter shade of black, but no signal greeted him.

"OK, so what's the plan then?" Aurora asked. "I'm hungry and I could use a hot bath, which reminds me, if we don't have hot water, I'm gonna grab some shampoo and sit in the pool. And I kind of want to get drunk." When Zephyr stared at her, she shrugged and added, "What? Sorry. It's true. We've kind of had a shit night, dude."

Then she turned to Jordan. "You don't care, right?"

"No."

"See?"

They all claimed their bedrooms. Naturally, Jordan wanted to sleep with Zephyr again and didn't respond well to the prospect of her own room. However, when he assured her that his quarters were adjacent hers, she gave a little, and when he bribed her with the possibility of investigating Disneyland at their earliest convenience, she relented and allowed the separation. He felt guilty about it, but they couldn't continue sleeping together forever, particularly if he and Aurora were going to—what? What would they be doing, exactly? His heart skipped a beat as he pondered the likelihood of going to bed with her. Not even sex. Just sleeping next to her. Curling up with her. He recognized for the dozenth time that she held so much power over him. Did she even know that? And did he hold the same power over her? He thought probably not.

They were too exhausted to rummage for food, so they ate from their snack bags— a dinner of Doritos, peanuts, donuts and water— everything a growing body needed. When they were all finished, Aurora marched off to see if the water ran hot and returned minutes later beaming. She told them she planned to take a long, "scalding hot" bath and that, like before, they needn't wait for her.

"Can't we go swimming instead?" Jordan nearly begged. "The pool water is hot."

Aurora shook her head. "We don't have any swimsuits." Then she looked at Zephyr with a raised eyebrow as she always did when presenting him a challenge.

"Lemme guess," he said. "You want me to find some."

He returned a half hour later with a bag full of swim shorts, bikinis and one-piece bathing suits in different sizes and colors. He started out with the plan to pillage some rooms for these items, but was relieved to learn that the hotel was home to its own clothing shop and once he finally unearthed a key to it, he also discovered a robust supply of options.

"OK, mission accomplished," he said and handed the bag over to the girls. "No idea what sizes you are so feel free to try some of these on. I grabbed everything I could find so something's gotta fit."

Jordan dug through the bag first and then skipped into the bathroom with several bathing suits in her arms. When Aurora finally investigated the contents, she looked up at him, frowning.

"How come only the bikinis are in my size?"

"What? Oh, uhm, I don't know." He met her gaze and smiled. "I mean, I really couldn't say."

"Uh-huh." But she smiled back. "This is how it's gonna be, is it?" She stretched a skimpy bikini bottom before him to accentuate her point. "And I suppose you found a thong for yourself?"

"Sadly, none in my size."

"I guess they don't make them that small," she mused.

"Nope," he said, ignoring her. "I think just the bikinis run that tiny."

They each seized a bathroom and changed. Zephyr slipped out of his clothes and into the swim trunks in seconds and then stood in front of the mirror and studied himself. His hair was a little longer, but he thought it worked. He looked taller, leaner, his muscles more defined than they had been just weeks ago. It was the world now— nothing came easy. Everything required work. And their idea of fun was shooting practice. Yes, his eyes were a little bloodshot and looked tired. Still, for the first time in his life, he thought he looked more like a man than a boy, and he felt good about it.

He found a bathrobe and pulled it tight over himself before stepping back into the living room. Jordan joined him minutes later, but Aurora made them wait forever. He was about to go knock on her bathroom door to make she sure was all right when it finally swung inward and she emerged wearing the same white, fluffy bathrobe that adorned him.

"OK, ready?" she asked.

He rolled his eyes. "Yeah. For about an hour."

"Hush."

There was, of course, no way of knowing if the hotel was as unoccupied as it appeared to be and Zephyr insisted on a proper probe before any of them could go swimming. Jordan groaned, but Aurora said it was the smart thing to do. So, dressed in bathrobes and armed with guns, the three of them explored the entire grounds, knocked on some doors, and looked for any recent signs of activity. Save for some leftover clothes, though, they never discovered any evidence of anybody.

His paranoia never quite dissipated, and yet the pool was too good to pass up. When they finally set their weapons down nearby and approached the waters, a smile crept over his face. He loved to swim. Was pretty good at it, too. He'd been a standout member of the high school swim team before the world broke down. When he dipped his toe in, he discovered it not just warm, but Jacuzzi-hot, and without looking back at the girls, he disrobed and dove.

"Is it great?" Jordan called to him when his head came topside again. She was practically vibrating with excitement on the edge of the pool, her robe now tossed in a pile behind her.

"It's nice and hot. Come on in."

She didn't wait for another invitation. Aurora, meanwhile, watched them from her perch on a nearby lounge chair, her arms crossed as though trying to hug away the cold.

"What're you doing?" Zephyr called. "It feels great. Hop in here."

She reached into the pockets of her robe and pulled out bottles of shampoo and body wash respectively, placed them both at the edge of the pool, started to disrobe and then glanced at Zephyr, at which point she stopped.

"You coming?" he asked.

"OK, so..." She studied her fingers. "I can't get in with you looking. I thought I could. But I can't."

"Why not?" He knew he was enjoying this much more than he should, but he couldn't stop himself.

For once, she didn't have a response to his query, and if the sun had been shining and there was any real visibility at their little oasis, he was sure her cheeks would prove bright red.

"All right," he finally relented and turned around. "Better hurry, though, because I might be tempted to take a little peek here."

"Don't!"

"I'm just kidding. Take it easy. Get in already then."

There came a little splash as she lowered herself into the water and even then he kept his promise and stared in the opposite direction.

"All clear?" he finally asked.

"Yeah."

She submerged herself and moved toward the far end of the pool with the broad, sweeping strokes of a practiced swimmer. As he watched, Jordan's head appeared beside him and he had no time to react as she spit water directly into his face. When the giggling girl tried to swim away, he gave chase, caught and then tickled her until she threatened to pee in the pool. Then he hoisted her high and dunked her. She came up laughing. The two of them played in this way for several minutes and finally Jordan surrendered and swam to the shallow end of the pool to practice hand-stands. So he paddled over to Aurora's corner and when she saw him coming, she allowed herself to sink deeper into the water.

"What's going on over here?" he asked as he drew near.

She was neither standing nor fully swimming. Instead, she treaded in place, and every so often used her arms to push and float.

"Just enjoying the warmth."

"I gotta admit, it's pretty nice." When she made no reply to this, he asked, "All right, is something wrong?"

"No—I just…" She finally met his gaze. "It's a little different now. Us. Since we kissed. Don't you think?"

"Different in a good way or bad way?"

"Good. No, definitely good. Just, different."

"How so?" he asked.

"I don't know. I guess I'm afraid you're…" She broke off. "It's stupid. I like you, Zephyr. I just don't want to mess this up."

"I like you, too. And you won't. I mean, if anybody will, it'll be me. Because I'm an idiot. I think we can both agree on that."

She laughed, moved closer, and wrapped her arms around him. He kissed her, and she didn't pull away. Rather, she pushed into him, meeting his lips and body with her own. It was electric, magnetic, and wonderful. A little too wonderful.

"So," he fumbled, backing away, "I'm just gonna… I'll be over there. I apologize. It's not you. Or, I mean, it is. That last kiss. I'm… I'll be back." Then he started in the opposite direction.

For a second, she only stared at him, then she cradled her mouth with both hands and giggled. "No, baby, come back," she called. When he didn't, she swam after and eventually caught up to him.

Zephyr held his arms out to her. "Seriously," he said and laughed. "Just gimme a minute."

"Is that all you need?" she asked and stuck her tongue out.

"Honestly? Probably."

An hour later, the three of them shivered back to the suite and then divided into their respective bathrooms. Zephyr thought the hot shower felt even better than the pool. After he toweled off and slipped into a tank top and sweatpants, he beelined to the kitchen and prepared a quick snack, and as he sat on the living room couch eating Cheeze-Its crackers and wondering why swimming always made him ravenous, Jordan appeared in a brown sweatshirt and flannel pajama bottoms. Her long blonde hair was brushed and pulled into a ponytail that dangled to her back and she looked altogether cozy.

"Can I have some?" she asked and plopped down beside him as he handed her the box. Then he leaned back, yawned and fixated on the ceiling. Jordan started fiddling with the television remote, but he barely noticed as he slid deeper into thought.

What kind of answers did the people of Alpha really have? And how? He pondered this for a long time. No matter how he attacked the question, he always slammed into the same brick wall, which was that the event itself was so widespread, so encapsulating, that it could not possibly be manmade. And if that really was the truth of it, how could mankind hope to understand it?

"Turn to Channel 101 to see the latest Hollywood hits," a voice blared to some vapid jingle and he nearly rocketed away from the couch before his eyes snagged on the television. Somehow, Jordan had cued the hotel's in-room entertainment service on the screen and it was still functional, which meant that they could rent movies or even play old Nintendo 64 games. Or so he thought, anyway. Much to the little girl's chagrin, when they actually tried this, an error message and a suggestion to contact the front desk appeared on the unit.

"Sorry, Jord. Looks like the hotel needs our credit card info before we can rent anything, and there's nobody left to take it," he said.

She grumbled something about how nothing ever worked anymore and then meandered into the kitchen, popped the lid on a can of Pepsi, and drank. As she was doing this, Aurora's bathroom door squeaked open and she moseyed out in her fluffy bathrobe, her hair still wrapped in a towel. Somehow, she looked even more sedated and snug than Jordan.

"Hi," she said, and smiled. "What time is it? Any idea?"

He studied the television and finally saw it on display in the upper-right corner of the screen. "Almost ten."

"Getting late."

"I know, I know," Jordan said. "I'm going."

"No, that's not what I meant—you can stay up as long as you like."

"It's OK. I'm tired, anyway." The little girl skipped to Zephyr, hopped onto his lap, hugged him and then pecked him on the cheek. "I'm gonna keep the door open a little."

"OK."

He squeezed her back, and then she rose and embraced Aurora before she bid them good-night and retreated into the bedroom. When she flipped the light off a few minutes later, the door was completely ajar, so Zephyr pulled it to a sliver.

"Not all the way," she called.

"It's still open. Night."

"Night."

Aurora lay on the thick, leather chaise beside the couch, and she smiled at him as he made his way back to the living room.

"So?" she asked.

"So, what?"

"Any thoughts on how we can spend our last pre-Alpha night together or do you just want to go to bed?"

His heart quickened at the thought of it. He had to admit, now that the possibility seemed almost within his grasp, it wasn't exclusively exciting, but terrifying. Just sleeping next to her—

he wasn't sure he'd be able to get any real rest. And if it was the other thing — well, what if he sucked? Aurora was the unattainable prom queen, not the girl next door — whom, by the way, was out of his league, too. He still couldn't believe that she had any interest in him and held true to his conviction that she would, for whatever reason, eventually discover him to be a fraud and then abandon whatever it was they had going. A bad performance in the bedroom might accelerate that inevitability.

"You still want a drink?" he asked.

"Sure. What do we have?"

The suite was stocked. Not just a skimpy mini-bar with a few airplane sample bottles of alcohol, but a large cabinet overflowing with high quality brands of whiskey, vodka, gin and more. The two of them settled on a bottle of The Glenlivet single malt Scotch whiskey, which had apparently been aged for eighteen years. Zephyr hoped that meant it was good. He rounded up two whiskey glasses and poured until each was about a quarter full of the dark brown liquid. Then he handed Aurora a glass and sat down beside her.

"Thank you."

"Cheers," he said, clinked his glass against hers and then sipped. It hurt. His throat burned and he couldn't seem to get oxygen through. Aurora swallowed hers without any issue and giggled when she saw him wiping at his eyes.

"Have you ever gotten drunk before?" she asked, amused.

"Of course," he said. "I usually drink vodka, though. Never been a big Scotch guy." That was a half-truth. He had indeed tried vodka, but he was by no means familiar with it. He'd sampled it only twice before.

"We have vodka, dude. Get a bottle."

"No, it's OK. Just let me get a taste for this," he said, and sipped again. This time it went down a little smoother. Not to be outdone,

Aurora clinked her glass against his and then tipped it to her lips. This time she coughed and then gagged.

"Have you ever gotten drunk before?" he teased.

"Fair enough," she said, still wincing, and then cracked up. "OK, you're right. It's gross. I think I need a chaser if we're going to keep this up. You want one?"

"Oh God, yes."

She returned a moment later with two cold cans of Pepsi. Then she leaned over him and whispered, "Should we go into the other living room? Jordan can sleep and we can be a little louder."

"Yeah," he whispered back and then followed her through the living space, past the kitchen, and straight into another expansive room complemented by its own set of couches, chairs and television. He turned on the TV and cued the hotel's directory of channels, studied it and eventually found what he wanted. Then he punched in a number on the remote, the picture faded to black for a moment and just as he was about to change the channel, they heard it.

—pires walkin' through the valley, move west down Ventura Boulevard. And all the bad boys, are standing in the shadows. And all the good girls are home with broken hearts. And I'm freeeee! Free fallin'! Yeah I'm free! Free fallin'!

"How did you?" Aurora asked.

"They have satellite radio. Didn't think it would work, though." He was still amazed that it actually did. "Might be the same song for the next decade, but beggars can't be choosers."

So they sat down on the couch, poured shots, talked, asked questions and really listened, laughed, refilled empty glasses, stared at one another for a little too long, and repeated, as Tom Petty's heartbreak song played out over and over and over again around them. Not that it mattered. Not really. In fact, by their third refills, they found themselves singing along. Aurora choked up as she spoke about her dad. She told him she barely knew Sarah and felt horrible because she was glad it happened to the older lady and not her. Zephyr, of course, dismissed this, said there was nothing she could've done and that it was natural to feel as she did. She wondered if Sarah was all right now and admitted that she worried about her a lot. And he told her that he worried about everything. Her. Jordan. Yes, Sarah too. But also about all the things they couldn't possibly consider or predict.

"Everything out there," he said and nodded to the window.

Aurora sighed. "The hanging man."

"Yeah, pretty fucked up, right? We see a dead man—someone obviously murdered, right—and we drive on, and then go freakin' swimming. Like we're on vacation."

She nodded. "That's how it is now. Survive first, live after. You gotta take it where you can get it."

That rang true. It was precisely the way he existed; the way they all existed now. And he knew it was philosophically inverted to the way Merrick, Brad and Ben had viewed their continuation.

"Exactly," he said, nodding. "That's exactly right, Aurora. So fucking right."

She was smiling at him. "You're wasted, aren't you?"

"What? No."

She leaned and then pushed against him. "Yes, you are."

"No, seriously. Not wasted, but I definitely feel it. Don't even try to tell me you don't."

"I do," she admitted, and stared at him.

"What?"

"I don't know." She ran a hand through her dark hair and then concentrated on her lap. When she finally met his gaze again, it was fleeting.

"What?" he asked again.

"OK," she sighed. "Just... do you want to kiss me?"

"Yes," he said. "Pretty much always. But I'm drunk enough to know that if I start, I won't be able to stop. So maybe I shouldn't."

"Yeah, you shouldn't," she agreed, and smiled. "Stop, I mean."

So he kissed her. At first, small, and light, and then harder, wetter, longer. And it was far more intoxicating than any bottle of alcohol. Her body against his, her hot breath on him, his hands through her hair. Their exploratory touches and kisses quickly became desperate, frantic, feverish, and then his shirt was off, her robe pulled open, and he was on top of her.

"Should we..." He kissed her. "A bedroom?"

"No, no—we'll just be quiet, OK?" Then she pulled him closer and they said no more as Tom Petty waxed on from some faraway place that seemed to grow fainter at the speed of light.

I wanna glide down, over Mullholland. I wanna write her, name in the sky. I wanna free fall, out into nothin'. Gonna leave this, world for a while.

35
Answers

Los Angeles drivers didn't carpool, ever, and the resulting traffic never slept. Even during the late hours of the event, the streets were obviously a nightmare. They finally arrived at a pileup that stretched across the entirety of their passage and Zephyr understood that there would be no skirting it. In the distance, shiny buildings that reached skyward and a beautiful sunset so red and rich that it looked unnatural. It was. Aurora noted that the splendor was the result of the local smog, which hung in the air like some misty ghost waiting to pounce. There was something else, too. When his eyes fixated again on the picturesque scene, the blemishes bled back in. Some of those distant skyscrapers were damaged. Pieces missing. Like some gigantic monster took a bite out of them. It was the first time he had seen this kind of ruin for himself and it triggered both sadness and fear. It was all the proof that mankind's imprint was not so deep and everlasting but shallow and fragile— a smear that could be wiped away.

"Well," he said as he killed the ignition. "Santa Monica is straight that way. For another fifteen miles or so, from what I can tell. You guys want to take a hike?"

"Leave the car?" Aurora asked.

"Yeah." He nodded to the mess ahead of them. "No way we're

getting through in this thing. Maybe if we had some bikes. Maybe. But I'm not even sure about that. I think we're gonna have to climb over some of these crashes."

"Maybe if we climb the cars, we can steal a better one on the other side," Jordan offered. "Or maybe the traffic will get better."

"Good idea, Jord, but I wouldn't hold my breath. We're in the heart of Los Angeles here. If anything, I bet it gets worse." He sighed. After a minute's consideration he added, "OK. So here's what I propose. We either decide to get moving and make as much time as we can before the sun goes down—we probably have about forty-five minutes— or we just buckle down and camp here until morning. Then we can do the rest of the trip in daylight."

"There's no way we're going to make it all the way on foot before the sun goes down," Aurora said. "So what do you want to do when it's dark then? If we try to walk it right now, I mean."

He shrugged. "Find somewhere to go. I bet we can make it to the next off-ramp before sunset if we leave now. Then, we find the nearest place— hotel, house, whatever—

and hole up there for the night."

She nodded. "Yeah. Yeah, OK. That works."

"Jord, sound good?" he asked.

"Yep."

"Good. Let's move then."

They carried their guns, all of which were armed and ready should anybody spring upon them. And we know how to use them, assholes, Zephyr thought, so if you're out there and you've got any designs, stay the hell away.

Progress was a fight. Whenever they could, they maneuvered around the obstructions, but most of the time the collisions were widespread and couldn't be sidestepped. So they climbed over the cars and wrecks. The sun was their guide. It stayed with them, dipping ever lower, until at last it seemed to be level with the highway, and then its rays finally disintegrated and the sky glowed dark red before the blues and blacks of the night suffocated everything else. It was then that the three of them found themselves walking alongside an off-ramp toward La Brea Avenue.

"You see?" Aurora asked and he nodded.

It was several miles to the west. A single, brilliant light beamed straight up into the sky like a beacon. That appeared to be the point. There was no way of knowing for certain if it was a marker for Alpha, but it probably was. Smart, he thought. And they still have electricity. In fact, the entire city did, based on the glowing street lights and illuminated shops down the block.

"I think we're here—wherever here is," Aurora said.

They found a liquor store in shambles. Someone had stripped it of almost all snacks and drinks and then destroyed it for good measure. Shelving systems lay on their sides and all of the glass refrigerator doors were shattered. None of these details offered any reassurance. At least in New Mexico they could pillage without competition.

"Looks like about maybe ten more miles," he said, ignoring the destruction around them, and then showed the girls the map. He fingered a junction point. "That's where we are. And we want to follow this path until we get…" He traced Venice Boulevard until it dead-ended at the beach. "… right here."

"OK," Aurora said.

"Yeah. It should be a pretty easy trip, knock on wood."

He was about to ask if they wanted to complete the journey tonight when Aurora shushed him.

"Do you hear that?" she whispered.

He didn't, started to say so, and then he did. He cocked his head and stared into the night. Faint at first, but soon the thumping was unmistakable.

"Someone's blasting music," Jordan said, and Zephyr knew she was right.

"Follow me," he said.

The three of them hurried out the door and found a hiding spot behind a parking lot dumpster.

The music grew louder, stronger, and more recognizable. It was definitely a car stereo and the beat was rap of the old-school variety. Straight up gangsta rap. Deep bass and shallow lyrics, baby. The only words Zephyr could make out were f-bombs. Before long, the bass resonated through their parking lot and sent vibrations through anything that wasn't glued or nailed in place. When he tried to peek around the dumpster, he couldn't make out anything beyond headlights. And just as quickly as the music came upon them, it dulled and drifted into obscurity until only taillights gleamed a deep red from somewhere down the road.

"Well, then," Zephyr said as he pushed open the gates. "Have you guys decided what gang you want to join yet?"

"We have to join a gang?" Jordan asked.

Aurora punched his arm. "No, don't listen to him, Jord. He's just being an ass."

"How do you know? That might've been the mayor of Alpha."

"Shut up," she said, still smiling.

"All right, first things first." He turned to Jordan. "Can you run back inside and look for any leftover snacks? Candy bars, chips—anything you can find? I just want to make sure we have plenty to eat. And while you're doing that, we'll figure out our next move."

"Yep," she said and then started for the store.

When Zephyr felt she was far enough away from them, he pulled Aurora closer and whispered, "So, no way they were friendly, right?"

She raised an eyebrow and stared at him. "Not that I disagree, but why do you say that?"

"Oh, I dunno. The whole *Fuck the Police* vibe ain't great, but blasting music like that seems like they're daring someone to try something. I got the impression they're looking for a fight."

She considered this for a moment and then nodded. "Yeah, I agree. So what do we do? Should we just find a place now? I don't think we should be out and about."

"On the one hand, yes, I like the idea of finding a safe place to sleep. On the other hand, though, are we really better off traveling by day? I'm not so sure. At least at night, we'll be able to hide, ya know?"

"In other words, you want to keep going."

"Well, no," he said. "I mean, I don't know. I think it's worth contemplating, that's all. We have our guns and we have the element of surprise. So if we do this now, we stay out of the light and we just keep moving toward the beach. We see any cars or people, we hightail it to a hiding spot."

"And what if we can't?"

He raised his weapon. "Hopefully, that won't happen, but that's why we have these."

"Jesus, Zephyr. I don't want to get in a shoot-out here."

"Neither do I." He put his arms around her and kissed the side of her head. "We won't. We'll be careful. All I'm saying is, if we have to, we use these." Then he cupped her cheek with one hand. "Aurora. Promise me. Whether we travel tonight or tomorrow. Shit goes down, we use these. Do you promise?"

She nodded. "Yeah, I promise."

Jordan returned a few minutes later with a packet of gum, an energy bar, a torn bag of stale pretzels and a few cans of Mountain Dew. "Found these in the back," she said and held up a can. "They're warm. Still good, though."

The streets watched as the three of them moved with measured stealth across dirty sidewalks and past sketchy shops. Every so often,

Zephyr or Aurora would stop and stare into the distance for something that never came or listen for something that never sounded, and then they would resume their silent trek. The wind bloomed beyond whispers to a regular breeze as they passed city blocks and drew closer to the unseen ocean. Their voyage stretched on forever—not minutes, but hours, with every gambled intersection a lesson in slow torture and a test of their collective determination.

Alpha wouldn't be difficult to find, at least. The spotlight still shone, not just a lighthouse for the ghost ships at its back, but a signal to everyone on land near and far. *Here we are. All you have to do is come.* Zephyr couldn't believe they were finally almost there. Would these people really have the answers? Even some of them? If they'd travelled all this way and endured all they had to hear another story about the Rapture, he thought he might be sick.

When at last they were close enough to hear the crashing of waves against sand and rock, they saw it. Two gray buildings, the tallest of which stood maybe a dozen stories, tethered together by a suspended walkway. Aurora pointed out that a handful of armed soldiers peppered the perimeter of the lowest roof and before Zephyr could process the information, an amplified voice boomed into the night.

"We see you there—don't move!" He searched for the source of the voice but couldn't find it. "Repeat: Do not move. We have our weapons locked on you now."

Jordan's hand found Zephyr's and she started to say something before he quieted her. "It's OK," he told her loud enough so that Aurora could hear. "Let's do as they ask."

Soon after, the glass double-door's comprising the building's entrance swung open and out piled several more figures, all dressed in casual clothes and armed with rifles. Two men, three women. It was still impossible to make out age. Zephyr lowered his gun to the ground, kicked it away, threw up his hands and told the girls to do the same. A man and woman approached them, their weapons still aimed. Surprisingly, he wasn't afraid. True, this wasn't the welcome party he'd hoped for, but this had to be the people of Alpha, and surely they would be friendly. Eventually. He hoped.

"Good evening," the woman said.

Her hair, cropped and hot pink, was as short as she was. Zephyr could make out the dark imprint of a tattoo on her neck, but couldn't tell what it was. She looked him over, nodded to her partner, himself a lanky man with long hair, and said, "My name's Catherine. My friend here is Pan. You're all gonna take three big steps backward and he's gonna walk over and take those guns. If you do anything except watch, I'll have to shoot you. Now, I really don't want to do that, and I'm pretty sure you don't want me to do that. So let's agree to work together on this, shall we?"

"We agree," Aurora said.

Zephyr stepped backward. "We do. But, those guns do belong to us. I'd appreciate it if we got them back at some point."

"We'll see about that. One thing at a time," the girl replied. "What's your name?"

He told her.

She surveyed Aurora and Jordan. "And you two?"

They told her.

"Why are you here?"

"That depends," Zephyr said. "Is here… Alpha?"

"Yes, it is," she responded. "So you saw the message then." This wasn't a question so much as a confirmation.

As her partner stood guard, she spoke into her walkie-talkie and nodded to nobody. After a minute of imperceptible chatter, she said, "Yup, out," and turned back to them.

"Where you coming from?" she asked.

"We're a bit scattered," Zephyr admitted. "But we happened upon your posting while we were in New Mexico, so I guess you could say we're from there."

"Oh? Well that makes you three our farthest travelers yet then."

She studied them a moment. "So listen, I'm not particularly proud of our meet and greet here, but as I'm sure you know, there's lots of bad news out there and it pays to be careful. I know you've got questions. Come on inside and we'll see if we can answer some of them."

She waved the rest of her party over and made perfunctory introductions. Then she turned back to them. "Now, I like you three already, but that doesn't mean I trust you just yet. Pan here is gonna follow behind us in case you're thinking about trying anything you shouldn't. I assume we're not gonna have any problems."

"You assume correctly," Zephyr said.

"Good. When we get to the entrance, we're gonna pat you down and then you'll be allowed to enter with me." Satisfied that they understood, she started off.

Half an hour later, the three of them found themselves at the head of a long marble table in some conference room, only the flicker of the fluorescents to keep them company. It might have been any meeting area in any office building across the country, but there were no real windows and the door locked from the outside. There was, however, an approximation of a window cut into one wall and adorned with black glass. A focus group test center turned interrogation room.

"Well, this is fun. So now what?" Aurora asked.

"We wait. Not much else to do." He turned to Jordan and stroked the little girl's hair. "How you holding up, kid?"

"Good. I hope these people are nice."

"I think they are," Zephyr said.

"I have to say, this isn't what I was expecting," Aurora began. "I mean, I don't know what I was expecting, to be honest, but it wasn't this."

"Hippies and cornfields?" Zephyr mused.

"Maybe." She smiled. "I sort of... yes, actually. Hippies and cornfields."

"Maybe that's how they started, but someone probably came along and shot them and burned the fields. And here we are," he said. It was a joke, but Aurora definitely didn't get it, or if she did, she didn't like it, so he added, "Or I don't know— maybe the hippies and cornfields are in the back?"

Just then, the lock turned, the door opened and in came four people, their pink-haired escort the only recognizable figure in the group. Zephyr braced himself for old men and women in lab coats, military garb, or both, and was instead greeted by civilians in daywear, all of whom looked to be in their twenties save one. A single man and three women, counting Catherine.

The man was easily the oldest of the assembly. He was short, bald, with tanned skin, a small nose adorned with glasses and eyes as unrevealing as the window behind him. He was well groomed, his black hair shaven, his nails trimmed. He took a seat at the table next to Zephyr and smiled.

"My name is Alec," he said with the thinnest of accents. Middle Eastern. "To my left is Janis and to her left is Karen. Nice to make your acquaintance." The man extended his hand and Zephyr shook it.

"You're probably wondering what's going on, who we are, what our purpose is, and so forth, and we will, of course, get to that in due time. But first, we have to ask you some questions. Will this be all right?"

Zephyr Nodded. "Sure." Both Aurora and Jordan replied in turn.

"Good. We understand you journeyed from New Mexico to find us. Why?"

"Well, New Mexico was beginning to run its course. But mostly because you said you have some answers," Zephyr said.

"And why do you carry your weapons?"

Was this a trick question? Zephyr glanced at Aurora. "For protection."

The man locked eyes with him. "Mr. Zephyr, have you engaged in warfare with anybody since the disappearances?"

He asked in the nonchalant tone of a man querying about the time of day, and yet Zephyr felt the weight of the question.

"Engaged in warfare? What… I don't understand. What does this have to do with anything?" he asked in return. "We've traveled halfway across the country to find you. Look at us. We're a couple of teenagers and a little girl. What do you think we are?"

The man's face showed nothing. He could've bluffed anyone in Vegas. "I ask you again. Have you engaged in warfare? It is a simple question."

"Well then, no. My simple answer is no. I have protected myself. And these two—they've never even used their guns."

"Please explain how you protected yourself," the man said.

"What does it matter?"

"Humor me."

The boy sighed. "Fine. Sure. Whatever." He met the man's gaze. "I've protected myself. That's all I've ever done." And so he began, first recounting his friendship with Ross and what came after, and next with the story of the twins and the nightmare scenario that followed. Although the retelling was summarized, he touched upon all the major events, omitting none of the incriminations. When he was done, he met the man's eyes. "That enough for you?"

"Yes, that'll be enough, Alec. Thank you," said the blonde woman. He thought her name was Janis.

"Very well." Alec rose, thanked Zephyr for his candor, and bid them farewell.

"You might have lied, you know. Why didn't you?" the woman asked. Her blonde hair was pulled back into a tight pony tail that revealed a pale, bony face. Not anorexic, but in the neighborhood.

"What the hell is the point of this, anyway? If I murdered someone, I'm unfit for your little city, is that it?"

When she didn't answer, his anger surged. "I woke up one morning and my parents were gone. The first person I met was a psychopath and the second was a sweet little girl. None of us know what the hell is going on. We're just trying to survive like everyone else. But I'm not a murderer, so if that's not good enough for you, you can go screw yourself. How's that? I'm done answering these questions."

She stared back at him in silence and after an awkward moment, she finally asked, "Feel better?"

"Not really."

"I admire your tenacity, Zephyr. I do. But you've come to our house, so show a little respect for our process. We are here to determine if you belong in one or another group of post-apocalypse survivors." She found his eyes and nodded. "As you said, one is allowed entry into our community. The other is not."

The woman clasped her hands together and let them fall back into her lap. "May I continue now?"

He shrugged.

"You said it yourself. You met a psychopath. And then you met a sweet girl." She looked at Jordan and smiled. "Thankfully, girls like her have never proven uncommon, but the other kind—

the aggressive, the violent, the sociopathic, the altogether deranged, these are, shall we say, less prevalent in modern society. So don't you find it a little odd that in this new world with such a dwindled population, the first man you encountered fit the latter bill and not the former?"

"I'm not sure," he said. It wasn't a lie.

"What if I told you that everyone living today could be categorized into non-aggressive or aggressive, non-violent or violent, empath or sociopath or worse yet, psychopath?" she asked. "The old man you met. The slave men who killed your friends. Whoever hung that dead body at the state limit. I can cite dozens more examples from my own experiences."

"I would ask, what are you getting at?"

She smiled. "Well, first off, I'm letting you know officially that I don't think you're a sociopath, and second, that you, Aurora and Jordan are welcome here. Third, I'm sorry that you don't appreciate the way we came about this, but I assure you that it is a necessary part of our process—a process developed over months and not unscathed by serious setbacks. Mishaps that we are hopeful shall never be repeated."

"Thank you," Zephyr said, and relaxed a little. "Look, I'm really sorry. I know I went on the defensive there, but I just felt like I was being attacked. Trust me when I say that we all understand that you need to be careful."

"Yes, and we all appreciate that you are allowing us to stay," Aurora added.

Janis flashed a genuine smile. "We are happy to have good people. We frankly need all the good people we can get."

"Your website called Alpha a city, but from what I can tell, it's more of a compound. No offense intended," Zephyr said.

"None taken," she said and laughed. "Yeah, we get that a lot. I think it's important to remember that Alpha is just the beginning of something bigger." She nodded at her companion. "It's already grown so much. Not long ago, it was just us. Karen here is my younger sister."

Sister? Another sibling. How was this possible? It had to be more than just coincidence. There was a resemblance, but the similarity pronounced itself only now that the two of them confirmed the relation. Her hair was a little darker, her features smoother, and her voice softer.

"When the world ended," Janis continued, "I was in San Francisco and she was down here. I made the journey to find her and then we were two. We met some good people, and then we met some bad people. It was after the bad ones that we realized we needed to band together with the good."

"We stayed in my apartment for weeks," her sister added.

"By chance, one morning while I was out scavenging the grocery stores for water—this was shortly after the pipes ran dry here—I met a man named Trey Sorrenson. Then we were three. And Trey, well he's one of the great ones. A former engineer. He changed everything for us."

"Yahoo," Karen added.

"That's how we got the website, and that's when it came together. It's only been a couple months since then, but we've grown from two to three to dozens and now hundreds. We've taken over a city block. We've got smart people working on big problems and we've got an army so that we can protect our own."

"We may not yet be a full-fledged city, but I'm guessing we're the closest thing left. In fact, we might represent the largest community of humans alive. And we're growing every day," Karen said.

Hundreds of people. Compared to the former population, it was a microscopic figure, but none of them had seen more than a few survivors at a time in months.

"What kind of big problems are you working on, if you don't mind me asking?" Aurora asked.

"The obvious ones, for starters. Clean water and sustainable food. To that end, we've tapped back into the city's water supply. It's not what it used to be, but we're able to purify it. We've been sending parties out to the purification plants to gather intelligence on automation and we think we're getting closer. In the meantime, we do it manually, and it takes some time, but it works. Food is harder. We've got storage units full of canned goods and freezers packed with perishables, but frankly our system isn't yet sustainable. That's why we're remaking the landscape—doing away with the old roads and planting for the future."

"Why not just move to farmland?" Zephyr asked.

Janis leaned back in her chair. "That has its own set of issues. Water supply is harder. Electrical is a joke. And we'd lose access to the benefits of the city. There are dangers, yes, but we have strength in numbers and more often than not we can still find what we need here, whether it's Internet access for guidance—and believe me, that alone is worth it—gasoline for generators or access to medical supplies. On top of everything else, we already have the structural facilities to support a growing community here. The more people who join us, the more buildings we occupy. Out in the middle of nowhere, we'd have to build, and we're not there yet."

"Sounds pretty smart," Aurora said.

"Thank you, Aurora. Like I said, though, those are the obvious ones. We also want to unravel what exactly happened to cause the disappearances. And why the people left are the way they are."

So they didn't really know what happened, Zephyr thought. "Why the people are the way they are?"

"Yes. We touched on this earlier, Zephyr. Empath or sociopath. All of us at this table, and the hundreds more in our community, fall into the former. Let me ask you something. Have you ever been so angry that you just wanted to punch something or someone?"

"Sure," Zephyr acknowledged.

"What stopped you?"

"I don't know," he said and shrugged. "I guess I just realized that it wasn't going to help."

"Yes, but that is cognitive reasoning and cognitive control at work. Self-control, in other words, not to mention a dash of social conscience. You are able to imagine the worst, but you respect the boundaries between imagination and reality." She surveyed the entire group. "The differences between us and the outsiders is that we possess those cognitive resources and they do not, but more importantly, they are dangerous on top of it all. These are people who may feign normal behavior but when pushed, they will throw cognitive reasoning out the window and turn instead to ultra-aggressive behavior without consideration of the consequences. Not just prone to violence, but underneath it all, violent."

Aurora looked at Zephyr and then back to Janis. "I'm sorry. Huh?"

"I think I see," the boy said.

"But I'm not sure that you do," Janis replied. "It has never been so black and white. Not before. The spectrum was a long, stretching gradient. You might have been cognitively able and still sociopathic. Or maybe lacking full self-control but just a pain in the ass. A child throwing a tantrum, not a serial killer. You understand? But this is not so today." She locked eyes with them. "In our experience so far, everyone – every single person we've met—leans hard into one group or the other."

"OK, you're right. I'm actually not so sure I understand what you're getting at here," Zephyr said.

"I definitely don't," Aurora agreed.

"Imagine," replied Karen, "that the world is a chess board. Now how might the game change if someone removed all the pieces except for the two kings? On one side, white. On the other, black."

Goose-bumps raced along Zephyr's flesh. "Good and bad. That is what you're saying."

Karen spread her hands in acknowledgement. "Yes. Polar opposites. First and last. Beginning and end. Alpha and Omega."

"And make no mistake—this is chess," her sister said. "The disappearances are not randomized. Someone or something has methodically set up the board."

"So Janis believes, anyway. We don't know that. Not for sure, anyway. What we do know is that everyone alive today— good or bad, empath or sociopath, however you want to define us —— we all share something in common."

"What?" Zephyr asked.

She smiled. "Come on. I want to you to meet someone."

Janis, Karen and Catherine led them into a large lobby appointed with a series of impressionistic paintings depicting beaches, sunsets, shells or fish. Zephyr thought it odd to decorate in this fashion when tourists could see everything in these prints and more by walking outside.

"This main building is home to all of our amenities," Janis explained, making mock quotations with her fingers to emphasize the last word. "Restaurants turned into kitchens and cafeterias on the first floor. Outside, the pool, which is used far less for swimming than it is community bathing, although it's still a hit with the kids. The second-floor gym has been converted into a training center for our soldiers. The equipment is still there for those who want to use it, but there are also weapons and melee instruction, which Cat can tell you about when we're done here."

"Happy to," the pink-haired woman said.

Janis continued, "The third floor used to feature meeting rooms, but we tore down the walls and set up our operations. That's where we're headed now."

"What's in the other building?" Aurora asked.

"Just people. How many now, Kar?"

"Well, we have 350 rooms, every one of them occupied with at least two people."

"Wow—sounds like business is booming," Aurora joked. "So when you say Alpha houses hundreds, we're really talking closer to a thousand?"

"We're just about there, yeah. Partly why we've needed to expand. We're out of room."

In the elevator, Aurora's hand found his and she smiled. Zephyr took Jordan's in his other. For the first time in a very long while, he felt like he had family and community — at least, the closest to both these days. It certainly didn't hurt that the simple action of riding an elevator was as much a part of the old world as fast food and amusement parks.

The doors parted to reveal a vast, open floor gutted of nearly all extravagance. The marble tiles of the lobby were gone. Whatever material had covered the floors previously had been stripped away until only chalky gray cement remained. Thick, round pillars of concrete, chipped and cracked, extended from floor to ceiling at regular intervals, the only architectural obstruction between the elevator and enormous windows that gazed forever upon the forgotten sea. The space was huge. The size of an underground parking lot. Which, come to think of it, was exactly what it looked like. However, this facade was shattered the minute Zephyr glanced up, for those same crystal chandeliers hung from a ceiling covered in an oily mural of angels and horses flying across a wispy cloudscape.

Great, stretching portions of the space were empty, but a conglomerate of oak desks, with just as many computers and monitors, laptops, television sets, and other mystery mechanisms, was positioned at the center. Medical machinery rested in one corner. And wires of all kinds ran in every direction. At least a dozen people sat before monitors peppered throughout the space.

"As you can see, we keep a steady eye on our perimeter, but also the outlying buildings and city blocks. Anybody steps within a mile of us, and we'll see them coming. We saw you folks sneaking around about an hour before our shooters stopped you. We can also see and communicate with those manning our expansion units from here. And there's plenty more, from research to outreach," she said, waving a hand at the desks. Then she pointed to the medical configuration. "And that's where we're headed, but first, you need to understand why."

She turned around again and motioned for someone to come. A man with the thickest beard Zephyr had ever seen — it seemed to consume his face — hurried over. Zephyr could see immediately that this one would never bald. He wore a dark t-shirt stretched over a protruding potbelly. There was no way to judge his age. He might've been in his late twenties or early forties.

"This is Carl," she said, grasping the man's shoulder. "Say hi, Carl."

"Hi, Carl," the man said, and smiled.

"Before the disappearances, Carl worked at a laundry mat. Afterward, Carl made the single most important discovery about the disappearances."

The man shook his head. "She makes this introduction every time and every time I say that it was dumb, stupid luck."

"And every time I respond that luck may have played its part, but that it was his intuition that got the ball rolling." She faced the group again. "Everyone who comes into our community meets me, Karen and Carl. After, we'll draw your blood, but I'll let Carl explain why."

"Sure. Sure," Carl started. "So, the little one is probably a little too, uh, little, but how many of you use computers — or used them?"

"I know how to use a computer," Jordan interjected, clearly cross with his presumption.

"I'm sorry. I'm sure that you do."

"We're all pretty familiar with them, I think," Zephyr said.

"Good. Good. So hold on, I'm getting ahead of myself. As you know, Janis and Karen are sisters and yet they're both still here. This strikes you as odd given how few of us are around and about these days, yes?"

The three of them nodded in unison, Jordan mostly to be polite.

"Yes, well it struck me as odd, too, when I first met them some months ago. So I started to think about how that could be, and it occurred to me, as I'm sure it has to you, that we survivors must share something in common. And that maybe Janis and Karen could simply tell me what that something was because they both had it."

"Which is when the questions began," Karen interrupted.

Carl smiled again, pearly white teeth engulfed by beard. "Yes, I know. How many times must I apologize?"

Karen's voice deepened in mock impression. "Let me see the color of your eyes. Do you have any birthmarks? What about genetic defects? Are you diabetic?"

"Well, it's a needle in a haystack," he said.

"What do computers have to do with it?" Zephyr asked.

"Oh, right, well that is how I explain it, that's all. And actually it might be a bad analogy here because you're all pretty young. But anyway, I love computers. Always have. When I was younger, I used to program in Q Basic, which is useless today. Anyway, this was before and during Windows. First, we used Microsoft DOS and then we shell—"

"You're going way off the path here, Carl," Janis interrupted.

The man snorted. "Sorry."

"Blood type," she reminded him.

"Sure, sure, that first. So how many of you know what blood type you are?" he asked and then raised a hand. "Now don't tell me what it is if you do."

"I do," Aurora said.

Zephyr had no idea. Neither did Jordan.

Carl turned to Aurora, whose face showed skepticism, and said, "You're AB negative."

The revelation wiped her expression clean. "How?" she asked, clearly astonished. "And... yes."

"It's not a lucky guess. We all are," he said and nodded toward

Zephyr and Jordan. "You as well. Everyone on this floor. Everyone still breathing oxygen on this planet, in fact. It's at least one trait that all of us share. And very likely the reason we're still here."

"So the set up over there," Janis said. "That's where we confirm everybody is AB negative. And everybody is. Hundreds tested. There's nobody here who isn't."

"It was when I started to think about myself, and what I might share in common with Janis and Karen, that I hit upon blood type," Carl said. "I knew I was AB negative and I knew it was rare — although, just how rare, I had no idea. So eventually my questions turned to blood type and that's how we hit upon it. Later, we secured the equipment to test it and that's when we confirmed it."

"I seem to remember us getting pretty drunk after that," Karen said.

"I'm glad one of us can remember," her sister joked.

"Do you know how many people in the United States are AB negative?" Carl asked. When nobody answered, he continued. "Well, it's different in Caucasians, Hispanics, etcetera, but we whiteys are the most likely to have this blood type. And we max out at one percent. Let me just say that again. One percent of the population, at best. And more likely, something like half that considering all the different makeups of people."

"Wow," Aurora said.

"Yeah, that about sums it up," the man agreed. "Now, if you do the math, and I have, you start with roughly 300 million people here. And by here, I mean America, of course. Then you do away with all the other blood types—all the variants of Os, and As, both of them more prevalent—you exclusively use Caucasians as the high, and you've got maybe three million folks left across the country. But that's not accurate, either, because America isn't just comprised of whites, and the number happens to be considerably less for everyone else. Only 0.3 percent of African Americans are AB negative. It's 0.2 percent for

Hispanics. And 0.1 percent for Asians."

"Thank you, Internet," Karen joked.

"Well, no, seriously, you're right," Carl agreed. "We had to put this together from nothing and without that kind of resource at our fingertips, we'd be in a much darker spot than we are. Granted, we've got a long way to go."

"So if three million isn't an accurate figure, what's your best estimate?" Zephyr asked.

"Maybe a million. Maybe a million and a half, tops, but I'd bet against that. I'm thinking it's less than a million. Not just because of the dwindled numbers when you consider whites versus everybody else, but because I suspect many of the survivors earned themselves very short-term leases on life. Accidents. Suicides."

He shielded his face from Jordan, and mouthed "murders."

"The general inability to survive under the circumstances. You three are young and able, but how many aren't? And then there is still the X factor, some intangible genetic code that we can't possibly ever identify which somehow categorizes people into empath or sociopath, good or bad. Or so we like to theorize, anyway. If that's locked away somewhere within us, nobody's ever found it, to my knowledge. Supposing we accept that we survivors are somehow marked with that cellular zero or one, if you will, then anybody who fell into the gray zone might have disappeared even if they were AB negative."

"Let me translate to English," Karen interjected. "If your blood is AB negative, you don't disappear. We think. Then we have a theory—my sister does, really—that all the survivors are either good or bad based on some unknown factor. If you're in the gray zone — you're a selfish asshole, but you're not gonna kill someone — we think you disappear, so that takes away a lot more folks. Those of us left are AB negative and lean hard into the empath or sociopath categories."

"And it's a test," Janis said. "Or a game."

Zephyr nodded. "But you don't really have any evidence of that."

She ignored the question. "Let me ask you this. After our little interrogation, if we had turned you away, what would you have done?"

"What do you mean?" the boy asked.

"I mean just that, what would you have done?"

He thought about it. "I don't know. I'd have been pretty peeved, I guess."

"I can answer this one," Aurora said. "We'd have flipped you guys a big bird and been on our way. Maybe to Disneyland, actually."

The woman laughed at this. "Yes, and that would be perfectly reasonable behavior. I could understand that. But you see, we only turn the bad ones away, and they always resort to violence." She studied them a moment. "Always."

"How so?" Zephyr asked.

"Oh, you name it. Try to fight us, stab us, shoot us. Worse. It's all happened."

"Which is why we keep their weapons now," her sister said.

"Not sure that's really proof of it," Aurora remarked. "We'd be severely pissed if you took our weapons, too."

Zephyr considered it and agreed, of course, but he also thought that fear would outweigh anger. Stripped of their weapons out here, they'd be defenseless, and he figured their first course of action would be to find a safe haven, not retaliate.

"We always explain to everyone why we're turning them away and keeping their weapons," Carl clarified. "We do actually try to reason with them. We do. Believe me on this. And this is why I think there is something to the theory Janis puts forth. They simply cannot be reasoned with. I really cannot overstate this. Those turned away are always violent."

"If that's true, then every time you turn someone out, you're creating an enemy," Zephyr said.

Karen nodded. "Yeah. Hence the protection."

Zephyr turned back to Carl. "Sorry, what do computers have to do with it?"

"We almost made it," Janis sighed.

"Ah, the analogy," Carl continued. "Like I was saying before, I grew up dabbling in the era of DOS and then Windows. Back in the DOS days, we had a command we used to batch rid ourselves of unnecessary files. Delete star-dot-whatever. So, if I wanted to delete all the text files in a directory, I'd simply type delete star-dot-t-x-t and all the text files in the directory would be erased in one fell swoop. You understand?"

"Not. At. All," said Aurora.

Carl chuckled. "I'm sorry. I'm not really great at this stuff." He ran his hand through his thick beard and continued. "So, imagine you have a bunch of photos in a folder on Windows. But in the same folder, you also have a bunch of Microsoft Word documents. Now, let's say you went in there, drag-and-dropped all your photos to the trashcan but kept the documents. You follow me?"

"Um," Aurora said.

"OK, sorry. Like I said, bad analogy, but that's the best I can come up with." He looked around the room and then spread his arms wide. "I think that's basically what happened to all of us. To everyone. To mankind. Something selectively deleted our asses. Or drag-and-dropped us to the trashcan, so to speak. You see? You, me, Zephyr, everyone in this room, everyone still alive. We're the leftover documents."

He looked over the table. "Now, I pose a question to you. Are we all still here by accident or on purpose?"

36
Gray

Jordan's dresser was overflowing with clothes. Gowns and dresses of all varieties. Jeans, corduroy, spandex, and sweats in multiple colors. Jackets, hoodies, long-sleeves, and T-shirts. No shortage of choice — a definite perk of growing up in a city short on children, not on children's clothes. So why was choosing her outfit every morning such a battle?

"I don't want this one," she whined one daybreak after he tossed an orange hoodie to her and asked her to get ready for lessons.

"Fine, I don't care. Pick another then. But hurry up or you're gonna be late."

"I want you to help pick."

"I tried, Jordan. Either put on the hoodie or dress yourself. I'll see what I can find for breakfast." He could hear the steady rhythm of water as Aurora showered in the nearby bathroom. "Figure it out."

Figuring it out was what they did these days. In the four months since they had moved into the apartment, they'd developed a clumsy routine. Wake up, scramble toward some goal, make it somewhere, do something, and then race back and pass out before starting the process again. Jordan's something was lessons, which was the closest thing to school in the aftermath of the disappearances. An elderly woman named Mrs. Brackle taught her and nine other kids ranging in ages from five to twelve about reading, writing, math, and the world around them. Much to Zephyr's surprise and frustration, there was no sugarcoating the latter topic, as he learned when Jordan returned from lessons one day and announced that her teacher said her mother was probably dead.

"OK, it's harsh. But I don't know—it's probably for the best," Aurora said when he told her about it.

"For whose best? Hers? Why take away hope here? She's a little kid."

"I know that. But we're not living in a world with Santa Claus and the Tooth Fairy any more. I get that you want to keep the magic, Zeph, but it's not doing her any good."

"Easy for you to say," he muttered.

"What's that supposed to mean?"

"Nothing."

She stared at him, her hands on her hips.

"It means," he said, and then lowered his voice, "that you're not the one who has to answer her at bedtime when she asks if her mom might still be alive despite what her damned careless teacher said." He shook his head and sighed. "Listen, I'm sorry. I'm just tired."

"I get it," Aurora said and kissed his cheek. "I'm sorry, too. How about we both get one be-an-insensitive-dick pass today, OK? I gotta go."

They were both scouts, but they never ventured out together. If Aurora was scheduled for a city search one day, Zephyr stayed back at base and either subbed in as monitor or spent the day in weapons practice. And if he was on reconnaissance, she remained and found something equally important to do with her time. Although it was never discussed, there was unspoken logic to this methodology, which was that one of them must always survive for Jordan's sake.

Zephyr hurried the little girl to lessons, kissed her goodbye and then rode the elevator up to their palatial estate on the seventh-floor. What a joke that was. The room couldn't have been larger than 450 square feet and the living space was singular. No bedroom. A microwave and a tiny sink comprised the entirety of the kitchen. The bathroom barely fit one. Compared to the mansion they seized back in Las Cruces, this was a dollhouse. Still, they had neighbors, which meant people, conversation, friends and colleagues, community, and therefore the gains were considerable. Living on the outside had its advantages, but when darkness came, so always did the fear. And it was a relief to fall into a comfortable sleep at night. To feel protected. Besides, Janis promised more expansion soon and said they would be at the top of a short list for suites, possibly even one of the penthouses in the high-rise across the street, because they cared for one of Alpha's children. It couldn't happen soon enough.

Deployment was in two hours, which meant he had the room to himself. He considered a return to sleep or masturbation and dismissed both. Instead, he changed into dirty sweats and then made his way down to the gym, which was crowded despite the disappearances. Some things never changed. The facilities, stretched across an entire floor, were divided into two unique spaces. The first looked like a regular gym complete with free weights and resistance machines. The second was a wide-open section covered in dark rubber floors populated by several sparring rings.

He spent an hour alternating between jumping jacks, push-ups, planks, and push-up side-planks. When he had first started this routine more than a month before, he could only do 30 push-ups and not even 10 push-up side-planks. Now he could easily bark out 80 and 30 respectively. In fact, even after three or four repetitions, his lows were superior to his previous highs. His arms and chest burned and sweat dripped and fell while he gritted through his makeshift program and he finally understood the adrenaline rush that came with regular exercise.

He'd been a skinny little runt before the disappearances. In the aftermath, a combination of forced diet and pure survival had turned him wiry, and he'd developed, shot up and filled out. Now, coupled with his regular exercise, his muscles announced themselves with definition and he stood tall. Taller, even, than Aurora, who now cocked her head skyward to kiss him.

A little while later, with a fresh shower and clothes to boot, Zephyr stopped into the weapons unit and signed out a .30-30 rifle complete with shoulder strap. This was a luxury afforded him after a three-week firearms course piloted by a beer-bellied black man nicknamed Heffer. With all of his previous practice, Zephyr was a natural, and whizzed through the program in five days flat, an accomplishment that he brandished to Aurora whenever possible because she still hadn't passed and could therefore only carry a revolver into the field.

Trey Sorrenson was the engineer who hijacked Yahoo and transformed it into an advertisement for Alpha. He was a big deal around the upstart city because he was one of the few names Janis and Karen dropped to newcomers. Although the leadership was informal, if there existed an executive branch, he would have made the board at the very least, which is why it made perfect sense that nobody wanted him on the survey teams. No man or woman was expendable, they said, but post-disappearances or not, a good engineer was not someone you just pissed away, especially if he was a celebrity in his own right. Trey was either the most naive and oblivious person still alive, or he just didn't care, because the man volunteered for every scouting exercise that opened up.

"Well, well, well," he said as Zephyr entered the deployment center's grungy locker room. "Look who's finally here. It really is nice of you to show up."

He was a short, lean man in his mid-twenties with a pale complexion and cropped brown hair, and he always seemed to be grinning. The two of them had bonded right away on a mission three months before when, while waiting for a team to return from an inspection, Trey asked Zephyr if he liked to play video games. That was all it took. A few hours later, the two of them had discussed, dissected and debated the finer points of the Metroid Prime trilogy, a Nintendo first-person adventure series starring heroine space bounty hunter Samus Aran. Trey argued that Metroid Prime 2 was the best game of the bunch because it was far and away the most difficult and therefore most rewarding, while Zephyr contended that the first was revolutionary and had superior pacing. By the time the conversation concluded, they were officially friends.

Zephyr made a mock glance at his watch. "Yup. Right on time, as usual."

"The late time, maybe."

"Maybe you should spend more time hacking second-rate search engines and less time worrying about me."

Trey rolled his eyes. "Pioneering search engines, you mean."

"Just because a search engine was last relevant during the era of pioneers doesn't make it pioneering."

"All right, that wasn't bad. I'll give you that," the man conceded. "You're still a Google-loving bitch, though."

"Where we going today? You hear anything yet?" Zephyr asked as he sat down on a bench next to his friend and opened his locker.

"Nada. Fifteen of us, though. Roderick is on point."

Spencer Roderick was a bald Latino man in his fifties or sixties. His skin looked like worn leather and the palms of his hands were so calloused they might've been rock. He was also ultra-conservative and easily spooked, which annoyed Zephyr.

"Short trip out today, I guess," he sighed.

"Uh-huh."

Thirty minutes later, Zephyr and Trey bounced up and down from the bed of a rusty pickup as it jostled along Santa Monica's famous 2nd Street. Two more trucks held ten others, everybody armed. Today, they were scheduled to hit a row of restaurants in search of salvageable food or drink and likewise any bars or taverns that might still hold alcohol, which was always at the top of the pedestrian most wanted lists.

He found nature's reclamation of the world astonishing. A year after mankind's near-extinction, the streets and sidewalks of Santa Monica were cracked and freckled with protruding weeds and grass. Windows broken everywhere, some clearly because of vines and vegetation that lay in wait of its chance to thrive again. Much of the foliage was thick and foreign to Zephyr. These days, he saw squirrels, rats, scrawny dogs and stray cats scattered about the grid, which didn't seem extraordinary. They were always city-dwellers, he told himself, even if their numbers were greater than ever. Deer, however, were not, and when he first glimpsed a doe as it dashed and then leapt across a major thoroughfare, it was equal parts astounding and surreal.

The streets still held cars. Some sat dormant in front of parking meters that would never be ticketed again. Others were scattered about the lanes, leftover blockades for the new world commuter. And yet many of the roads had already been cleared by Alpha cleaning crews, whose purpose was to tow away the remnants and harness whatever they could.

The trucks rolled to a stop outside of a mall on 2nd Street somewhere between Colorado and Broadway. Modern, beautiful, more sophisticated than any retail outlet had any right to be, and even a little ostentatious. It was called *The Market*, and he wasn't sure if a grocery store was actually part of the attraction, or just a conglomerate of restaurants and shops. There'd likely be surplus either way, and it was large enough that the potential gain was definitely worth the risk.

"All right," Roderick said as he hauled himself down from one of the beds. "Team two surveys today." He pointed to Zephyr's group. "Get a move on. All five of you in. Start at the base, work your way up. Verify your communications, people. I want status checks every forty-five seconds."

He turned to the two other trucks. "You five—take the premises and set up a defense. Look for high-ground advantages— get your snipers there. The rest of you, across the street," he said and waved them away. This was the typical formation: an equal split of "men in, men on, and men out," as Roderick defined it. The strategy was sound. Send a small group in to search while another held the defense of the building. The final unit was to be hidden nearby where it could surround and ambush any attackers.

Zephyr, Trey, Miles, Shannon, and Rudy comprised the scout unit today. Everybody was armed with their rifle or automatic of choice and also carried a handgun on their person. Additionally, everyone wore bulletproof Kevlar vests and tactical headsets, both rescued from the Santa Monica Police Department, thank you old world. Should anything go wrong with the scouting group, all units would break formation and breach the building.

Trey leaned into him. "Remember," he said. "If anything goes down, you do what everyone in Alpha would want you to do. Protect me."

"Get out of here," Zephyr said and pushed the man away, but he couldn't curtail a smile.

Trey held up his hands. "OK, OK. Just sayin'. Celebrity here."

"Your claim to fame has a short shelf life, buddy boy. You better pray the juice lasts for as long as possible or you'll be out here digging farm systems with the rest of the jackals who can't shoot a gun."

"I can shoot the only gun that matters," Trey said and grabbed his crotch.

"Really?"

Zephyr's earpiece buzzed. "Focus, you idiots." It was Roderick. "Your tacticals are on automatic and the whole squad can hear your shenanigans. Switch to manual and stop playing around."

"See what you did?" Trey asked after he muted his mouthpiece.

"Now the entire group knows you're not a team player."

Inside, it looked like Chernobyl. What was not long ago a bustling marriage of pristine architectural minimalism and high-end boutiques and restaurants now stood in silence, marred and weathered by regrowth, broken and tainted by men. A brown moss covered portions of the floors and ceilings while stretches of ivy wrapped around sculpted statues of half-naked Greek gods and any bannisters it could grasp and choke. Furniture and trash were strewn around in reckless abandon, and inarticulate spray-painted messages adorned some walls, posts, and floors. The place smelled of smoke, mold and rot. It was a sad, haunting display that seemed to embody everything mankind had built and lost in one fell swoop.

"Jeeze Louise," Trey whispered, clearly awestruck. "This reminds me of some of the buildings in Detroit after the car bubble burst. It's... awful."

"Sort of beautiful in its own way, too, I think," replied Shannon, whom neither Zephyr nor Trey knew, as she aimed the beam of her flashlight throughout the dingy expanse.

Trey shook his head. "Not seeing the beauty here. All I see is a combination of tragedy and horror-movie scary."

The mall proved huge and difficult. The power was out, which meant that large portions of walkway were shrouded in blackness. The massive glass dome several tiers higher allowed some light to bleed through, but few rays cast down to the bottom level and when they did, their potency was diluted. They heard dripping water, the occasional beating of wings, and other unidentifiable things moving somewhere from within the murkiness.

"Hey, it's Trey. I mean, Trey to Roderick," said the man into his tactical, altogether ignoring the accepted communication nomenclature, which was *Search* and *Command*. "We've got a Footlocker here and it looks clean. Shoes galore. Pretty big score."

"Food and drink are the priorities, Search," a voice popped back. "Go ahead and mark it, but let's stay focused on the task at hand. Forty-five-second status checks, please. Command out."

"Should I say roger?" Trey asked. Zephyr couldn't tell if he was joking or not.

"Let's keep moving," Rudy responded, ignoring the question.

The mall had been looted, as if that wasn't obvious from all the wreckage and graffiti, and yet the plunder was evidently selective, not all-encompassing. Footlocker survived. So did The Gap. The store window wasn't even broken, which Zephyr found amazing given that people needed clothes and in particular warm winter coats. In contrast, all the jewelry stores were picked clean — another mystery given that not even diamonds were useful in today's environment.

"Any damned restaurant is a loss," said Shannon. "There's no food here."

"Just the bottom floor," Zephyr reminded her.

"Command, this is Search. First floor is a bust," Rudy said to the wider group. "No sign of provisions at all."

"Understand, Search. When you're sure it's clear, proceed to second level. We have no contact here. Command out."

"Provisions? Just say food, for crying out loud," Trey whispered, but Rudy ignored him. This was becoming a regular exchange.

The escalator to the second tier was wet and mossy. The climb up felt squishy and unnatural to Zephyr, who did his best to restrain a grimace, not that any of them could see it. Shannon illuminated the broken display and counter of a Mrs. Fields Cookies which no longer contained any edibles. Meanwhile, a nearby Microsoft Store had been altogether consumed.

"OK, of course I get the food and I even get the jewelry. But what the fuck with phones and computers?" Shannon asked. "Really?"

"Electricity still works in some parts," Zephyr said.

Trey nodded. "End of the world or not, people gotta have their Internet porn, am I right?" He threw up a hand, waited for a high-five that never arrived, and then continued on. "Seriously though, they're creature comforts, that's all. Makes sense to me. I'd loot a phone just to load up some music… if there was actually a single damned unit left in there. They have these battery cranks out in the world somewhere. You find one of those, you can power your music forever, even when the electricity is long gone. Well worth it."

They found some cooking sauces, baking mix and bottled jams in a William-Sonoma, radioed it in, and stored the leftovers in their packs. It wasn't much. A ransacked Chick-fil-A yielded only a warm freezer full of something petrified. They were rummaging through the paltry remains of a chocolate store— they'd amassed four dozen boxes, although Zephyr couldn't say if any of the treats were still good— when Shannon shushed them.

"What was that?" she whispered.

"What?" Trey said.

She raised her finger. "Quiet. Listen."

So they did. At first, only the unbroken silence met their ears, but then something sounded from beyond the store. A distant… what? Reverberation? A faint clanging, maybe. Zephyr thought it came from up above and then said so.

"I think you're right. Some kind of animal?" Shannon asked.

"I honestly don't know. I think we should check it out, though."

"Let's do it," Trey said.

Rudy fingered his tactical and whispered, "Command, we're hearing something, maybe on the third floor—banging or something. Permission to investigate."

A pause. Then a voice buzzed back, "Hold on, Search."

Here we go, Zephyr thought, and braced for the inevitable. Surely Roderick would order them out of the building now because this was what he always did.

"OK, Search. You're clear to explore, but proceed with extreme caution. Firearms at the ready and safeties off, please. Keep your tacticals on automatic. Status checks in thirty-second intervals. You hear or see anything, I want to know about it. I don't care if it's a dog farting in the dark, you call it in."

"Roger, Command," Rudy said.

They were ascending the mossy escalator, itself covered in discarded chairs, tables, and trash, when another noise disrupted the silence.

"Did you hear it?" Shannon whispered.

"Sure did," Trey breathed back.

It sounded like more banging to Zephyr, but there was something else in there. Less pronounced. No echo or reverb to it. Lighter. Fleeting. It might've been footsteps. Maybe. But then again, perhaps he imagined it. He turned to Trey, who merely shrugged.

"All right, let's just do this," Rudy whispered, and started to walk.

"Search, please keep status checks at thirty-second intervals," Roderick advised into their headsets.

"Roger, Command. We are maneuvering through obstructions blocking both lanes of the escalators to the third level. Single file up the right side, which seems a little less cluttered."

"Roger. We're still clear at the perimeter."

They made quick work of the barriers, and yet the process was an affront to the senses — one amplified by its polarity to the stillness before them. Zephyr winced at every piece of furniture that they cast aside with loud disregard.

"Hello!" Trey called out. "If anybody is up there, we—"

Rudy quieted him. "What the hell are you doing?"

"What's it look like? The whole world can hear us coming, man. We may as well announce our intentions at this point."

"Jesus, Trey. You think you can clue us in here before you make decisions that impact all of us?" Shannon hissed.

He seemed about to say something, thought better of it, and then responded, "You're right, sorry. It just seemed obvious."

Their tacticals popped. "Search, guns up, keep your eyes open, but proceed with contact now that the cat is out of the bag. Trey, we'll talk about this later. Command out."

Trey ignored him and started to call out into the darkness again as Rudy cleared the final table that separated them from the level.

"Hello! If anybody is up here, don't be afraid. We're the good guys!" His words reverberated across the remnants of the domed ceiling and seemed to call back to him. His echoing voice was, however, the only that returned.

"Well, I guess this explains the mess on the escalators," Zephyr whispered.

The top floor was home to The Market Fine Foods Court. Yeah, right, he thought. If your idea of fine food is Hot Dog on a Stick and Tommy's, maybe. The restaurants ran the gamut of the floor, which was an immense circle. McDonald's, Zephyr recognized. Pho Tastic Noodle House, Tres Amigos and When in Rome, however, were all foreign to him. A stale, greasy, putrid smell permeated the air and seemed to accentuate this truth.

"I'm not gonna lie, man. I'm feeling pretty nostalgic right now," Trey said. "And yes, I'd be all over Hot Dog on a Stick if that shit was open. Haters be damned."

From the looks of the court, Trey wasn't the only one fond of fast food. Every restaurant had been demolished. Obliterated in some cases. Worse than any of the destruction that befell the retailers on the previous floors. The signage remained, but windows were smashed, countertops were destroyed or missing, registers toppled, and more graffiti blanketed walls, tables and floors. The light was thin, and yet he could see into some of those kitchens and they looked gutted if not altogether terminated. Furthermore, big, white and brown splotches of what Zephyr thought must be bird shit bathed the floors and furniture. He looked up and marked the countless penetrations in the once-magnificent dome and thought, all of this splendor reduced to a huge toilet in a year's time.

They stayed in formation and canvassed the floor. Occasionally, Trey called out into the environment with promises of peace and friendship, but no more sounds returned. McDonald's was drained of all food and any signs of life. So too, he thought, was Pho Tastic Noodle House, but someone had wrapped a heavy chain lock around its double-freezer doors, which was promising. The group spent almost fifteen minutes hammering away at it—literally, as that was the only tool in their collective possession capable of the job— and finally broke the lock. When Rudy at last unlatched the chain and tugged the doors open, Shannon gagged and backed away.

Pretzeled together inside were two corpses, both naked from head to toe, both disfigured and well decayed. Zephyr doubled over and nearly lost his breakfast when it dawned on him that it was those rotting bodies and not petrified food that they'd all smelled.

"Jesus," Trey whispered, pinching his nose.

"Command, we found a couple bodies in a freezer," Rudy said into his headset. If the revelation bothered him in the slightest, he didn't show it.

Two very long seconds passed. "Roger, Search. Come on back. I'm calling it."

"Roger," Rudy acknowledged and motioned them back out of the restaurant.

Their tacticals popped. "Keep your guards up, Search."

"Roger."

"What the hell happened to them?" Shannon asked. She looked pale, shaken.

"Murdered, obviously," Trey said. "Good grief. What a way to go."

Miles, who was a short, bulky man in his fifties, spoke for the first time since they'd started the survey. "Probably some fight over rations got out of control."

"Doesn't explain why they were naked, though," Zephyr argued. "Or crammed into a freezer, for that matter."

Trey nodded. "Whatever this was, it was vicious shit. Someone stripped these people, mutilated and murdered them, tangled them up and stored them away."

"Let's just get back," Shannon replied.

"Maybe they were meant to be food," Trey pondered, ignoring her. "Maybe when they were all done pillaging the place and food ran dry, someone went cannibal on them."

Shannon shook her head. "Jesus, Trey."

"What?"

"There's still plenty of food to be scavenged around the city. I don't think cannibalization is necessary. At least not yet," Zephyr interjected. Although, the corpses were pretty torn up, he admitted to himself. It was always possible that some lunatic planned to eat these people. Jeffrey Dahmer lived during an era in which food was abundant, but that didn't stop him.

Rudy halted and silenced them. He was peering at the Tommy's directly across from their position. Zephyr was about to ask what the holdup was when he noticed a thin layer of smoke hanging in the air like some lonesome cloud across the restaurant's dimly lit kitchen.

"You see it?" Trey whispered.

"Yeah. I do now."

"What are you—" Shannon began and then stopped. "Oh… shit."

"Guns," Rudy hissed.

"Search, what is happening?" their tacticals buzzed.

"We have smoke coming out from Tommy's, Command. Signs of life here, maybe," Rudy whispered.

"OK, vacate the premises, Search. Status checks at fifteen-second intervals."

"Roger, Command," Rudy said.

Trey, though, had other ideas. He was halfway to the restaurant before the group realized what he was doing.

Rudy darted after him, crying, "Get back here!"

But Trey tore free of his grasp and backed away. "I'm tired of this play-it-safe bullshit," he said. "I didn't come out here for nothing, man. We might have survivors so if you want to help, great, cover me. If not, I'll catch up to you guys."

His pursuer started into the logical counterargument but Trey dismissed it with a flap of his hand and began calling back toward the restaurant. "Hello! If anybody is here, don't be afraid. We are not going to hurt you. If you're armed, put your weapons down. My name is Trey, I'm super nice, and I'm coming in!"

He pushed through a flimsy double doorway and into the kitchen.

Zephyr counted.

One second.

Two seconds.

Three.

He couldn't wait any longer, so he bolted for the kitchen, his weapon raised and ready, and like dominoes the others fell behind him.

Distantly, he heard Shannon shout, "Trey! Say something, for God's sake!"

Another second — a lifetime in slow motion. Then a muffled voice from somewhere inside.

"It's OK. Come on in, guys."

Zephyr realized he'd been holding his breath, exhaled, and then pushed open the door.

Tommy's was a greasy dive. The kind of fast food best served at three in the morning to a gathering of drunken, ravenous teenagers as they struggled to keep their eyelids from closing. Zephyr had never been, but the chain held a permanent place on Trey's exhaustive list of *Things I Would Devour Immediately if the World Returned to Normal.*

But as he stepped through the double doors into the kitchen, the only thing remarkable about it was that it was clean. No mold. No shattered plastic plates or discarded wrappers, no graffiti, not even any perceivable dust. The industrial equipment held its stainless steel shine. The floors were spotless. Then he saw Trey, his back to the group, squatting on both legs, his weapons on the ground beside him. And just beyond his friend, huddled together in a dark crevice between an oversized stove and dishwasher, two smaller figures held each other and stared back at him.

"It's OK. We're not going to hurt you," Trey said. "See? I've put my guns down. My name is Trey. What's yours?"

No response. Zephyr strained to see them, squinting into the shadows as Trey tried again. Somewhere behind him, Rudy whispered updates to Command.

"All right. I understand you're probably freaked out right now. I would be, too. So let me just tell you why we're here. This is my friend Zephyr," Trey said and thumbed backward. "Behind him are Shannon, Miles and Rudy. We came up here to see if there's any food or water and we've got our guns just for protection, not to hurt anyone. That's all. We didn't expect to find any survivors, so we're really happy to see you. I'm just going to sit down on the floor here and we can get to know each other, cool?"

Zephyr felt obliged to chime in and yet he didn't know what to say. He settled on, "Hi, I'm Zephyr," gave a little wave, and then sat on the tile, too. Shannon did the same, then Miles, and after a moment's hesitation, even Rudy, although he held tight to his weapons.

"Great," Trey said. "So you wanna try again? Can you tell me your names?"

Silence stretched on for a long time. Zephyr heard whispers, but couldn't discern the words. Then one of the silhouettes finally nodded.

"Sam." Soft, low, but unmistakably young. If he was a teenager, only just. "My name's Sam."

"Hi, Sam. Who's your friend?" Trey asked.

More enthusiastic now. "He's Nathan. I watch him."

"OK, great. Now we're getting somewhere. Thanks for talking to me, guys. How old are you two?"

"I'm not really sure any more. I used to be eleven. Nate used to be eight. Do you know what month it is?"

Trey nodded. "Yes. It's November. It's actually been more than a year since folks went away, so you two are probably twelve and nine now."

"No, my birthday's June, not November," the other boy said.

"He means your birthday's passed, Nate. Mine too."

"Oh."

Zephyr thought of Jordan and his heart sank. She'd gone only a day or two by herself and that was grueling enough. How long had these two been at it? More than a year on their own? Did they have any help at all?

"Are you really good?" Nate asked.

"Yes, we are," Trey said.

Zephyr flashed the boys what he hoped was his brightest smile. "Hi Sam and Nathan. Can I call you Nate?"

"Yep."

"Thanks. It's so nice to meet you. I was wondering, how long have you two been here, and are you alone or do you have any friends to help you?"

"Just us," Sam replied.

"For how long?"

"Since whenever everyone went away was. We met a grown up girl a while ago but someone took her, and ever since that, it's just been us."

Jesus, Zephyr thought. He understood that life was unfair, now more than ever, and yet these two living out here by themselves for more than a year— it was unfathomable.

"Sam, do you and Nate want to scoot on out from there now?" Trey asked. He placed his thick flashlight on its heel so that the beam shone at the ceiling. Immediately, the space was brighter, and Zephyr could see the kids much better. They were both skinny, both dirty.

"I don't know," Sam said. "You seem nice, but maybe we'll just stay here if that's OK."

Now Rudy spoke up. "If we wanted to hurt you or your friend, we would've done it already."

Well done, Mister Tact, Zephyr thought before he and Trey tripped over each other's words in a clumsy attempt to overcompensate for the outburst. They needn't have bothered, however, because somehow the big man's simple, ugly truth proved most effective.

"OK," Sam said and the two of them emerged from their hiding spot. Slowly at first, but they both came and finally took seats on the floor before Trey.

"Just so you know, we have no plans of hurting anybody," Trey said.

"Thanks," replied the older boy. He scratched at his thick, auburn hair and fidgeted. Zephyr estimated that mane housed a full colony of well-fed lice. Freckles covered his face and arms. He wore jeans, a collared shirt and sneakers. Nate, meanwhile, was shorter with dirty brown hair and donned a similar outfit. Both were skinny, but not malnourished. Somehow, they'd been eating. He wondered if the smoke was related.

"Hey guys," he said without moving from his perch. "I have to tell you that I'm really impressed with how long you two have been out here by yourselves. Are you hungry or thirsty? We can feed you."

The boy crossed his arms as if to warm himself. "No, thanks. We ate already. But, you know, thanks."

"Sure. So this is where you guys live?"

Sam shrugged. "I guess, yeah, for the most part. We stay around the mall, but we've been here for a while. We go out sometimes, though." He studied the tile. "Just not very much because some of the people out there are, well…"

"Bad guys," Nate interjected.

"How do you eat? Where do you sleep? I mean, Jesus, what do you do every day?" Trey asked.

Nate started to rise. "You wanna see?"

The boys pushed aside an empty shelf to reveal a huge walk-in pantry stocked full of canned, jarred and even zip-sealed foods. A dozen unopened bags of potato and tortilla chips— probably all too stale to be good, and yet rare commodities all the same. Canned beans, oranges, peas, corn, and carrots. Stacks of soda cans. Candy of all kinds. Crackers, jars of peanut butter and jelly, apple sauce, and much more. It seemed like all the preservable food from the old world, and in abundance. Zephyr figured this supply would last these two at least another year, if not longer. It was a gold mine.

Trey whooped and twirled as he clutched something in his hands. "Holy shit, man. Taco-fucking-Doritos. They have Taco Doritos!" He clutched the bag as someone might a trophy. "Sam, Nate, I will give you my left nut for this baby right now. Good grief! I never thought I'd see these again."

Sam shrugged. "You can have 'em if you want."

"Seriously?"

"Go for it."

"Man, you just made a friend for life. No joke. Your legend will be passed down through my family for generations because of this."

"Cool."

"How did you get all of this?" Rudy asked.

"We found it here or at some of the places nearby. We've been saving as much as we can so we can make it last longer."

Rudy didn't waste any more time getting to his point. "Is there more somewhere?"

"I… think so."

"Where?" the man asked. It seemed to Zephyr less a question and more an order.

"Why don't you lay off a minute, man?" Trey said, holding up his hand. "It can wait."

"We're on a mission here, in case you forgot."

Shannon stood between them and met his scowl. "Back off, tough guy. In case you forgot, they're just kids."

He leaned in, his eyes locked on hers, and Zephyr thought he might take a swing — that he actually might throw down with a girl, which would probably ignite a full-blown brawl. Something, anyway. None of them would stand for that kind of behavior, outmatched or not. Seconds dragged on as Zephyr considered all of this and prepared for the worst. However, the punch never came. Instead, the big man grunted. "Whatever. I'll be on the horn with Command. Get your priorities straight." Then he turned and stomped back toward the entrance.

"Asshole," Trey whispered, and then winced before he fingered his tactical. "I really gotta remember to set this thing to manual."

In the middle of all the food lay two mattresses covered in blankets and pillows. The boys had also dragged in a small television surrounded by piles of movies and video games.

"So this is what you do," Trey said.

"This is our room, yeah," Sam replied. "Power went out a couple weeks ago and we haven't been able to watch or play very much since. Just a little."

"Yep, it's been pretty sucky," Nate added.

"Sounds like an understatement," Trey said. "Wait, though, how do you watch anything at all?"

"We found some of these mega batteries, and then we got the TV working again. But the charges don't last very long. Like, a few hours. So when we want to watch a movie or play something, we gotta take the batteries up a few blocks and recharge them."

Trey whistled. "What a disaster."

"Why not just move to one of the other buildings then?" Zephyr asked.

Sam shrugged again. "We have all of our food here and it'd take forever to move it and we like it here, anyway. It's not so bad getting the batteries recharged."

Zephyr couldn't take it any longer. "You guys, it's cool that you've been surviving out here, but you know you could leave this all behind and come live with us, right? It's safe. I mean, we can protect you. We've got a whole city of people, with electricity, our own rooms. It's a lot warmer than the mall, too, I can tell you that." He paused. "We've even got a big swimming pool."

If Sam was impressed by any of this, he sure didn't show it. The kid was really hard to read. Zephyr expected giddiness and saw only blank composure in its place. Another star poker player in-the-making, no doubt. The boy's calm, thoughtful manner was simultaneously striking and pitiable for the same reason, which was that it stripped him of his adolescence. He acted older than he had any right to be. In stark contrast, Nate was beaming. The younger boy tugged on Sam's shirt and murmured something indistinct, but it went ignored.

"It's not far from here," Zephyr continued. "It's a new city. Really more like a handful of buildings. There's all sorts of people and we're try—"

"No," the boy blurted and then regained his equilibrium. "Sorry –

but no, that's all right. Thank you, but we're pretty good here. We're," he started to say something and then stopped. "Thanks, really. Thanks a lot… for the offer, but we're fine here."

"Why not?" Nate pleaded. "Can we go, Sam? We should go."

"Not now," he whispered.

"Nate has the right idea on this one," Zephyr joked, but Sam didn't look amused.

"No. I just think you guys should go because we have stuff to do here. OK?" When nobody said anything, he turned to Trey. "Go ahead and take the Doritos."

Trey grinned at him. "Hey, thanks, kid. You did me a legit solid, so let me do you one in return. He ain't too bright, and he sure as hell ain't pretty. This once, though, Zeph here is actually right. You're free to do what you want, but you should really think about this offer. We're living pretty large compared to your little setup here. There are others your age, too."

The boy nodded fast. "Sure, thanks. I'll think about it. Thank you. We're not ready to do anything just yet."

"I'm ready. I want to go, Sam." Nate implored now. "Please. They have electricity there, and I want to go swimming. I'll let you have my 3DS if you say yes."

"I don't want your 3DS."

"It sounds like Nate wants to give it a try," Trey said.

"I do – can we? Please? You can have any of my games, I don't care."

Sam shook his head. "Not yet, Nate. I don—" he started to say and then paused, but not before Zephyr heard the tremble in his voice. Was he scared?

"All right, totally your decision," Zephyr started, and threw up his hands. "I get it. You don't know us and it's a pretty messed up world out there. You're playing it safe and I totally understand that, believe me. I was in your position more or less a few months ago and I didn't have good reason to trust anybody, either. All I'm gonna say is – and there's no way to convince you but look at me and you'll see that I'm telling the truth here – we are genuinely trying to help. That's all. We're not here to hurt anyone. We really are the good ones. I mean that as literally as possible. And—"

He stopped mid-sentence, struck by his own words. The good ones. Maybe the problem was that not everyone saw it that way.

"Sam, do you already know the place we're talking about?" he asked, inspired.

The boy shrugged.

"Sorry – does that mean yes?"

Sam seemed to study his shoes for a moment and then nodded.

Word had spread then. Had some of those turned away told lies about the city? If so, maybe Sam believed the hearsay. That would definitely explain his behavior.

Nate tugged on the older boy's shirt. "Know what?" But the question was ignored.

"What's it called?" Zephyr asked.

Sam shrugged. "What's it matter?"

"Humor me."

He met Zephyr's gaze – and, yes, he saw fear in his eyes. "Alpha."

"What's happening here, dude?" Trey asked. "I'm not following this."

"I think someone's been telling some tall tales about Alpha and poor Sam here believes them." He turned back to the boy. "Let me guess. Alpha is a city of – what? – evildoers, or Satan worshippers, or what have you? Maybe something like we chain up our people and hold weekly book-burning ceremonies? Drink the blood of goats and that kind of stuff? Any of that ringing a bell?"

The boy stared back at him and gave no response.

"I'm right, aren't I?" Zephyr asked and when no reply came, he smiled. "Sure, I am."

"Dude, we need a fucking public relations department —this shit is nuts," Trey joked.

Zephyr continued. "Listen, whatever you've heard, it isn't true. And anybody who says otherwise, I don't know how to tell you this, but if they're badmouthing Alpha, it's probably because they were not allowed in. We have a system—it's a long story, but the short of it is, we have a screening process."

Trey snorted. "Yeah, and the irony is that we only turn the bad guys away, so talk about the pot calling the kettle fucking black."

"Yah, that's a good one," Sam practically spat. "Except, I didn't hear anything."

Then, unprompted, he turned his back on them, lowered his head, and tugged down his collar. A scabby 'X' stretched across the full of his nape. In bad light, it might've been a tattoo, but there was no mistaking the wound now.

"You see it?" the boy asked.

"Hard to miss," Trey replied. "What in the sheep fuck happened to you, kid?"

Sam turned back to face them. "Don't play stupid. You can go back now. I think we're done here." There was an edge to his tone that hadn't existed before.

"Sam, seriously, what happened? We're not fooling around. We really don't understand," Zephyr said.

The boy chuckled. "What happened?" Now his words quivered with emotion and Zephyr understood that the unruffled demeanor was merely a well-worn facade. "What the hell do you think happened? Alpha happened, as if you didn't know that," he said.

"What do you mean? Spell it out, kid," Trey said.

The boy's face showed a mixture of incredulity and rage. "This is for real, huh?" he asked and shook his head. "I went there, but unlike you, they turned me out. Surprise, surprise, I'm not good enough for your precious city. 'Sorry Samuel, good luck' and all that. And the best part is that they were kind enough to burn this 'X' onto my neck to mark me. Because they're— you're— the good guys, right?"

Shannon gasped. "Who did this to you?"

Sam rolled his eyes. "Ask me a serious question."

She laid her hands on his shoulders. "Sam, why is that mark there?"

He shook free of her grasp. "Why the hell do you think? I'm one of your so-called bad guys, you idiot."

37

Three hours later, Zephyr paced the length of the same clean, white hallway that they'd been escorted through months ago. Nearby, an armed, expressionless guard blocked his way from the sterile interrogation room, now occupied by Janis, Karen, Alec, and at least one newcomer. All he could do was wait for the conversation to be over, and yet waiting seemed an impossibility under the circumstances.

The kids had been turned away. Again, apparently, in Sam's case. Zephyr couldn't fucking believe it, especially because he'd spent the better part of an hour convincing the boy to follow him back through the mall to their scouting party with promises of righting some terrible misunderstanding. When, however, he explained the predicament to Roderick, the man examined Sam's neck and promptly denied him access to the caravan. Just like that. And nothing Zephyr said could convince him to reconsider.

"I told you, it's not my call. Rules are rules, and if you can't appreciate that, I suggest you take it up with someone above our pay grade."

He nearly reminded him that pay scales were obsolete and then thought better of it. Instead, he asked, "What about Nate?"

"Is he marked?"

"No." He realized, though, that he'd never actually checked. "I don't think so, anyway. Nate, show him your neck, OK?"

"He's not marked," Sam said, emphasizing the last word.

Roderick nodded. "Then we can take him."

"Is Sam coming?" the boy asked.

Zephyr turned back to Roderick. "Is he?"

The tanned man shook his head. "No, he's not. And don't push me again or you'll be sleeping out here, too. Understood?"

"That's real big of you, Spencer. Really earning those stripes today. Hero mode all the way," Trey said.

"Go fuck yourself. Some of us actually abide by the laws we have in place."

"I want Sam to go. I do—" Nate started to say and then Sam hugged him.

"I can't, Nate. But you can go if you want, I won't mind. I swear. I won't be mad or anything. If you want to stay with me, that's cool, too. It's totally your choice."

The younger boy surveyed the caravan of soldiers and then whispered something to Sam.

"What's the word, compadre?" Trey asked.

Nate looked to his friend again and Sam shook his head. "It's your choice."

"I want Sam to come. If he can't come, then I'm gonna stay too," he said.

And that was that.

A half hour later, the trucks pulled out from the battered shopping center and the two boys faded away in the rearview mirror as Zephyr obsessed over the branded 'X' and its implications. He wasn't naive or stupid. Yes, there were bad guys out there and no, they were not allowed access to the city. But Sam was just a kid. And a kid who cared for another at that. A kid who had just displayed one of the most selfless acts he'd seen since the disappearances.

The door to the interrogation room opened and two men Zephyr didn't recognize stepped out. Behind them trailed Janis, Karen and Alec. Zephyr waved them down, Janis said something to her sister and Karen nodded before rejoining the party down the hall. Janis flashed him a winning smile and then embraced him.

"What can I do for you, Zephyr?"

He was actually surprised she remembered him. Alpha was a city a thousand strong and growing. That was a lot of faces and names to keep on mental file.

She laughed. "I don't actually recall everybody's names," she said, reading his mind. "But your name's hard to forget. And besides, you and Trey are thick as thieves so you're something of a celebrity by association. What can I help you with?"

He thought about how and where to begin and couldn't settle upon an elegant summary. "Where to start."

"What is it?"

"There's a lot, actually," he said. "I guess the short version is that I was on a scouting mission today, we were searching an abandoned mall down on 2nd and we found a couple kids living in one of the restaurants."

"Inside the mall?"

"Yeah, and I tried to take them back with us, except it turned out that one of the kids—Sam, is his name – he didn't want to go. Which made no sense because where they are now, they don't even have real power, and they're on their own out there."

"OK," she agreed.

"The kicker is that it turns out Sam came to Alpha once before and he got escorted out."

She sighed. "I see."

"But that can't be right, though, right? I mean, Sam isn't even a teenager. He wouldn't get turned away, right?"

He searched her face and was disappointed with her expression, which hadn't changed.

"Oh, Zephyr, I love your optimism. I wish I still shared it," she said. "You know as well as I do that children can kill just as well as adults. There's no age restriction on this stuff. I know it's not what you want to hear and I wish I could tell you that it's not the way of the world. I've seen it happen with my own eyes, though."

He met those eyes, his heart racing. "Are we really burning brands onto people? Onto kids? He's twelve years-old. You should see the back of his neck."

When she didn't respond, he added, "I thought we just turned them away and took their weapons, if they had any. And for adults, not kids. Now we're mutilating people, too?"

She considered her words and then said, "It's not ideal, I'll give you that. But it could always be worse. We could be killing all of the bad ones. The suggestion has been made more than once."

"Yeah, great way to distinguish the good guys from the bad. By killing a bunch of people," he blurted loud enough for others to hear. He could feel himself losing control. Could feel himself trembling. "First, you ask the eight-year-old a few questions, then you magically determine he's 'bad' and then it's off with his head, right? That sounds like a great plan to me."

"That's enough."

"Why even bother with the interviews? Hell, maybe the geniuses upstairs can create some kind of undetectable poison that we can put into milk bottles and we'll just distribute it freely to all the barely-surviving mothers out there. Get the bad guys before they have a chance to grow up."

He might've continued onward if the back of her hand hadn't slapped his train of thought right out of him. He'd taken a few punches over the years and hers stung and rattled as good as any balled fist.

Before he had any time to recover, her fingers were in his elbow as she marched him down the hall toward the interrogation room.

"That… was not very smart," Janis said after she had closed the door. The words came unflustered and yet her hands still balled into fists and she drew a long breath before finally facing him again. "Not smart at all, Zephyr. But I shouldn't have slapped you, and I'm sorry."

"Whatever."

"Pouting now? It doesn't suit you."

He searched for a witty response but she ignored him and launched into conversation again. "One thing I will not tolerate is public insubordination. If you want to have it out with me, that's fine. Come to my office, close the door, and get whatever you need to get off your chest. I'm not saying I won't scream back, but I welcome that kind of dialog. Out in the hallways of my building, though, and in front of my people…" she said, and shook her head. "No. That, I won't stand for. And you just learned that."

She stared at him for a moment and then her features softened. "Back to your boy, I want to ask you, do you think we make any of these decisions lightly? Denying the leftovers access? Sending them back out into this damaged world? And yes, even marking them? In case you have any doubt, let me reassure you, the answer is no. Absolutely, unequivocally, no. We all have to make excruciating decisions to keep the ones we love safe. That sometimes means doing things that might keep us up at night. Things that don't always feel right."

She paused and sighed. "All we can do is trust in our convictions, what we believe in here, because when everything is said and done, we are trying to do good with the limited tools and skills we have left and I truly do believe by that measure the end always justifies the means. I think there are a lot of people within these walls who would agree, yourself included. Deep down, whether you want to openly admit it or not right now. I really do."

It was easy to understand why Janis was in charge. Her charisma sparkled and she possessed a nearly-indiscernible deftness for disarmament. That he somehow felt responsible for his recent lashing was proof enough of that. And yet, he couldn't let go of the simple truth underneath it all, which was that whatever she asserted, and however she spun it all in her favor, she agreed with a fundamental philosophy that denied sanctuary to kids like Sam.

"Zephyr, do you know how many murders we've had at Alpha?" Janis asked.

He rolled his eyes. "Let me guess. Zero?"

"No," she said, and smiled. "Actually, two. Both of them were early on, before we tested. The first — a gentlemen in his forties strangled his girlfriend. Ugly business, but not as bad as the other. That one — a ten-year-old boy. His name was Charles. Only ten. And do you know what he did?"

She didn't wait for him to answer.

"Let me tell you," she said and stepped closer. "He stabbed his mother to death while she was sleeping. And why? Because she blocked him from playing video games on the weekend."

Her hands found his shoulders as her eyes locked with his. "The things we do, we do for the good of the city."

Zephyr pulled away from her. "The other kid with Sam didn't have a mark," he said. "He could've come back with us if he wanted to. And guess what? Sam didn't flip his shit or try to kill anybody when he found this out, either. He just turned to the kid — Nate — and told him that it was OK to go, and that he wouldn't be mad at all."

He started toward the door, looked back, and added, "That's the monster you burned and abandoned. So why don't you think about that when you're curled up in your warm bed tonight."

38

Aurora literally bit her lip and studied him as they sat at their tiny kitchenette table and he spooned watery cereal into his mouth. Milk was now a luxury seldom attainable, at least until the farm and ranch systems were operating at full capacity.

"So?" he finally asked between swallows.

"I dunno," she said and then plucked at one of her cuticles.

Here we go, he thought, stopped eating and glared at her.

"Fine. If I'm being honest—and don't get mad at me, because you asked for my opinion— I can kind of see both sides."

"For fucking real?"

"Baby, how many kids were in gangs and shooting each other before all this happened? Or, you know, when you turned on the news, every so often you'd hear about some crazed kid who killed his classmates or whatever. Or another who strapped bombs to himself and blew people up across the world. I'm just saying that it's not impossible."

He realized Janis had nothing on Aurora. She had a way of relating to him and circumventing his defenses when few others could.

"You didn't see what I saw, though, Rory. He's a good kid. He's out there protecting a little boy the same age as Jordan, for fuck's sake. And he's been doing it by himself all this time with no help at all from any of us."

She leaned across the table and placed her hand over his. "OK, so don't jump all over me for saying this, either, all right? I'm on your side here."

He sighed. "Go ahead."

"You said you found some bodies in a freezer up there," she said and then winced as though the words themselves pained her.

"What?"

"Two dead bodies in a freezer. You said that, right? Because just to play devil's advocate here, there's no way those kids didn't know about them if they've been living there as long as they said they have. And maybe they more than knew about them."

"No," Zephyr said more to himself than her. She was right, though. She was fucking right. And why hadn't he made that connection at all? They must have discovered the bodies at some point — the smell permeated the area — so why would they just leave them there? The simple answer was that they never jimmied the doors open.

"OK," he said. "OK. It's a little weird. I admit it."

She slid her flimsy chair closer to his and then wrapped her arms around him. This simple display of affection always overpowered him—words alone never satiated her, and it was one of the reasons he cherished the girl.

"You're a good person, baby," she said and kissed him. "You always see the best in people."

He ran his fingers through her thick hair. "You might be right. Maybe Sam is all messed up, and maybe they were right to turn him away. But they're still burning kids and leaving them to die without any legitimate proof of anything. If we're all supposed to be categorized into hard good or hard bad, where does that kind of shit fit in?"

39

Saturday night, almost three weeks after the expedition, Zephyr and Trey found themselves lounging in lawn chairs with a twelve-pack of beer as they studied the skyline from their perch on the rooftop of a newly-appropriated building. It was a hotel, actually. He was drunk and couldn't remember the name, but it might've been The Bittington. Or maybe The Burlington? That was in another life.

Alpha's expansion teams had secured the structure a week prior and he and Trey ventured over two days after that to determine if the living quarters were more suitable than their own. They were. They all moved the next day. Their little makeshift family had risen higher in the new world and now dwelled in a spacious flat with a view of the city that money could not buy. Literally could not buy, he thought, and chuckled.

"What's so funny, jackwad?" Trey asked, reached for his bottle, knocked it over, and then cursed. "You know, I had to barter a box of movies to get this and now look what you made me do."

"Try not to be so wasted and dumb all the time," Zephyr said.

His friend ignored this. "But maaaan, come on—look at that view."

It really was magnificent. The sun had already dipped into the ether that separated sky from sea, and rich tones of red still radiated and stretched into the dark blue above.

When the darkness finally blotted out those final stubborn rays, they rotated their chairs so that they could gaze into the opposite direction, the sea and wind at their backs. A great pile of skyscrapers, motionless, but still breathing with electricity, greeted them, and this too was arresting. Except, Zephyr knew that this particular view would not always be there for the ogling— that unlike the rising and setting sun, which would outlast him and millions of his descendants across thousands of millennia, the sparks of power which illuminated this skyline were fleeting, destined to sizzle and pop into extinction sooner than later.

He swallowed a foamy mouthful of beer. "In a thousand years, do you think people are gonna look at these buildings like they do the pyramids?"

"Holy shit, that reminds me. Well, yes, first off. But I've been meaning to tell you about this theory of mine and I think you hit the nail right on the head, man." He held up his index finger. "Hold on a sec. Lemme just…" He popped the cap off a new bottle with a hiss and chugged.

"Well?" Zephyr asked.

His friend let go of a noisy belch complemented by two smaller ones.

"Pig."

"You know it," he said.

"Theory?"

"Well, I was thinking about our little… predicament. The event, and what have you. And I was thinking about, why now? And then it occurred to me that maybe this shit isn't unique at all, but systematic. A reoccurring phenomenon, right? And that made a whole shitload of sense to me."

"How so?"

"Think about it," Trey said. "All of these great civilizations just up and disappeared on us. The Greeks. The Egyptians. The Noks. The Mayans. The Aztecs. The Atlanteans."

Zephyr laughed. "Well, first of all, the Greeks, Egyptians and Mayans are still around. Were still around, anyway. And second, the Atlanteans?"

"Maybe a stretch, but who the hell knows these days? Doesn't seem as farfetched to me as it once did. And the Greeks, Egyptians and Mayans fell from grace big time, man. In weird ways. Think of Greece. It was the most civilized of all ancient civilizations. Centuries ahead. Plato, Aristotle, Socrates, these ridiculous philosophers. And it just faded away. And by the way, Plato wrote about Atlantis, so deal with it. Supposed to be this huge continent with a bunch of kings and a devastating naval force. But then it all died off, too. Sank into the sea." He took another big swig of his beer. "Egypt, yeah, sure, whatever, but tell me who built the pyramids, and then tell me how."

"I thought it was common knowledge that they were built by aliens."

"Anyway," Trey continued, ignoring him, "I'm just saying, what if something happens at the pinnacle? When a society, a culture, whatever, hits a certain point of advancement, something comes in and stamps it out. Maybe not entirely. Just does some serious damage. Kind of resets the process, you know. Like this whole blood type thing with us. America as we knew it—that's gone, man. But you and I, we're still around to tell the story, to keep the history, and maybe there's something to that. And, I don't know, but maybe all the Greeks and Mayans still alive today—or, at least they were before all of this—maybe they were the one percent, too."

Zephyr nodded and contemplated it. It was an interesting theory, but of course they were all fascinating. The problem was that there wasn't any proof.

He swiveled in his chair so that his feet touched the ground and looked at his friend. Yeah, he was definitely drunk all right. It wasn't so much the variance in his perception of the world as it was the suspension of low-grade fear that gnawed forever at him. For now, everything felt as right as rain. He sipped at his beer and then replied, "So what you're basically saying is that a god force or aliens or whatever wipes us out once a millennia or so to make sure we don't advance beyond a certain point."

"Pretty much, yeah."

"It's plausible," Zephyr conceded, and smiled. "Actually, it's a pretty good theory. Not an iota of proof, mind you, but I like it."

"Well, thanks for your approval."

"Let me present you an alternate theory, though," Zephyr said.

"All ears."

"Everything I've heard so far—the Rapture, aliens, this thing about wiping humanity clean, and your addendum to that, they all presume that we are the center of the universe. Whether it's God or E.T., they're really interested in messing with humanity."

"Why not? We are pretty awesome — especially me, as you know."

"But what if we're not? What if everything we know and everything we are—it's all some infinitesimal speck buried a trillion layers deep within endless universes? Think of it like this. What if Earth was just one of an uncountable number of cells within the bloodstream of a flea hidden away in the mangy fur of some dumb dog, itself unsubstantial, its neighborhood inconsequential, its universe one in a zillion? And then let's say that the dog was finally given a long overdue flea bath, and the ramification of that was a poisoning of the flea and a breakdown of its cellular structure. Now, this is an event that takes seconds in its universe, but spirals into infinity for us, and as those cells are tainted, the result is an unexplainable change in the reality we know—in this case, the widespread disappearances of people." He met his friend's gaze. "And that's it. No design. No epic plan. Just cause and effect, but not one that we will ever understand. Certainly not one that gives one solid shit about us."

Neither one of them said anything for a while, and then Trey broke the silence. "OK, a couple things to say to that. One, you're not even twenty, so stop this pessimistic fatalism bullshit. I get that you've been through a lot, but from my point of view, your life could be worse. Your place is rockin' and you're with one of the hottest girls in Alpha by far. By far, dude. So maybe try to sprinkle a little more optimism into your life."

"It's not fatalism," Zephyr began and Trey talked over him.

"Two!" He flashed the peace symbol with one hand. "Two! Even if we are microscopic flecks on a puddle of vomit in some bigger universe's toilet bowl, that still means there is another universe. And that if you climb the universal ladder high enough, maybe there is some method to the madness. Some version of the Wizard of Oz, my man. And whoever or whatever that is, wherever they exist, and however they exist, I choose to believe that they understand the balance and keep it, even if we never will. That whatever happened here happened for a reason."

Zephyr considered all of this, took another drink, and then smiled. "Dude, let's keep my girlfriend out of these little chats, huh?"

"All right then. But no promises where my dreams are concerned."

"Pervert. And no offense, but you're a little old for her, grandpa."

"Experienced, you mean, and go fuck yourself," Trey said and then held out his beer. The two of them clanked their bottles together and then drank.

"I've been wondering, with the world being what it is, if you could go anywhere and do anything, what would you do?" Zephyr asked.

His friend scratched his neck and thought about it. "I've considered that a few times. I think maybe I'd get a boat, sail to Fiji or something. Stupidly beautiful, by the way—vacationed there before all of this happened. White sands, aqua blue ocean. You can look right through the water and see fish swimming around. And the weather is perfect. Not too hot, not too cold. You just wanna bask."

"You could, you know. You could just take a boat and do it. You're a smart guy."

"Sure, but it's not sustainable. I'm not a farmer or a fisherman. I need help to survive. And don't act like you don't, you idiot." He was about to take another swig of beer and he stopped. His eyes narrowed, and he said, "You're scheming—I can see it in your face. What're you getting at?"

"No, nothing. It's just a question."

Trey surveyed him a moment longer. "Yeah, not buying it."

"It's really nothing, seriously. I've just been thinking a lot about the future and what I should be doing with my life, that's all."

The older man swiveled in his chair and faced him. "Translation: Where you should go. And you started thinking about this right around the time we met those kids in the mall, am I right?"

"You don't have to be a dick about it," Zephyr said.

"I'm not. But let's face it, man, you've been moping around for the last couple weeks and everyone around you knows exactly why. And, by the way, I'm not saying that you don't have every right to be pissed off because that shit ain't cool and we both know it. At the same time, though, I can see the other side of this an—"

Thunder crashed around them so loud that it walloped them, obliterating the argument. And did lightning flash, too? Fading colors pulsed and swayed in his vision. He blinked, then glanced at the sky again and confirmed the moon and no clouds.

They both listened, their heads cocked like confused dogs, and Trey was about to say something when several new booms sounded from some unseen place. They gaped at one another before they both understood, rose and raced for the edge of the rooftop even as more gunshots cracked and roared five stories below. To Zephyr, it sounded as though thirty minutes of fireworks had been condensed into a few seconds and he knew before he saw anything that some terrible battle must be underway.

Trey tripped over something and released a series of profanities as he stumbled and fell. "What is it?" he called from the ground while he clutched a knee and groaned.

"I… hold on," Zephyr began and peered over the ledge as his friend struggled to rise.

His first assessment blazed and burst in a millisecond. Strobe lights, a street party with strobe lights and fog…. and then, a Halloween party? What? No, that couldn't be right, he thought. And then his eyes focused and his mind overwrote the ludicrous diagnosis with a truer one: muzzle fire, guns, lots of guns, smoke everywhere and all the people. *Oh my God, so many people. So many damned people!*

The assault was colossal in scale — easily hundreds and possibly thousands of combatants surrounded all sides of Alpha's base. The street lights had likely been blown out and yet the muzzle fire from hundreds of weapons shot in unison illuminated the scene in radiance that flared and dimmed unpredictably. The structure's first floor was on fire, a half-incinerated car still protruding from a gaping wound in what had formerly been the barred entryway. Something big exploded, the crowd roared and Zephyr nearly lost his footing as his own building shook and glass disintegrated all around them.

"Get down!" he yelled and ducked, but Trey was still on the ground and nothing came at them.

"What the fuck!" Trey bellowed.

"They're attacking the headquarters!"

He hurried over to the ledge, leaned over and gawked at the building across the street. "Jesus, they're boned. They're fucking boned, man! We have to do something."

"Check it out!" Zephyr pointed to the top of the structure. "Our guys are still up there!"

As if on cue, a thick stream of fire and smoke erupted from that precise area and javelined down to the city street below, lighting up the night as it flew. For just a second—had he blinked, he might've missed it—the strobe light effect was overtaken by uninterrupted brilliance and he gasped at all of the people. Then, a monumental explosion ripped through the pavement and the resulting inferno spiraled flailing, broken bodies into the air with terrifying force. Now, as screams rang out in chorus on the streets below, more Alpha gunmen took aim and sniped people at will.

For a moment, Zephyr hoped the crowd might actually disperse, that this simple show of force would end the uprising, but clusters of people reformed as quickly as his idea and he shook his head. They aren't gonna last like this, he thought. There are too many out there.

"Our weapons," he said. "We need to get our guns."

"Yeah, let's do it," Trey replied.

They hadn't made it halfway back when the rooftop door swung open and they skidded to a halt—Trey stumbled again and nearly ate cement this time.

"Relax — just me," Aurora said and tossed Zephyr a spare rifle. She wore a long flannel, some shorts, and her feet were bare. "Please tell me you're seeing this."

He nodded. "Hard to miss. Where'd we put the bug-out bags, you remember? We need to get all of our weapons and get…" He gripped her shoulder hard as understanding seized him.

"Aurora," he said. "Where's Jordan?"

She cupped her mouth and shook her head, tears already forming in her eyes, and he knew. She didn't need to say a word, and couldn't anyway.

"I… She…" was all she could manage between the agony that disabled her.

"Where?" Trey interjected.

"Across the street," Zephyr said. He felt sick.

"At fucking Alpha?"

"Yes. At fucking Alpha." He turned back to his girlfriend and tried to embrace her, but she wouldn't let him.

"It's OK. We'll try around back. Or go through the sewers if we have to. We'll figure this out." It wasn't a lie. He'd get her back or die trying and it was just that simple.

"I sho—shou—uld've picked her up earlier, but Sonia… Sonia sss-s-said she'd bring her when they were done playing," Aurora cried, her face contorted. "Why didn't I get her? I should have fucking gotten her!"

She was going to lose it and he knew it, so he took her face in his hands and met her eyes. "We will get her. I promise you. No matter what." And he was unwavering in his resolve. She must've seen it on his face because she nodded and seemed to regain herself a little.

"Guys, something's happening. I think you should look at this," Trey called and Zephyr's ears confirmed the change. The gunshots had halted. Scattered bangs and cracks still sounded from nowhere, but the cacophony of deafening noise had subsided. All at once. When he and Aurora finally leaned back over the edge of the building, the light show was finished, and they saw crowds of faintly lit shadows retreating backward into the darkness.

"They're leaving," she said.

"Maybe the big boys on the roof scared them off," Trey replied. "The bazooka or missile or whatever the fuck they shot down below tore up those assholes pretty good."

Zephyr shook his head. "Yeah, but why now? It was one big explosion and the crowd reformed right after it blew up. I don't get it."

"Who cares? Let's go get Jordan before they come back," Aurora said.

They had scarcely started back when more gunfire rang out behind them and Zephyr turned just in time to see that it was all coming from Alpha's rooftop. The snipers now lined the perimeter of the structure and had forgone any particularity about their targets. Muzzle-fire layered the border of the high-rise. Shot after shot after shot. They were firing everything and not stopping to breathe.

"Christ, here we go again," Trey said as the three of them ran back for a better view.

Then he spotted it. A monstrous diesel truck made an accelerated beeline for Alpha's front doors, the rooftop soldiers unable to inflict any real damage upon it. Shoot another one of those rockets, you idiots, Zephyr thought and nearly screamed, but it was too late, no good, and he knew it. Seconds passed underwater and then the 18-wheeler plowed through the entryway of the building as though it were tissue paper until it was obscured from view.

"Are they carrying fighters inside it, you think?" Trey asked.

"I don't kno—" Zephyr started before a blinding hot light raced through the lower extremities of the structure and a massive detonation howled into the night and knocked them on their asses even as their own hotel seemed to shake and sway on its foundation. Zephyr watched the stars blur in and out of focus and thought he heard more explosions, although they seemed distant now. A low humming gave way to ringing, he cupped one of his ears and found it wet to the touch.

"Oh God!" he thought he heard Aurora scream from some faraway place as he fought against his senses to regain verticality, faltered, and toppled forward. He couldn't seem to restore his center of gravity and every time he tried to stand firm he oscillated and fell instead.

"It's blowing!" Trey shouted. "Man, it's blowing! We're fucked!"

"Help me get up… help me get up," Zephyr said. Or he hoped he said. The ringing in his ears still outshouted everything else. He was about to ask again when Trey and Aurora obliged.

He looked out beyond the perimeter of their own building just in time to see Alpha trembling, its footing shaky, its standing uncertain. His mind surfaced images of the old party game Jenga seconds before a misplaced block sent the puzzle to pieces. Then, before he could even contemplate the totality of such a change, his former home crumbled into itself, level collapsing onto level as any recognizable architecture transformed into broken concrete and metal and splintered wood and great shards of glass.

He screamed something that might've been the name of a little girl and then a black cloud of billowing dust and debris swept over him.

40

This couldn't be happening.

The city horde roared somewhere down below. Aurora screamed and cried from another universe. And for the first time since the disappearances, Zephyr's fight left him. He lay there on the cold rooftop, stared up into layers of smoky darkness and searched for the stars and moon beyond it. If he could just find one twinkling light in the night sky, he felt certain he'd wake from the dream and everything would be right again. His parents downstairs in the kitchen, maybe. No scourged new world. Just the old one, reality shows and traffic jams and thirty-two-ounce sodas and report cards and the fucking Internet and…

"Get up, Zeph!"

Faintly he heard this, the ringing still louder in his ears.

Trey's dumb face stooped before him and Zephyr almost pushed him away so that he might focus on the sky instead, but these thoughts fluttered away into the cloudy aftermath above and he finally allowed the circumstances and the horrible truths that followed to crush him.

He loathed himself for every time he promised to find Jordan's mother and for every time he sent her off to school so that he could savor his pointless solitude. And he blamed Aurora for letting this happen. He knew it wasn't fair and wasn't right, but he couldn't help himself. As the tears cut paths through the ash and dirt on his cheeks, he wished it was him underneath that destruction and swore a silent oath to murder whoever orchestrated the attack on Alpha. That was what mattered now. Not anything else.

Then Trey's hands were upon him, shaking him, and pulling him up. His friend shouted something that Zephyr couldn't understand and now Aurora was beside him. He waved her off but she ignored him.

"We've gotta get him—" Zephyr heard before the ringing overtook his senses again. Far away, a great crowd of people cheered. That collective jubilation reverberated outward and he bawled his fists in response. So many innocent lives lost, and for what? What had really been gained this night?

"Oh my God," Aurora said and then asked something Zephyr couldn't decipher.

"Dunno, but it's not pretty, that's—"

"I can walk," he said. "Let go of me. I can walk."

But they continued on as if they hadn't heard this declaration or didn't care, each holding an arm and dragging him closer to the rooftop exit. He tried to shake them off but couldn't. When they finally pulled the door open and after his eyes adjusted to the emergency lights inside, he saw that his shirt was soaked with sweat. Dark red sweat. And something was jutting out from it. Something foreign. He reached down to touch it and passed out.

41

"Now what?" a voice breathed.

Another replied, "Bedroom closet. Three black bags. Get them all."

Zephyr opened his eyes and searched the sky again for moon and stars. Dark against darker. The blast cloud still dominated his panorama. He blinked and nothing changed. Tired. Cold. Nauseated. He tried to sit up and couldn't move his arms.

Cognition sparked to life and he recognized two new and important details. First, that he was no longer on the rooftop, but in his dining room. This was not a reassuring revelation— only disorienting and concerning. Worse, he seemed to be lying on his dining room table, itself cleared of plates and silverware, not to mention books and toys and whatever else littered the surface on a daily basis. Second, and most important, he was bound to it.

A pattering of footsteps. "I've got 'em," Trey whispered from somewhere nearby. "Good fucking Christ, this is not what I signed up for. Is he awake?"

"Yep," Aurora said and then her face was over him, her hair dangling down onto his cheeks as it always did. She smiled, but he saw at once that it was disingenuous.

"Zephyr, baby. You're hurt. Not too bad. But we have to fix you and then we have to get the hell out of here." She cupped his face with both hands and kissed him. She was sweating and breathing heavy. "You following all this?"

"Yeah." The world lagged a little and he felt dizzy. "Why am I tied up?"

"Because it's gonna hurt. A lot, baby. You've got a big piece of wood in you and I have to pull it out. We don't have anything to stitch up the wound with and even if we did, we're not sure we'd know how to do it. Plus, those people are still out there, which means we've got to go, and the sooner the better."

"Just leave me," Zephyr said. "Take the bags an—"

She slapped him hard enough to rattle his senses. "Don't," she growled. "You never say that to me, ever. You fuck. That is not up for argument."

"Aurora," he started, and she ignored him.

"So we're going to cauterize the wound. It'll be quick, and it's going to work—Trey is positive it'll work just fine— but it's going to hurt."

"It'll work, dude," Trey promised. "But yeah, she's right. Not gonna be a rocking good time."

"You're probably gonna wanna scream," Aurora continued. "That's why we have to gag you, too. The last thing we need is people hearing that. I'm sorry, baby."

Zephyr tried to argue with her and again she cut him off. "If you're going to ask me to leave you, I'm going to beat the shit out of you, damn it."

"All right, don't leave me then," he said. "And thank you. Where am I hit?"

Trey answered him. "Somewhere between your left shoulder and chest, man. You're actually pretty lucky, even if you're not feeling like it right now."

"And you're going to yank out a big piece of wood and then… burn me?"

"More or less, yep. The good news is that we already broke off the tail end of the post — or whatever it is. So we basically just have to pull what's already in you out of you. Not sure how big the wound is gonna be, though, so I've got a small sauce pan heating up on the stove and—"

Aurora thumped him. "That's enough."

Zephyr winced. "Good grief. OK. Just do it. Do we have any more alcohol? I don't care what. Just give me three more shots of something."

Aurora returned to his side a few moments later with a large glass of bourbon and lifted his head so that he could drink some of it. He choked as much of the poison down as he could and then bit down on tube socks rolled especially for the occasion before offering a tentative thumbs up from his binds.

"You've never looked sexier, babe," Aurora said and he flipped her the bird as best he could.

"I'm ready over here… I guess?" Trey whispered.

"Look away," she said. "And close your eyes."

He nodded and did as she asked.

"On the count of three, OK?" she lied, and yanked.

Zephyr's back arched and his eyes rolled into their sockets as he coughed something guttural into his gag and pounded on the table. The pain was so intense that he thought he might black out again and his heart palpitated as he struggled for air, his nostrils flaring as beads of sweat formed on his brow. Then, as quickly as it had come, the pain started to dissipate. He had no time to savor it, though, for a new torment was upon him before he realized it. Burning, searing, torture enveloped his shoulder and chest with a hot hiss as Trey slapped a glowing iron pan on the hemorrhaging hole. This was the worst of it— the pain before was a mosquito bite. Without thinking, he spit out his makeshift gag, vomited all over himself, and passed out.

He woke to cold tile and colder shivers. Now he wore only a wet washcloth on his forehead. He'd been stripped of everything else and the lingering odor of fresh puke explained why. Aurora brushed his damp hair from his face and whispered something to him. He tried to lean forward, and she pushed him back.

"No, don't move. You've been through a lot." She sniffled and wiped her nose. "In a few minutes, we're gonna have to move, and you better believe you're getting up then. Until then, relax. You've earned it."

"You got the thing out of me?" he asked in a voice raspier than he liked.

"Yep. And you're cauterized. Trey did a good job of it."

"That's a first," he said and attempted to smile.

"Yeah, very funny," Trey replied from somewhere beyond his periphery. "Lots of good ones tonight. Like wiping you down after you blew chunks. That was hilarious. Me and your ball-sack are on a first-name basis now. That's... not great. Your dick is pretty funny, too, by the way. Lemme tell you something, the mystery of your relationship with Aurora continues to grow, my good man."

"Jealousy's unbecoming," Zephyr said.

"Your dick is perfect, baby," Aurora interjected. "Quiet, Trey."

"I'd like nothing more than some peace and quiet, actually. Can we get out of Dodge now?"

"I can't go," Zephyr said.

Aurora's posture tightened. "Don't start that shit with me, Zephyr. You're gonna be fine and you are going."

He shook his head. "No, Rory. I'm staying," he said and squeezed her arm. "I'm sorry, but I'm not going with you this time. And you guys aren't done operating on me just yet, either."

42

They trudged through the blackness forever as Zephyr drifted in and out of consciousness. Footsteps and heavy breaths and distant shouting and gunfire and laughter and the crunch of broken glass and whispers that he struggled to comprehend before slipping away again. He sometimes woke to the sound of his own snoring, to himself drooling, and struggled against it, to find his footing, and couldn't. When he moved, there was pain, the world thinned and wavered before him, and so he didn't. He wondered if she had screamed for him when the building came crumbling down. If she had been in mid-sprint when it all crashed and fell. If she had done anything at all, some last desperate wide-eyed action; some final grasp for help, before her skull collapsed into her windpipe and then shattered the rest of her frame and—

"Zephyr," a voice said. "Zephyr, baby, wake up."

His throat was as dry as the desert, his eyelids crusted over. He struggled to see and tried to rise, but a gentle hand pushed him back again.

"No, no, don't move," Aurora said. "Here, drink this." She guided a cup of water into his hand.

He swallowed and grimaced. The liquid hurt going down, it tasted wonderful and foul simultaneously, and still he drank until she stopped him.

"Slow."

He choked and coughed. "I can't open my eyes."

"It's just some sleep," she said, licked a finger and rubbed his lids. "You've been out of it for a while. Better?"

When he blinked, smeary, watery vision returned. Her hair, normally brushed and straight, was disheveled, her eyes swollen, and her tank top stained in blood, likely his. She still looked beautiful. The window behind her showed daylight.

"Are you OK?" he asked.

She nodded. "I'm just glad you're OK."

"I feel like I ate a cat," he said, his voice dry and cracked, and massaged his neck.

"Yeah well, you've been asleep for two days, baby. You're dehydrated."

Two days? He was going to ask what happened, and then the memories battered him.

"She," he started, and couldn't stop the torrent of emotion, the sudden inhalation, his wobbly voice, and the tears. "Ssh-shhh—"

Aurora had him, and she was crying, too, and hugging him and kissing him and telling him that there was nothing any of them could have done. He held her back, the two of them silent for a long time.

He ran his fingers through her hair. "I love you," he said, and he wasn't embarrassed; for the first time, it didn't matter if his feelings were reciprocated. "You must know that by now, but just in case there was any doubt."

"I love you," she said, kissed him, and he could feel her body spasm with the throes of each silent sob.

They hadn't left the penthouse. She and Trey must've dragged him to their bedroom, but that was as far as he'd gone since the explosions. Somewhere in the city streets below, Alpha and all of its people had been reduced to crumbled piles of stone and bone. It was a truth that he didn't want to think about. Not now — maybe not ever.

"Where's Trey?"

"He's on the roof making sure we're all good," she said, and caught herself. "Or at least as good as we can be considering the circumstances."

He was coated in sweat and, he discovered, still naked except for a damp blanket that he let slip from his waist as he tried to rise.

"No way," Aurora said and pushed him back. "Not a good idea."

"I need to pee. Help me up then."

So she did, and they were both a little surprised when he could walk unaided. At first, his tingly legs and feet stung with every step, but very soon his circulation flowed true and, although the weakness held, movement was manageable. He sat down on the toilet seat and pissed because he wasn't sure he could stand that long without passing out or throwing up.

"I feel like death," he said, his voice still scratchy.

Aurora stood in the door frame and peered at him. "I know, but the important thing is that you're getting better. You need to drink more water, then eat something, and you'll start to feel like yourself again."

He met her gaze. "So," he said. "Do I wanna see this wound?" All this time, he'd avoided it, wasn't sure he was ready for it.

"Don't be such a wuss." There was a hint of a smile back upon her face. "The truth is, it's pretty bad, but not as bad as it was a couple days ago," she said. "Besides, we've got it taped up. There isn't much to see."

Now he did glance down and confirmed the amateur Band-Aids. Wide, silver stripes formed multilayered Xs across a baseball-sized patch of skin where chest became arm. They'd used duct tape and he thought it made him look a little like a patched-up android. He moved his arm — barely, and then some more.

"Doesn't really hurt," he said.

Aurora chuckled. "That's because you're way high. We've been slipping the good stuff in your water every time you drink."

"Oh."

Now that he thought about it, yeah, it wasn't just exhaustion and fever. Or maybe it was both of those things with a healthy dose of drugs on top. Either way, he wasn't in any real pain, and however temporary the relief, he was glad for it.

A door squeaked open from somewhere behind Aurora, and Zephyr ignored it while he studied his hands and the walls in a futile effort to comprehend just how wasted he really was.

"Oh, for the love of Christ," Trey said, cutting through the silence. "First, your balls, and now I gotta step into you taking a shit?"

Aurora elbowed him. "He looks better though, doesn't he?"

"He does," Trey agreed, and he was smiling.

43

Four more days had risen and set as he cycled between sleep, drugged tranquility, nausea, and lucidity, the latter of which came with a heavy price tag paid in pain and memories.

Occasionally, Aurora or Trey left the penthouse to scavenge food or other supplies from the surrounding rooms, or to survey the city from the rooftop, but usually they remained inside with Zephyr, hid, and waited. Hid from the banter, gunshots and footsteps far and near. Waited for him to heal.

The disaster across the street had taken all the electricity with it. When they looked out at night, the city was black. Luckily, Trey's generator still worked, and they hadn't run out of fuel yet.

"Where did they all go?" Zephyr asked.

"No idea," his friend answered as the three of them spooned mouthfuls of canned beans into their mouths and watched television.

TV wasn't what it used to be. Most of the satellite broadcasts had failed since the event. Many stations aired static logos, messages with promises that would never be honored, or nothing at all. Now, though, the selection had dwindled until just two channels played anything worthy of an audience. The first was CNN, which looped a short, grainy video of a marching band as it performed a somber melody over and over and over again. Trey joked that *MTV* had finally returned, but Aurora said the footage was freaky, so they seldom tolerated it for long. The second was TBS. When they had first browsed upon the station months ago, its grayscale transmission had been a welcome surprise and a small comfort — a reminder, perhaps, of the old world and better times. Late at night after Jordan and Aurora had slipped off, Zephyr would sometimes turn the channel on and watch the movie as it lit up the screen on infinite repeat, and it always made him feel a little better. Now, though, as the townspeople piled into George Bailey's house and spread holiday good cheer, not to mention their money, the irony licked at him like hot flames, and he realized that he would rather watch the marching band play the world away.

"They pretty much disappeared," Trey added, and then corrected himself. "Not like that. I mean, they left. Took off."

He shoved another spoonful of cold beans into his mouth. "Mind you, I didn't even go out to look until the second day because we were, one, focused on getting your ass better and, two, pretty much terrified that someone would search this place and find us. But when I finally did, there was nothing to see. Except, you know, the aftermath."

"We've heard people, though," Zephyr said.

"Yeah, well, of course — I mean, they're obviously still out there. I just don't know if they've still got an army. They seem to have scattered again."

"I think someone needs to go out and look."

"Don't start," Aurora snapped. "What we're going to do is get you all the way healed, and then we're going to find some place far away from here and we're going to be safe and happy, like we were in New Mexico. I can't believe I'm saying this, but I actually miss that boring old mansion."

He missed it, too, he realized, but he only shook his head. "We were never that safe there. Not really. And I'm not leaving until someone pays for what they did."

She glared at him. "Yeah, and it's gonna be you. With your life."

He didn't turn. "Aurora," he said. "I haven't stopped running since this all began. Hell, I ran most of the way to California, usually trying to get away from something rather than face it, because I've been scared. Always. But I'm not scared now. And I owe it to Jordan to see this through. I need to see this through."

His plan was simple, and if they had listened to him as he lay bleeding and on the verge of passing out several nights ago, the hard part would already be finished. The ones who attacked Alpha, who blew it up, who murdered Jordan… they had something in common beyond their horrific crimes: they were branded. Not all of them, he understood, but more than a few. So he would wear the brand, too, and he would walk among them, get to know them, work his way to their leader, and kill him.

"Setting aside that this is a death sentence — that you will never get out of there alive, even if you could pull it off," Trey argued for the umpteenth time. "You expect me to believe you're just going to waltz in there and blow some dude away? Yeah right. You're not a murderer."

Zephyr shrugged. He thought of the man he'd killed in that awful ransacked Target so many months ago. "I'm telling you, I will," he said, and he meant it.

That night, as Trey slept in the next room, Zephyr and Aurora made silent, intense love: the release of pent up tension transformed into passion and fueled by a downpour of every emotion left unchecked. She had done most of the work — his arm was still barely functional and using it in any capacity brought bursts of blasting pain. When they finished, she spooned into him, wrapped his good arm around herself, and whispered, "If you insist on doing it, then fuck it, I'm going with you."

He didn't say anything but his body language, a tightening, a straightening, all instinctual, must have spoken for him, because she launched into the defensive before he ever opened his mouth.

"Don't you dare say no, you asshole," she said and rolled over to face him in the dark, her face so close that he could feel her breath. "You have no right to say no to me. It's my decision, just like it's your decision, and I'm going."

He tried to kiss her, to diffuse her, and she turned her head.

"No. I'm going, Zephyr."

"I can't let you," he started and when she pushed away from him, he caught her. "Wait a second. Let me… Aurora. Wait."

"Fuck you."

"They are killers. Like the men I rescued you from. And you are the single most beautiful girl anybody has seen — trust me on this," he said, and when she didn't respond, he continued. "Me? They won't give a single shit about me. But you? You're priceless in this world and they will fight over themselves trying to get at you. They'll kill me just to take you. To own you, Rory."

44

Four days later, Zephyr moseyed along the stretching sidewalks of Santa Monica Boulevard and pondered the golden hue that blanketed the city, a gradient that seemed exclusive to Southern California. Even in the winter, that beautiful summer tone hung over the landscape and belied the hazards at every footstep, he thought, as he traced the painful scab on the back of his neck with one finger.

He was alone now, just as he had been that first morning. Trey had understood at once that there'd be no deterring him, but Aurora had fought with everything she could muster, threats and tears included. Turning them away was an exercise in torture — maybe not as agonizing as the physical kind, his throbbing neck a constant reminder of that — but miserable all the same.

"Please," she had cried, her arms around him. "Promise me you will meet us there." And he had nodded, knowing that there was no guarantee.

There, in this case, was the luxury resort in Palm Springs. The hotel where he'd surrendered his virginity. With a little luck, Trey and Aurora would be back there by now, or arriving soon. With a lot more luck, Zephyr would rendezvous with them in fewer than thirty days. Any longer than that, and they would move on. Aurora didn't want to stay in California any more.

"If we're not there, we'll be in New Mexico at the old house," she had told him. "Or, at least I will. I haven't even asked Trey yet."

He'd sighted them with his scope and watched them go from his window. First, to cover them if anybody should impede their progress. But mostly, just to see them. To catch one last glimpse of her and hold it in his mind's eye.

Nothing extraordinary had befallen him in the days since they walked out of his life. He had his rifle, some rations, including a backpack full of protein bars and two bottles of water. And best of all, his health seemed to have stabilized. He no longer felt nauseated or dizzy as he rose or after standing for extended periods. He could walk, which is what he did. He walked the city unabated and unafraid.

There was no army.

Sometimes he came upon people but the encounters were more depressing than anything else. The first day *After Aurora*, or *1 AA*, as he now thought about it, he saw a fat, scruffy, red-headed man in his late forties. Zephyr came upon him as he explored the city and saw movement from his periphery. There in some blown out store window was the man, relaxing in an armchair and watching a lifeless television while flames leapt and danced from an oversized cooking pot at his feet — an improvised bonfire. On *2 AA*, he happened upon a gathering of four teenage boys, draped in blankets and drinking beer at the beach. When they saw him, they turned and sprinted into the opposite direction and nothing he shouted could bring them back. On *3 AA*, a bicycle fell from the sky and crashed against the sidewalk only a few feet before him. When Zephyr looked up and then examined the windows on the building adjacent him, a lone hand flipped down the bird from a window several stories up.

Later, as he rummaged through the leftovers of a ransacked grocery store, he heard a noise, turned, and found a man and a woman with their guns on him. He dropped his rifle, explained that he wasn't looking for a fight, peeled back his hoodie to show his brand, and this actually seemed to do the job. They lowered their weapons and a mostly-one-way dialog began; he could tell that they still didn't trust him, but it was nevertheless progress. They revealed that they were going to Oregon, and not much else. Zephyr fed them his practiced lies about amnesia, and waking with a terrible wound, and they nodded. When he asked where he might be able to find more people like him, however, they only shrugged, and he didn't think they were lying.

Today wasn't great, either, but at least nobody had tried to murder him with a bike. Mid-afternoon, and still nothing to show for his wanderings except a cold breeze and a colder sweat. What he wanted to do was go find a bed, either in one of the empty high-rises or houses, and sink into it. And yet, when he thought about Aurora waiting for him, and about the days ticking down to zero until she didn't, his feet kept moving. So he walked, and walked, and walked some more after that. And as the sun dipped behind some medley of buildings and darkness came, he finally spotted a flickering of flame in the distance and beelined for it.

As he drew closer, he saw that it wasn't just a flame, but a massive bonfire set outside the entrance of what looked like a former car dealership. The adjoining lot still held a hundred or more vehicles that would never be sold. The blaze was huge — the kind of controlled inferno that Zephyr expected to see at some desert music festival, not here. Strangest of all, though, was the crowd. Not just a few people, but at least fifty — some of them standing and chatting, others dancing, still more sitting or sleeping, all of them sucking up the heat.

Here they were at last, he thought, and felt that familiar pang in the pit of his stomach. The crowd was the biggest he'd seen since the attack on Alpha, and although this display looked almost primal, he still took some small measure of comfort in discovering so many people together. It happened so seldom these days — it was like looking up to see a rainbow on a misty afternoon. Except, of course, rainbows couldn't kill you. He unlatched the safety on his rifle and slung the weapon back over his shoulder. Just in case. Probably, he'd be fine, but just in case, he told himself.

It was a party, and these people didn't seem to care who knew about it. As he approached, the music was blaring so loud that he could've fired off a couple rounds from his gun and nobody would've been the wiser. The bonfire flared and leapt, pinpricks of glowing light popping into the darkness, as people swayed and whirled. Beer and liquor bottles stood around the flames like some sacrificial offering to them. Some people were passed out, others on the verge.

Nobody noticed him. Or, if they did, they didn't care. The party went right on raging, people shouting and laughing and writhing against the music and the fire. A thick cloud of smoke and the strong odor of marijuana permeated the expanse — a room designed to showcase cars, not host primitive raves. Beyond the radius of the fire, the area grew darker until he couldn't see anything except for the stray embers of cigarettes burning in the darkness like stars in the night sky.

Zephyr had almost expected to find cannibals with tangled hair, tribal face tattoos and teeth sharpened to fangs, but the truth of it was, circumstances aside, most of these people looked normal. Well, normal for spring break in Florida was probably more accurate. Most of the men lacked shirts, and the women, of which there must be at least twenty, he noted, wore bikini tops; this attire despite the cold weather outside. But otherwise, they looked like him. Just happier.

Something was out of place, though, and when he finally ascertained what, he understood that not everybody present was celebrating. The inferno raged atop a massive cinderblock just outside the showroom. It looked like a car engine. Except, someone had fastened chains to the perimeter of the block, and most of the people he thought were asleep, or relaxing, were in fact in shackles. They were prisoners. Five women and a man, locked at the ankles some ten feet from the blaze by chains stretched to break. Zephyr realized with disgust that they were all naked from the waists down.

He pondered how the same fate might've befallen Aurora if he hadn't arrived when he did, and something inside of him wanted to unsling his weapon and start shooting at these people, oblivious as they were, cheering and dancing in the face of this injustice. He didn't, though. He knew they'd be on him in seconds, and then he'd likely be the next chain on the block, or worse.

Two women holding hands slid by him and as they did, the trailing one turned, blew smoke in his face, and giggled.

"You're welcome," she said, barely audible through the cacophony of raw noise, waved good-bye, and followed her friend into a mass of dancing bodies.

Zephyr coughed and was about to turn away when he noticed that the two of them came out again on the other side of the mob and made for a faintly illuminated exit on the opposite end of the room. No electricity — it was hard to see anything outside of the fire's range, but there was some other area back there. Of course, he still hadn't devised anything resembling a plan — his modus operandi for too long, he accepted — so he shadowed them.

As he stepped through the frame, he came into a smaller cavity lit by dozens of candles scattered across wall shelves. The two women he'd followed in had already fallen into one of several plush couches that comprised the only furniture in the smoky space. Once his eyes adjusted, Zephyr saw that this shabby lounge was undoubtedly an office in another life. Now, at the end of the world, it was a speakeasy.

"Hey stalker," said the woman who'd blown smoke in his face as she draped a skinny leg onto her friend's lap. She wore her long blonde hair in a ponytail, her skin as pale as milk.

"Hi," Zephyr said, surprised that he could hear her, and examined the room. There were a dozen more bodies laid out on the couches, most of them sleeping.

The woman patted the space beside her and smiled. "Don't be shy — come sit with us."

"I'd love to," he lied, "But I'm actually just on my way out. I really need to get some sleep or I'm going to fall on my face. I was hoping you could help me out real quick, though. I'm a little… confused."

"He's confused, Jules," the woman's friend snickered.

He ignored her. "Jules, is it? Hi. I'm Zephyr. Nice to meet you both." He offered them what he hoped was his most disarming wave.

"Here's the deal — and I'll make this quick, I swear. I guess the short version is that I woke up outside of a crumbled building a couple days ago and I had this," he said, and lifted his shirt to showcase the patched wound on his chest. "Obviously, something happened. I just don't know what. I can't remember anything."

The women exchanged a look, and then Jules said, "Come sit with us, and then let's chat." She scooted sideways so that a space developed between herself and her friend and then motioned again for Zephyr to join them.

He did. It was an awkward exercise, not only because sitting between them meant that he faced neither, but also because he needed to unsling his weapon first. After he sat, he placed the rifle on the floor at his feet.

"Look at you," the still-unnamed woman sighed as she ran her fingers through his hair. "A beautiful boy."

There was nothing malevolent in her tone; she just sounded stoned. *She's probably coming down from a weeklong bender*, he thought. Even so, he wanted to pull away, to get out of there, and yet he never so much as flinched. Instead, he thanked her, and was about to ask his questions again when Jules interrupted him.

"Do you remember the building?"

He fumbled for a response and then found it in the truth.

"Alpha," he said.

"Alpha," the nameless woman whispered. "Yes, Alpha."

"What happened to it?" he asked.

"Do you know what was going on there?" Jules replied in turn.

He'd practiced for questions like these.

"It was some kind of community," he said. "I went there once. The bastards gave me this." And he pulled back his hoodie to reveal the star of tonight's show, his own personal all-access pass to the city post Alpha. When he did, he felt the other woman's soft touch across his scar.

"He's like us," she said.

Jules nodded and then threw her arm around him. "We blew it up," she said. "Well, not us, but people like us — like you and me and Heather here. People who still care about this world."

"What do you mean?"

"That place was just… bad. The people there…" She trailed off for a moment and then regained herself. "I've got the mark, like you. They kidnapped me, mutilated me, took everything I had, and threw me back out to die. They did that to hundreds. They did it to kids. And they would've kept right on doing it if we hadn't fought back."

"How the hell did we do it?"

After the woman had recounted the battle from her perspective — a version that mostly mirrored his own — he finally asked her who had organized the army, who was behind it all.

She only shook her head. "I don't know. Word just spread to meet at the boulevard after dark and be ready to fight."

"Because two wrongs always make a right," the other woman — Heather — interrupted.

Jules rolled her eyes. "All right."

"No damned better."

"I'm seriously not in the mood, bitch," Jules said.

Zephyr pressed on. "So who leads your group here?"

"Nobody, really. Or maybe all of us?"

"The men do," Heather interjected.

"That might actually be true," Jules agreed. "We're pretty much back to the basics now. Hunter and gatherer bullshit, and all that stuff. So I guess we fall in line with the men here, but it's not like we're their slaves or anything. We can leave if we don't like it."

She lit a cigarette and dragged on it. "Honestly, though, it could be a lot worse."

"So why are those people chained up?" Zephyr asked.

"Oh, those are prisoners of war."

"From Alpha. From the battle?"

"Uh-huh."

"And they're naked?"

The woman looked away. "Yep."

He wasn't sure what he expected to find tonight. Maybe it was the so-called hard bad, the sociopathic or psychopathic so often hypothesized about, so far removed from empathy that they would be easy to vilify and easier to hate. But these women were just lost. They might be desperate and even misguided, but underneath it all, he thought they were scared, and he pitied them.

Heather squeezed his thigh. "We can be naked, too," she whispered. "If you want."

How come it had never been this easy before the disappearances? He only chuckled at the suggestion, though.

"I'm flattered, but I'm also exhausted."

He lay awake in the bedroom of some captured house that night, his legs restless, his mind racing. He missed the buzz and pop of electricity. What he wouldn't have traded for just one more hour of *It's a Wonderful Life* to lull him into dreams. Instead, he shifted in his bed and thought only of Aurora and Trey, and whether or not they had made it to the hotel in the hot desert of California. What would they be talking about now? Would they be swimming, as he had? Or scavenging those freezers for leftover food? And those contemplations inevitably led to visions of Jordan and then to the crime committed upon her by people who weren't necessarily as immoral and depraved as he pictured them — as he hoped they were. It would all be so much more convenient if they had just been cannibals.

By *AA 15*, Zephyr was ready to go — shadowy leader of the enemy army be damned. It was an atrocity. It was unforgivable. And it was done. But the more survivors he encountered, the more he understood that there was no *Red Skull* calling the shots. No ruthless dictator. No central power at all. However the strike had developed, it had been carried out without singular leadership, a sporadic hive assault. Nothing more, nothing less. He could search forever and he'd never find the boogeyman because he didn't exist.

He missed Jordan. He missed her tiny hand in his own. He missed reading to her at bedtime. He missed her silly questions and her sillier perspective on everything. He missed the way she mispronounced the words she had picked up from her books. *What does im-bee-kill mean?* He missed the way she laughed and threatened to pee her pants when he tickled her.

He spent the next few days at a big hotel off one of the major boulevards. At night, he heard a steady beat of movement, but he never saw anybody in the place during the days. The street was a different story. He periodically surveyed the stretching road and sidewalks with his scope and oftentimes spotted a passerby or a gang of people as they went about their business. Sometimes he walked out to talk to them, but mostly he let them go without interruption.

On *AA 17*, he decided to leave. There was no point in staying any longer. His vengeance lacked a culprit and target. He guessed he could stick to the area and snipe at random groups — people who had likely played some part in the attack. They might have slaves and maybe he could save a few of them. But more likely, he would die, and that would be that.

The hotel was drowning in extravagance, its crystal chandeliers and marble pillars and gold-trimmed bannisters and designer bedding. And yet, Zephyr couldn't turn a light on and when he tried to take a shower, the faucet pissed out cold, brown water on him.

He busted through the doors into a few of the hotel rooms nearest his and stole whatever snacks and water bottles he could. He had more than enough supplies to sustain himself for several days. And he possessed a map, just in case he forgot the way back to Palm Springs. Which he wouldn't.

Later, dressed for the weather, his backpack full of food and water, and his gun slung over his shoulder, he walked the boulevard toward the nearest freeway onramp. What a difference a tragedy made. He recalled their mad dash to Alpha, sneaking through the city streets in the cover of darkness, all three of them terrified that they might be seen. Now, though, there was no such fear. He just didn't care. And if for whatever stupid reason someone wanted a fight, a fight they would have.

He liked to think he was prepared for battle, but he wasn't looking for one, and indeed took precautions against any potential hazards. Periodically, he raised his scope to his eye and scanned into the distance, searching for abnormalities, motion, anything at all that might be dangerous to him.

He was doing exactly this when he sighted on a man and girl outside a gas station several blocks ahead. The man was tall, thin, with graying hair and a short beard to match. He wore a flannel over jeans and carried a wooden baseball bat in one hand. With the other, he led the girl, who was short and blonde. She was dressed in a black jacket over a yellow sundress and boots; the colors of a bumblebee. Zephyr thought she could've been Jordan in another life.

He steadied the reticule against the wind, his heart thumping in his chest, his breath suddenly shallow. Wait, he thought, as he locked on her again. As he studied her through newly smeared vision. As he struggled to stay his focus. To keep his composure. To stand at all.

That *is* Jordan.

45
Jordan

It's her, he told himself. It is. And you know it.

Everything in him yearned to confirm it. To examine her, to embrace her, to validate her existence, to exorcise any lingering doubt. But he couldn't. He had to be smart about this. He had to do it the right way. He couldn't mess this up.

Zephyr loathed that man, whoever he was. He watched them walk to a nearby shoe store whose glass windows had long ago been broken out. When they stepped inside and he couldn't see them, it took everything he had to stay his ground when all he wanted to do was run screaming ahead so that he might substantiate the reality of her again. He was petrified she might never come out of there, that he'd chased a ghost, that he'd finally lost his mind.

How could she have survived? The entire building had collapsed. They'd all died. Everybody. Except, he knew that wasn't true. The scattered slaves were proof enough of that. Might she have been one of the lucky few who'd been pulled out of the rubble unscathed? He recalled the terrorist attack in New York and the catastrophic loss of life so long ago. Even then, there had been survivors.

Zephyr squinted into his scope, tried to locate them and couldn't. He thought he could shoot and kill this man from his vantage point and knew he would never risk it. Not with Jordan so close. And there was the possibility that her captor was no kidnapper at all. He had no intention of murdering an innocent man, as much as believed him to be just the opposite. And if he really was a scoundrel, a thief of little girls, then he would die slow and hard.

There she was again, clutching a shoebox as the man guided her back onto the sidewalk. The two of them trudged along and talked as they made their way up the street on a path that would lead right to him. He needed to take shelter, he realized, and made slow, deliberate movements to back away from his crouching spot. When he was confident he would not be seen, he sneaked around to one side of a rundown *Denny's* restaurant and took refuge behind it.

The long walk toward him seemed to stretch out into infinity and he thought again of all the shit that had gotten him here. He might be in Palm Springs or New Mexico now, but he had chosen to stay, and nothing could sway him of that decision. A commitment to avenge the little girl who was the closest thing he had to family in this world. And after all of it, here she was, still alive and coming right to him.

Zephyr remembered something one of the Alpha sisters had said. That some higher force had reset a cosmic chess board — the leftovers the pawns of some grand strategy beyond understanding. Now here was a circumstance that seemed utterly outside of coincidence. Could the series of events that took him back to Jordan have been part of that design, set in motion by the same guiding power that had ripped so many billions of lives from the planet? Or, was he just another example of mankind's preserving arrogance – an everlasting belief that there are no coincidences, and that the sun revolves around the Earth?

The answer, he found, was that he didn't care.

So long as she was really real, so long as he could hug her and kiss her and take her away with him, it didn't matter. And if he never understood what had changed the world forever, or why, he could live with that.

Patience, he learned, was not one of his virtues. When Jordan finally walked beyond his hiding spot, he rose — to hell with playing it safe — and sprinted to them. By the time the man finally heard his footsteps, he was on him, his rifle trained and ready to fire.

"Your hands up!" he shouted. "Put your fucking hands up!"

"Zephyr!" Jordan cried, and ran to him.

"I'm here, Jord," he said, as she plunged into him with a thud that knocked him slightly off balance and then wrapped her arms around him.

Zephyr never looked away from the man, who had taken a step closer.

"Wouldn't do that, if you want to live," he said, and reasserted his weapon.

"Don't hurt him. He's nice," Jordan said. "He's been taking care of me. He's nice."

"What's your name?" Zephyr asked.

"Brian," the man said and rubbed his peppery beard.

"How'd you find Jordan?"

He stared back at Zephyr, but gave no reply.

"When the bad people blew up the—" Jordan began but the man shushed her.

"I've got this, Jordan," he said.

Zephyr shook his head. "No," he replied. "You don't. Now let her talk."

She let go of Zephyr and wiped her eyes. He wanted to pick her up and bear-hug her, but wouldn't. Not yet.

"After the building blew up, some other people took me. Brian got me from the bad people and protected me."

"Jord, how did you get out of there?"

"Where?"

"Alpha, kiddo," Zephyr said. "How did you survive the explosion?"

"I was already outside. We were coming back home and I just ran down the street when all the people were shooting."

The man took another step closer and Zephyr backed away with Jordan.

"I don't know what you're playing at, but rest assured I will shoot you," he said.

Brian nodded and didn't move, his hands still raised, the bat still clasped in one of them.

"Drop the bat," Zephyr said. "And back away. Five steps. Then we'll talk."

The man nodded, started to lower the weapon, and then swung it at the rifle. It was a valiant effort, but Zephyr was ready for it, and he fired the gun just as the wood connected with it.

Three things happened simultaneously. First, Jordan screamed, and seemed to go right on screaming. Second, Zephyr's gun flew from his hand and he scrambled in slow motion to retrieve it. Third, a hole opened up on the side of the man's neck and blood spurted out from it as he slipped and then fell backward.

Zephyr dove and snatched up the weapon just as the bleeding man was coming for him, oblivious to his hemorrhaging wound. He squeezed off another shot that tore through man's cheekbone and ripped off half of his face, but it might as well have been a mosquito bite for as much as it slowed him. Then the figure was on him, and cracking him in the face with blow after blow. Zephyr fought back, punching and kicking and thrashing and screaming while the battering rained down upon him. A gory face blocked the sun from view and snarled spit-drenched obscenities at him.

Jordan was wailing from some muffled, faraway place and Zephyr thought, I'm sorry. I tried. I almost did it, Jord.

When he looked into the man's eyes, there was nothing in them except blank rage, and he knew this was finally the end. That there would be no relenting. He was going to be beaten to death in front of a damned Denny's in a city with imported palm trees. In direct view of the little girl he'd tried to save.

He kneed his attacker's balls with the last remnants of his energy. The man howled and the assault halted, but it wasn't going to be enough and Zephyr had nothing left to give. He stared up into those terrible eyes once more and as he did, the man's head detonated.

That was the only way to describe it. One second he was whole, about to mount another powerful offensive, and in the next, he was headless, his face and skull blown clean off his body, a fountain of red pulp an eruption from the savage wound.

Zephyr screamed, struggled to free himself from the corpse, and rolled over. He tried to stand and fell, so he rose again, and slipped. He had to get to Jordan. They needed to get off the street. To hide somewhere while he recovered.

Then he noticed them. Four new legs. When he looked up, Trey and Aurora stood behind him, smoke still billowing from his girlfriend's shotgun.

"He's dead," she said almost to herself. "Really dead."

"I'll say," Trey added.

Zephyr plopped back onto his back. He heard Aurora call his name.

She leaned over and kissed him, her beautiful face blocking the sun, her hair falling over him. It was his favorite thing.

"You didn't actually think I'd leave you, did you?" she asked. "That was never on the table. I told you that."

He smiled at her. "You bitch."

In some remote place, another galaxy maybe, he thought he heard Trey singing Jordan's name, and then the world faded from view.

46
Going Home

Fishing was a pain in the ass.

After Zephyr returned from the library with books that covered the subject and more, Trey told him he was wasting his time, but both Aurora and Jordan encouraged this newfound interest. So whenever he found a moment, he scoured the books for useful advice and techniques, and before too long, he thought he understood the concepts. He knew how to kill a fish in the most humane manner. How to gut and clean it. How to ignite a spark for a fire and then nurture the flames so that they didn't burn out. How to design an enclosed space so that he could smoke and preserve his catches.

But first, he had to catch a damned fish, and that just wasn't happening.

In truth, he didn't think he had much chance of ever starting a friction fire, anyway. He admitted to himself that there was just no way he possessed the ability or patience to rub sticks together until they produced an ember. Thankfully, he had a lighter and it worked just fine for now.

Trey's mouth also worked just fine, and it never closed. Even now, as Zephyr, Aurora and Jordan waited for anything to bite, he heckled them from his grassy perch thirty feet off.

"I think it's gonna happen this time," he called, ignoring Zephyr's plea for peace and quiet. "Yep. Get ready, Jordan. Record-breaker incoming. I can feel it."

Nearly two weeks had passed since the beating and Zephyr's face still wore signs of it. His broken nose, now forever crooked, had given rise to blackened eyes that were only just fading. Meanwhile, his lower lip still held three stitches that had taken Aurora the better part of an hour to sew. He looked a little like a healthier version of Frankenstein.

He still didn't have the slightest idea why the man hadn't listened to him or why he'd attacked instead. Jordan hadn't yielded any answers. She only reiterated that he was nice to her. Whatever his motives, they died with him, and that's just how it was.

"I think I'm gonna call it for the day," Aurora said as she spooled in her line. "Better luck tomorrow, right?"

Trey feigned excitement. "What's happening — did you catch Jaws? Jordan, get away from the water. Aurora's hooked Jaws!"

"You seriously have nothing better to do?" Zephyr asked.

"Nope."

He didn't think Trey was lying. His friend seemed to take great pleasure in antagonizing them. When he wasn't doing exactly that, he was listening to the AM/FM radio he'd found while Zephyr had been solo-exploring Santa Monica. Or drinking. He might have been an engineering genius in his former life, but these days, he was just a dystopian hipster.

They'd had big plans for Palm Springs, but by the time they finally started a car and drove out there, they discovered that the city no longer hummed with electricity. Cold weather and, with no juice to heat it, a cold pool, too. The luxury resort no longer held its luxuries and the allure was gone, so it wasn't long before the four of them moved on.

Jordan was back from the dead and everybody fawned over her. More compliments, kisses, hugs, and squeezes had befallen her than in all the months they'd lived together prior, and when she asked to sleep with them, Zephyr and Aurora always obliged her. He still couldn't believe she was real and sometimes studied her face as she slept, too afraid to look away lest she disappear.

One night as they slept together, he caressed her hair and whispered, "Jord, I don't think we're going to find your mom."

"I know," she whispered back, and hugged him.

"I'm sorry."

She cried into his chest and he cried with her.

When at last she pulled back, she said, "I'm glad we're together."

"Forever this time. Or until you get sick of me."

"I never will."

The lake was located about eighty miles east of the state border. They were somewhere in Arizona now. Good old Arizona, he thought. Where nobody had ever tried to murder them. Where no buildings had crumbled before their eyes. This was a state they'd driven through without incident. Of course, he reminded himself, they hadn't ever voyaged to the bigger cities like Phoenix or Tucson and that's probably how they'd sidestepped the localized dangers. Their good fortune would likely continue then because they didn't intend to explore those cities now, either.

He was going home. Back to Firefly Valley. They all were.

Aurora first raised the idea. She said she wanted to see his hometown. He resisted the suggestion from the start for all the obvious reasons, Ross primary among them. How long had it been? Surely not just a year. Could it be two? Zephyr didn't even think he'd be recognizable to the man now. He was much taller, stronger, weathered. No longer the boy Ross remembered.

"There's really nothing left to see anyway. The bastard burned down the one thing I could've shown you."

"I know," she said and laid her pole on the ground. "It's not like we've got any other pressing plans, though. Besides, I think it would be fun to see the city you grew up in."

"Except, there's a gun-toting maniac hanging out back there, and we didn't exactly leave things on the best of terms."

"You know what I think?" she asked.

"Do tell."

"I think that's the old you talking. The new you was born to this world. That's the guy who killed a man to rescue me and who went out to die for Jordan's honor when he didn't have to. I don't think Ross is prepared for that Zephyr. You're probably a better shot than he is now."

"Rory, what I realized out there is that I don't care about anything else but us." He looked to Jordan, Trey, and then back to her. "Our family, I mean, as dysfunctional as we sometimes are. I risked all of that for some pointless act of vengeance. It was dumb. I don't want to do it again."

"And if you hadn't, Jordan would still be dead to all of us — we'd never have known to look for her, let alone have actually found her." She rose, patted the dirt from her jeans, and added, "Listen, all I'm saying is, think about it. Every brave thing you've done has been good. It's worked for you."

She kissed her hand and then touched his cheek. "Whatever you want, we'll all support you."

"It could go badly."

"Don't worry, baby. I'll rescue you," she said and smiled. "Oh, that reminds me. We're even on the rescuing front."

He smiled at her. "What about New Mexico? I thought you wanted to go back."

"Let's stop in and check on Sarah. No rush, right?"

47

Firefly Valley. Population: Five.

The snow came down hard and fast as they crested the peak that glared down upon his hometown, itself covered in powder. They drove slow, cautious of the slushy roads and of the man Zephyr had told them all about. Trey was the worst shot among them, Jordan included, so he held the wheel, and he never stopped complaining about it.

"Make the guy from California drive into a snow storm. That's what we'll do. Because he's been in the snow before. Once. When he was blasted nine years-old."

"If you didn't handle a gun like a little girl, you wouldn't be driving right now," Aurora said.

"Hey!" Jordan objected.

"I didn't mean you, Jordie. Trey wishes he could shoot as well as you do."

"I'm not above crashing this beautiful beast to make a point," Trey said.

The beautiful beast was a Mercedes-Benz G-Class SUV, silver, with a twin turbo-charged V8 engine, seven-speed automatic transmission and full-time all-wheel drive. Zephyr had no idea what any of that shit meant, but it was Trey's dream car, and he never shut up about it. The vehicle was another gift from Arizona, which was rapidly becoming

Zephyr's favorite vacation destination in the new world. Arizona: No murdering and dream cars aplenty, folks, he thought. There's a campaign that just about any leftover would find appealing.

They passed through New Mexico almost a week ago and it was both depressing and wonderful. Main Street reminded him of Ben, so lovable and funny, decomposing in a forgotten department store. He thought of Merrick and Brad in their final resting place beside an incinerated death bus and all of the old guilt came crashing back. He and Aurora prepared Jordan for the bleak possibility that they might find Sarah in a similar state. But when they finally entered the old mansion, not only was she still alive, she was plump, with good color, and she was smiling.

She also had company. Shortly after the three of them made off for California, Sarah was scavenging for supplies when she met Paula, a stocky, short-haired fifty-something, and the two of them became fast friends. Zephyr wondered if they might be more than friends, but didn't say anything. They'd been living together ever since, which was, as the group discovered, not at all the happiest surprise.

Sarah had given birth to a baby boy. Robert Weskler Jr was tiny, pink, with a tuft of deep black hair. When Paula carried him downstairs, his impossibly small balled fists opened, his arms stretched out, and he yawned, which elicited oohs and ahhs from everyone. He was only six months-old.

"What? How?" Zephyr asked, still unable to believe what they presented him.

"Oh my God, Sarah! Congratulations!" Aurora threw her arms around the older woman and the two embraced. Afterward, she wiped tears away and surveyed the new mother. "This is happy news, isn't it?"

"Yes, dear, very happy," she said, and smiled. "Early on, I might've had a different answer, but look at his face." She caressed her baby's scalp and nodded. "It's happy news."

Zephyr finally understood. He thought of all the days Sarah didn't feel like eating, all the days she had retreated to her room, and realized that, even then, she knew. He couldn't begin to imagine the struggle she'd endured and wondered if the outcome would be the same if not for Paula, who had obviously served as a coach through it all. A baby conceived in hate and born into love. He liked the sound of it. Ironic, he thought, that they had gone to Alpha in chase of hope and purpose and found only despair, while Sarah's despair had ultimately delivered both.

They stayed for several days, savoring the smell of home-cooked food and doting on the infant boy. Zephyr liked Paula, who was a brash, blunt woman with a good heart. Whether in the yard watching little Robert on the grass or sharing snacks table-side, they focused on the present, or recounted great stories from the distant past. The future, and what it carried for Zephyr, Aurora, Jordan and Trey, seemed off limits. Maybe Sarah knew that they were headed off somewhere to settle scores, or perhaps she didn't want to know, but she never asked them where they were going next, not even when they bid her and hers farewell.

Zephyr could only imagine two possible outcomes for today's encounter. Either he, Aurora, Jordan and Trey were going to die, or Ross was. He hoped it was the latter and figured they at least had numbers going for them, although he had no intention of putting Jordan in harm's way. She was going to stay behind, even if he had to tie her up himself. She wouldn't like it and it didn't matter.

Darkness was integral to the original plan. They would sneak into Firefly Valley, just as he had crept out of it. But then the storm had come along and presented a new opportunity. Surely, nobody would be out in this freezing mess, especially Ross, who was probably already bundled up and asleep in his shabby little house. Or, more likely, passed out. So now they could drive in broad daylight, park a half mile from the man's residence, and spring upon him.

The springing upon him part was what he still needed to work out. That might prove tricky, even in a snowstorm. If the old man so much as glanced out his window at the right time, they might have a battle on their hands, and that's exactly what Zephyr didn't want. The advantage of surprise was integral.

"Last chance to back out, people," he said. "If anybody in this car isn't feeling it, speak now or forever hold your peace. No hard feelings whatsoever."

Snowfall and the steady rhythm of the windshield wipers; nothing else.

"Let's deal with this house-burning, murdering bastard," Trey said. It was both comical and sobering.

They drove by the same wrecks that Zephyr had come upon the first morning of the event. A stalled truck across the intersection into town. A pole leaning forever to one side. The snowy streets were peppered in animal tracks — likely deer, no longer afraid of men.

He still feared Ross, though. And as much as he told himself otherwise, he knew that when they finally encountered the old man, he'd be afraid. But also angry. And he was counting on the latter emotion to drive him through the day.

They parked behind an old comic book store about five blocks away from the house. There was no direct line of sight to the place, which was good because it meant that Ross couldn't see them, either. They'd trek the rest of the way on foot. Take it slow, careful, and smart. They didn't need to speed into it.

Zephyr was double-checking the ammo in his gun when Jordan said, "You promised you'd never leave me again, remember?"

"Jord," he started before she cut him off.

"You promised. And I'm a better shot than Trey, anyway."

"I know, but this is dangerous. The last thing I want is for you to get hurt."

"I'll stay back a little ways if you want. I just don't want to be apart from everyone."

Zephyr considered it and then nodded. "OK," he said. "But no matter what happens, you hold your position. Got it?"

"Got it."

When they were close enough to see the house, he stopped them. It looked the same, the only difference a thick layer of snow covering the roof and curtains of it falling before them. He squinted against the storm, struggling to see anything resembling motion, fire, smoke, and couldn't.

"What's the plan, Zeph?" Trey asked.

The best idea he could come up with was borrowed from their days as Alpha scouters, and when he explained it, Trey and Aurora understood at once.

"Flank attack," she said and nodded.

Zephyr nodded back. "So I'll take center. Trey, you'll want to skirt around this shop and go at his place from over there." He pointed toward an old laundry mat a block away. "And Rory, you'll come at him from there." More ramshackle houses that bled into the same neighborhood where Ross lived.

"What about me?" Jordan asked.

"You'll stay right here. You've got a clear view of everything, including his house. So if you see anything suspicious, your job will be to signal us. Got it?"

She nodded.

"But I don't want you to move unless you see something suspicious, Jord. And if you do, you fire off three rounds." He put his hands on her shoulders and faced her. "Three rounds. And then get to cover. Understand?"

"Yeah."

Zephyr's heart thumped in his chest as he prowled down the street in direct view of the house. He held his scope to his eye and studied the scene for anything that might confirm the old man's existence. Nothing revealed itself.

Snow fell all around him and ice crunched under his boots with each step, but he never looked away. Any movement. Any motion at all, and he'd be ready. Even amidst the downpour, he was certain his aim would hold true and the bullet would find its target.

Trey was the first to appear within the radius of Zephyr's sight. He sneaked to the side of the house and hunkered down against a medley of bushes. Then he flashed Zephyr a hearty thumbs up. Aurora appeared on the opposite side of the structure and waited, the shotgun huge in her arms.

Still no other movement in his scope.

He walked on, visions of his mom and dad in his head. He was a killer now. He had allowed people to be killed. He had killed people. Aurora too. His parents could never have imagined this fate for him, and certainly wouldn't have condoned it. But then, they were gone, their house and everything they owned burned to ash. He was still here, still living, still fighting for survival.

This, though, was not survival. This was deliberate. This was straight up murder. And the more he thought about it, the less he liked the idea of it. Even if the victim in this case was a murderer himself. Even if he deserved to die.

The screen door was closed, but Zephyr could see through it into the living room beyond, which meant the front door was wide open. On a freezing day, no less. And with no sign of electricity or fire. No heat. What the hell was the old man up to? Had he abandoned the place? Zephyr had never considered the possibility. Ross was, if nothing else, he figured, a creature of habit.

He pulled away from the scope and surveyed the house before him. He was close enough now that he could sprint to that entrance and smash into the dingy interior it protected in a matter of seconds. He glanced back, hoping for a glimpse of Jordan before he committed himself, but the snow came down too thick and he couldn't see her.

Zephyr signaled for Trey and Aurora to stay their positions as he mounted the stairs to the porch, each step a careful exercise less he give them all away. One of the floorboards squeaked under his weight and he stopped, his breath visible before him. He could reach that screen door now. This could be over in seconds. It's now or never, Zeph, he thought, and gave the signal.

They all pounced. Zephyr, through the front entryway, Aurora through a window on the far side and Trey through another. It felt louder, slower and clumsier than it really was. Although the entire semi-coordinated assault played out in seconds, for Zephyr, it was eons, more than enough time for Ross to react and shoot them all.

Only one gun fired, however, and it belonged to Trey, not Ross. For once, his aim was accurate. As he fell from the windowsill into the old man's living room, he shot him dead on. Right in the chest. It would've been fatal for sure.

The old man, however, was already dead.

The armchair held only a badly decomposed corpse, half man and half skeleton, a chunk of skull missing. A dusty blanket covered most of the body. The old man had shot himself, and by the looks of it, he'd done it a long time ago.

Aurora hugged Zephyr with one arm.

"I'm glad," he told her, finally able to breathe again. He felt as though a great, invisible weight had been lifted from him. "I didn't want to kill him. It's bad enough, the things we have to do to survive. But I don't want to be like him."

She nodded, and then kissed him, as she always did. "I love you."

"Maybe you could have let us in on this epiphany of yours before we ran guns blazing into this shithole," Trey said as he shook glass from his jacket.

"Sorry about that. But hey, man. Nice shot."

It was finally over.

They were about to turn away from the grizzly scene when Zephyr stopped dead in his tracks. It was the corpse before them. There was something wrong with it. At first, he couldn't figure out what, and then the anomaly sucker punched him. It was the skull. Its front teeth were missing. Had been blown clean out, in fact.

"Oh, no," he said as the tiny hairs on his nape stood erect and his pace galloped.

"What?" Aurora asked.

He motioned them all down and surveyed the living room as he fought to steady his nerves. Where was the gun? His eyes darted to and from as they hunted the floorboards for some rusty pistol, but none presented itself. As much as he wanted and needed it to appear, to be made visible as proof that everything was all right, there was no weapon in sight. This was no suicide.

"Zephyr," Aurora whispered, "what's going on?"

"It's not good."

He knew what he'd find waiting for him beneath the corpse's blanket before he tugged it away, and still the outcome rattled him. Not a hunter's flannel and jeans, or an old pair of overalls, but a black suit and tie. Shredded and stained a faded crimson in parts, undoubtedly the aftermath of the hungry animals which had torn meat from bone in the months it had sat here. And yet, old and rotted as it was, unmistakable. This wasn't Ross. It was Jerry. And cradled in Jerry's bony hands was a black walkie-talkie, its red power indicator presently aglow.

"No," Zephyr whispered.

"How is that walkie-talkie on?" Trey asked. "Dude, how is that fucking thing on?"

"Oh my God," Aurora said.

Zephyr shook his head. "The asshole's alive. This body isn't him — it's the guy he killed. This whole elaborate thing is for me." He nodded in the direction of the walkie-talkie. "He wants me to take it."

"Tell me you're fucking kidding," Trey said. "Obviously, no. I mean, no. Screw him. That's the solution. Leave it and let's get out of here."

Zephyr unleashed a series of expletives. "It's no good. He'll be watching for us now. He obviously knows we're here. The walkie didn't just turn itself on. Somehow, he knew we were coming."

He wondered if Ross was clever and crafty enough to rig a mechanism like a trip wire designed to reveal trespassers. If so, they could've driven right through and triggered it on their way into town. Such an obstacle had never even occurred to them. Even if Ross was capable, though, and he wasn't so sure, there was more here. The body. Jerry. He had to move the corpse, and from the looks of it, he did it a long time ago. Maybe he set it up as a decoy after Zephyr threatened to attack him on his home turf so long ago. But how did he know Zephyr would come to his house?

"Maybe he comes and charges the batteries every other day, man. He might not even know we're her—"

The device in the skeleton's hands crackled and beeped.

"Well, well, would you look at ya'll," a voice said. Zephyr recognized it right away.

"Welcome to my humble home. Sorry about the mess, but I ain't lived there for some time now. I mighta' cleaned up a little if I knew ya'll was coming for dinner, but nobody saw fit to tell me."

Aurora caught Zephyr's eyes and mouthed, *how?*

"Go ahead now, smile for the camera. You're on Rossy TV," the voice continued and laughed itself into a coughing fit.

Trey pointed to one corner of the room and there, perched on a shelf, was a wireless camera. The man plucked and examined it.

He whispered, "Analog, battery powered. These don't have long ranges. You go too far away and the connection will be shit. He's close, man. Probably in one of the nearby houses."

Then he hurled the camera against the wall and it broke into several pieces before tumbling to the ground again.

"Well, that's just rude," Ross said and cackled. "I sure did like looking at your purty lady friend. If I had a swing like that, I'd ride it every night, know what I mean?"

Zephyr withdrew the walkie from the bony clutches of the corpse's hands and pressed the talk button.

"Old man, I missed you."

"Well now, that you, boy? Was beginning to wonder if you had the ball sack to make a peep. Woulda' figured against it based on the way you done tuck tail and run last time you saw me."

"It's been too long," Zephyr said, ignoring the insult.

"Looked like you sprouted a bit. Don't matter. Still spineless, or you'd have come at me like a man."

Aurora took hold of the walkie. "Why don't you show yourself then if you're such a big man, you fat piece of shit?"

"Whoo-whee, this one's got a mouth on her, don't she?" Ross said in unmistakable amusement. "I sure know what to do with girls like her. I sure do, yes sir."

Zephyr motioned his companions into a huddle and started into a whisper. "He's goading us. He wants us to get angry and sloppy now, so don't fall for it. I'll do the talking from now on, Rory." He focused his attention on Trey. "My man, I love you, but you're a shitty shot. I wasn't comfortable with you coming when I thought we had the jump on Ross, and now, you gotta go."

"Shove it as far as it'll fit, you cocky son of—"

"Trey, Jordan's out there."

That's all he had to say. He saw the words strike their target as intended and Trey's features softened before he looked away.

"Fine," he hissed. "Fine. But how the hell am I supposed to get out without getting my ass shot off?"

The walkie squeaked and popped in Zephyr's hand. "Boy, you ever get tired of being outsmarted by your old pal? 'Bout now, you gotta be thinking to yourself, 'Why didn't I just leave Ross alone? I should've known I'd be no match for the likes of him.' And you'd be right in thinking that because..."

The boy let him drone on, the words fading from focus, as he locked eyes with his friend. "You said he's close. This is a corner house and there's nothing but a snowy field behind us. There's a full block of houses to our right and more across the street. But you should be fine if you take the field."

"He's probably next door, man. The shit-eating clown thinks he's a genius, but the camera is a giveaway. Like I said, it's analog. The range is crap. He might not know that, but I do. I don't even think it'd work if he was in one of the houses across the street. You ask me, he's right there," Trey said and pointed in the direction of the house adjacent their own. "We could bum rush the place and take him."

"No," Zephyr said. "Jordan is your priority. Circle around to her, get the hell out of here. The last gas station we stopped at before Firefly Valley, do you remember where it is?"

Trey considered his question and then nodded.

"Good. That's where we'll meet. If Aurora and I don't show up by nightfall, you take Jordan and you get as far away as possible."

"Just come with me now. Fuck this asshole."

"Can't. Ross is no dummy. I'm going to need to stay behind and create a distraction for you, just in case."

"How?"

"Leave that to me. I've got an idea."

Ross really didn't need an audience. He could, as it turned out, entertain himself with a one-sided conversation. He blathered on about how Zephyr lacked the "testicular fortitude" to do anything but remain stupid prey, and that this world was about the survival of the fittest, and that the weak would be weeded out until only the strong were left, and on and on and on. It was all some warped, psychopathic justification for the old man to behave in whatever wicked fashion he desired, and it was easy to ignore. Only the occasional reply from the Zephyr was necessary and the old man was on to a new diatribe.

As he scoured through the garage, Aurora ransacked the kitchen and together they found the items they needed. The boy wasn't sure the old house still held possession of the integral ingredients, but his luck struck true and he felt confident that the plan, however sketchy, might just work.

Visibility was worse than ever, which also proved fortuitous. Zephyr didn't think Trey would be seen when he scrambled away to safety. And not because the old man wouldn't be looking for them — he would be; despite all of his talk, he was certain the bastard was still searching for any opportunity. To him, it was all part of the hunt.

"You know what's sad, Ross?" Zephyr asked.

"Your aim'd be my guess."

"Funny, but no. You know where I've been for the last… what? It's gotta be pushing two years, wouldn't you say? I'm sure you've been counting the days. You could probably tell me exactly."

No reply from Ross.

"What's sad is that in all of that time, I've barely thought about you. I explored the country. I met all of these great people. I swam in the oceans of California. I fell in love with a beautiful woman," he said, and looked at his girlfriend. "And I have a family. I have friends."

"You," he continued. "In all of this time, what have you done? Sat here with a dead man as your only companion. A man you murdered.

Sat here on your fat ass and plotted. Waited, and plotted, and hoped that one day I might return to your miserable existence."

With Aurora in tow, Zephyr drew closer to the den, the only room in the house with a window out to their nearest neighbor, and presumably Ross.

"Is that supposed to irk me, boy?" the old man asked. "You gonna need to try a little harder than that. Fact of the matter is, you came back, so I guess that makes you every bit as pathetic, don't it? Sheeoot, I musta' really left an impression on ya if you did all those things and still came back to see your ol—"

"Now!" Zephyr hissed, Trey ran, and Aurora's shotgun erupted.

It was a direct hit, and two windows exploded: theirs, and an identical one in the home only fifteen feet away. Zephyr sprinted toward the opening and hurled the explosive cocktail — a canister of old gasoline topped with a lit paper fuse — across the short divide between the houses. His aim was true, and in slow motion he watched the bomb soar through the air and into the gaping wound on the other side before a heavy blast shook both houses and glass and wood shattered and splintered. The force of it knocked him to his ass with a heavy thud and he sat there dazed before Aurora came to his rescue.

"The asshole shot you!" she shouted.

"What? Where?" For that matter, when? And how? He didn't feel injured.

"Here," she said and palmed his shoulder. There was a bullet wound all right, and yes, now that he'd regained his senses, it hurt like hell. Ross must've been waiting for them, and had just enough time to squeeze off a good round before the blaze came at him.

Aurora examined the rest of him. "It's gone through the other side. I think you'll be all right. You've definitely seen worse."

"Let's get the motherfucker then," Zephyr said, the ringing in his ears robust, and rose. At first, his balance resisted, but powered by nerves and hate and determination, his steadiness rebounded, and they were off.

The house across the way wasn't just on fire — it was already an inferno, and it was spreading. The flames licked at their own house, which was in the process of catching. Good, Zephyr thought. This is right. This is the way it ought to be. Let him watch his own house burn to the ground now. But when they peeked through the frame for Ross, he was nowhere to be found.

"He's running," Zephyr said, and they both knew it was true.

Except, it wasn't. Not exactly, anyway. They hurried out the front door and spotted the old man, his back to them, at the snowy sidewalk. He wasn't running, though. He was limping, and even that was an exaggeration. His once-meaty scalp was bloodied and crisped, the hair burned away, along with most of his shirt. Even amidst the snowfall, Zephyr could see the blistered skin across his back and neck. The fire had done its work.

"Ross, old pal, where you going?" Zephyr called, but the old man ignored him. "Now, don't be that way — come back here! We can't have a proper reunion party without our guest of honor!"

Aurora spoke with her shotgun. It blasted into the air and Ross heard that loud and clear. He stopped, seemed to reconsider, and then finally turned to face them. He wore a smile on his face, but it was disingenuous. He was terrified, and Zephyr knew it. Moreover, he was cooked. Figuratively and literally. Half of his face was a mesh of burned tissue and jagged edges of white bone protruded from his cheek and eyebrow. His upper chest was a rubbery, melted goo of skin that bled into visible collarbones. And his right leg seemed to hang from its socket; it was obviously broken and torn beyond repair. Ross stood on his left. He looked like a zombie about to play hopscotch.

Even with modern medicine and technology, he was unlikely to survive this brand of injury. Without the aid of either, he was a dead man, and this was plain to see. Only Ross seemed oblivious to this truth.

"Well, I guess everybody gets lucky now and then," the old man rasped. "Go ahead and gloat, boy. Ya got one on me."

"This isn't a game, you psycho. We are real people and there are real lives at stake. And you just lost yours."

"You don't have the guts, you little turd."

"Ross, it's already done."

"Bullshit."

Zephyr stepped closer to him and Ross tried to pedal backward, staggered and nearly fell.

"You've always been arrogant, so maybe that's playing its part here. Or possibly you're just in shock," Zephyr said. "But sooner than later — and really soon because there isn't much of a later in your future — you're going to realize that you're already dead. Agony, and then it's curtains."

Now the boy was close enough to smell his burnt flesh. "And when that epiphany finally dawns on you, I want you to think of me, and my girlfriend, and my family. I want you to think about how we beat you, and took everything from you."

Zephyr locked eyes with him. "And then, old man, you can die."

Epilogue

Six months had passed since Ross, and now Trey was leaving.

"You don't have to go," Zephyr told him one morning as they hung their clothes out to dry on a line by the campsite. The Colorado weather had warmed enough for them to go swimming in the lake, but the water was still brisk.

"I know I don't have to, dude. It's just time. You have Aurora and Jordan, but I'm kind of like this weird third wheel an—"

"You're not a third wheel. Your part of the family, as much as any of us," Zephyr said.

Trey held up a hand. "OK, a not-third-wheel who masturbates alone while you and your crazy supermodel girlfriend retreat into your tent every night. That's cool, too, right?"

Zephyr smiled. "So you're gonna go look for a girlfriend? That's the big plan?"

Aurora and Jordan had spent the morning in the garden and now they came clutching red peppers and tomatoes in both hands.

"Yeah. Plus, I have family in New York, or had — whatever. I feel like a road trip again."

"Did you see what Jordan grew?" Aurora asked, as she and the little girl came camp-side.

Zephyr and Trey made a dramatic show of how impressed they were with this latest crop.

Fresh veggies were a big deal now. He was impressed that the girls had taken up gardening and more impressed by every new vegetable or fruit they produced. If only his regular hunting excursions were as productive. He tried not to beat himself up too much about it, but it was frustrating that he hadn't killed a single deer yet. They lived primarily on the goods they looted and the fish he caught.

Aurora stood before them. "So what's going on, boys?"

"Trey's taking off," Zephyr said. "He's going to New York."

"Oh." She didn't look surprised.

"Wait, did you know about this?"

She twirled her hair and pivoted on one foot. "OK, don't get all pissed off, but yes. We've talked about it. I told Trey I wouldn't say anything until he was ready, though."

"I can't believe this."

"Don't go getting your panties in a bunch," Trey said. "I wasn't sure I was going to do it, so there was no point in bringing it up. But now I am."

Aurora sighed. "And you're going to let Zephyr in on the real reason, Trey."

"I did. I told him because I want to check out the East Coast."

"Nuh-uh," she said. "Fess up."

Zephyr turned to face him. "What's she talking about?"

His friend rolled his eyes. "Damn it, Aurora. I told you`

"He deserves to know."

"You deserve to know my ass," he said.

She stared at him, her hands on her hips. "That doesn't even make sense, genius."

"It sort of does, if you think about it." The older man raked his fingers through what was left of his hair. "Fine. You win, as always."

"Good. Start talking."

"OK, hold on," he said and jogged back to his tent. When he returned next, he held the portable AM/FM radio that seldom left his side these days.

"This," he said, "is why I'm going."

Zephyr raised an eyebrow. "An old radio?"

"Yeah. When you were out on your revenge quest back in California, when we were tracking you, I found this little bugger in an old drug store. At night, I'd turn it on, put on my headphones, and listen to anything I could find. There wasn't a lot, but I'd usually find at least one or two songs playing."

"One night, though," he continued. "I heard a broadcast. National. Out of New York."

"They're saying they found something out there," Aurora said.

"Hey, that was my big reveal. I was working up to that, damn it. Anyway, yes, they found something. Some kind of big white wall with weird writing all over it. Whatever the hell it is, it's not manmade."

"How do you know it's not a bunch of bullshit?" Zephyr asked.

Trey considered the question. "I don't. But it's worth checking out."

"And even if it's there, then what?"

"No idea."

Later that night, after they laid Jordan to bed in her tent, he and Aurora moved back into theirs and made quiet love. When they were finished, she asked, "Do you think we'll ever know what happened?"

He thought about it for a long while and then said, "I don't know that it matters. Maybe we'll find out, maybe not, but it's not going to change anything."

"I'm happy you found me," she said as she snuggled into him.

"Me too."

Tomorrow, they would need to decide whether they were going to join Trey on this new adventure. Of course, his friend was opposed to them coming. He insisted it might be dangerous. And there was the camp and the garden to think about. The fish in the smoker. All of their supplies. But those were all considerations for the daylight. For now, he just wanted to soak in the darkness, to enjoy the moment, the warmth, and to drift.

He dreamed of great skyscrapers covered in stretching vines, and cracked, grassy highways peppered in deer and wolves. He dreamed of tattered men and women huddled over bonfires in underground railways. He dreamed of an enormous white, pulsating wall with words he couldn't read, words that seemed to transform anew as he studied them.

And when the man's eyes fluttered open in the morning, dim sunlight bleeding through the tent, he rolled over to touch her and smiled, because he wasn't alone.

THE END